This series is dedicated to all
U.S. military veterans of all branches
who served in times of peace and war,
for your families who stood by you,
for all of you now serving our country,
for all now waiting for a loved one to return,
and for all those whose wait has ended in tragedy.
God's love is for you.
The Homeland Heroes series is for you.

HOMELAND HEROES

★

Book Four

STANDING STRONG

DONNA FLEISHER

ZONDERVAN.com/
AUTHORTRACKER
follow your favorite authors

Standing Strong
Copyright © 2007 by Donna Fleisher

Requests for information should be addressed to:

Zondervan, *Grand Rapids, Michigan* 49530

Library of Congress Cataloging-in-Publication Data

Fleisher, Donna.
      Standing strong / Donna Fleisher.
          p. cm. -- (Homeland heroes bk. 4)
        ISBN-10: 0-310-27256-4
        ISBN-13: 978-0-310-27256-4
        I. Title.
      PS3606.L454S73 2007
      813'.6--dc22

                                      2007026420

Interior design by Michelle Espinoza

Printed in the United States of America

---

07 08 09 10 11 12 • 21 20 19 18 17 16 15 14 13 12 11 10 9 8 7 6 5 4 3 2 1

For Shannon.

Thanks, lady. Mia thanks you too.

ACKNOWLEDGMENTS

LORD JESUS, WHAT A JOURNEY this has been. A fun eleven years; these four books; these two amazing imaginary friends; one story of friendship, faith, and hope. Of peace. The kind of true peace only You can give. Thank You for the privilege of being Yours, for finding me here in this place, for pouring this story through me. And thank You for all those who encouraged me along the way. Thank You, Lord, for . . .

★★★

MOM AND DAD, CHRIS, THESS, Christine, and Mario. My family.

Zondervan. For all they've done, and all they do.

Thank You for Gayle and Margaret and Francine. And for all my readers and friends, both online and real-time. Special thanks for Shannon, Susie, Vickie, Heather, Melisa, Trish, Steph, Jeanna, Denise, June, Lynn, Jacci, Brooke, everyone at the Sandcastle, Jenness, Christina, and Sherrie, Rel, Susan, Susie, Judy, and Camy. Especially Camy.

And thanks for Wayne Watson and his powerful songs "It's Time" and "Friend of a Wounded Heart." Chris's songs, played at max volume straight into my brainpan over and over as her world was revealed to me. You do, indeed, Lord, meet us where we are, always faithful, even to the end.

Thank You, Yahshua, for being so good.

STANDING STRONG

AUGUST 1996

ONE

Screeching tires. Thumping rap music. Moving closer, growing louder.

With one foot on top of the shovel blade ready to push it again into the soft dirt, Chris McIntyre froze, her eyes narrowing against the breeze blowing through the trees. Tires screeched once more, slamming a car to a brutal stop. A horn blared but was quickly beaten back by angry shouts and booming hip-hop.

A shudder ripped through her. She stared past the back corner of the gym out over the side street. The car's engine roared, once again pushed to its max. Heading straight for Chris's neighborhood, the fools were using Kimberley Street as their own private drag strip.

She tightened her grip on the shovel's handle.

For the past several weeks, rival gangs from Portland's Outer Northeast explored the easternmost fringes of Kimberley Square, determined to add turf to their territory. Police patrols had been stepped up to counter the increased violence, leaving everyone, including Chris, a bit wary. Even after all she had endured as a veteran of Operations Desert Shield and Storm, this new type of warfare was unlike anything she had ever seen.

She forced herself to breathe as the racing car, its booming hip-hop music, and its screeching tires seemed to be aimed straight for her. Just the thought of what that car carried stirred up tendrils of pure terror, electrifying her blood.

Slapping footsteps echoed off the houses across the street. Peering over the thin azalea bushes lining the sidewalk, Chris waited. She didn't have to move. By the sounds of it, whoever was running would pass the very spot where she stood.

A boy appeared. Sweating, desperately out of breath, a young boy no more than ten years old ran down the middle of the street, feet clomping in his oversized sneakers.

Enrique? Was that his name?

He hopped the curb and ran down the sidewalk just a few feet from Chris. His head turned her direction. Her presence must have startled him. He skidded to a stop, quickly looked over his shoulder, then burst through the line of azaleas and ran at Chris. "*Señorita!* Chris! *Por favor!*"

She dropped the shovel and faced him, hands up, palms out. "Easy now—"

"Help me! *Ayúda!*" He pointed back down the street.

Those same screeching tires brought the car onto the side street. Frozen in place, Chris watched it as the boy ran behind her and grabbed her arms, using her as a shield.

The tricked-out late-model sedan slid through a quick right turn and skidded to a stop in the gravel of the gym's back lot, no more than twenty feet away. The hip-hop spewing out of it shook the fillings in Chris's back teeth. Dust filtered up from the tires and floated on the breeze.

Enrique's fingers dug into her upper arms, and he bent with her as she reached down for the shovel. "*Le suplico,*" he whimpered. "*Le suplico!* No ... no let ... *no deje que me agarren!*" His terror zipped through his crushing grip and settled in the pit of Chris's stomach.

She couldn't move. As she stared at the car, her breath hung suspended in her throat.

A sudden, complete silence fell.

Four grinning young men, teenagers, all wearing tight black nylon skullcaps and chains of silver around their necks, peered at Chris through the open passenger-side windows of the sedan. "Do it," the driver shouted. "Let 'em have it!"

One of the teens in the backseat pointed an assault rifle at Chris. It looked brand-new. Shiny. More like a pistol, the short length and small diameter of the barrel defied its ability to spray a world of hurt at anything standing in its way.

Enrique pulled at her arms. "No, no! *Señorita, por favor* ... no let them!"

Cruel laughter rumbled from the car. The boy in the front seat wore bright gold caps over his two front teeth.

Their laughter turned to taunting curses. The barrel of the miniature machine gun swung side to side as the teen holding it stared Chris down, his dark eyes glinting with unchecked delight.

Chris slowly raised the shovel, centering the tip of the handle in the dirt between her feet, the blade over her heart. With the weight of Enrique's grip pulling her arms down, she struggled to hold it steady.

The cursing taunts increased. Each vulgar name they called her struck deeply. The driver's shouts carried through the chaos of profanity and insults. "Wanna die? Yo, stand there and die." Wicked grins. Violent, horrible promises of pure evil, of what they would do to her after they settled their score with the boy behind her.

Lord God ...

"Nah, spray 'er now, Bones," the one with the gold teeth said. "Cut 'em both in half. Do it."

The swinging barrel slowed and steadied on her.

She glanced down at the shovel blade. The way she held it against her chest, any bullets from that pistol striking it would deflect directly into her stomach. Or her face. Feeling a bit sheepish, she spun the handle to turn the blade so it curved out. Teeth clenched, she tried to stem the tremble that had overtaken her jaw.

Hideous laughter spewed from the car.

Chris stared into the gunman's eyes. Waited.

He glanced away first. Then he laughed and pulled the barrel of the gun to his lips and kissed it.

Enrique's fingers dug so deeply into Chris's arms, her pulse throbbed under her biceps. She struggled to keep the shovel centered over her heart. To keep her balance. To keep the boy from pulling her down. *Come on, kid. Keep cool ... Wait 'em out ...*

The car's engine thundered. The back tires spun, shooting rocks and dirt across the street, then dust into the air. Before tracking in to propel the car forward, the tires stopped, but the engine continued to roar. Confined to its spot, the sedan seemed to scream for mercy, begging to be released.

Silence fell. Except for loud laughter. Purely evil taunts.

Ahh, man, Enrique. What did you do?

Chris blinked as Mr. Gold Cap pushed his door open. His right foot, encased in a huge Nike high-top, plopped into the dirt.

She took a step backward, but her knees almost buckled when Enrique suddenly pushed away and sprinted across the lot toward the trees, screaming in his panic, arms raised to protect his face as he slashed through some rhododendron bushes.

A slow growl rumbled up from Chris's throat. If the boy continued in his current direction, he would end up in Ben and Sonya's backyard. Or at the church. He'd find open arms to protect him, even as he drew the gangsters deep into the heart of Kimberley Square.

The sedan's engine revved, drowning out laughing shouts of cruel and profane delight. Mr. Gold Cap quickly jumped back inside and slammed his door shut. Hip-hop once again boomed as the driver spun the car in a tight circle in the gravel, kicking rocks and dirt at Chris. She cowered beneath the spray, eyes pinched shut, hearing pinging sounds as rocks hit the shovel blade. Back on the street, the car's tires again screeched. Chris slowly straightened and blinked open her eyes. Leaving black smoke in its wake, the car raced to the intersection of the first cross street and then turned right once more to follow its prey. She rested her head against the back of the shovel blade.

Enrique ... is that even your name? Her arms trembled so hard the blade bounced off her forehead. *Okay ... okay ... breathe ...*

Maybe he wouldn't stop at the church. Maybe he'd keep running all the way home. Though he needed someone to take him in, Chris whispered a bit of a selfish prayer. She didn't want him stopping to hide anywhere near the homes of her best friends.

She needed to find her cell phone and call Ben to warn him. But she knew it was too late.

She needed to move. Her feet felt skewered to the ground.

Trembling overtook her. The shovel fell away. She dropped to her knees, then let herself fall the rest of the way down. She rolled onto her back and stared up at a patch of brilliant blue sky peeking out from behind thick puffy clouds.

Okay. It's okay. Her heart thumped against her chest as she tried to relax. *Yeah. It's okay. He'll be okay.* She blinked. *Um ... Lord? I mean ... like ... what was that all about?*

✯✯✯

BEN CONNELLY LOVED KIMBERLEY SQUARE. But he could certainly do without living in a city. Sometimes it seemed to weigh on him. All the cars, the houses, the people. Oh, he loved people. Most people. But sometimes it seemed as if all the people surrounding him were sucking up more than their fair share of space and time and breath. He wasn't of the mantra: Live and let live. Yet if he had to draw a line somewhere, it would be there. *Just let me live as I let you live. I don't want to hurt you. Please don't want to hurt me. Or those I hold dear.*

He wished he could speak the words aloud to the kids in the brown sedan who obviously dug their obnoxious music and somehow found their way into the back parking lot of the Kimberley Street Community Church. From the kitchen window of his house, Ben watched the sedan turn sharp circles, its smoking tires leaving ugly black circles on the pavement. The boys inside whooped and hollered over the thump of their rap music as black smoke slowly curtained them from the world. A tiny bit of justice. Ben hoped the thick smoke would hurt their lungs and make them cough as they breathed it.

A small sigh. *No, Lord, I don't hope that. I just hope they leave.*

The car stopped. Laughter and loud thumps of bass continued to reach the spot where Ben stood. The glasses in one of his kitchen cupboards rattled.

The longer the car remained on church property, the more it necessitated Ben leaving his kitchen to go out and try to persuade them to leave. Or at least to try to persuade them to cease their current activities. As the clock above the sink continued to tick and the glasses continued to rattle, he prayed he wouldn't have to go out there. He already knew what he would say and how he would say it. A soft answer always turned away wrath. But these days, with these kids, even a soft answer could potentially be answered with gunfire.

"Benjamin?" His wife, Sonya, slowly padded down the stairs. "Should we call the police?"

He strained to see into the car. Each new tick of the clock gave witness to the truth. He needed to go out there.

"Sweetheart?" Sonya moved in beside him.

"No. I'm giving them ten more seconds."

"Oh, honey, don't go out there."

"You better call Andy. See where he's at."

Sonya reached for the phone.

As the church's senior pastor, Andrew, Ben's oldest son, was probably somewhere inside the huge building. The back door, the one just a few feet from the gang of troublemakers sitting in their smoking car, was probably unlocked. It was rarely locked. One of the ministries of the church was to be open and available to all who needed its safe retreat. But these kids didn't need a safe retreat. These were the type of kids who would abuse a safe retreat and twist it to suit their own evil intentions.

"No answer."

Not good. Where was his son? "Try his cell."

The kids sat in the car, gazing at the church's back door. As the smoke dissipated around them, Ben took notice of the car's make, model, and license plate number.

"No answer on his cell either. Are they gone? Did they leave?" Sonya again stood beside him. "Oh, sweetheart. I think we should call the police."

"So far they haven't done anything wrong. Except for cutting a few cookies."

"What do you think they want?"

"Ahh, they're just blowing off steam. I'm sure that's all it is." He pushed away from the sink. "I'll just go out and make my presence known. Keep trying Andy." He gave his wife's cheek a quick caress. "And don't worry. It's just another fun day in Kimberley Square."

"Yeah, right." Her pale green eyes darkened. "Please be careful."

He hated to hear such concern in her usually pleasant Southern drawl. "Always, my love." He kissed her soft lips. "Be back in a minute." He turned and walked out onto his back porch, focusing his gaze once again on the sedan.

The front passenger side door opened and a tall, thin boy stepped out. Ben took immediate notice of the black nylon cap wrapped around the boy's head. His steps quickened toward the church.

The boy's face bore a huge grin as he lifted his hands over his head and stretched. Thick chains of silver jewelry, one sporting a huge cross, hung down so low they reached beyond the bottom of his black T-shirt. His blue-striped boxer shorts puffed out from under his jeans — jeans that looked ready to fall down any second. Shorts. Though they reached below the boy's knees. He let out a deep yawn, all the while staring up at the church. Until his eyes caught sight of Ben. The music dropped to a volume considerably more conducive for conversation.

"Can I help you guys?" Ben spoke over the rap, yet kept his voice soft and devoid of concern as he moved closer. The boy's two front teeth were capped with gold. Ben tried not to stare. "That's some interesting music you've got playing. And quite a nice piece of artwork you left there on the pavement. You must have some serious horses under the hood."

He tried not to take offense as the boy slowly reached down to give Ben a sign of ultimate disrespect.

Snickers of laughter came from inside the car.

Ben took three more steps and stopped. Close enough, he figured, yet far enough away to be safe. He stood firm, back straight, then crossed his arms over his chest. Raised his chin just a bit. Pulled his expression into one of authority. Narrowed his eyes.

"Jus' lookin' for our friend, yo. He might've gone in there." The boy tilted his head toward the church.

Ben waited. He kept his eyes from glaring.

"We was waitin' to see if he'd come back out."

"Just passing the time, is that it?" Ben stood completely still, yet lowered his weight until his knees bent slightly, and rocked forward just a little to stand more on the balls of his feet.

The boy grinned. Sunshine sparkled off his gold teeth. "Yeah. Guess you could say that." He glanced back into the car where his buddies laughed and flicked gang signs at him.

Eastsiders.

Even with all his experience as a brigade commander in the army, this was not a bunch Ben wanted to mess with.

He lightened his tone. "Well, there's a Bible study starting soon." It wasn't exactly a lie. If the definition of "soon" could be stretched to mean about five hours. "You are all certainly welcome to stay and take part if you'd like."

Relief flooded through him at the boy's reaction. He didn't let it show.

With disgust pouring from his scrunched face and rolling eyes, the young gangster flicked a sign at Ben, communicating his thoughts on the matter quite clearly. "Forget dat, old man. Yo, we're outta here." He folded his long frame back into the sedan and slammed the door. Two seconds later, engine screaming, tires squealing, rap music once again blasting, the car sped out of the lot and turned toward downtown, but quickly turned onto the side street and burned a path past the side of the church. As it moved out of sight behind it, Ben let out his breath, yet kept his ears focused on the car's whereabouts. It turned once more, then roared down Kimberley Street, past the front of the church and Ben's house, heading east, hopefully heading home.

Portland's Outer Northeast. Away from downtown. Away from Kimberley. That was their turf. That was usually where they stayed.

Until now.

***

"Ben?"

He spun quickly at the sound of the familiar soft voice.

"Are you all right?"

The fear on Chris McIntyre's face unnerved him. It was one thing he usually didn't see in her eyes. "Are you? What happened?"

"I'm good, sir. They just paid me a visit before heading this way."

His jaw dropped.

"I wanted to warn you somehow." Sweat lined her forehead. She sounded slightly out of breath.

"Are you sure you're all right?"

A small smile. "Yeah. Good as gold."

"What did they do? What happened?"

"Ahh, they just ran their mouths off a bit. And pointed an automatic pistol at me. Did you get to see it?"

Ben tried to close up his mouth. "Um, no. Didn't have the pleasure." He wished he had his cell phone with him so he could call the police.

Chris laughed. "Thank goodness they left. Back to the hole they crawled out of, huh?" She looked around. "Did you see the boy they were chasing?"

"Chasing? They said he was a friend."

"Yeah, well, if they always chase their friends like that ..."

Ben turned to gaze at the back door of the church. "They said they thought he went inside. They said they were waiting for him to come out."

"Uh-oh."

He hurried to the door, comforted somewhat that Chris followed close behind him.

Inside, the big basement was quiet, and cooler than the late August afternoon. Ben focused to hear any slightest sound.

"There. Last room."

He blinked. Then almost cringed. As much as he hated to admit it, he was getting old. His hearing definitely wasn't what it used to be.

Chris led the way to the Sunday school classroom at the far end of the basement. Ben's heart surged with relief when Cappy Sanchez stepped out.

"Hey, you guys." She seemed just as relieved to see them. "It's all right in here. What about out there? They gone?"

"Yeah. They're gone." Ben pushed the classroom door open wide and peered inside. Sitting at the small table in a child-sized chair, a young boy drank from a water bottle, then slowly rocked forward and back as he swallowed. Sweaty, red-faced, and clearly Latino, he stared at the table, his dark eyes wide.

"He won't tell me his name, but he did tell me a wild story. I think we'd better get Child Protective Services in on this one."

"I think his name is Enrique." Chris leaned around the door frame for a look.

"You know him?" Cappy asked.

"He's been in the gym a time or two."

Ben pulled the door closed and looked at Cappy. "What did they want with him?"

"Well, to hear him tell it, they basically wanted to hang him from the nearest light pole. But I doubt it's that bad."

Ben glanced at Chris.

"Well, Cap, I wouldn't be too sure." Chris gave Ben a weary grin.

"Who were they?" Cappy folded her arms around her chest and leaned against the door frame.

Ben headed for the basement's kitchen and the cold bottle of water he needed at that moment. He pulled two from out of the refrigerator and handed one to Chris. Turned back to Cappy. Chugged a long drink from the bottle.

"They were Eastsiders." Chris's voice barely carried the words.

"Seriously?" Cappy's eyes widened. "Well, no wonder the little Bandolero was afraid."

The word caught Ben's full attention. "You think he was with the Bandoleros?"

"He's got the brand on his arm."

"He does?" Chris closed her eyes for a second. "Great. That's just great."

"But I thought they pretty much disbanded after Miguel got arrested." Ben could only hope.

Cappy shook her head. "Who knows."

"He doesn't look like he's more than ten years old." Chris lifted off the cap on her water bottle. "That would've made him, what, seven or eight when they first organized and handed out the brands? How is that possible?"

"Like I said, who knows." Cappy turned to push open the classroom door. "I'll ask him what they wanted with—"

The door flew open and the boy ran out, colliding head-on with Cappy, sending her sprawling as he pushed away and darted for the back door. In a brilliant flash of daylight, he disappeared. The door slowly closed.

"Ouch. *Ay caramba.*" Cappy sat up and held her wrist. "Dumb little brat."

"You okay, girl?" Chris left her water bottle on the table and moved in to help Cappy up.

Ben took a step closer, watching with concern, but their playful banter blended into the myriad of thoughts running through his mind. Was this kid really a Bandolero? Were they back in action? Had they somehow crossed the Eastsiders? *Oh ... please don't let it be so, Lord. I've seen enough outright warfare in my time.*

"I think you hyper-extended it. Put some ice on it to keep it from swelling."

Ben pulled his attention back to the two women standing beside him. Two of his fellow Gulf War veterans. Two of the four female warriors who had found their way to Kimberley Square. He tried not to grin as Cappy waved off Chris's diagnosis.

"Nah. I'm all right, *hermaña.*"

"You sure?" Ben gently squeezed the top of Cappy's shoulder.

"Yes, sir. Nothing's hurt."

"You bounced pretty well, Cap. I'd give you an eight point five." Chris walked toward the freezer, probably to fix up a bag of ice.

"Little ingrate. What'd I ever do to him?"

Ben tried not to smile. "Well, we can only hope he'll find his way home safely."

"Yeah." Cappy let out what sounded almost like a grunt. "Let's hope the little ingrate finds his way merrily home."

"A BANDOLERO?"

Ben wished he could give his wife a different answer, but he couldn't. "Yep. That's what Cappy said." He threw his empty water bottle into the garbage under the sink in his kitchen, then grabbed up the phone on the wall and dialed the Portland police's non-emergency line.

His wife blew out a deep breath through puffed cheeks. "Not good, Benjamin. I thought they had straightened up."

Cappy's words filtered through his thoughts. *Who knows.*

"I had hoped they had abandoned their little gang aspirations."

"They may have. This one boy may have dissed the Eastsiders somehow." The pleasant voice in Ben's ear asked for him to hold. "Great. They put me on hold."

"Must be a busy day." Cappy sat at the dining room table and picked out a piece of hard candy from the bowl Sonya kept there.

Chris leaned against the wall just inside the dining room and watched quietly.

"You know, this is so after-the-fact, making this call may be a total waste of time." Ben shifted the phone to his other ear.

"No, no. This is important. Who was this boy, Benjamin? How old was he?"

"Young." Ben sighed. "Maybe ten. At most. Something he pulled the Eastsiders from their home turf."

"Ten? Lord, have mercy."

Cappy pulled the candy out of her mouth and studied it. Chris stared down at the floor.

The pleasant voice returned. "Thank you for holding. How can I help you?"

Ben quickly cleared his throat. "Well, this happened about ten minutes ago, but I wanted to call and report it." He gave the dispatcher his name and address, then explained the situation. He glanced at Sonya as he recounted what the gangsters had done to Chris.

Sonya's face blanched. "Lord ... Lord! Child!" She hurried over to Chris and pulled her into a quick hug. "Are you all right?"

Ben looked away and finished telling his tale, complete with make, model, and license plate number of the sedan.

"All right, Mr. Connelly. We'll send a unit by your place to check things out. Thanks for the call."

"You got it." He hung up the phone. "They're going to send a unit over."

"What, to take pictures of the cookies they cut in the parking lot?" Cappy leaned back in her chair.

"Yes, well, at least they'll know what happened." Sonya rubbed Chris's shoulder and then made her way closer to Ben. "Oh, let's hope this is the last we'll see of those boys for a long, long time."

"Amen to that." Ben lifted his arm and gave his wife a comforting embrace.

"Well, I've got to get back to the gym." Chris pushed away from the wall, her cheeks glowing red.

You made her blush, love. Ben gave his wife a wink.

"Let me know how things go." Chris waved and started out the screen door.

"You should stick around, lady." Cappy grabbed a piece of candy from the bowl and threw it at Chris. "They may send the good cop Richardson out here to check up on us. Wouldn't it be cool to see him again?"

Chris caught the candy with one hand, then let the screen door slap shut. "Very funny, Cap. You're hilarious."

"Yeah, I'd give myself a nine point five. Maybe even a ten."

Ben savored the laughter between the two friends even as he enjoyed his own. He squeezed his wife against him, then leaned down to kiss the tip of her nose.

★★★

CHRIS UNWRAPPED THE CANDY AS she walked and pushed the wrapper into the front pocket of her jeans. Kicked a rock out of her path. Then popped the sticky root beer barrel into her mouth. She hummed a bit as its root beer sweetness spread across her tongue. And laughed again at Cappy. Not aloud. Just in her heart.

The good cop Richardson. Sugar Ray, as Jason called him. Though Chris saw the police officer every Thursday night at the rec league basketball program she ran at the gym, she hadn't seen him fulfilling his official duty since that day last May. The last time things in her world went a little haywire and got a bit out of hand. The words he said to her that day wormed their way back into her brain.

"Now, don't worry. I'm not going to label you a troublemaker. Not just yet. It takes three innocent incidents to label one a troublemaker. At least in my book."

Chris had two innocent incidences in the man's book. And she certainly hoped today's little incident wouldn't qualify as a third.

To avoid slashing through the same rhododendron bushes the young Bandolero slashed through, Chris turned left and followed the sidewalk to Kimberley Street, then turned right and followed Kimberley to the front of the gym.

Though it still looked much like an old warehouse on the outside, and purposely so, she had to admit she was quite pleased with how the inside of the gym turned out. She loved how the children's laughter and the bounce of their basketballs echoed across the cavernous depths. She loved how the floor had been carefully and successfully set in place by the many volunteers from the church who showed up on a Saturday last spring to help. She even loved those reinforced rickety old bleachers that had been donated by a local elementary school. After she finished sanding and painting all the metalwork, then sanding all the benches and laying down several thick coats of polyurethane, the bleachers looked almost new.

She let her eyes follow the words Sonya elegantly painted in dark blue across the pale gray background of the wall facing the street. *The Kimberley Street Gymnasium. An outreach of the Kimberley Street Community Church.* Smiling a bit, Chris turned down the gym's front walk and stopped at the big set of glass double doors. Slowly, she looked back over her shoulder.

Now, more than ever, she appreciated the wisdom of the man in charge of converting the old warehouse into the gym. It had been Isaiah Sadler's idea to close and seal the warehouse's front and back entrances and to put in the new entrance at the side of the building. By eliminating direct access from the street and back lot, it was hoped only those who purposely meant to arrive at the entrance of the gym would be able to do so. The back lot offered plenty of parking for the rec league nights. The extra security lighting and motion sensors brightly flooded the walkway and entrance, and yet the trees blocked most of the light from disturbing the neighbors.

Chris had spent hours clearing away brush from under the trees and debris from the walkway. In the back lot she weeded and turned every patch of ground not covered with gravel. Flowers now fluttered in the breeze. New sprigs of grass pointed skyward, tender shoots that would multiply and thicken into a carpet of lush green. With no lack of winter rainfall in the Pacific Northwest, the grass would flourish. By December she would be out there mowing it. Her just reward for planting and nurturing it.

She let her gaze wander across the treetops, enjoying the contrast of the brilliant greens against the deep blue sky, back to that place she loved. Though it was just a parking area, the back lot had become a refuge for her, a place to sit among the towering Douglas fir, to listen to the breeze softly rustle the leaves of the hardwoods. A place to savor the luscious colors of the rhododendrons when they bloomed. A place to watch ladybugs and other crawling critters make their way across the long green leaves after the blooms faded.

This entire place. Kimberley Square. Portland, Oregon. Light-years away from anywhere she ever dreamed she would live. Even now, almost eight months since her first breath of the inner city's heavy air, Chris still awoke most mornings amazed that this place had become her home.

Laughing a bit, she savored the moment, until a new thought tore through her.

Every consideration had been made, and she felt safe working alone on the property. She knew with confidence they had built a safe place for the neighborhood children — and even the neighborhood adults who still wanted to act like children — to come and play.

If only.

If only the Bandoleros really were still out of business.

If only the Eastsiders stayed in their own neighborhood, on their own home turf.

Her teeth clenched. *This is my turf. My home. And if you come this way again, flashing that weapon at anyone I love ...*

Sonya's sweet Southern drawl swept back to play in with Chris's thoughts. *"Let's hope this is the last we'll see of those boys for a long, long time."*

She sighed. "Yeah." Just a whisper as she turned again to the doors of the gym. "Like Ben said. Amen to that."

She pulled open one of the doors and stepped inside. The last of her root beer barrel dissolved away on her tongue as she enjoyed the sight of Kay Valleri diligently working her aerobics class to the beat of a jazzy tune.

Kay gave her a quick wave between side-stepping lunges.

Chris returned the wave and then lifted her eyebrows and mouthed the words, "Is everything all right?"

Kay nodded as she smiled at her class and answered the question with a thumbs-up. "We're doing great, aren't we, class?"

Over the music, Chris heard several different replies from the group, and though none carried Kay's enthusiasm, all agreed with her assessment. Chris wanted to laugh. She still couldn't imagine anyone willingly paying money to be drilled into shape like this three times a week.

She glanced around the open room one last time, returned Corissa Foley's warm smile, then headed back outside to the lot to finish up the day's work—work she happily had been doing before she was so rudely interrupted. Maybe, if Kay wanted to stay after her class and keep an eye on the kids who would soon be arriving, Chris could finish planting the last of the daffodil and tulip bulbs before cleaning up for dinner. Or maybe she'd just grab her stuff from the back lot and call it a gardening day.

She kicked a small clod of dirt from the walkway on her way around the side of the building. Then another, though it exploded as she kicked it, sending a cloud of dust over her shoe. More dirt and gravel. What a mess. She glanced at the deep ruts the gang's sedan tore into the gravel lot. She needed to sweep the entire walkway and then rake the gravel to smooth it back out. She sighed deeply. So much for planting bulbs.

She turned the corner and stopped abruptly. Her heart seized as she gasped for breath. Her eyes slowly surveyed the entire back lot.

Deep tire tracks not only cut into the gravel lot, but into every patch of soft dirt over by the trees where her newly planted grass had been growing. Dirt and debris lay scattered across the lot. Dirt in the gravel. Gravel in the dirt. Grass hung like tinsel from a branch of a rhododendron. Over by the sidewalk, grass hung from several azalea bushes.

She moved a few steps closer to the middle of the lot, her mouth hanging open as she barely breathed.

Her gloves lay where she had left them. Along with her rake and water bottle. But where was her shovel?

Her eyes shifted, turning her entire body as if the strange markings spray-painted on the back wall of the gym literally pulled her in for a closer look. Over the pale gray paint she so carefully laid down months ago, the Eastsiders had left their tag. Huge, violent, black letters displayed mesmerizing artwork. Obscenely beautiful. Terrifying to her core.

Desperate to pull her eyes away, she glanced down, only to see all her flowers in the strip against the building lying broken and trampled into the dirt. Huge shoe prints, with perfect imprints of Nike Swooshes centered in each one, covered the ground. Ground she had so carefully turned. Flowers she had planted and watered and cared for and loved.

Her feet carried her back a few steps, away from the sight of it. Trying to move farther away, she almost tripped, but caught her balance. Suddenly dizzy, she knelt to one knee, then forced her eyes to close. Her hand came up to cover them, yet the sharp lettering in the artwork of the tag remained in her mind's eye.

EASTSIDERS.

Oh, Lord . . .

Her stomach hurt. She turned to sit in the middle of the lot, her back facing the wall, her eyes searching the comforting branches of the Douglas fir above her for signs of life, for the flutter of a chickadee or the furry gray tail of a squirrel.

Her eyes closed as the breeze chilled the moisture on her forehead. She wiped her face with the shoulder of her T-shirt.

They returned for only one reason. To leave a personal message for the woman holding that shovel. They had no idea who she was, but she stood her ground and stared them down. They didn't forget that. And they never would forget that.

But she didn't purposely set out to stand her ground. With Enrique effectively pinning her down from behind and with nowhere to run, what else could she do?

Couldn't they see the terror in her eyes? Didn't they know how much they terrified her?

Lord Jesus . . . help me . . .

They saw her terror. And returned to inflict just a wee bit more. Fine. It was enough. Now they would leave her alone.

Right?

Would they be back?

She needed to clean up the mess they left behind. ASAP. Before anyone else saw it. Before anyone else suffered from the terror they hoped to inflict.

Kay had been teaching her class. With the music blaring, they all had been oblivious. And they were still oblivious. The Eastsiders didn't disrupt her class; they didn't even appear to have attempted to enter the gym.

They didn't go after Kay and her class. They knew their limits. This wasn't about Kay and her class or about anything else going on at the gym. This was about Chris. The crazy woman standing

there holding that stupid shovel. Standing between them and a terrified kid. A kid they wanted. A kid who did something to set the
entire chain of events in motion.

That kid. And the woman staring down the barrel of that
automatic pistol.

Enrique, what did you do? You've put us all in danger. Why?

Her eyes pinched shut. She rubbed her forehead.

The boy was gone. And safe.

Was she safe? Would they be back?

Clapping noises drifted toward her on the breeze. Kay's class.
Happy and free. Oblivious.

They made no attempt to enter the gym.

Could she keep this moment just about her? Could she clean
up the mess and paint over the tag without anyone else knowing
about any of it?

If he wasn't already, the good cop Richardson would soon be
in the area. It was a good chance after Ben told him about the pistol being pointed at Chris, Richardson would want to talk to her.
He'd eventually show up at the gym, looking for answers, looking
for evidence that the Eastsiders had been causing trouble in his
precinct.

She couldn't hide this from Ben. He owned the property and
needed to know exactly what happened. Pictures needed to be taken
of the entire lot. Evidence.

Would charges be filed?

Lord, don't let this get any more out of hand. Please?

Filing charges would only exacerbate the entire mess.

She needed to get up. Immediately. She needed to call Ben.

Maybe the good cop Richardson was busy on another call.
Maybe they'd send out a cop who didn't know Chris McIntyre or
about her two previous innocent incidences.

She didn't move. Only breathed. The breeze played with the
stray strands of hair that had worked their way out of her French
braid. One strand tickled her cheek.

No. With her luck, they'd send Sugar Ray Richardson. The good cop would definitely find out about everything. And this would probably classify as a third innocent incident in his book. Officially labeling Chris McIntyre a troublemaker.

Great. Just great.

She needed to go back inside the gym, crawl into a corner of her office, and pretend the day never dawned.

She pushed up to stand and brushed herself off. She'd give Ben a call and wait for Richardson to show up to take his pictures and ask his questions. Immediately afterward, she'd dig out the Brillo pads and gray paint and attempt to remove the hideous graffiti before anyone else in the neighborhood saw it.

Before the Eastsiders returned to gloat over it. And inflict more terror because of it.

No. If they returned, they'd see nothing but a freshly painted wall. All their hard work scoured away and painted over. But they'd still be able to see what they had done to Chris's hard work. Most of the flowers and the tender new grass would not survive.

They'd still gloat.

If they came back.

A part of her dared to pray they would never come back. Yet, somehow, deep down inside her, she knew they would. They'd find the wall freshly painted and laugh at the terror that had caused Chris to so quickly paint it over. They would laugh at Chris, just as they laughed at her before. They'd laugh at Ben, and at the Kimberley Street Community Church. They'd laugh at anyone foolish enough to stand in their way.

No doubt about it. They'd be back. It was just a matter of time.

TWO

Erin Mathis secured the tapes of the diaper around her squirming baby daughter and closed the snaps on the bottom of the Winnie-the-Pooh onesie. And then couldn't resist blowing a loud raspberry into that soft, plump belly. Her wiggly little one promptly clamped both hands around her mommy's hair and pulled. Erin's laughter gave way to a slight shriek. "Hey now! That's not playing fair." She eased the tiny fingers apart and tugged her hair out of the ferocious grip.

The huge smile on that chubby face proved the game had potential, but only if the parameters changed just a tad.

Erin held her daughter's hands in both of her own, felt the tiny fists clamp onto her index fingers, then leaned in again for another loud raspberry. "Got you that time, little boo." She blew one more against her daughter's belly, then pulled away and watched pure laughter dance in those gorgeous brown eyes, in those tiny kicking feet. "Little Kicking Feet. That's what we should call you. From day one I've loved your little kicking feet."

So amazing. Basking in the wonder of motherhood, Erin played patty-cake with her little one even as her heart burst within her. Prayers of thanksgiving and praise flooded her.

Again.

And she knew they would never stop. This was a forever moment. Overwhelmed with motherhood, and with being her Father God's own. Being loved and cherished by Him even more than she loved and cherished this little babe, flesh of her own flesh. Never before had the level of her Father's love meant so much. Never before had she cared for anything so precious.

"Mia Renae ... how your daddy and I love you."

Perfect tiny fingers, such perfect little pink fingernails. Quick to reach out and grab whatever dangled close. Quick to pat Erin's cheek.

Such a gentle pat. Such inquisitive eyes. Erin could almost hear her daughter's thoughts at that moment. *Are you my mommy? You are. You are! Let me look at you. Hold still! When's dinner? When can I borrow the car?*

"Oh, that deserves another raspberry." And she let her have it, long and loud against the Winnie-the-Pooh onesie as she dodged those kicking feet.

"What's that vulgar noise I hear?"

Erin pulled away and gazed wide-eyed at her daughter. "Is that Daddy? Why, yes, I think it is."

Mia's smile carried a hint of laughter as her head turned toward the sound of his voice.

Definitely Daddy's girl. Erin couldn't deny it.

"Did you just get a change? My little boo-boo-boo." Scott rubbed Erin's shoulders and lowered his voice to a sultry level. "And how are you, my big boo-boo-boo?"

"Perfect." She leaned into his sideways embrace and kissed him. He gave her no other choice.

"Mmm, you smell good." He kissed her again.

"And you smell like you stopped at Sal's. Meatball sandwich?"

"With extra provolone. I would've brought you one ..." He leaned over to nuzzle his daughter's cheek.

"Yeah, I know. It's the thought that counts. Especially with Sal's meatball sandwiches."

"Mmm. You smell good too. My two sweet-smelling girls." Scott picked Mia up and held her over his head for a second, then lowered her to his lips. Loud smooches followed. He lifted her again. "Why is there a cop parked outside Ben's house?"

"What?"

More boo-boo noises and loud smooches.

Erin walked to the front screen door and peered across the street. Sure enough, there sat a City of Portland police car. "Hmm. I have no idea."

"Why don't you go check it out? We'll be here."

She looked over her shoulder and gave her husband a playful smirk. "Sure. Why not? I've been here all morning while you've been gone. I'd love the chance to get away."

Scott carried Mia over to the love seat. Seemed oblivious to what Erin just said.

"Actually, I'm going to take your Mustang and head to the coast for a few days."

"All right, dear." Totally engrossed in baby talk. And he knew better. They both read somewhere that they should talk to their child in complete sentences. It helped her learn language faster. But Scott couldn't resist any more than Erin could.

She stifled a grin. "I may be gone for a whole week."

No reply. Except for more baby talk.

Erin turned once again to peer across the street. "I'll be back in a few minutes."

"Okay. We'll be here."

She laughed. Couldn't help it. Gave them one more long look. Then ran her fingers through her hair to straighten the wayward curls, pushed her feet into her clogs, and headed across Kimberley Street to see what was happening at Ben and Sonya's house.

Maybe it was nothing. Though Erin did hear tires screeching earlier. Sounded like a bunch of hooligans up to no good. But was that enough to bring out the cavalry?

Another thought almost stole her breath. *Where's Chris?*

She wanted to laugh even as a thread of fear wrapped around her.

Why would she think of her best friend now? Just because a police car sat in front of Sonya's house, why would that involve Chris?

Well, maybe because the last few times I've seen a police car ...

She let the thought drift away on a breath of laughter. And refused to think about it for another second. It had all the makings of classic association anxiety. She needed to work on that.

She knocked on Sonya's front screen door and gave her a warm smile. "Hey, lady."

"Erin. Sweetheart. Come in." Sonya pushed the door open. "How's our precious baby-child?"

Sonya's Southern drawl tickled Erin's ears even as the woman's soft kiss tickled her cheek. "Fine. Great. Better than great. But what's up over here?"

"Oh, sweetheart, there's been some excitement. The officer is just checking things out for us. We're out back." Sonya led the way through her dining room to her back door.

Erin followed her out to the back porch. And there stood Cappy Sanchez. Surprised, Erin sidled up to her friend. "Hey, you. What's up?"

"*Hola, mamacita.*" Cappy flashed a wide smile. "Blew the coop for a spell, eh?"

It wasn't as if Erin spent every single minute of her life in her house with her new baby. She did get out every once in a while. "I was sent on a mission to find out what's up. So what's up?" She shielded her eyes and squinted across Sonya's backyard to the parking lot of the church where Ben and a tall African-American police officer stood.

"Bandoleros."

Her hand dropped as she met Cappy's gaze. Her stomach flopped.

"They have arisen from the dead."

Her knees felt as if they would give out any second.

"And they dragged a few Eastsiders into our neighborhood."

Erin closed her eyes and lowered her head. "Stop, Cap. I don't want to hear any more." A resurrection of the Bandoleros was bad enough. But finding out the hooligans that were up to no good earlier were actually part of one of the worst gangs in the city was beyond bad. She dropped into one of Sonya's deck chairs.

Cappy sat beside her. "So. How was your morning?"

Erin gave her friend a growling look.

"Ahh, just when life gets boring, along comes another adventure."

"Don't wax poetic, Cap. Not about this."

"What's not to wax? We knew it would eventually come to this."

But how hard they had all prayed that it would not?

Erin glanced up at Sonya. The soft look of resignation she received told her they obviously had not prayed hard enough.

"One of them even pointed a mini-assault rifle at Chris."

Erin's heart slammed to a stop. "What did you say?"

"Yep." Cappy pressed her lips into a firm grin. "Chris has all the luck, doesn't she?"

"Where is she?"

"Back at the gym." Cappy softened. "She's fine, Erin. They were just playing with her. They were after the little Bandolero kid. Chased him for blocks, I guess."

"Is he okay?"

"Disappeared. But I'm sure he's all right by now." She peered across the yard at the church, then sat up and raised her head an inch. "Ahh ... this can't be good."

Erin turned to see Ben leading the police officer back toward the porch at a quick pace. His right hand gripped his cell phone.

Cappy whispered something in Spanish.

"Chris just called." Ben's face bore an intensity Erin hadn't seen in a long time, not since they worked together in Saudi Arabia during Desert Storm. "We're heading over to the gym."

"Benjamin?" Sonya moved to his side.

"They paid the gym a return visit. Painted their graffiti on the back wall and pretty much made a mess of things."

The words fell over Erin like a smothering blanket. *Oh, Lord ... Father God ...*

Cappy jumped out of her chair and headed down the stairs.

Erin closed her eyes for another second and let the rest of her prayer find voice in her heart. *We need You.*

She pushed out of her chair and followed her friends and the police officer down Kimberley Street to the gym.

✵✵✵

MAKING THE CALL HAD BEEN agony. Now waiting for them to arrive about drove her insane. Trying not to alert Kay and her class, Chris carried out a cardboard box full of everything she would need to clean up the mess the minute she received the green light. Brillo pads, garbage bags, a paint brush, a gallon can half full of the gray paint they used last spring to paint the outside of the gym, a stirrer, a bottle of water, a roll of paper towels, and her bottle of aspirin. She had already taken three. If they didn't start working soon, she'd take two more.

It wasn't fair. But what was fair, anyway? Why did Enrique have to see her standing there? He could have ducked into any hiding place and waited them out. Why were they chasing him? What did he do? And why did he think she could protect him from them? How in the world was she supposed to do that? Beat them all unconscious with her shovel?

They didn't care at all about her. Not at first. They wanted him. Poor kid. And they didn't care one bit about the gym. Even on their return visit, they didn't enter the gym. This wasn't about terrorizing everyone. Just the kid. And Chris.

Well, they pretty effectively carried out that mission.

But what did they do with her shovel?

She plopped the box down at the end of the walkway and sat beside it. The early afternoon air was warm, but not hot. Except for the few weeks of hundred-degree weather in early July, for the most part the summer had been pleasant. For a mid-August afternoon, Chris could not complain. She hated hot weather.

She missed her Colorado home. Missed the mountains. The fresh, clear air. The deep peace she used to know there. Back before it all blew up in her face.

Lord Jesus, how can You stand to be near me right now? Quite a pity party I'm throwing for myself, huh?

A long, deep breath carried scents of car exhaust, fresh dirt, and a hint of fir. Closing her eyes, she focused on the sounds of the city. Passing cars on the street. An airplane on ascent out of Portland International. The slight breeze blowing through the dry leaves of the rhododendron bush beside her.

Footsteps behind her. Cappy's voice. *"Ay caramba, hermaña."*

Her head lowered until her chin almost touched her chest.

"Can't leave you alone for one second. Look at the trouble you've once again found yourself in."

She pushed up to stand. "Say another word, Cappy, and I'll stuff a Brillo pad in your mouth."

Silence.

"Chris?"

The new voice made her smile. She turned to her best friend. "Hey, Rinny."

"Are you all right?"

Erin moved in close, then Sonya and Cappy crowded around her. Chris was fine, and she told them so.

Cappy walked over to gape at the Eastsiders' handiwork. Sonya took a few steps into the lot and stopped, her hand covering her mouth as she stared at the mess. Erin stayed close. Quiet. Chris couldn't look at her. She fought against the heat threatening to engulf her cheeks.

But then Ben stepped into the lot, followed closely by Officer Ray Richardson.

Almost groaning aloud, Chris wanted to find her shovel, dig a huge hole with it, and bury herself alive.

Well, what did you expect? Of course, of all the cops in Portland, it would have to be him.

He gave her a quick smile, then took a long look at the gang's tag. "Well, they certainly left no doubt as to who is responsible."

She laughed in spite of herself.

"So, Miss McIntyre, how have you been?" The officer wore dark sunglasses, hiding most of the laughter in his eyes. But not all. "It's been a few months since I've officially interrogated you. I may be a bit rusty."

"I doubt it." Chris tried to rein in her grin. It was difficult.

Richardson pulled a small camera from an attaché case and handed it to Ben. "Would you take some pictures while I talk to Miss McIntyre?"

"Certainly." Ben winked at Chris, then slid his cell phone into the front pocket of his jeans and took the camera. He immediately went to work, with Cappy by his side pointing out the highlights of the mess for him.

What a pain that girl could be. Chris needed to call her *Capriella* more often. Exact some revenge.

Richardson softened his voice. "So what do I need to know about what happened here this morning, Chris?" He lifted off his shades and smiled.

"You heard about the Bandolero kid?"

He pulled a black notebook from the attaché. "Some. But I'd like to hear it again from you."

Chris told him. But she left out the part about the kid leaving red marks on her arms. She was glad her T-shirt sleeves covered that small detail.

Richardson wrote in his book. "And about the Eastsiders?"

She told him.

"Can you describe any of the boys?"

"I can describe them all. Scary. Mean-looking. Obnoxious. Rude. And loud."

Richardson's eyebrow lifted. "Anything more ... specific?"

Chris glanced at Erin and felt a bit of comfort in the smile she saw on Erin's face. It amazed her once again how much like sisters they had become.

"Mr. Connelly said one of the boys had gold caps on his front teeth. Did you see this boy?"

How could she miss him? "Um, yes. He seemed to be one of the loudest mouths."

"Yeah, he is. And his name's Antwoine. Definitely one of the loudest in the bunch."

Antwoine. Mr. Gold Cap now had a first name.

"And one of the more dangerous. Did he say anything specific to you? Did he threaten you in any way?"

Chris glanced again at Erin, then at Sonya. If they heard too much of the story, both would never let her live it down. She cleared her throat. "Well, he did happen to mention a few rather unpleasant things he'd like to do to me. But they seemed pretty occupied with the kid." She needed to change the subject. "Oh, and the one with the pistol had a total baby face. Though he looked older. I think they called him Bones."

Richardson made a note in his book. "Hmm. That may be Terrance. He usually goes by T-Bones. Original, huh?"

"Do you know these boys?" Sonya moved a few steps closer. "Just how dangerous are they? Do you think they may be back?"

The cop scratched a spot on the back of his head. "Well, ma'am, I know a few of them. Mostly the older boys. And it's hard to tell if they'll be back. They're a fairly dangerous gang, but for the most part, they stay on their own turf. Whether or not they come back depends on if they're actively seeking to expand their territory. With their increased activity lately, it appears that may be on their mind."

Chris glanced at her friends. The words seemed to hit them all the same way. Hard. And no one seemed to know what to say in reply.

Ben handed the camera to the officer. "Got most of it."

"Thanks. I'll send all this to our Youth Gangs Unit. They'll sort it all out." Richardson turned to face Ben. "Are you sure you don't want to press charges? Not that I'll blame you if you don't. From what I've seen, it may just make things worse."

Ben shook his head and looked at Chris. "I wish if we did press charges, it would stop. But I know it won't. And we're all right." His eyes implored, as if he sought reassurance from Chris in that moment. "We've been through worse."

She savored the sight of his warm smile. "Yes, sir." Her voice shook a bit. "We have."

Ben turned to Richardson. "So I guess we say thanks, but no thanks. But we'll certainly let you know if they show up again anytime soon."

The officer nodded. "Yes. Please do that. We're close by. And we care. You know that." He looked at Chris. "See you Thursday night?"

"You bet. And bring that jump shot. You're gonna need it against Fire. Jason's been bragging about how they're going to take the league."

Richardson snorted. "That boyfriend of yours is a windbag. I'll make him pay."

Chris tried not to laugh, but it spurted out anyway. True, her boyfriend loved to taunt the other teams in the league, but to call him a windbag? That was a stretch.

But to call him your boyfriend isn't?

The thought struck her. Boyfriend. The word sounded so juvenile. But the way she felt around Jason Sloan, the way he swept into her life and captured her heart, the word certainly fit. Even if he sometimes could be a windbag.

Richardson said his good-byes and started down the walkway toward the street. Before Chris could object, Ben scooped up the box of supplies. Without even a glance her way, he headed for the gym's back wall with Sonya following him. Erin grabbed Chris's rake and joined Cappy over by the azalea bushes, where she started cleaning up as Cappy pulled the uprooted grass from the bushes.

Chris stood still and silent, allowing the sight to settle her heart. Of course, her friends wouldn't leave her alone to clean up the mess. And with their help, it wouldn't take long until the lot looked presentable once again.

She wouldn't need to take the extra aspirin. At this rate, her headache would soon be gone.

But a sudden thought caused her to turn and yell after Richardson.

He stopped and looked back.

"Not only were they loud, rude, and stupid, but they also stole my shovel!"

At first the cop didn't say anything. He didn't move, and he was too far away for Chris to tell if he was hiding his laughter. Finally, he said, "Okay. I'll make a note of it."

"If you find it, I want it back."

"All right, Chris. If I find your shovel, I'll definitely bring it back."

"Thanks, Ray."

"That's Officer Richardson to you, Miss McIntyre."

His playful words reminded her of another dilemma. "Does this qualify as my third innocent incident?"

He tossed her a dismissing wave. "Nah. Not even close."

Whew. "Okay. See you Thursday."

"Tell your boyfriend to be sure and bring his game."

"He never leaves home without it."

Rumbling laughter followed the man as he turned and headed back down Kimberley Street.

Chris watched him go, enjoying the sound. Until the gym doors swung open and several sweating, chattering ladies walked out. They glanced Chris's way and smiled, but then must have noticed that something was happening in the back lot, for all of them ceased smiling and chattering and turned from their previous course to head straight for her.

Great. Just great. So much for cleaning up the mess before anyone else found out about it.

So much for hoarding the Eastsiders' inflicted terror all to herself.

It's always polite to share anyway.

Gasping in horror, the women surveyed the scene.

Chris tried not to smile at their antics, and wasn't surprised when they dropped their belongings and joined the others. In a matter of minutes, the work was done. Except for the smell of fresh paint, the sight of the bare dirt that used to hold flowers and new shoots of grass, and the pile of garbage bags full of the broken flowers and wilting shoots, no one passing by the lot would ever imagine anything amiss took place there earlier that day.

But a little while later, as Chris walked home with her friends, dread fell over her entire being. She knew the image of that mini machine gun pointed at her chest would haunt her dreams. And the sharp, violent lettering spray-painted on the back wall of the gym would remain in her mind's eye for a long time.

★★★

ERIN WALKED QUIETLY BESIDE CHRIS, holding a small bouquet of broken pansies in her hand. She remembered the day Chris planted them in the strip of dirt by the gym's back wall. The simple brilliance of their shape and color captured her. The tenderness with which Chris planted them now saddened her. All that effort wasted.

But it wouldn't take long. New flowers would soon be planted. Until then, these pansies would adorn the ledge under Erin's kitchen window.

She wished they would last forever. But she knew they'd eventually die. Tiny casualties of the Eastsiders' senseless cruelty.

She glanced again at Chris. Though she wanted to, she wouldn't fuss. She wouldn't ask Chris again if she was all right. Chris was fine. She had certainly seen and survived much worse in her lifetime. All of them, as former U.S. Army soldiers, and

Sonya too, as a lifelong army spouse, had seen much worse. Yet Erin could tell the events of the morning left all her friends shaken. Even Cappy seemed spooked. Her usual friendly joking with Chris seemed tempered. But maybe that had something to do with her not wanting a Brillo pad stuffed in her mouth?

Arm in arm, Ben and Sonya led the way home, and they did not hurry. The short walk settled into a leisurely pace. Erin didn't mind. Scott still had another half hour of free time before he needed to take over for Kyle at the clinic, and Erin fully expected to go home and see both her husband and her three-month-old daughter asleep on the couch, enjoying their afternoon naps.

The thought made her smile.

She glanced again at Chris. And again looked away before Chris could catch her in the act.

Ben's voice sifted into her thoughts. *"You worry too much about her."* He said the words months ago after they talked for hours about the time they spent in Saudi Arabia, about Erin's friendship with Chris and how it had developed as Operation Desert Shield gave way to Storm. They prayed hard for Chris that night. The memory, their prayers, and Ben's words returned often to play on the fringes of Erin's mind. She couldn't deny his words were true. She did worry too much about Chris, but she also knew it was worth it to worry.

Besides, wasn't that what friends were for?

Chris would not be pleased if she knew how worried Erin was for her at that moment.

Chris had been shaken by the Eastsiders. And it wasn't often that Erin saw Chris McIntyre shaken.

The sight unsettled her, even as they walked quietly, side by side.

Lord, I hate feeling this way. I hate worrying about her. But yet I love it. You know it's true.

To love someone was to worry about them. To always want to see that smile in their eyes. To know all was well with them. To know there was nothing to fear. No reason to worry after all.

I don't want to worry about her. I trust her to You. She belongs to You anyway. Her heart is Yours.

She relished that thought, and the memory of that night when her friend's life became new.

And yet there was still so much to learn about Chris. So much she kept hidden, even after all they had been through. Always trying to protect Erin. Always trying to make light of things, to water down the truth to make it palatable. Ever so considerate. And ever so infuriating.

After all the rush and chaos of Erin's delivery to the time she brought her new baby home from the hospital, and with her parents visiting for as long as they did, Erin still had yet to hear the entire story about Chris's trip to Colorado when she faced her father for the first time in fourteen years. Chris traveled all that way to tell her father she forgave him for everything, for a past so terrifying and cruel. To forgive and forget and then to move on.

Chris had forgiven her father. But since then, in the past three months, had she been able to forget and move on? Erin didn't know; they had not yet found time to talk about it. Not really. Not nearly as deeply as Erin wanted to.

Time was hard to come by these days. Life was certainly getting in the way.

And that kicking little babe was certainly making her presence known to all the inhabitants of Kimberley Square. Maybe even the entire city by now.

Ben and Sonya slowed to a stop in front of their house and turned to face Erin, Cappy, and Chris. "Y'all are most welcome to come in for some lemonade." Sonya slipped her arm around Ben's waist. "Or some sweet iced tea."

"None for me, Sonya. But thanks." Cappy moved past them and took a few backward steps toward the church. "I need to check in with Isaiah. He's probably wondering what happened to me. I'll see you all later tonight." She gave them a wave and turned, but immediately turned again as she walked. "Oh, and Chris? Try to stay out of trouble at least until then, okay? Let's not have to put Officer Richardson's number into our speed dials."

"Yeah, yeah." Chris pointed in the direction of Cappy's feet. "You better watch where you're going, Capriella. You may just step in what you're dishing out."

Laughing heartily, Cappy turned and quickened her pace toward the church.

"That girl." Sonya shook her head as her lips pressed into a firm line.

"She's loco. I'm telling you." Chris pouted for a second, then let herself smile. She looked at Sonya. "And thanks for the offer, lady, but I think I need some serious Mia time." She turned to meet Erin's gaze.

Erin grinned. "Me too. I've been away from her now for what, almost an hour?" She winked at Sonya. "See you two tonight."

"Let's hope we can locate our son by then." Ben looked down at his wife. "Notice how he conveniently missed out on all the excitement?"

"He's around here somewhere. Or at least he will be for the Bible study." Sonya ushered her husband toward their front door. "And if I don't get a move on, there won't be any cookies baked in time." They both gave Chris and Erin one last wave before heading inside.

Chris returned their wave and said, "See you later," but her voice barely carried the words.

Strange. Erin didn't think Sonya or Ben even heard what Chris said. And as Chris's hand came down, her eyes still gazed at the front door of their house. She didn't say another word. Yet Erin heard every word Chris didn't say just fine.

I love you guys.

Loud and clear.

A second later, Chris turned to Erin and sighed deeply. "So. Can I come get some Mia time?"

"Um ... well ... not if I get to her first!" Erin took off across the street, trying not to fall in her clogs, trying not to hurt her already-damaged pansies. Chris easily caught up with her and passed her. Which was fine. This was one race Erin planned to let Chris win anyway.

Chris bounded up the stairs of the duplex, then softened her steps and tiptoed across the porch to the front screen door. Giggling softly, she turned to Erin and lifted her finger to her lips. "Shh. Sleeping baby."

Erin stepped closer and whispered, "It is about that time."

"Sleeping husband too?"

"Probably."

Chris pulled open the door. Sure enough, daddy and daughter lay snoozing. A delightful sight.

"Gotta wash up. I'll be right back." Chris headed upstairs to the bathroom.

Erin left her clogs by the door, walked into the kitchen to put her pansies in a glass of water, then sat on the coffee table beside the couch. She resisted the urge to touch her tiny daughter. To take the hand of her sleeping husband.

Lying on his stomach, he breathed soft and slow, and the pillow pushed his thick brown hair askew. His chin sported an early five o'clock shadow. His hand rested on the lip of the wooden cradle he had made for his daughter. Their little one, growing so fast, getting so big, lay nestled deeply in it. Gently rocked to sleep. Until the rocking carried away her daddy as well.

Such sweet rest. Another moment to cherish for all time.

Erin eased up and then sat on the love seat across from them. She put her feet up on the coffee table and slouched low in the seat so her head could rest back against it.

Chris tiptoed down the stairs and into the living room to sit next to Erin. For a long while, neither of them said a word. Erin treasured the silence. The hush of her husband's soft breaths. The quiet ticking of the clock on the kitchen wall. The presence of her best friend beside her. A perfect addition to the moment.

"Daddy's a bit tuckered out," Chris whispered.

"Yeah. He didn't sleep well last night."

"You sleeping any better?"

"Yeah. She's doing better. And so am I."

A pause. "Good."

Erin turned to give Chris a smile. "You want her now?"

"Let them sleep a bit longer."

"He needs to get up. He's due at the clinic."

Chris didn't reply.

But Scott did. He stretched and groaned. Then blinked open his eyes. "Yeah, poor Daddy's got to go back to work."

Poor, poor Daddy. Erin grinned but kept her thought to herself.

"Yeah, me too," Chris said to him. "But I needed some Mia time to make things right."

Scott pushed up to sit on the couch, then ran a hand through his crumpled hair. "Things not right in your world, Chris?"

"Never a dull moment in my world. You should know that by now." She looked over at Erin. "But it's nothing to worry about. Nothing major."

"Nothing a little Mia time won't fix." Scott's sleepy brown eyes carried his smile.

"Exactly."

"Funny how she makes everything right." He reached down to caress the back of her hand. "Daddy'll be back, sweetheart."

"At least you won't be that far away."

"Yeah." Scott pushed up from the couch and stretched again. "That is true. You gotta love that commute." He stepped around the cradle and coffee table, leaned over the love seat, and kissed Erin deeply. "Come see me later, okay? Or I'll get lonely."

"Oh, my. You poor, poor man." She kissed him again, then smoothed his cheek where the pillow left a crease. "I'll bring you some coffee."

"Yes. Please do. I can't handle that stuff Kyle drinks." Another quick kiss. Scott moved around behind the love seat. "See you tonight, Chris." He gave Chris's braid a tug before pushing through the door leading into the other half of the duplex housing the clinic.

"Later, dude." Chris watched the door swing shut behind him, then turned to Erin. "I thought he'd never leave."

Sudden giggles made it hard for Erin to push herself out of the love seat. "Listen to you."

"Don't tell him I said that." Chris kicked off her sneakers and situated herself sideways into the corner of the couch with her back against the pillowed armrest and her feet up on the cushions. She stuffed a rolled-up receiving blanket under her left arm, then draped another over her left shoulder and chest.

Erin gently lifted her sleeping daughter from the cradle and placed her in the crook of Chris's left arm so her head rested against Chris's shoulder. She stepped back and watched the familiar scene play out.

Chris snuggled down into the couch, pulling her knees up and resting them against the back of it. She stared at Mia, holding her as if she were a priceless porcelain doll. Fragile and precious. Wonder and awe seemed to gush from every corner of Chris's being.

At that moment, Erin could wave her arms and dance a jig and Chris wouldn't notice. She could stand and gawk at the sight, but she didn't want to intrude on the moment. She sat back on the love seat and kicked her feet up once again. Hugged a pillow to her chest and toyed with the idea of taking a nap. Mia would sleep at least another half hour. Maybe more. And Chris would sit still and quiet, just watching the little babe sleep.

Another moment engrained deeply in Erin's heart.

Tears blurred the sight. She let her eyes close as a deep breath washed through her.

These precious tears. These, and all the others recently shed. They were simple gifts from God to replace her many tears of anguish, worry, and fear. All the years of praying and wondering. For every moment Erin spent crying out to God on Chris's behalf, it seemed He gave her a moment like this to savor. A reminder of His love. A glimpse into His ways. A reward for her perseverance. For her obedience. And for her love.

Where would Chris be at this moment without Erin's perseverance? Or her obedience to get up and go when her Lord asked her to go?

But it wasn't that easy. Erin didn't gallantly travel to Colorado last winter to dutifully obey her Lord's call to go. She didn't even know if she should go. Scott didn't exactly want her to go. If she honestly assessed her actions of last January, she would have to admit she actually disobeyed her husband to go to Colorado.

Disobeyed, perhaps, but not to dishonor. The urgency of the situation demanded a quick decision. She just decided to do the one thing her husband asked her not to do. He didn't understand the urgency. Didn't understand how deeply Erin had been brought into the plan working out between Chris and her Creator. Chris's Creator longed to become Chris's Father. And He needed Erin to complete His plan.

Only now was that plan fully recognizable. At the time, no one knew what was going on. Especially Erin.

A part of her wondered what the future held. What more of His plan had yet to play out?

Whatever You need, Lord, I'm with You. Thank You for Your plan. Thank You for using me in it.

A part of her wondered where Chris would be right now, at that very moment, if she hadn't flown to Colorado last January to be by Chris's side.

A shiver of fear worked its way through her. She knew where Chris would be. But she hated to consider it for even one second.

It's done, Lord. She's here. You've worked out Your plan. And she's ... alive. Oh, thank You for saving her. Thank You for making her Your own. And for putting her here with us. With me.

"Rinny?"

Erin opened her eyes and blinked to focus. Chris's whisper was as faint as a breath. Saying Erin's name in the way only she said it.

"You awake?"

"Yeah." Erin whispered as well.

Chris didn't look up. Didn't take her eyes off Mia. "Rinny ... she is so ... beautiful." The whisper cracked. Chris still didn't look up. "I'm gonna cry again."

Erin's breath carried a hint of the laughter inside her. She hoped Chris didn't hear it. "Do you need a tissue?"

"No. Not yet."

"Let me know when you do and I'll get you one."

A pause. "Okay. You better get me one."

Her laughter escaping, Erin pushed up from the love seat and walked to the small table at Chris's end of the couch. She pulled up three tissues and laid them on Chris's chest, then squeezed Chris's shoulder. "There you go, lady."

"Thanks." Still just a whisper. And Chris still did not look up.

"Need anything else?"

"No."

Erin sat again on the love seat, then pulled her feet up and leaned against the arm of it. With a pillow under her and her head resting on another, she would fall asleep, if she allowed it. In a heartbeat.

Chris slowly lifted her head and looked over at Erin. Her eyes glimmered with tears as she smiled.

No words were spoken.

Nothing more needed to be said.

Chris picked up a tissue and dabbed it at her eyes. Then once again gazed at the sleeping babe in her arms.

For just a few seconds, Mia's tiny lips pursed as if to suckle as she dreamed.

Erin closed her eyes and fell into the abyss of a glorious afternoon nap.

THREE

His name was Jamaal. Not Homeboy, Homie, Dawg, Boy, or G. But no one called him Jamaal. Except his mother. His posse sometimes called him Maal. It was close, and he figured it was as close as they would get. If he stayed with this crew, he'd have to be down with that.

But he never called his friends their real names either. Marcus and Earl and Andre and Michael. They were Q-Tee, Rummy, Dre, and Emmin. Or Homeboy, Homie, Dawg, or Boy. Or anything else that fit the sitch.

"Yo, G, don't get flexed, boy. Be quick, yo. Dance and dee-light."

"Word up, G." He pounded fists with Rummy.

G. Everyone was G. Everyone wanted to be a gangsta. Like one of dem gangsta rappers. Like Jamaal's big brother, Jerome. Now there was a gangsta. King of da crib, he was. Word up, he ran tall and did his thang. Until he got himself dead.

Jamaal glanced around at his homeboys. All of them seemed to fondle something. Their rides, or their hotties, or whatever they was packin'. Or smokin'. Life with this crew was starting to wear thin. He loved his homies. But he loved his brother more.

Too whatup, this scene. Sometimes they all hung tight like best bros. Other times, they'd turn on him and be his worst enemies. One flash they'd be all hangin' and chillin', the next, something would happen to get them all trippin'. So fast they'd turn. And turn against him. They'd be all up in his bi'ness, flappin' their jaws and getting all loud and wigged, like he didn't matter one iota in the crib. But then they'd take notice to his stock and back down.

He wasn't no youngin wannabe. Some punk wangster. He paid his dues to carry his stock in this crew.

And he was paying them still. Called out like some scrubbin' fool.

Duncey done called him out. Duncey da dunce, so dumb he couldn't make two and two. But wanting to move up. Wanting to pull down some of Jamaal's stock and make it his own.

Simple little callout. Two dawgs and their blades. One on one, they'd dance and dee-light. First to draw blood would move up the chain. First to be drawn would slip a link. And if the drawing laid one of them out, for the other, all the better.

It wasn't a fight to the death. At least, it wasn't supposed to be. But if it turned out that way ... who would care. Just one less homie in da hood.

Duncey da dunce. In Jamaal's stock, Duncey wouldn't last a hot minute. But he talked the talk. Soon it'd be time for him to walk the walk.

The better blade would win. The other would just bleed.

Jamaal sat on the front corner of his ride and forced himself into total impassivity. Surrounded by his boys, he wouldn't give up how his stomach quaked. A part of him ached to step off and walk away. Still too vivid—knowing Jerome lay in that 'fin, his face too far gone for anyone to want to lift the lid and take a last look. Eastsider ways kilt his big brah. And Jamaal was starting to figure if he didn't bail soon, they'd lead to his killin' too.

Soon, if he continued to move up the chain, his callouts would be fights to the death. Or as close as they could get to it. If he drew Duncey's blood this day, he'd move up. Another link on the way to the top, where Jerome once stood. But Jerome toked out. He rode that wave of swirlin' death until it done swallowed him up.

It was the crystal, or maybe the rock, that did him in. His death about broke their mama in two. She swore her boy Jamaal would stay clear of the Death of the Street. But she didn't know how fully entrenched her boy already was. She couldn't hold him down, couldn't lock him away from those who sucked him in.

It was Jerome who first brought him in and made him part of the crew. An Eastsider. Got him the tats and lined up his beatin'-in. And if Jamaal continued to move up the chain, he would one day stand with Twoine or Bones, or maybe even with Cee Train and Rafer. An Eastsider to the depths of his raggedy soul.

It would straight up kill his mama.

He boosted a cigarette and a light from Rummy. Pulled in a deep drag. Blew out the smoke through his nose.

He couldn't be thinking about his mama now. The way his stomach hurt, thinking about her would only send him trippin'.

He didn't want to hurt his mama. Not like Jerome did. Jerome, at first, was a good boy. But he grew up too fast. Became a man too soon in da hood. And was kilt by his own dawgs. Not kilt outright by them. No Eastsider put that gun to his head. No brah stuck that needle in his arm.

Flying so high. Not a clue the bullet would blow off half his head.

Jamaal's fist clenched. Yet he kept his face as hard as stone. Gritted his teeth. Then sucked another long drag from the cigarette.

When Cee Train gave the word, Jamaal would open his blade and get to work. He'd strike for Duncey's gut. No way Duncey could move like Jamaal. Jamaal was quicker, a bit younger, smarter. Meaner. No way Jamaal would let this dawg take him down.

Deep booming thumps of a hip-hop groove carried toward him. He flicked his burning cigarette into the gutter and turned slightly on the corner of his car to take a look.

Sho nuff, Shree's brown Chevy Impala crept up the street, forcing the homies and hoodrats to make a hole. Some of the rats were so young. Truly just boys. Hangin' wit da homeboys. Each one a hungry young wannabe.

Go home, y'all. Don't hang wit us. Don't be like us. Live.

He shifted his eyes to Shree's ride and watched as two of his fellow Eastsiders got out.

Twoine and Bones. Just in time for the show. And all braggin' about their trip into town. Bones showing off his new piece, pulling it up to kiss its stubby barrel. Jamaal glanced again toward Shree's car. Was that Cee Train? Did he go with them? It would appear that way. No wonder the man was nowheres around the crib. He was off joyin' with Shree.

The entire little entourage worked their way toward him. Jamaal didn't move. Didn't smile or say a word.

"Yo, Cee." Twoine's wicked grin flashed his golden twins. "Looks like our boy Maal is ready to raah-humm-ble. He's got his game face on." He put an arm around Jamaal's shoulder. "Slice and dice, boy. Duncey ain't no match for you. Cut 'im up, dawg."

"Word up, T." Jamaal's voice cracked from cigarette smoke stuck in his throat. Hoping they didn't notice, he pounded fists with Twoine and Bones, then relaxed a bit when they moved on. He could tell they were both high from the ride. Wherever they went and whatever they did, it left them pretty stoked. Once Duncey's callout was complete, the whole crew would probably go off somewhere and get half baked.

"Yo, boy." Cee Train gave Jamaal a smirk. "You ready to get it on?" He glanced at Duncey. "Whatup wit you, dawg? You ready?"

Duncey was too ready.

Cee Train stepped back into the middle of the street and held out his hands. "Then, my brothas, let's get this on." He drew his hands together and stepped back far enough to sit on the hood of Shree's ride.

Jamaal slowly stood, lifted off his long chains of silver, handed them to Rummy, then stepped away from his car. He reached into the pocket of his lowriders and gripped his blade. It fit just right, felt fine in his clammy hand. Warm and dry. He pulled it out and flipped it open. The steel glittered sunlight, but he glared at Duncey. "Last chance to back out, dawg."

"Yo. Don't be trippin' wit me, Maal. Come on. Let's see wha-cha got." Duncey stepped toward him.

Blade on blade. First to draw blood.

With his homeboys shouting, Jamaal moved in and went to work.

✯✯✯

CHRIS ONCE AGAIN TRAVELED THE familiar route across Kimberley Street and down the sidewalk two blocks to the gym. But this time, with the way her heart seemed to soar inside her, she resisted an overwhelming urge to skip. Prayers of gratitude whispered up from her soul. She could almost see her Lord Jesus walking beside her.

Can I take your hand, My love? Can we skip and dance together?

She hopped over a crack on the sidewalk. *That'll have to do, Lord. For now.* She didn't want her neighbors thinking she was any stranger than they already thought she was. The time to step out and dance would have to wait for the morning, when Chris first arrived at the gym and enjoyed having the place to herself for just that purpose.

She slowed her pace and gazed up at the sky. A thin haze diffused the usually brilliant blue expanse. Puffy white clouds floated along, though the haze tinted their edges dingy brown. The city needed a good hard rain to cut the dust and clean the air. She lowered her head, then smiled as His sweet words echoed again through her soul.

At times, His voice seemed to sneak into her thoughts. His words, so tender and kind. And they would stay with her, working their way to rest deep inside her. Maybe it was just her imagination. But she didn't think so.

"If you listen for God's voice, you'll hear it. You may even hear His thoughts as He hears yours."

The words stuck in her mind long after Pastor Andy spoke them. They seemed too wonderful to be true. But she knew they were true, and just like her Lord Jesus to speak so tenderly to her mind's ear.

Father, help me to always listen to You. And to Your Son. And not just to listen, but to hear.

Still so much to learn about her Father God. Sometimes she felt exactly like Mia, just a babe snuggled up in His arms.

And You love me so much more than I love her. Which I can't fathom, Father, because I can hardly handle the love I feel for her.

She skipped. Couldn't help it.

She's so amazing, Lord. Thank You so much for her. And for Rinny.

Just up the block, in front of the gym, a big white ambulance sat parked against the curb. Chris slowed to a walk.

Thanks for Scott too, Lord. He's such a good daddy. And a good friend.

An extremely familiar ambulance. Not only had she seen it before, but she had ridden in it. Had it really been over three months ago?

And thanks for the handsome man who belongs to that ambulance. But what is he doing here? And ... where is he?

She looked inside the cab. Empty. Then turned for the gym. She made it halfway down the walk when she heard two men talking, their voices filtering to her from the back lot.

"This is insane. I can't believe this!"

"Now, it's not that big of a deal. They were just strutting their stuff."

Curses. And other not-so-nice words.

Chris snuck up to the edge of the building and peeked around the corner. There stood her boy, Jason Matthew Sloan, all decked out in his paramedic's uniform, his cheeks glowing red, the long veins in his neck sticking out.

"They were here, Coop. This could have been so much worse."

"Ahh, man, don't let it get to you. Come on, let's get out of here."

"She'll be here soon. I'm waiting for her."

"Fine. Whatever. I'll be in the bus."

"Yeah. Go wait in the bus. Go ahead."

Chris stepped away from the building. "Aww, boys, don't fight now."

Her handsome paramedic brightened at the sight of her. He moved past Cooper and pulled her into his arms. "Chris. Are you all right?"

She let the embrace linger a second longer, then pushed away, keeping her hands on his chest. Her smile came easily, though his question angered her. "Why wouldn't I be?" She glanced at Cooper. "Hey, Coop. What are you guys doing here?"

Jason grabbed Chris's hands and held them. "Ray said Ben didn't press charges. Why not?"

"What doesn't Ray tell you? Does he have you on his speed dial? Every time something happens to me he's got to call you?" She would thank Cappy later for the joke. Or not.

"He's my friend. And yeah, he made the call."

She twisted her smile into a playful smirk. "You should've heard what he called you today."

"Chris, why didn't Ben press charges?"

"Jase . . ." She squeezed his hands and studied the ever-so-faint circle around the base of his left ring finger. "Like Coop said, it's not that big of a deal. And it's over. They had their fun. They won't be back."

"You don't know that for sure."

The tone of his voice forced her to meet his gaze. "If we don't pay attention to them, why would they want to come back? What fun is it for them if we just ignore them?"

"You're a target, Chris. They targeted you."

"Come on." She let go of his hands and turned for the gym's glass doors. "Mr. Cooper, can I buy you a cold can of Pepsi?"

The big man quick-stepped up to her. "Sure can. I'll let you."

She held the door open for him, then tilted her head at her frowning boyfriend. "I'll buy you one too, Mr. Sloan, but I'm not delivering it. You have to come in and get it."

"We're not through talking about this."

"Well then, I guess I'll remain eagerly anticipating the day when we can continue this delightful conversation. But right now I need a Pepsi." She waved her hand as if to shoo him toward the door. "After you, sir."

Jason stared at the ground as he walked toward her. If his bottom lip worked that frown any harder, it would stick that way.

The thought of it sparked a flash of terror inside her. Chris let the door swing shut, then grabbed Jason by the front of his shirt and pulled him close. "Gimme that frown, buster." She stood on tiptoes to kiss his pouting lips.

He kissed her back, though not with burning enthusiasm. When he pulled away, his frown remained.

Chris lowered her head and gave him a hairy eyeball.

"I'm sorry, but I'm worried about you."

"When are you not?"

"Can't help it."

"And you know how insane that makes me."

"Well, I can't help that either."

She folded her arms across her chest. "Fine. But if all you're going to do is frown at me, then I don't want to look at you." She grabbed the door again. "I'll go look at Coop. He's pleasant on the eyes."

"*What* did you say?" Jason's arm came around and pulled her back against him.

Chris let out a shriek and tried not to laugh as the glass door once again swung shut. "Either we're going in or we're not."

His whiskery chin tickled her neck under her right ear. "Just listen to me for a second." He pulled her backward, away from the doors, then turned her and gently pushed her back against the wall. He moved in close, so close she could feel the worry oozing out of him. His hand cupped her cheek, then caressed the side of her neck. "I've seen what these Eastsiders can do. They're for real, Chris. I've been there to clean up the mess they've left behind."

She knew exactly what he meant, yet couldn't resist playing with him just a bit more. "And now, so have I. And all it took was a bunch of Brillo pads and some gray paint."

Breath ground out of him as he pulled his hand away. "Why won't you ever be serious? Do you have even a clue as to what you're dealing with?"

The concern pouring out of his pale blue eyes sent warm fuzzies fluttering through Chris's belly. At the moment, it amazed her that she didn't want to fight, argue, or push him away. But she didn't know how much longer the moment would last. If any more of his oozing worry fell over her, she feared it would trigger something she didn't want to have triggered. She kept her voice soft, the expression on her face even softer as she spoke her next words. She even smiled a bit, hoping the words would make sense as they came out. "Mr. Sloan, are you asking me if I understand the senselessly cruel and violent nature of the enemy? Or if I fully appreciate their ability to spread a world of hurt on innocents across the board, without regard for humanity, compassion, or decency?" She paused to let the words sink into her man's worry, to temper the fury he was fighting to control.

His grinding breath flowed easier.

"Yes. I understand it. And I appreciate it. I've faced some pretty out-of-hand enemies in my day."

His eyes lowered to study the sleeve of her T-shirt as his head slowly nodded.

"I know this gang is trouble. And I know they're making a play for our neighborhood. But I am not a target. I'm just another nobody standing in their way. We're all standing in their way. We're all in this together. And we'll face them together. As one. All of us covering each other's six."

His eyes lifted to meet hers, a hint of confusion wavering his intense gaze.

Chris couldn't force back the grin pressing her lips. "Our backs, Jase. We'll all be covering each other's backs. So nothing creeps up on us from behind." She let out a deep breath. "We'll be fine. I'll be fine. Whatever happens, we'll just take it with our eyes open ... and with a lot of prayer."

He glanced away. She could tell her last word didn't sit well with him.

At least most of us will be praying.

The warm fuzzies fluttering through her grew cold as she stood there. The sudden chill made her heart ache.

In the past few weeks, it seemed as if Jason wanted to hear less and less about the Lord. At first he said he enjoyed going to church, but then he skipped a Sunday to work an extra shift, and since then never returned. It was as if he didn't want to talk with Chris about God anymore, even though they talked about Him quite a bit at the beginning of their relationship. After she returned from Colorado. After she processed and put away the disappointments of that trip.

She still had not told him everything that happened on her trip to Colorado. And since he seemed to be less interested in God and more interested in worrying about every little thing that happened to her, she was sure it would be best never to tell him. Some things were better left unsaid anyway. In the quiet times they spent talking, she tried to pursue the more important things about how she loved her new life, and how she trusted her Father God with every part of it. How she loved her friends and her Lord Jesus Christ with all her heart. How she loved her home, and loved the growing relationship she shared with Jason. Deep down she was beginning to think maybe she was falling in love with the man. But in the last few weeks, the more she dared to love him, the more her heart trembled at the thought.

Standing there, she studied the clean line of his jaw to the patch of three-day whiskers on his chin. Her eyes were drawn to his lips, though she hated how tightly pressed they were. She watched his eyes, waiting for him to look at her, but he wouldn't. He didn't move or say anything. But at least his breathing steadied and didn't seem so forced.

She wanted to melt into his arms. Wanted those firm lips to stop frowning so they could smile at her. Wanted those sad blue eyes to stop being sad, so his smile could set them alive. "Jason, please stop worrying. Worrying never helps. You know that. I'm not worried." She reached up to gently turn his face toward her. "They got my attention. I'll be more alert now, that's for sure. And I won't put myself in a precarious position."

His eyes finally met hers. A hint of doubt compounded the concern.

"What. You don't believe me?"

"Precariousness seems to find you."

She lowered her hand and looked out over the back lot. "Yeah. Thanks for reminding me."

"It's because you put yourself in its way."

What once felt like warm fuzzies in her belly now felt like burning sulfur. She tried not to glare at him. "Don't say that."

He softened a bit. "I'm sorry. I'm certainly not here to lecture you."

"Good. Now come inside with me and get a Pepsi."

"You know, maybe that is why I'm here."

"See, I knew you were thirsty." She leaned toward the door and was about to take a step when his hand on her upper arm stopped her.

"Listen to me first, Chris. Listen to what I'm saying."

She straightened against the wall and waited, resisting the urge to again cross her arms over her chest.

"I am worried about you. And for good reason. Please, all I'm trying to say is ... be careful. Ask for help when you need it. Keep your cell phone with you at all times, and call the police if something happens—don't just call Ben or Erin. Call 911 immediately so they can do something about it. Don't even think about it. Just do it."

A breath of quiet laughter spurted out of her. "All right, all right. I will."

"You're just saying that. You know? I haven't known you very long, but I can tell deep down you don't trust the police to do their job."

Confusion swept over her, leaving her dumbfounded.

"Maybe it's because of your past. I don't know. Maybe it's because you think you're smarter than they are, that you can handle anything and don't need their help."

"Stop it." Enough was enough anyway.

"No. Hear me out."

"No, Jase! You started out okay, but what you're saying now doesn't make any sense at all."

"I think it makes perfect sense. You didn't call them three months ago, and you didn't call them today. Both times you figured you could handle the situation all by yourself."

She could only stare. Quick and nasty responses jumbled into a chaotic mess in her mind, but she allowed none to find voice.

"What happens tomorrow? Or the next day. Huh, Chris? Will you call the police the next time something serious happens? Or will you just blow it off? Like you did today. You didn't call them today because you figured you could take what happened and deal with it all by yourself."

The truth in his words startled her. But she didn't let it show.

"That's how you work, isn't it?"

"What is your problem? Do you actually think I'm going to take these guys on all by myself? I just told you we're all in this together."

"So that's why Ben didn't press charges then?"

"What does Ben have to do with this?"

"You're all cut from the same mold. You and Ben and Cappy and Bettema. Even Erin. If it wasn't for Scott—"

Chris spread her hands against his chest, wanting to push him away. "Wait one minute, Jason."

"No, Chris. I heard what you said." He stood his ground and kept his eyes on hers. "You all think you can stand together and take on these gangsters. Well, I'm telling you, you can't. I know you were all soldiers, that you were in a war and you know how to face an enemy. But these kids are not like any enemy you've faced before. They're urban guerillas. They'll shoot you, rob you, beat you, then try to sell you some smack. They'll stomp all over this neighborhood in their size-twelve Air Jordans, then turn around and grind what still stands into the dust."

"You have a rather high opinion of them."

"I've seen them in action. I know what they can do."

A hint of fear laced his words. Chris almost felt sorry for him. "What's this all about, Jase? Cut to it. What's eating at you?"

In a huff, he pushed away from the wall and walked into the back lot.

Chris slowly followed. "It's okay that you're upset. So am I. These guys scared me big time. I'll admit it. And they stole my shovel, which flat-out ticks me off."

Jason didn't turn around. "Yet Ben would not press charges."

Chris moved in beside him and started to put her arm around him, but he pulled away. She drew in a deep breath and held it. Then let it out slowly. "What charges were we supposed to press, Jase? They killed my flowers, painted a tag, cut cookies in the parking lot of the church, and scared a little Bandolero kid ... who probably did something in the first place to initiate this entire fiasco."

Jason didn't miss a beat. "Menacing. Reckless driving. Disturbing the peace. Vandalism. Harassment."

Chris was impressed. The list sounded serious enough to nail every one of those bad Eastsiders. With this many charges against them, the judge would certainly toss them all in the clink and throw away the key.

"And assault. With a deadly weapon."

Please. "You should have this discussion with Ray, not me."

"I already did."

Oh. Chris didn't dare say the word aloud, especially the way she heard it play out in her mind. She really needed a Pepsi. She hoped Cooper wasn't still waiting for his. Surely the man would have been able to find his own way to the refrigerator in Chris's office all by himself.

"He agrees with me. He said he was surprised when Ben refused to press charges."

"I don't believe you." The words slipped out.

Jason spun to glare at her. His upper lip quivered.

"He may have been surprised, but he told us he understood. Which makes sense. None of those charges would last a split second in court. And even if they did, the slap on the wrist those boys would get for all their hideous crimes against humanity would only aggravate them. It would stir up their entire little hornet's nest. You know this, Jason, so admit it. Stop being so pigheaded."

"I'm not being pigheaded."

"You most certainly are."

"Sometimes, girl ..." His hand lifted. He made a fist that shook for a second, but let it drop to his side as he let out a deep sigh. "You seriously make me crazy sometimes."

"Well, right back atcha, dude."

A faint laugh.

She enjoyed his smile as it lingered. "You know? I think you care about me."

When he gazed into her eyes, she wanted to drop to the ground and melt into a big puddle. "I do care about you. Please tell me you know that."

Her heart thumped. "I do know that, Jase." She took a step toward him. The words replayed in her mind. *"I do ..."* They seemed to open a place inside her that had never been opened before.

Would she one day stand before this handsome man and say those words to him? And mean it with all her heart?

His eyes, once flooded with worry, now reflected what she knew poured from his heart. She took another step toward him, and he grabbed her and pulled her to him. The intensity of his grip startled her—his hands, his fingers finding the same places on her upper arms where Enrique's grip left her sore.

She closed her eyes and prayed Jason hadn't noticed. Smiled. Opened her eyes. And knew what was coming by the look in his eyes. Her heart fell inside her.

Jason's mouth hung open, his eyes narrowed as he shifted his grip to her lower arm and then slowly lifted the sleeve of her T-shirt.

"Please, Jase ..." She tried to back away, but his grip intensified. A whisper. "What is this?"

Her eyes closed tightly. By now the red marks were probably starting to bruise. "It's nothing."

A curse. Jason quickly lifted her other sleeve. Chris lowered her head and kept her eyes closed as he vented his anger in a string of vile profanity.

When it stopped, she dared a glance. His nostrils flared as breath rushed through him. She again tried to pull away, but he held on to her even as he softened. His Adam's apple bobbed as he swallowed deeply.

Everything inside her struggled with the moment. Desperate to run away, helplessness overwhelmed her. Everything he said, everything he felt in his heart for her. Everything she felt for him. At that moment, what did it all mean?

His breathing settled as the grip on her arm eased. Jason slowly lifted his hands and touched her face, his thumbs tracing her lips. He caressed her cheeks as his eyes seemed to ache from his own struggle raging inside him.

He moved in to kiss her cheek, then to breathe in her ear. "I love you." He kissed the side of her neck and breathed the words again. "I love you."

He had tested the waters before with these words. Always play-fully. Never with such heartfelt honesty. And desire. The words ricocheted through Chris until chills left her trembling. Her arms reached out to pull herself closer against him.

"I love you, Chris. Please know that I do."

His embrace closed around her. She pushed her face into his shoulder. *I do ... I do ... I do ...*

"Don't say anything. Let that be enough. For now."

It would always be enough. To be loved and held by this man ... so tender, yet so strong ... She turned her head to nuzzle against him.

He held her close and didn't say anything more for a long while.

Cooper's holler shattered the moment. "Hey, Romeo, we gotta fly. Fourteen-sixty-three Duvane. Again."

A growl rumbled through Jason's entire body. "Not again."

"Let's move, dude! Thanks for the Pepsi, Chris."

She pushed away, yet Jason still held her hands. "You better go."

He nodded. And pouted.

She put her finger on his lips. "No more pouting today."

He leaned down for a quick kiss. "See ya."

"Please come to Ben's tonight?"

By the time he replied, he was already halfway to the bus. He turned to take a few backward steps. "Can't. Long shift."

"Then maybe tomorrow night?"

"Maybe. I'll call you afterward. For sure."

"Okay." Chris lifted her hand to wave, but Jason didn't see it. A second later, he ran around the front corner of the gym and disappeared.

★★★

Jason struggled to buckle his seat belt as Cooper cranked the bus's steering wheel to complete a sharp U-turn. The bus sped back down Kimberley, but Jason didn't look up from the dispatch list in his hand. Past the gym, past Ben Connelly's house, past the big church on the corner. He tried to ignore Cooper's inquisitive glances as well. It was difficult.

That was all he needed. Cooper getting on his case about Chris.

He tossed the dispatch list onto the seat between them, sucked in a deep breath, and let it out slowly. The effort seemed to drain him dry even as the bus's roar lulled him. After his childish outbursts back at the gym, he almost wanted to crawl into the back of the bus and take a nap on the litter.

"Well?"

He laid his head back against his seat. "Well what, Coop." His eyes closed. He let them stay closed.

"Is it love or isn't it?"

It is. But he kept his thought in his head.

"Sure looked like it to me."

The horn sounded to clear the intersection, yet the bus slammed to almost a complete stop.

"Come on, get out of the way!"

Aggravated, Jason leaned forward and grabbed the last of his watered-down Mountain Dew from lunch out of the cup holder. After one drink he put it back.

"And what's not to love, huh? Man, she is one fine woman."

"You would drive better if you kept your mouth shut."

"I'm driving just fine." The horn blasted again. "Come on, moron, pull over!"

Jason turned his head and stared at the houses passing by.

He did love her. And she was one fine woman. Her dark eyes burned in his memory. Her soft kiss. The way she snuggled against him. He just wished he hadn't seen what that Bandolero punk did to her arms.

He wanted to strangle the kid. Just how bad did it get? Ray said the Eastsiders in the car were some of the worst members of the gang. And the Eastsiders were one of the worst gangs in the entire Northwest. Transplanted straight from LA.

Even among the worst gangs, not all of them carried assault weapons around with them. But these gangsters did. And not only did they carry one into Chris's neighborhood that morning, but they actually had the nerve to point it at her.

They couldn't get away with it. If someone didn't stop them, they would be back to do it again.

Joyin' was the word Ray used. That was how he said the Eastsiders described it. They were out on a joy ride, and leaving nothing but terror and destruction in their wake.

Someone had to stop them.

Jason knew how he wanted to stop them. He wanted to kill them all. One by one. If any of them ever returned to threaten Chris or her friends again, he'd find a way to take out every last one of them.

Big talk, boy.

Yeah, well, someone has to do it.

But deep down, despite his grumbling misery, he laughed at himself. He knew all his big talk was just that: big talk. If he ever came face-to-face with an Eastsider packing an assault rifle, he'd probably start bawling like a baby.

Chris stood face-to-face with them.

But she had been in the army. She knew how to assess her enemy. When to act. And when to stand still and wait them out.

That was what Ray said about it. But the man's words did nothing to help ease Jason's misery. They only intensified it.

It just didn't seem fair to Jason that his girlfriend had more guts than he did.

"You gonna move over or are you gonna make me have to rearrange your bumper?" Cooper laid on the horn. "I can't believe these morons! Is it a full moon or something?"

Maybe that was it. Maybe that explained it.

Or maybe it's all just an act of God.

That would definitely explain a lot.

Chris would scowl at him if she knew he was thinking that way. She would smile and tell him how much God loved him and was working things out for his good.

Sure He was. Just like three years ago when He let that drunken moron get behind the wheel of his car.

Cooper steered the bus onto Duvane Street and parked in front of the familiar house. "Fifteen bucks says there's actually something wrong with the old biddy this time and we really do need to transport her."

Jason shook away the memory of that night before it could set in. "You're on. And make it twenty." He unhooked his seat belt, but didn't exactly hurry to get out and grab his kit.

"Woo, you must be feeling lucky. How about if we go all out. Fifty bucks, and the loser throws in a pizza if she's admitted."

"You actually think something's wrong with her this time?"

"Hey, you never know. Today may be the day."

Grinning at his partner's optimism, Jason pushed out of the truck and grabbed his kit. He didn't feel lucky or even one ounce of compassion at the moment. The lady in the house was just yanking their chain. Again. Wanting a free ride downtown. Which was fine, since fifty bucks of Cooper's money, plus the pizza, would cover Jason's insatiable desire to go out tomorrow night, get fed, and get drunk.

The lady back at the Kimberley Street Gym called out to him once again, her voice carrying to him on the light afternoon breeze. *"Please come to Ben's tonight?"*

For a second, his heart ached, but he forced it away and trudged up the front walk of the house.

He was almost glad he had to work. But tomorrow night? No matter what happened later, pizza or no pizza, getting drunk or not getting drunk, going to the Kimberley Street Community Church for a prayer meeting did not fit into any of his plans.

✯✯✯

He said maybe, but he wouldn't be there. Chris knew it. Though she asked Jason every week to come to the Tuesday night Bible study at Ben's house, he showed up only one time. And never again. She also asked him to come to the larger Wednesday night prayer meeting at the church. But he never showed up for that. Not even once.

And yet she loved him.

As a group of neighborhood children played indoor hockey with Kay Valleri, over their shouts and laughter, Chris sat at her desk in her office and pondered what her heart was telling her.

It was true. She couldn't deny it. Couldn't hide from it any longer. Somehow, over the course of the last three months, she had fallen in love with Jason Sloan.

But even as the realization settled over her, bringing sensations of joy she had never known before into the farthest reaches of her being, a wrenching fear gripped her. Since that day in Floyd Walker's living room when Jason's genuine concern first pierced her walls of resistance, with each passing hour she seemed to fall more deeply into the possibilities of their relationship. And yet, with each passing hour, as they grew ever closer, Jason seemed to fall farther and farther away from God.

Her fingertips moved in slow circles over her temples, pressing lightly to soothe the ache building behind them.

Lord ... what am I gonna do?

She never loved a man before. Except for Travis. But she never told him she loved him. And she wouldn't tell Jason until ... later. Much later. Until things sorted out. Until he once again at least made an attempt to share her love for Jesus.

She leaned over her desk and rested her head in her arms.

He once loved You. I know he did. Before the accident. And he was trying to deal with his anger, but it seems as if he's given up. Why?

I know he once hated You for what happened. Oh, Father ... does he still?

Hate was a strong word. When they talked about it, which wasn't often, Jason never went so far as to say he hated God after his wife and unborn daughter were killed. He had loved God before the accident and shared that love with his wife. But losing her—losing his entire family in one tragic heartbeat—tore out his heart, his soul, and his faith by the roots.

Chris knew how that felt. Walking, breathing, living a worthless life while every part of her had already died.

Jase ... I'm so sorry. What you've been through, what you're still going through ... I know you're still hurting. I've felt that kind of hurt. I know how hard it is.

Travis didn't deserve to die. Chris couldn't stop Wayne LaTrance from killing him any more than Jason could stop that drunk from crashing into them. All three deaths were senseless, unbearably tragic. Nothing could turn back time and make things as they once were. Nothing could bring Travis or Jessica or little Elizabeth back.

But here we are, Lord. You've put me here, and You've put Jason here with me. We've both been through it, and we both need You. Lord, I can't make it without You.

How was Jason doing it? After once knowing the Lord and loving Him, how was he now making it without Him? How could he constantly push God away ... and still have reason to live?

He never cornered Chris about her faith, never asked her to give it up or tone it down when they were together. She certainly didn't flaunt her faith around him, but her decision to believe the truth about Jesus Christ was what breathed new life into her dead body.

You gave me my life back.

Her eyes drifted shut. Happy shouts of hockey-playing children only added to the moment threatening to overwhelm her.

He needs to live again. He needs You to breathe through him once again.

But even as she prayed the words, she knew it would be difficult. How could he find a way to start loving God again when his heart lay shredded six feet underground, buried in the box that held the body of his first love and the precious little girl he would never know or hold in his arms?

No.

Her eyes flew open.

Jason's heart no longer lay shredded. He had just given it away. *"I love you. I love you. Please know that I do."*

And given it to her.

Oh, Lord ...

She lifted her head and smoothed back her hair, attempting to tuck the stray strands back into her French braid.

She needed to get up and do something. Clean the bathroom. Put away the stuff in the box they used to clean up the mess in the back lot. Anything.

Anything to keep away the flurry of thoughts invading her mind.

With a huff, she lowered her elbows to her desk and hid her face with her hands.

Why was Jason giving up his fight against his anger toward God? Why was he giving up on God's love? Well, why not? He didn't need God or His love anymore. He had Chris to love now. He didn't need God anymore because he had been slowly replacing that need with Chris. He needed her love more than he needed God's love. Especially when God's love demanded so much more from him than hers did.

More than being loved by his Father God, Jason desired Chris's love.

And if she gave it to him, it would take him one more step farther away from God.

Oh, Lord Jesus. Please! What am I gonna do?

Her head fell again to rest over her arms.

Please help me know what to do.

FOUR

"WHACHA DOIN', CHRIS? ARE YOU all right?"

Normally, that question asked by anyone other than Erin Mathis angered Chris to her core. But hearing it asked in Alaina Walker's nine-year-old sing-songy voice sent shivers of pure love and gratitude flooding through her. She lifted her head just enough to rest her chin on her forearms. "Good as gold, Lainer." She hoped her smile convinced the girl. "Taking a break from the game?"

"You need to come play with us. We need you on our team."

"You do, huh?" She pushed away from the desk and leaned back in her chair.

"Yeah. They have Kay on their team. So we need you. Come on."

That beautiful face, those big blue eyes, that mouth stuffed with a wad of chewing gum. "What did I tell you about the gum, Lainer?"

A sheepish look. "Aww, don't make me spit it out. I need it to play good."

Giggles swept over Chris, and she did nothing to hide them as she stood and walked toward the door. "Spit it out, girl. You won't be playing good when you have it stuck halfway down your throat."

More complaints and grumbles, but Alaina spit the wad into the trash can by Chris's desk.

Chris sniffed the air. "Oh, too bad. Watermelon, huh?"

Alaina stomped out of the office and grabbed her plastic hockey stick. "Yeah. And it was good too."

"Still want me on your team?"

The girl spun around and flashed a brilliant smile. "Positively, dudette!"

Chris's giggles returned as she grabbed up a stick.

Just like her Lord to send an angel to rescue her.

Every Tuesday night this same group of people sat in his living room. And every Tuesday night Ben Connelly gazed around the room, wondering if his heart would inflate to the point of explosion. From the pride he felt as he prayed silently for each one to the praises swelling inside him. If the buttons on his shirt didn't pop off from the last cookie he ate, surely the joy puffing out his chest would send them flying.

These people were family. Some literally, and some through the process of friendship refined by fire. For most of those family members, that fire was as close to a literal fire as one would want to get. The scalding temperatures in Saudi Arabia during the first few months of Operation Desert Shield left them all gasping for breath. As they went about their duties on the Tarmac at King Fahd International Airport, it seemed as if they walked on the surface of a frying pan sitting over a raging fire. Even through his khaki-colored canvas boots, Ben's feet sizzled. It took all his concentration to endure it at first, to keep from hopping like a leprechaun toward any container of water and climbing in. And it wouldn't have been proper for a U.S. Army brigade commander with the dignified rank of full-bird colonel to be seen hopping around the Tarmac.

He'd never forget those days. And even though he enjoyed his entire army career and carried no regrets because of it, he still had to laugh at himself when he realized he never wanted to experience anything like those days in Saudi Arabia ever again.

They ranked right up there with the time he spent in Vietnam.

He retired for good reason. And besides, he wasn't a young pup anymore.

So the old dog came home to this new place, the place he called Kimberley Square, and commandeered a new theater of operations. That his family and dearest friends would join him in the new mission God placed on his heart was a joy he could hardly contain.

Especially when he watched the newest member of the family smile and blink her beautiful baby browns. Since before she was born, Mia Renae Mathis generated a soft spot in Ben's heart. Before the night was over, he would definitely hold the squirming little one in his arms and play cuddle-and-coo.

He could not look at Mia and not think of her mother, the former first lieutenant trauma nurse he assigned to the helicopter medical evacuation team from Alaska. Young, pretty, and fiercely determined, Erin Grayson later received a Purple Heart for injuries sustained at a Dustoff gone bad. Ben would never forget the day he pinned the medal on her USS *Mercy* T-shirt. His lame joke about the color of the medal matching the deep bruises surrounding her eyes left him rubbing the bruise she left on his arm after she slapped him. Good-naturedly, of course. All in good fun.

He could not think of Erin Grayson and her Purple Heart without thinking of Christina McIntyre. After all the years, he still could not believe the former medevac medic actually had the audacity to turn down his recommendation for the Bronze Star. He didn't think he would ever fully understand what made the woman tick. But whatever it was, he liked it.

At the moment, Erin could not look more radiant. And Scott could not be a better man to take on the job of Dad. Chris's face beamed as she stood Mia in front of her, using her knees to steady the wobbly new legs. Mia's little hands patted Chris's cheeks. Much to Chris's delight.

Ben wondered about Chris's new boyfriend, Jason. A fine young man, though he carried a load of hurt far too heavy for his young shoulders to bear. Ben lifted a prayer for the paramedic and for the relationship developing between him and Chris. *May it only grow sweeter, Lord. And ever closer to all You desire it to be.*

Which reminded him of Bettema Kinsley. Would Mason ever get wise and ask her to marry him? What was the boy waiting for? Maybe Ben should give the boy a good talking-to. But if Sonya ever found out, she'd have his hide.

Bettema deserved to be happy. Her selfless attitude and willingness to work with the children of Kimberley Square would always endear her to Ben as close as a daughter. A true sister, sharing the same Father.

Which brought him to Capriella Sanchez. Ben would never forget the first time Bettema suggested he bring the former Humvee mechanic and fellow Gulf War veteran onboard at Kimberley. He stared bug-eyed at Bettema that day and said, "Cappy Sanchez? Are you kidding?"

He didn't think it possible that Cappy would say yes to his offer. If she agreed to come and be a part of their outreach to the people of Kimberley Square, Ben would provide a place for her to live and a paycheck besides. With her widely varied expertise in all forms of mechanics, both electrical and structural, she would, if she said yes, be a huge asset to Isaiah and the other maintenance workers running ragged around the center.

Much to Ben's surprise, Cappy said yes. Not only to him, but to the Lord Jesus Christ as well.

One of the happiest days of Ben's life.

Like the day Chris McIntyre first walked into his living room, five years after he watched her exit his command tent in Dhahran, Saudi Arabia.

And now they're both Yours. Oh, Lord God, how can I thank You enough for the family You have surrounded me with here in Kimberley Square?

Isaiah Sadler and his wife, Emily. Kay Valleri and her husband, Rick. Ryan Jensen and his new wife, Susan. Ben's own son, Andy, pastor of the church at the cornerstone of the outreach. Andy's wife, Sarah. And their three rambunctious little ones. Grandpa's complete undoing.

Tuesday night. Family meeting night. And all were present and accounted for, gathered as one to hear the Word of the Lord.

Ben cleared his throat in an authoritative manner and waited for the group to quiet down. As he waited, he prayed. Before turning the meeting over to his son, he would make sure everyone in the room knew about the trouble that had found them earlier that day. For even though this group was family, they were also warriors. And if he asked them to, they would join with him to stand as one to fight, if necessary, to protect the neighborhood they all claimed as their own.

No gang of immature hoodlums would invade and overtake this neighborhood. No one would intimidate them or stand in the way of the work they had yet to do.

Not if Ben Connelly had anything to say about it.

SUNSHINE OVERPOWERED THE THIN CURTAINS hanging from the rod above Jamaal's bedroom window. Birds chirped and screeched, grating his eardrums.

At some of his homies' cribs, they hung heavy black sheets over their windows to help them sleep late. Some of his brahs even taped tin foil against their windows to keep out the light. But Jamaal liked taking in the light of the new day. It didn't mean he had to get up. His days usually didn't start until at least noon. But it did do something for his soul. It was one of the few ways for him to know for a fact he did indeed still have one.

And straight up, he liked his crib decked just the way his mama decked it, curtains and all. She knew enough not to touch his stacks of hip-hop and reggae CDs. And she steered clear of his closet where he hid his stash of weed, his .44 Magnum, and his brother's black leather jacket with the word *EASTSIDERS* plastered across the back of it.

He didn't keep much of his brah's stuff, but he kept his jacket, even though he knew he'd probably never have the nerve to put it on.

Sunshine and chirping birds. A new day awaited him. He dreaded the thought. Lying on his stomach on his double bed, entangled in the sheet, he lifted his head against the pillow and tried to read the numbers on his clock radio. 10:17. A groan carried through him, which wigged out his throat, making him cough.

"Baby? You 'wake?"

"Yeah, Mama." His voice croaked.

"You ready for breakfast? I can make up some waffles 'for I'm haftin to leave for work."

He didn't move a muscle. "Nah, you go on. I'll see you later tonight."

"You all right, honey?"

She must have took notice to the bloody wrap he left in the bathroom garbage. "Be easy, Mama. Yo. I'm a'ight."

Her pause told him she didn't believe him. "Well, be sure and eat something 'for you leave. I'll see you later. I love you, baby."

"Love you, Mama. Peace. Yo." He hoped she heard the words since he meant them, but his voice cut out and didn't deliver them straight up as he hoped.

His eyes weren't ready to open. His entire arm ached. The deep cut on the underside of his forearm throbbed in perfect rhythm with every beat of his heart. As his mother pulled the back door closed on her way to work, Jamaal drifted off to sleep. His last few thoughts carried him away.

If you ain't dead by now, Duncey, word up, when I see you next, you will be.

Peace. Yo.

Such a laugh. He didn't even know the meaning of the word.

WHAT IS WRONG WITH THESE people?

Heartsick, Chris glanced around the small crowd that had gathered for the Wednesday night prayer meeting. This group of retirees, school teachers, business owners, and bankers made up the backbone of the Kimberley Street Community Church. Their amazing volunteer efforts, not to mention their incredible financial sacrifices, kept the church's outreach alive and thriving. They lived in Kimberley Square and made it what it was: a friendly neighborhood within the confines of Portland's inner city. They lived out their Christianity in the way they cared for their neighbors, gave of their time and money, and prayed earnestly for the Lord to keep His hand on the Square. They prayed for those working within the outreach, and Chris would forever be grateful for them. And indebted to them. She loved these people. They were her sisters and brothers—some of them, the grandpas and grandmas she never had.

And though she understood their concern about the difficult things Ben discussed with them all, she couldn't make sense of the fear she felt flooding out of them.

They live in a city. They know the dangers of living in a city. And they know how good You are, Father. You'll take care of us all when things get out of hand. If I know that, and I'm just getting to know You, what's up with these people who have known You forever?

"Are the police going to increase patrols around here?"

"Should we start locking the church doors?"

"Should we close the gym? Maybe it's too dangerous to keep it open."

She squirmed in her pew and struggled to keep cool even as her heart screamed, *No, we shouldn't lock up the church. And we shouldn't close the gym! Are you crazy? It's safe. And it's my job to keep it that way!*

Standing in the aisle between the rows of pews, Ben held out his hands to quiet the group. "Now, I know this is something we've all been dreading, but I don't think it's reason enough for us to panic."

You tell 'em, Ben.

"It would go against our mission to lock the doors of the church just because a gang of hoodlums cut a few cookies in the parking lot. And it would be terribly irresponsible for us to even think about closing the gym just because that same gang of hoodlums painted graffiti on its back wall."

"But that's not all they did," came from Myron Dungrass.

Ben slowly nodded. "Yes, you're right, Myron. But think about it. If all the churches and businesses that suffered at the hands of these hoodlums ceased operations because of it, the entire city would be an abandoned wasteland."

A few chuckles. Chris forced her clenched teeth to part.

"We're not locking the church." Ben spoke each word carefully, though forcefully. "And we're not closing the gym." He glanced Chris's way.

She wanted to hug the man right there on the spot.

"But we will take measures to increase security across the board. Those of us who man the outreach, so to speak" — he flashed a grin at his daughter-in-law — "have already discussed ways to do just that."

"But what if they come back?" Corissa Foley's voice shook. "What should we do?"

Chris felt sorry for the lady. Corissa's face had paled to a weird shade of green.

"Like the other emergency situations we've faced before in the Square, the first thing we need to do is pray." Ben paused to let the words sink in. "Next, we need to be alert and aware of what is happening. If the boys in this gang are just driving down one of our streets, they are not doing anything wrong, so we should treat them as we would anyone else who traverses our neighborhood."

"Well, maybe if we stop thinkin' of these boys as hoodlums — no disrespect, Ben." Velda Jackson gave Ben a playful smirk.

The expression on his face quickly turned from serious to silly.

"Yes, these boys can be loud and a bit frightening," Velda went on to say. "And yes, they can sometimes cause trouble. Sometimes big trouble. But if we let 'em keep us scared and all holed up in our houses, we're doing nothin' but encouraging them. And in the meantime, we're missing out on good livin'. The Father doesn't want us livin' in fear." Her voice lowered to a whisper. "Thank You, Jesus."

It was all Chris could do to not stand up and applaud Velda's words.

"But what if they do something that breaks the law?" came from Myron Dungrass's wife.

"Mercy, Nadine." Velda turned her ample frame to look over her shoulder. "If the youngins break the law, then call the po-lice! Do it joyfully!"

You go, girl. Chris laughed along with several others in the room. She couldn't wait to get her hug from Velda later. Hugging Velda Jackson was like hugging the Pillsbury Dough Boy's grand-mother. One soft, plump, smothery hug.

"Of course, that is always an option." Unlike Velda, Ben seemed to purposely keep the tone of his voice conversational rather than confrontational. "No matter what happens—and please, don't feel bad if it comes to this—but if you ever feel as if you or your family or your home or your car or whatever you own or love is in danger in any way, for any reason, call the police. They'll answer your call in a matter of minutes."

And they'll do it joyfully! Chris squelched a grunt as Ray Rich-ardson's face popped into her mind's eye.

Sonya Connelly walked over to stand beside her husband. "But let's all keep in mind that our God is one big God." Her slight Southern drawl softened her words. "He knows what these boys are up to. And He knows why they're making waves here in Kimberley Square. We need to pray for *them*, y'all. Not just for ourselves. We need to pray that their hearts will be changed."

Velda's soft whisper reached Chris's ears. "Yes, Lord. Please change these boys. They are so dear."

"We belong to our God, y'all." Sonya put her arm around her husband. "Our homes, our ministries, and all our efforts to serve Him belong to Him too. No matter what happens, we can trust Him to see us through. As long as we keep our eyes on Him, we'll be fine."

Chris glanced at Erin.

Erin's small smile reached her eyes, lighting them with a faint hint of mischief.

The essence of the warrior. The same essence inside Chris, whispering through her. *With our heads held high and our eyes on Him, standing strong, together, to defend and protect. Facing down the enemy, ready to fight to the death.*

Crazy. And she knew it. But she wouldn't trade that whispering essence inside her for anything.

✳✳✳

THE SISTER HANGING ON TWOINE'S arm was straight-up hot. And new. Jamaal had never seen her before.

"Yo, Maal. Wassup?"

His arm hurt, his last beer left him half sick, and his raggedy ride needed gas. But he said to Twoine, "Nothin' much, dawg. But *you* now …" He gave the hottie a good once-over.

"Word up, dawg. This is Sharrrr-nisha. Say yo, babe."

"Yo, babe."

The hottie could speak. Jamaal was impressed.

Twoine whooped it up. His gold twins flashed sunlight.

Jamaal leaned against his car and tapped out one of Rummy's cigarettes.

"Yo, boy, ride wit us." Twoine tilted his head toward Shree. "We goin' joyin'."

"Where to?" Jamaal lit Rummy's cig.

"I'll tell ya when we get there. Come on, dawg. Live a little." Twoine squeezed the hottie against his chest and she squealed with dee-light. "She's makin' me take her back to her crib. Says her mama'll get all wigged out if she's gone much longer."

Sounded like a personal problem.

"So come wit us. Yo. I'll show ya where we tagged a brick downtown."

Jamaal glanced at Cee Train. Since when did he clear for tag-gin' downtown?

Sharrrr-nisha giggled. Straight-up wannabe. "Maal. Is dat your name?"

"Word up."

"Short for Jamaal?"

Smart girl. He blew cigarette smoke in her direction.

"Yo, Jamaal. Meet my girl Meghan."

The girl didn't look like she wanted to be hangin' wit da homeboys.

"Say yo, Meghan." More Sharnisha giggles.

"Yo."

Jamaal gave her a tight grin. He begged to ax what she was doing so far away from her lily-white crib. Seeins how she was all lily-white herself. He couldn't resist. "You look lost."

She almost smiled. "I feel lost."

He tossed his cigarette into the gutter. "Then let's take you home."

Rummy started buggin'. "Hey, man. You keep wastin' my squares, I ain't gonna give you no more."

Jamaal took Meghan by the arm and followed Shree, Twoine, and Sharnisha, not turning once to give Rummy the what-for.

They settled into Shree's ride, and he drove toward downtown, the booming sub-woofers blasting hip-hop. With the music too loud to talk over, Jamaal relaxed back and chilled. His right arm ached from his shoulder to his middle fingertip. And it wouldn't stop throbbing.

It was fate he didn't meet up with Duncey that day.

Duncey would live another day.

Though Jamaal's homies taught the boy a lesson. They got his back. And Duncey got what he deserved. He'd never again dis the sitch of one of Cee Train's callouts. Duncey done called Jamaal out. But Cee Train laid it down how it would play out between them.

Blade on blade. First to strike blood.

And Jamaal struck first. Though it took longer than he thought it would. Duncey da dunce done turned out quicker and meaner than Jamaal ever knew. Their blades clashed a time or two. One time, the strength in Duncey's slash almost sent Jamaal down. But the last move Duncey threw cost him. Jamaal flicked in and cut the flab around Duncey's gut. Sho nuff, it drew blood. Duncey just stood there all trippin' and buggin'.

That was when Jamaal chilled out. The callout complete. He stepped up a link on the chain, while Duncey done fell to the bottom. Which didn't sit well with the boy. He slashed out at Jamaal's face. All Jamaal had time to do was lean back and throw up his arm to protect himself.

Duncey's blade cut deep. Felt like it sliced Jamaal's forearm almost clean down to the bone.

Houses flew by as Shree maxed his ride toward town. Beside him, Twoine and Sharnisha grooved with the tunes. Beside Jamaal in the backseat, lily-white Meghan stared out her window.

He wanted to talk to her, to ax her what she was doing so far from her hood. Sharnisha wanted to mix. How did Meghan end up along for the ride?

The girl wouldn't look his way. Her light brown hair danced in the wind around her shoulders. She was a pretty girl. Even if her skin was pale white. Wearing Levi's and raggedy Nikes.

The car turned a sharp left, another quick right, then slammed to a stop. Silence fell as Shree cut the jam. Jamaal peered through

Meghan's window as Twoine tripped. Big time. "No way, dawg! They dissed it already!"

Looking around, Jamaal saw only the back of a gray building. And some trees.

More trippin'. Twoine must have sprayed the tag himself. Some good work, no doubt. And who cared. Did he think it would last forever? The boy vented until Shree spun the car in the gravel and stopped at the street.

Jamaal glanced at Meghan. She seemed as if she wanted to speak up.

Sharnisha beat her to it. "Those goody-two-bit churchgoers."

Jamaal glanced again at Meghan. She looked downright miserable.

"Maybe we should pay those dissin' churchgoers a visit." Twoine looked at Shree. "You remember the way, doncha, dawg?"

"Sho nuff do, boy!" The car turned south, then west again at the next street. Hip-hop once again thumped so hard it added beats to the rhythm of Jamaal's heart.

Shree turned his ride once more and slammed it in front of a huge church. The Kimberley Street Community Church, from what it said on the sign. With its front doors open and parked cars lining both sides of the street, it looked like church was in play.

His head starting to ache as deep as his arm, Jamaal glanced out his window at the houses across the street. Nice houses. Flowers and big porch swings. One huge house had two doors. He squinted to see more clearly. One of the doors had writing on the glass. He struggled to read it.

Kimberley Street Community Clinic. Scott A. Mathis, MD. Erin Mathis, FNP. Kyle Sundevold, MD.

Hip-hop blasting, Shree and Twoine howling, the car launched forward so hard Jamaal's head whipped back against his seat. He let it rest there and closed his eyes.

The rest of the words on that glass door echoed through him. *You will not be turned away by your inability to pay.*

His arm was killing him. He needed to have it looked at. But he couldn't hit no ER. They'd ax way too many questions.

But maybe ... maybe tomorrow he'd put a little gas in his raggedy ol' ride and pay this hood another visit. Maybe. It wouldn't hurt to find out for himself what was what at the Kimberley Street Community Clinic.

SCREECHING TIRES. THUMPING HIP-HOP.

Déjà vu all over again.

Chris dared a glance Erin's way. As the hip-hop grew louder, Erin gazed at Chris, her expression grim.

The car stopped right out front of the church. Everyone inside turned to look, though no one could see beyond the doors leading to the foyer.

The main front doors were open, though.

Isaiah Sadler jumped up and hurried down the aisle to peer through one of the small windows in the foyer's swinging doors.

The car took off, tires squealing for quite some time as it probably laid two strips of rubber at least a block down Kimberley.

Isaiah turned from the door. "Well, as I'm sure you can all tell ... they're gone." He made his way back to his pew and sat with a deep sigh.

Chris stared at Erin.

"Who were they?" came from Corissa Foley.

"They were Eastsiders," Isaiah said.

Erin glanced away first.

So much for the essence of the warrior. The only essence whispering through Chris at that moment spoke paralyzing fear straight to her racing heart.

CHRIS SAT ON THE FRONT steps of the church as the last of the group filtered out and headed home. It took all her willpower not to look again at the long black tire tracks running down the middle of Kimberley Street. She could still hear the horrid screech when those tracks were laid down. It seemed to echo across the walls of her mind.

She gazed instead to the west and enjoyed the last few golden rays of the day's sun. It was a beautiful late-summer night, warm, with a slight breeze ruffling her hair, now free from its braid. With her head turned to take in the western sky, she didn't notice when Scott Mathis sat beside her on the step. It was the release of his deep sigh that caught her attention. She gave him a small smile.

"Nice night, huh?"

"Yeah. I was just thinking that."

"Why are you sitting here?"

"Don't know for sure." She thought for a second. "Just felt like sitting, I guess."

"You're avoiding crossing the street."

"Really? And how would you know that?"

"That's why I sat down beside you."

Her smile widened. "Erin may be the bravest one of us all."

"Well, when Mia says, 'Mommy, let's eat,' it's not like her mommy has much of a choice."

She couldn't argue with that.

"So, Chris, former combat veteran and Bronze Star rejecter, tell me. What's your take on this Eastsider mess? Should I pack up my daughter and her mommy and head for the hills?"

Laughter bubbled out of her even as she shook her head. "Nah. I wouldn't if I were you. Not just yet."

"People are on edge around here. I'd hate to see this thing escalate."

She looked him in the eye. "Are you on edge, Scott?"

His eyebrows lifted. "Well ... yeah. It's a serious matter."

"Are you afraid?"

He gazed at her awhile before answering. "Yeah."

An honest reply. Chris smiled, hoping he could tell she appreciated it.

"Yesterday I didn't sense your fear. Not really. But I'm sensing it now. You want to talk about it?"

Always the doctor. But she considered his words. And loved him for his genuine concern. "I guess yesterday I wasn't all that scared. Not until Jason stopped by the gym. And his fear ... his fear made me realize there might be reason to be afraid. I guess he scared me more than the Eastsiders did."

"What did he say?"

"He didn't like that Ben didn't press charges."

"That may change soon."

"Yeah. Ben won't put up with much more."

"But that'll be a good thing. Maybe the police can make some arrests and quell this thing before it gets out of control. Like with the Bandoleros."

That word didn't sit well with her. "Wish we could find out if they're officially back in action."

"Yeah. That's *all* we need on top of everything else."

The breeze blew her hair into her face. She tucked it behind her ear and wondered if she should ask the question playing on the edges of her thoughts. She met Scott's gaze. "Oh, wise one, may I ask you something?"

His smile showed a hint of amusement. "Sure."

"Is it harder for a guy to be a Christian than it is for a girl?"

She could tell that was not the question he expected. His expression showed surprise, then thoughtful consideration. "Well, I'm not sure how easy it is for a girl."

Laughter again filtered out of her.

"Are you thinking about Jason?"

She couldn't hold back her surprise. "Oh, wise one ... you're pretty smart."

He seemed to like that response. Then he set the record straight. "It is pretty obvious. You've been thinking about him a lot lately."

"Did Erin tell you?"

"She didn't have to. I could tell. You've been ... quiet lately. Like you have much on your mind."

"He told me yesterday that he loved me."

Scott stretched his legs out on the step below him. "Well. That would be cause for some deep thought."

"I think I love him too. But he's not interested anymore in learning about God. I don't think he's interested in loving God at all. He's too busy hating Him for what happened to Jessica."

A deep sigh. "Yeah."

"So do you think it's harder for a guy to love Jesus? I mean, us girls ..." Chris stopped to sort through her thoughts. "Well, *this* girl, at least. I love to imagine running into His arms, feeling His arms around me. I love to crawl up on God's lap and lean against His chest. Sometimes it's as if I can hear His heart beating. Is that something you imagine too?"

"That's really good, Chris. And yeah, I imagine it like that sometimes too. I see the Father as my own father, loving and gentle. I used to love to sit on my dad's lap. But now that I'm older ..." A laugh.

Chris didn't know what else to say.

"But when it comes to Jesus, I see Him as my brother. My friend who sticks closer than a brother. I don't imagine us getting too touchy-feely, but on that day when I stand before Him, I know—once I get up from the ground, of course—that I'll put my arms around Him and hug Him for all He's done for me."

"A ... slap-on-the-back sort of hug? Or a real lean-into-Him sort of one?"

Scott's eyes studied the tops of the trees behind his house. "Well, I'm not exactly sure what's going to happen on that day, but I do know I love Him with all my heart. So, I suppose I'll want to hug Him in a way that allows Him to come away feeling my love.

And my gratitude." He turned to meet Chris's gaze. "I'm not sure if I can accomplish that with just a good-ol'-boy slap on the back."

She enjoyed the way the sky reflected in his brown eyes. Then looked away and rubbed her nose. "You know Jason pretty well. Do you think he'll ever love Jesus like that?"

Scott didn't move and didn't immediately reply.

Chris looked at him.

"If you show him how. If you show him what true love is."

She glanced away. And heaved a deep sigh.

"Part of what makes you so loveable is how the Lord Jesus's love flows through you. I've seen it. It's amazing."

One more time she met his gaze. "Really?"

He leaned back and faked surprise. "Would I kid a kidder? Yes, really. I love how His love has changed you. I love how much you love Him. Jason has to see that. He feels it, even if he doesn't understand where it comes from. Someday he will. Jesus's love is irresistible, especially when it's lived out completely, honestly, and selflessly. That's how you live it."

Wow. She wanted to give in to her threatening tears and start bawling.

"So. Do I think Jason has it in him to love Jesus Christ with all his heart? Yep. You bet I do. I knew him when he was first married to Jessica. They were both strong Christians, very active in their church. And very happy."

Sadness swept through her.

"It was tragic, what happened. But once a person experiences the love of Jesus Christ, he can't soon forget it, no matter what happens. Jason will recover from Jessica's death. You'll help him do that. You are helping him do that. Nothing is as sweet as the love of Jesus Christ. Not even the love of a wife, or of a newborn daughter. And hey, that's pretty sweet."

She laughed even as she blinked her tears away.

"It's the love combined, working in concert with each other, that fills the heart. The love of your spouse, your children, your friends, your Christian brothers and sisters, all combined with the pure, irresistible love of Christ. Together, it's about as much love as a guy can stand."

"Makes you wanna hug someone."

"You bet it does."

Chris slowly leaned over and rested her head on Scott's shoulder. "Thanks, dude. You're the best."

His head lowered to rest against hers. "Any time, Chris. And right back atcha."

★★★

FULL OF COOPER'S PIZZA AND working on his fifth beer, Jason sighed. His night was almost complete. Three more beers ought to do it.

The Seattle Mariners had three more innings to complete their shutout of the Baltimore Orioles. Cooper, also full of pizza and almost as buzzed as Jason, shouted at the TV from time to time, encouraging his team on. Jason didn't really care one way or the other who won the game. Earlier that day, his team, the Atlanta Braves, handily defeated the Cincinnati Reds.

Once again, he thanked Cooper's bad luck and the sweet little old lady from 1463 Duvane Street for the festivities of his evening. Yesterday, the poor lady not only needed to be transported, but also needed an immediate IV to hydrate her. The attending doctor at the ER said the lady would be fine, but still admitted her even before Jason and Cooper left the hospital.

Leading to this delightful night. Cooper paid up like the chump he was, then invited Jason over for the doubleheader on his big screen. Jason couldn't ask for anything more.

And yet, the lingering image of his girl standing there in the back lot of the gym ate at him. The sight of her bruised arms wouldn't break free from his mind. The promise he made to her as she stood there nagged at him. Her face looked so sad.

He told her he would call her tonight. "For sure," he had said. But he wasn't going to call her. Not in his present state. That would really set her to worrying about him, and he didn't need that. It was his job to worry about her. And he did it so well.

He laughed aloud at the thought. Cooper turned to look at him.

Jason popped open another beer and hoisted it. "Go Mariners!"

"Woo-hoo!" Cooper raised his as well, and both men chugged huge gulps.

✦✦✦

CHRIS AND SCOTT FINALLY WORKED up the nerve to walk across Kimberley Street, but both stopped in the middle to study the ugly black tire tracks.

"Wow. If they keep this up, they'll have to buy new tires soon."

A breath of laughter spurted out of Chris as she stole Cappy's words once more. "They probably have Goodyear on their speed dials."

They continued across the street and up the stairs to Scott's house. Inside, Erin sat in her rocking chair holding Mia up on her shoulder. She patted Mia's back and gave them both a big smile. As soon as Chris closed the screen door and kicked off her sneakers, a hearty burp erupted from the babe.

"That's my girl." Scott moved around behind them and made wide googly-eyes at his little one.

Chris sat on the couch and cherished the moment.

"Daddy-o, would you like to give your daughter her bath tonight? I'll let you if you want to."

"You mean, a little splish-splish with my little fish-fish? Most certainly. But only for a kiss-kiss."

Laughing, Erin planted a few smoochy kisses on Mia's plump cheek, then lifted her head to receive several long ones from her hubby. As she blinked her eyes open, they seemed to shimmer with joy.

Scott lifted Mia from Erin's arms. "Come to Daddy, my love."

"I set everything out for you. Have fun." Erin pushed up from the rocker and tossed the burping pad on the coffee table. Then looked at Chris. "I need some fresh air. Want to join me?"

Chris quickly stood. "Sure do."

They walked outside and sat on Erin's new high-backed porch swing. A long, deep breath escaped Erin's puffed lips. Dark bags hung under her weary eyes. Chris's heart ached as she settled back on the swing. The sun was just starting to set. Deep shades of gold led into softer shades of pink and blue.

In silence, they rocked. Enjoying the night.

Until Erin turned her head to look at Chris. "What were you thinking tonight at the meeting? You looked just a wee bit ticked off."

Chris let out a quiet laugh. "I was, I guess."

"Were you surprised at what they were all saying?"

"I was glad Jason wasn't there to hear it. I didn't think they'd all be so afraid. Except for Velda. She didn't seem afraid."

"You're not afraid?"

She considered her reply. "I wasn't yesterday. But I'm getting to feel that way more and more."

"Makes it all that more important for us to pray."

"Yeah."

"And not just for us, but for them too. It's true what Sonya said."

"Praying for our enemies. That's living it out."

"And loving those who hurt us. Not easy words to obey."

She turned to meet Erin's gaze. "Did you ever pray for the Iraqis?"

A small grin. "I prayed they wouldn't shoot me. Or you." A laugh. "So I guess I got half my prayers answered the way I wanted."

Chris didn't know what to say. When she did, she didn't know how to say the words. "Rinny?"

"Yeah?"

"With all this Eastsider mess going on, promise me one thing."

Erin turned on the swing and pulled her knees up, then once again leaned back to rest her head on the top of it. "Sure, Chris."

"I mean it, Rin. If something should happen, promise me you won't do anything ... heroic. I saw the look in your eye during the meeting tonight. If anything happens, do like Ben said. Call the police. Okay? Promise me?"

Soft laughter. "I promise." A poke on Chris's shoulder. "Can I ask the same of you?"

"What. Me? Trying to be a hero? Are you kidding?"

More laugher. "Oh, yeah. What was I thinking? You've never done anything heroic."

"Not on purpose, anyway."

"Just don't try to. Please, Chris."

She gave in and let her own laughter surface. "Didn't I make that promise to you once before?"

"Yes, and you know how long that lasted."

"Yes. Yes, I do."

"Just be careful. That's all I'm asking."

When did this conversation get twisted around to become about her?

"And keep your cell phone with you. Put 911 on your speed dial."

"Cappy should get royalties on that line. She'd be a rich woman."

"Promise me, Chris."

She turned and grinned. "Okay, okay. I promise."

FIVE

SOME NICE CRIBS LINED THE streets in this hood. Garages, little white fences, flowers, and trees. Grass actually grew in the yards. Only a few cribs needed a fresh coat of paint. Less than that needed new roofs.

Very different from Jamaal's hood. Seemed like no one really cared about the outsides of their cribs in his hood. Which was weird considering how much time everyone spent outside chillin' on their porches or grilling up ribs in their front yards. Maybe the reason was no one had time to worry much about it. Every one of his homies who still lived in his mama's crib didn't get to see her that much. She was off working two jobs. Or maybe even three.

Jamaal's mom worked too hard, but there wasn't anything he could do about it, unless he ditched school this year. Or sold more weed to his homies.

Maybe he'd line up with Bones and Rummy. They talked about hitting a jewelry store out near Hillsboro. Crash and dash. A little ice to push instead of green. More lucrative. And slicker than working for a living.

No one in this hood pushed weed. He doubted very many moms in this hood worked near as hard as his mom did.

What was the big deal about this hood? Why was Twoine all trippin' about running here? All last night he wigged about his tag getting dissed. Served him right. Why waste the time spraying a place that people obviously really cared about? Of course they would paint it over. They wouldn't let anyone come in and mess with their nice place.

But the place was just an old warehouse or something. Big ol' square thing. Nothing special.

So what was it about that place that had Meghan all buggin'?

Everyone trippin' and buggin'. Big hairy deal.

But someone sure did cover over Twoine's tag in a hurry.

Antwoine Campbell. If the boy kept trippin', he'd bring down the whole brothahood. And Bones too, the way he was always up in people's bi'ness, flashing dat piece.

Disgusted, Jamaal pulled his ride over to the curb. He missed his hip-hop groove, but didn't want to announce his arrival all over the land. He wondered what he was doing here, miles from his crib, miles from his hood.

It took him all afternoon to dig up the guts to make the trip, but he knew he needed to make it. If he didn't get his arm stitched up soon, he'd have to pay a visit to an ER. And if the sign on the door of that clinic across from the church was true, he wouldn't be turned away, 'cause he definitely could not pay.

They would know sho nuff it was a knife wound. Would they call The Man? ERs were supposed to report gunshots and such. Did that include knife wounds? If he didn't get it stitched, wouldn't it eventually heal up on its own?

Could he wait that long? The way it throbbed and burned about drove him nuts. His whole arm was trippin'.

Do it, boy.

He cranked the car into gear and peeled a little rubber.

They wouldn't turn him away. Not in this hood.

Not unless they was closed.

Now that wasn't a good thought. Why did he wait so long to make the trip?

If they was closed, a'ight then. If they wasn't … he'd play it straight up and legit. His long-sleeved T-shirt covered most of his tats. He'd even ditch his silver chains and his skullcap. It would feel all buggin', but he could do it. He could give up his Eastsider ways for one hour if it meant getting his arm fixed.

Deep in his heart, he wished he could give them up for good.

***

THE SILENCE IN THE HOUSE felt strange. Sweet silence. Erin kicked up her feet onto the coffee table and laid her head back against the love seat. A long breath sifted through her. Left her refreshed. Revived.

But still her arms ached. She missed her daughter.

It wasn't as if Mia was miles away. She was just across the street with Sonya and Sarah. Ben, Andy, Ryan, and Scott decided tonight was their night for a round of golf. Sonya and Sarah decided it was Erin's night to get a little rest.

For the first time in many months, she faced the prospect of two quiet hours all to herself. What would she do?

Absolutely nothing. For two hours, she'd sit on her love seat with her feet kicked up on her coffee table and do absolutely nothing.

The thought left her smiling. And thanking her Lord for her friends.

She wouldn't doze off. No. She'd just sit and veg. Listen to the silence. And breathe.

But it didn't take long for a familiar sound to find her. Not a sound she wanted to hear. Someone walked over that loose board out on her front porch. The one by the clinic's window. The resulting squeak was undeniable.

She growled, hoping whoever it was would go away.

But they continued to walk, back and forth it seemed. She heard the squeak at least three more times.

Her front door was open to let in fresh air through the screen door. She was glad she had locked it. It wasn't something she normally did, but with two hours of solitary peace and quiet rest ahead of her, she didn't exactly want anyone barging in unannounced.

Definite footsteps on her front porch. Then a string of soft-spoken profanity.

Okay, okay. She pushed up to see who it was, and felt her jaw drop when she saw him. The nice-looking African-American boy was tall, his face cleanly shaven except for a flattering moustache and goatee. His face bore a lost look. "Can I help you?" She didn't open the door.

Her voice made him jump, yet his face brightened when he saw her. "Yo. Hey. How are ya?"

A smile tried to pull at her lips. "I'm fine. Is there something I can help you with?"

He tilted his head toward the clinic's door. "I was hopin' it would still be open. But I guess I'm too late."

"Yep. It closes at five on Thursdays."

A slow nod. "A'ight. Well, thanks anyway." He turned to go.

"Was there something you needed?" Erin released the lock and pushed the screen door open. "Do you need care?"

He turned around. "Actually, um … yeah. My arm got cut. I think I need stitches."

"Really?" She stepped out onto the porch beside him. "Let me take a look."

"You a doctor?"

"Sort of. A nurse practitioner, actually."

"Is dat you?" He pointed to the words on the clinic's door. "Are you … Erin Mathis, FNP?"

"I could be."

"What's the F stand for?"

"Fabulous."

The boy's brown eyes about popped out of his head.

"Family. It stands for family."

"Ahh." He gave her a long look.

"Really. I have the paperwork to prove it."

"A'ight." He slowly nodded, then held out his arm and pulled up his shirt sleeve to reveal a black bandanna wrapped around his lower arm.

The swelling and redness above and below the bandanna caught Erin's full attention. "How long ago did this happen?"

"Couple of nights ago."

Not good. Infection was setting in. "Don't move. I'll be right back." She looked up and met his gaze.

He didn't seem too sure at first. But then he smiled. "A'ight."

His smile exposed perfect white teeth. A handsome young man. Obviously not from Kimberley Square. And Erin would not be surprised one bit if the long sleeves of his shirt covered gang tattoos. Maybe even Eastsider tattoos.

A'ight, Lord. Whatever You say.

She went back into her house, closed and locked the front door, and hurried through the living room to push through the swinging door into the clinic. She flipped on the lights, then opened the clinic's door and waved the boy inside.

He didn't move right away. His expression reflected pure wariness. But he slowly walked in.

Erin closed the door, locked it, and led him back to the examination room. *He looks almost as nervous as I feel, Lord. Maybe even more nervous.*

Somehow, the thought set her even more at ease.

BE COOL ... BE COOL ...

Sweat lined his forehead. His stomach churned.

Come on, dawg, keep it together ...

Every bit of what made him up wanted to jolt out of the place. But he followed the lady back to one of the rooms. She motioned for him to sit on a padded table. So he sat. And watched her closely.

She washed her hands at the sink and dried them with a paper towel, then pulled a pair of rubber gloves out of a drawer. "So, you know my name, but I don't know yours."

He swallowed deeply. Should he tell her his name? Could he get away without telling her?

She tugged on the gloves and picked up a pair of bent scissors. "And I still don't. Aren't you going to tell me?"

Did she have to know? If he didn't tell her, would she kick him out? Another deep swallow. "Jamaal." His voice sounded wigged out.

The lady smiled at him. "Hello, Jamaal."

Something about her chilled his trippin'. Her smile. She totally seemed to mean it.

"Before I cut, do you want this bandanna back?" She waited for an answer.

"Um ... nah. That's a'ight."

She sliced through it, eased it away from the cut, and ditched it in the trash. Then poked around his cut a bit. "Well, Jamaal, you've got yourself a knife wound that's starting to get infected." She eyeballed him.

He looked away, waiting for the lecture. *Why didn't you get this taken care of sooner? Were you fighting? You shouldn't have a knife. You shouldn't be fighting.* He'd heard it all before.

But the lady didn't give no lecture. She poked again at the edges of the cut and shook her head. "It's deep. But it doesn't look like there's serious muscle damage. Can you flex your hand for me?"

He made a fist. Tried not to reveal how it pained him.

"Good. Lift your hand at the wrist?"

He lifted it.

"Yeah. That's good too. You've got good muscle response. I know it hurts, but with this much response, there's minimal damage." She again eyeballed him. "You are a lucky man, Jamaal."

He held her gaze. Her assessment of his wound—and of him—felt good.

Again she poked. "But it needs to be cleaned. With the infection starting, I'd say the knife that did this wasn't exactly ... sterile."

Still no lecture, no getting all up in his bi'ness. But that Duncey ... no doubt the fool laced his blade. No wonder the slice spoiled so quickly.

"I'll give you a local and numb it all out before we proceed. Would that be all right?"

Jamaal nodded. "Yeah. Dat sounds straight up."

"I'll need you to fill out a few forms, though. How old are you?"

Her question slammed him.

"Need to know. If you're a minor, I'll need to contact your parents at some point to keep it all legit." She waited for his reply.

"It's just me and my mom. Can't you keep her out of this?"

"She doesn't know you've been hurt?"

"Yeah." His racing heart started to ache. "She knows. Yo. It ain't like she don't care 'bout me."

"I'm sure she loves you very much. And I'm sure she's afraid for you right now."

"She ain't afraid."

The lady ... Erin ... only nodded.

"I told her I'm fine."

"And you are. It's just that I'm going to need to tell her about the care you've received here. It's part of our agreement with the good old U.S. government, who just so happens to be the ones who allow us to stay in business."

What a waste of time. Jamaal pushed off the table and made for the door. "Yo. Later." He didn't say the rest of what he wanted to say, the name he wanted to call her.

"Wait a minute, young man."

He didn't turn around.

"Jamaal!"

The lady was quick. She made it to the door before he did.

"Will you just chill? Please?" She yanked off her rubber gloves. Her choice of words amused him.

"All right. Forget the forms. But promise me you'll tell your mother all about this. If the infection gets worse, you'll need antibiotics, and I cannot prescribe you any without her consent. But I can certainly clean and stitch your cut. What have you been taking for the pain?"

He sized her up. Then regretted the name he had wanted to call her. This lady was proving herself to be cool. "Advil. Yo."

"Good. That's good. Keep taking it. Just make sure you follow the dosage directions carefully. Don't take too much."

He could do that.

"It'll keep the swelling down." She grabbed his good arm. "Come on, you. Let's get you fixed up." She pulled him back toward that padded table. "Sit, sir."

He sat.

She came back with an ice pack, gave it a good smack, then shook it easy to mix the stuff inside. "Here." She put a clean white cloth over his cut and laid the ice pack down over it. "Grin and bear it for a few minutes until it sets in." She looked at him. "Then I'll give you the local. A'ight?"

A grin worked its way across Jamaal's lips. He couldn't keep it back. "Who taught you to rap like that?"

She laughed and headed for a cabinet on the other side of the room. "I had a good teacher."

Jamaal's grin gave way to a fully cheesy smile. Nothing he could do about it. No way he could stop it.

"I HAD A GOOD TEACHER," Erin said, but she left the rest of her thought unsaid. *And I wonder what else he has to teach me before this night is over?*

She rummaged through the med cabinet's shelves for the lidocaine, a syringe, a stitching needle, and some silk, then pulled down a bottle of hydrogen peroxide, a bottle of Betadine, and some large gauze bandages.

What are You teaching me, Lord?

She filled the syringe with lidocaine, carried the peroxide over to the sink, prepared several sterile towels, and carried the syringe and stitching materials to the metal table beside her desk.

Lord? Help me to listen ... and to learn.

Sitting on the rolling stool, she dared a glance her patient's way.

He seemed to be studying the wall behind her with great interest. The wall covered with pictures of patients, family, and friends. Her glance caught his attention. "Who are all those people?"

"Most are patients." Erin pulled out another pair of gloves and slid them on. "Some are friends."

"Who are those soldier dudes?"

She purposely feigned nonchalance. "Marines we treated in Desert Storm."

Those eyes widened. "We? Like, as in you? In Desert Storm?"

"That's right." She let her amusement show in a tiny pressed grin.

"Straight up? Cool."

"Yeah. It was a fun experience." A laugh. "Well, for the most part. The war part was sort of a drag."

"Where are you?" He squinted at the wall.

Erin reached up to point at one of her favorite pictures, the one with her and Chris standing by the sweetest helicopter in the world. "That's me, right there. And my friend Chris. She was the medic on that Huey's medevac crew, and I was the trauma nurse. We nicknamed that helicopter 'Ticket to Paradise.'"

A soft cuss. "For real?"

"Riding on that helicopter as it buzzed the desert at about eighty feet was totally for real. Probably the most 'for real' experience of my life." Except for a few months ago when her newborn daughter arrived. She lowered her head as the thought carried through her, bringing a fresh touch of joy to her entire being.

Another assortment of soft cusses. But spoken on a breath of pure wonder.

Erin didn't mind the boy's bad language. At that moment, as he stared at the pictures on her wall, she didn't mind one bit.

★★★

JAMAAL STARED AT THE PICTURES, yet cringed inside, waiting for the lecture. *"Boy, don't use that tone with me! Mind your manners. You shouldn't say things like that."* But again, the lecture never came.

"How's it feeling?"

He blinked. "Huh?"

The lady smiled. "The ice. How's it feel?"

He grunted. "Cold."

"Well, that's good, I guess."

"You were really in Desert Storm?" His question sounded lame, but it didn't add up. This nice lady was in the war? She didn't look tough. Not like he thought a soldier should look at all. But maybe that was 'cause she was just a nurse.

"Yep. Right in the thick of it."

Her answer surprised him. "How thick. Like ... you were in combat?"

"On G-Day—that was the first day of the ground war—we patrolled the supply convoy all the way up into the heart of Iraq. Most of the worst of the combat had already been fought, but we had our own run-in with the enemy."

"For real?"

"Yep. It wasn't fun, I'll tell you that."

"Did you kill anybody?"

She laughed off his question and looked down at his arm. "Think you're ready for your shot now? I'll have to really clean out the wound. It'll take some doing."

That didn't sit well. He squirmed on the table.

"In two minutes you won't feel a thing." She touched his shoulder. "Don't worry. We'll wait until it's good and numb. I'll take my time and talk you through it. You should be out of here in about a half hour. Sound like a plan?"

He gave her a slight nod. And a grin. "Word. Sounds a'ight to me."

JASON SLOAN PACKED UP HIS gear and took it and his game to the Kimberley Street Community Gym. His old pal Sugar Ray Richardson would be there. And his girl. Christina Renae McIntyre. He loved how her name tumbled through his brain. Christina Renae, sweet and smooth. Blown away by the strength in her last name. McIntyre.

Some of the guys who also played in the Thursday night basketball league she set up at the gym called her Mac. She didn't seem to mind. But she didn't like being called Chrissy. Not at all. She set him straight on that almost from the get-go.

He parked his truck out on Kimberley Street to avoid laying eyes on that fresh patch of gray paint on the gym's back wall. As he walked toward the gym's propped-open doors, his heart picked up its pace. He needed to see her, needed to apologize for not calling her, for not going to church. For getting drunk. For just about everything.

She would forgive him. She always forgave him. Forgiveness was a big thing to her. She made that stupid trip to Colorado to forgive that monster she called Dad. Jason wondered again why she didn't seem to want to talk about the trip. He still didn't know the half of what happened in the week she was gone. He could only hope the trip went well.

He didn't hurry through the open glass doors. Leaning against the inside edge of the left one, he took in the entire sight before him, hoping to see her out on the floor laughing and shooting hoops with the guys. She had a sweet outside jump shot. A nice release. The ball would follow a high arching path to usually fall straight into the bucket. Sometimes she put him to shame.

But she hated playing defense.

He liked that about her. Competition didn't mean all that much to her. She didn't need to win. She just needed to be out there watching her high-arching shot tickle the twines.

And there she was. Toosh. From the corner.

Jason's heart swelled.

Two more points. This time from the top of the key. Followed by a huge smile.

You are so beautiful...

"Sloan, what are you doing?"

He recognized the voice immediately, but didn't move. "What's it look like I'm doing?" *I'm watching my girl.*

"Holding up the building?"

He turned to scowl at Harper, one of the firefighters who worked in his station. "Man, don't give me that."

Harper laughed and walked inside. "I know what you're doing."

Jason followed, ignoring Harper's smug response and keeping his eyes on Chris. An idea struck him, and he tossed his gear down against the wall to better carry out his plan.

She stood just about at half court. Jason moved in behind her, tiptoeing to soften his steps. Two feet from her, he lunged in and grabbed her from behind.

He never expected to hear the scream she let out, or to feel the twisting move that wrenched her from his grip. He stood there, his arms still out, feeling the dumbfounded expression on his face but not able to remove it.

"Why did you do that?" Her voice pierced his eardrums. Her hands lifted to push him away.

Jason stepped back to catch his balance, lowering his hands in the process. A quick glance around told him just about everyone in the gym waited to hear the answer to her question. "Dumb idea." He dared a glance her way.

"You better believe it was a dumb idea." She stormed to her office and slammed the door.

It took about two seconds for the entire gym to erupt in a cacophony of hoots and hollers. Standing in the middle of it all, Jason desperately wanted to take a bow. But resisting the urge to carry out his second dumb idea in as many minutes, he took his sorry self and his bruised ego to the door of Chris's office. Without knocking, he pushed open the door and closed it quietly behind him.

"I'm sorry," Chris said before the door even latched shut.

"Me too." Jason leaned back against it.

"Don't be." A deep breath seemed to leave her sagging. She stood, leaning against the far wall, not raising her eyes to look his way.

"I'm sorry I didn't call you last night."

Finally. Her soft eyes met his. "You should be sorry for that. You told me you'd call."

"I know. I got drunk instead."

A hint of surprise lifted her right eyebrow. "Another dumb idea."

"I'm just full of them lately."

She pushed away from the wall and grabbed up her whistle. "You better go warm up. It's almost six."

"Forgive me first."

Her eyes stayed on his as she moved in close. "Already done. Soon as you walked through that door."

Jason leaned down to kiss her lips. "What if I wouldn't have come in here?"

A smart-aleck grin gave way to a beautiful smile. "I still would have forgiven you. But not until after I slapped a few cheap fouls on you." She held up her whistle for effect. "Now go warm up. You've got ten minutes."

With Chris in his arms, Jason stepped her backward, moving away from the door, and kissed her once more. "Ice cream tonight." He pulled the door open. "After you close up shop."

"I think I'll allow that."

Her smile was so soft. He wanted to kiss her again. But turned instead and headed out the door.

He plopped down against the wall and dug his hightops out of his bag. And really wanted to kick himself in the pants. Why did he scare her like that? When would he ever learn?

But how could he have known she would freak out like that?

What in the world caused her to freak out?

"ALL DONE. YOU CAN LOOK NOW."

Jamaal lowered his eyes from the collection of pictures on the wall. The lady in most of those pictures sat beside him. With a pair of small scissors, she snipped the thread for the last time, then pushed the light away and leaned back in her chair. Jamaal leaned forward for a closer look.

"Some of my best work, I'll have you know. I've always wanted to stitch a quilt someday."

The long line of black stitches tripped him out for a second. Especially against the orange stuff she put down on his brown skin. But the sight of the tightly closed slice left him grateful.

"It'll leave a bit of a scar, but not too bad."

No prob. Scars were cool.

He watched as she cleaned the wound one more time and then wrapped a thick bandage around his arm. "Keep this on until at least Sunday afternoon. Don't let it get wet. I'll give you some gauze to take home with you." She cut the wrap and taped the ends down. "After that, change the bandage at least once a day. And try to keep the wound clean and dry. Use a little alcohol on a Q-Tip to keep it clean. After about a week, let it get some air during the day. But keep it out of sustained direct sunlight."

He glanced up at her.

"Okay?"

"A'ight."

"Come back in two weeks and I'll take the stitches out. And please tell your mother about this. Tell her everything. And be sure and tell her it's all taken care of. Bring her with you when you come back. We'll do the forms then. But if the swelling gets worse, come back immediately. I mean it. Don't wait. We'll do the forms, then I'll be able to set you up with a prescription for an antibiotic."

He nodded, not sure if he'd ever come back, or even if he'd tell his mom about any of it.

"And know this, Jamaal."

His eyes lifted to lock onto hers.

"You are always welcome around here. If you need anything, come back and talk to me. Remember my name?"

His guts were trippin'. Yet he said it. "Erin."

"Right. I'll remember yours." She walked across the room to one of the cabinets, came back with a roll of wrap and some tape, and handed them to him. "That should do it."

Jamaal stood and took the stuff.

"So. I'll see you in two weeks."

Nah. He wouldn't be back. And he couldn't look her in the eye as he realized it was true.

The silence dragged out.

"Hey. I hear you." Her voice was soft. "It's all right. They're easy to take out. Just be sure to keep everything sterile. Cut the stitch by the knot, then pull it out carefully. It shouldn't hurt. But you can numb it with ice beforehand if you want. Just be sure and keep things clean." She pointed to the tape in his hand. "Put about six or eight strips of tape across the cut once you pull out the stitches and clean the wound one last time. Leave the tape in place for at least a week. Then carefully soak off the strips. Don't just pull them. Don't pull open the wound. It'll still be vulnerable. A'ight?"

He slowly lifted his eyes. Laughter tripped around in his gut. "Yeah. A'ight."

She eyeballed him a bit longer, but not in a mean way. "Go with God, Jamaal. He loves you."

The words sent him buggin'. He headed for the door. "Yeah. A'ight."

She followed him but made no move to stop him.

He flipped the lock and pulled the door open, took a step to leave, but then needed to turn around, to check her out once more.

She stood by the front counter, leaning against it, just looking at him.

He gave her a smile. One of the first real smiles he had given anyone in a long time. "Yo. Thanks, Erin."

"Anytime, Jamaal. Take care."

He pulled the door closed and headed for home.

✳✳✳

ICE CREAM. JUST WHAT SHE needed. Something to seriously help her chill out.

Chris walked into the private bathroom in her office, closed the door, and leaned back against it. This was a weird place of escape, yet an effective one. The pitch darkness, thick wood door, and all the concrete surrounding her blocked out most of the noise from the gym and the street, seemed to muffle it just enough to make it palatable on those days when things got to be too much.

Those days didn't come often, but when they did, she was grateful for the escape.

The darkness closed in. She flipped on the light and squinted against it. Her heart still thumped. She drew in another long breath to try to settle it.

Why was she so spooked? Poor Jason. She embarrassed him in front of all his friends. At least Ray wasn't present to witness it. If he had been there, Jason would never have heard the end of it.

He scared her out of her socks. Which proved only one thing. She was scared to begin with. More scared than she realized. Or would ever admit.

The whole Eastsider thing was starting to play with her mind. Shadows were starting to creep in from all sides. She needed to pray. But with five minutes to go before the game she needed to referee, her prayer would have to be a quick one.

Where to begin?

"We need to pray for them, y'all. Not just for ourselves. We need to pray that their hearts will be changed."

"Lord, I do. I pray You'll change them. And that You'll keep them out of Kimberley Square."

Not exactly a compassionate request. Probably not what Sonya had in mind.

"Just keep them in their own little world. That's all I ask. On their own turf. But if they come this way again ... may they come in peace."

This prayer was going nowhere.

"Lord, Colorado is starting to sound better and better." Her eyes closed.

"Peace I leave with you, My peace ... let not your heart be troubled." My love ... do not be afraid.

The words echoed through her. Words she read in her Bible? Words from her favorite verse: John 14:27?

Yes. And so much more.

Thank You, Lord. I'll trade in my fear for Your peace any day.

She opened her eyes and enjoyed the warmth flooding her.

Especially today.

ERIN WATCHED THE DOOR OF her clinic close, heard the young man's footsteps stomp down the stairs. Just that fast, he was gone. And if Erin enjoyed placing bets, which she did not, she would bet at that moment the young man with thirty-two of her best-placed stitches in his right forearm would never again find his way through that door. He was gone. Never to return.

Sadness tugged at her. She did all she could do for him. Legally, she did too much. She could be held liable for treating him without completing the proper forms. But with no forms completed at all, who could prove he had even stepped foot inside the clinic? With no forms completed, she didn't even know his last name.

A shadow.

With a terrific smile.

The thought made her laugh. "We did good, Lord." Just a whisper in the silence. "Now he's in Your hands. Protect him. Kill that infection and guard his healing. Please?"

She glanced at the clock on the wall, then turned to clean up her mess. An hour of her assigned rest period was history, but maybe if she cleaned up in a hurry, she could savor the last hour on her love seat with her feet kicked up.

The clinic's door pushed open just as she walked into the examination room. Slightly annoyed, she turned to see who stood at the door.

"Hey ya, Miss Erin!"

The sight of a six-year-old terror brought a smile to her face. "Well, hey there, Jimmy Thurman." She walked into the front room and flopped down onto the couch. "What are you doing here this time of night?"

"Oh, I was just out and about." His toothless grin hinted of mischief.

"Out and about, huh?" Did he hear that from his mom? "Does your mom know you're 'out and about'?"

"Sure she does."

Erin hoped it was true. "It's almost dinnertime. I'm sure she's wondering where you are."

"Can I call 'er?"

Perfect response for a six-year-old's dilemma. Erin laughed and consented. "All right. But let me talk to her first."

"A'ight. Whatever."

Oh, Lord ... he's too young for that! She dialed Darnice Thurman's number, waited four rings, and said hello to her friend. She told her friend that Little Mr. Jimmy Thurman was, at that moment, sitting on a chair in the front room of the clinic.

"What? Send him home this instant!"

"Wait a minute. Let him hear it for himself. Say it again." Erin held the handset at arm's length.

"James Robert Thurman, you get home this instant!"

"Yes, Mama!" The boy tore out the door. "Bye, Miss Erin!"

Laughing, Erin pulled the handset back to her ear. "I think he's on his way."

"Goodness, I didn't even know he was gone. Sometimes I wonder what that boy's thinkin'."

"He said he was 'out and about.'"

"Did he now? Well, we'll see about that. Thanks, Erin. Talk to you later."

"Take care, Darnice." She hung up the phone. Laughter overtook her. She walked to the front door, made sure it was closed, then locked it. She flipped off the lights in the front room and turned once again to clean up her mess.

Jamaal and Jimmy. Two handsome young men just out and about. And, for some reason, both young men found themselves in Erin's clinic that night.

A night she wouldn't soon forget.

SIX

Bettema Kinsley needed to hang out at the gym more often. The kids adored her, especially when she'd palm the basketball with one hand and hold it away from their grabbing little hands. She could dribble the ball between her feet and even twirl it on her finger. One afternoon last week she lined up twelve of the kids to teach them how to twirl it on their fingers. Chris McIntyre, one of the twelve kids, could almost do it. Of course, Alaina Walker, Jazzy Sadler, and Jen White—all nine-year-olds—put the twenty-nine-year-old to shame. But Chris didn't mind. The three girls could flat-out play the game. One day, if they stuck together and ended up on the same high school team, they'd be invincible. In a few months, Chris would get a peek into the future when she coached the three girls on the AAU twelve-and-under team sponsored by the gym. The Kimberley Angels, they'd be called. Ben came up with the name.

He could not have chosen a more fitting name.

Chris loved these kids, and loved this old transformed warehouse. As each day passed, it seemed to transform her with the laughter bouncing off its walls and flurry of activity playing out on its floor. But after a full week of work she also loved heading home just after noon on Saturdays, knowing her week was complete and the next day and a half were hers to spend however she wanted. True, most of her Sundays were spent at the church, then at Sonya's house for dinner, then back at the church, then at Erin's house hanging out and cuddling Mia. But that suited her fine. No other place she'd rather go on her days off. No other people she'd rather spend them with.

Especially this weekend. Especially after her unbelievably long and ugly week.

Leaving the gym and the rambunctious children in Sonya's and Kay's capable hands, Chris and Bettema grabbed their gear, said their good-byes, and headed for the street. Both walked at a leisurely pace, enjoying the warm sunshine and the pleasant chatter of birds.

Glancing up at her African-American friend, Chris felt short in Bettema's presence. At five-foot-six, Chris was short compared to Bettema at five-foot-nine. And the woman carried herself with such confidence and grace, she reminded Chris of a New York City model. But Chris knew better.

Bettema was a warrior, just like Chris and Erin and Cappy. She shared the same memories of hot Saudi Arabian days and long Desert Shield nights. And the chaos of Desert Storm. The UH – 1 Huey helicopter Bettema copiloted on G-Day ferried scores of troops and tons of equipment into the forward operating base in south-central Iraq, even as Chris and Erin's Huey medevac patrolled the army's ground convoy snaking its way to that same base.

And now, as a high-level security officer at Portland International Airport, Bettema still trained and maintained that warrior's heart.

As they walked down Kimberley, making small talk and enjoying the day, another surge of gratitude swept over Chris. She cherished this woman's friendship, and could not thank the Lord enough for making them sisters.

A sudden and knee-high menace to society flashed by them on the sidewalk.

Chris turned and shouted, "Hey, Jimmy, slow down!" But already the boy was a half block away. Chris looked up at Bettema.

A heavy frown worked her friend's face. "That's not right."

She peered again down the street, but the boy was gone. "Something's got him seriously spooked."

A deep sigh. "Great. And we were having such a nice day."

Sometimes it seemed as if Erin craved fresh air. And the high-backed, heavy-duty wood-slat porch swing her husband bought for her as an early birthday present last month provided her with the perfect spot to breathe some in. Even if it was city air. Not the fresh, crisp air she breathed outside Chris's cabin last January high up in the Rocky Mountains of Colorado.

But, then again, with a westerly view of oncoming traffic on Kimberley and an unobstructed view of Ben's house and the church, she could sit and rock and breathe the city's best attempt at fresh air and keep in touch with the happenings of her neighborhood. Or her "hood," as Jamaal would probably call it. Erin's hood. She liked how that sounded.

At the moment in her hood, her husband worked in the clinic, examining Mr. Calpone's enflamed bunion. Her daughter napped peacefully in her cradle on the other side of the front screen door. And soon her hungry best friend would arrive for lunch, hopefully bringing Bettema with her. Until then, Erin would swing in her swing and breathe in her world.

The sun shone brightly, but not too fiercely; the air was warm, but not hot. A slight breeze carried the scent of sweet flowers and freshly mown grass. For a busy Saturday afternoon in the City of Roses, things seemed pretty quiet.

It was the final moment of quiet before the insanity of Labor Day fell upon them. The last hurrah of the summer, with school starting not long after that. Ben's grandson, Benny, would start kindergarten this year. Already he told his grandma he would go for one day to see if he liked it, and if he didn't like it, he would not go back.

A flash of her own daughter, brown-haired and five years old, standing at the front door of her kindergarten class, sent a shiver through Erin's soul. *Will she be afraid on her first day of school?*

The thought almost brought tears to her eyes.

But you'll be there to comfort her. She'll take one look at all the fun things to do and not even know when you leave.

A smile softly pressed her lips. *I hope so, Lord. I really hope so.*

She pushed out of the swing to peek in at her daughter once more. Nothing had changed from the last time she peeked. Mia slept soundly, her tiny hands resting up by her chin.

Sleep sweet, my little boo ... my beautiful Mia Renae.

She could stare at her daughter forever.

But footsteps approached. Erin looked over her shoulder through the screen expecting to see Chris and Bettema.

She saw two young Latino boys. Each wore a brown bandanna over his nose and mouth. Each wore a pair of dark sunglasses.

The sight lit up her belly. She pulled the main door toward her, reached around to lock it, then yanked it closed behind her, cringing as it slammed, knowing it would awaken her daughter. Letting the screen door close, she moved quickly to lock the clinic's door, then turned and leaned against it.

Not two boys, but four. All wearing the bandannas and dark sunglasses.

One took a step toward her. Against the clinic's window, Erin slid sideways to the far end of the porch. As two of the boys climbed the steps, she worked her way around the swing to stand behind it, free to escape, yet for some reason compelled to stay.

The tallest boy lifted his hand and made what Erin thought was a gang sign. "You the doctor who works here?" He spoke solid English.

Erin gave him no reply, only focused on what looked like soft black balls in their hands. Each boy carried one.

"You talk to that Eastsider the other day?"

Her stomach twisted. Her gaze flicked to the boy's dark glasses. Every part of her wanted to cower and hide behind the swing, to run around the corner and up into Chris and Cappy's apartment. Yet she straightened and narrowed her gaze. "You boys need to leave. I'm sorry, but that's just how it is."

"We came to tell you something."

"I'm sure you did. And you're welcome here. But not like this. You're committing a crime."

"Don't ever talk to another Eastsider. This is our turf. We own this hood."

That's what you think, you little ... Erin forced her teeth to unclench. "You're Bandoleros, aren't you?"

The tall boy gave his friends a nod. The boy beside him turned and pulled Erin's screen door open.

"No!" She rushed past the swing and ran at him, but turned at the last second and reached for the ball the tallest boy carried in his hand. As she grabbed at it, he pulled it away, squeezing it, exploding it in his hand. Thick black goo poured through his fingers.

Their eyes met. Through the dark glasses, Erin sensed the boy's terror.

Shouting wildly, the one by her door took off down the stairs. The two others standing on the sidewalk threw the balls they carried, but one of the balls popped over one of the boy's head, raining black goo down over him. In his haste to escape, he slipped in the mess and fell to his knees, but popped back up and sprinted away.

And still the tall boy stood in front of her.

Erin's mouth hung open as she struggled to make sense of the moment.

The boy flipped his hand, spraying goo from his fingers, then turned and ran after his friends.

Breath gushed out of her.

Screaming, Mia's screaming, and shouts of pure rage aggravated the chaos. Inside the locked door, Mia cried for her mommy. Wanting to rush to her, Erin's strength evaporated, dropping her to one knee. She gazed around, trying to take in what had happened. The shiny black goo looked like fresh paint. It seemed so out of place splashed over her hand and on the light blue paint of the porch. Two adults ran after the boys, and it took another heartbeat for Erin to realize those adults were her friends. It was Chris's rage she heard, Bettema shouting at the little brats to stop.

Cappy stomped down the outside stairs and appeared at the far end of the porch. "Erin? What the—?"

Erin pushed up to her feet and breathed deeply, in and out.

"You okay?"

"Yeah." She turned to her friend, but gasped when she saw the mess. Slowly moving closer to the front window of the clinic, she gaped at the ugly black paint oozing down the window and wall.

"Erin?" Scott touched her arm. "What happened? Are you all right?" He turned her sharply to face him. "Are you hurt?"

She couldn't look away from the mess. "No. It's their paint, not mine." The monotoned voice didn't sound like her own.

"What? Are you sure you're not hurt?"

She forced her eyes to meet his fierce gaze. Blinked to focus. "Mia's not happy."

"Baby, answer me. Are you all right?"

A smile broke her out of her daze. "I'm fine. I'm not hurt. Go see about Mia."

His eyes flickered with anger and concern.

"Go, love. I'm fine."

He didn't go. Instead, his hug squished the breath from her lungs.

"Who were they?" Cappy said softly. "Were they Eastsiders?"

Scott leaned back and gazed at Erin, waiting for her reply.

"They were Bandoleros."

His jaw dropped.

"No way. Those little creeps."

With her clean hand, Erin touched her husband's cheek, but turned to glance at Cappy. "Chris and Tee went after them."

Cappy's eyes bulged. "Really? Which way did they go?"

"West." Erin's heart surged when Cappy took off running in that direction. "Watch the paint!" She stared into her husband's worried brown eyes. "Don't slip on the paint." Just a whisper.

His hand lifted to squeeze hers against his cheek. "See to Mia. I'm gonna call the police."

She nodded.

"Please tell me you're all right." He kissed her palm.

"You feel me shaking. My heart hasn't pumped like this in a long time."

"Are you lightheaded?"

"I'm fine." She leaned in and kissed him, then pushed him to the door of the clinic. They both kicked off their shoes and walked inside. Smiling at Maria, the clinic's receptionist, and Mr. Calpone with his one bare foot, Erin hurried through the swinging door into her living room and beelined it to the kitchen sink to wash her hands. "Mommy's here, sweetheart," she said over the running water. "Mia ... Mommy's here." With just soap and warm water, the paint washed off quickly. Erin breathed a grateful prayer for the makers of latex.

Crossing the room, she peered into the cradle. Her squirming, red-faced little bundle of joy was not exactly a happy camper.

She lifted her and held her close. "Shh ... Mommy's here. Did you hear that bad ol' door slam? You were having such sweet dreams, weren't you." A few gentle pats on her back. "I know, sweetheart. I know."

The babe slowly quieted in Erin's arms.

"Yeah. That's it. You're all right." She lowered her into the crook of her left arm, used a soft tissue to dab the tears, and waited a few more seconds for the snuffling to ease, caressing the fluffs of brown hair. "Hey, I know. Let's go see Daddy."

She could almost hear her daughter's reply. *"Yeah. That sounds like a plan. I wanna see my daddy."*

"Yes, you are your daddy's girl." Erin carried her into the clinic.

"Oh. Okay. Yeah. Thanks." Scott hung up the phone and frowned at Maria and Mr. Calpone, but he caught sight of his girls and moved toward them to give them both warm kisses. He slowly looked up at Erin. "They're sending someone. He should be here any minute."

"Good."

"And guess what else. I wasn't the first one to call in and report it."

"What? Do you think Ben called? Sonya's at the gym."

Scott shook his head.

"Then who?"

His eyes flickered with amusement.

"Oh, of course. Our sweet little neighbor, Mrs. Taylor. You think it was her?"

"Who else?" He reached out to take his daughter. "Come to Daddy, my little boo. Are you all right? Did the bad guys wake you up?"

Erin's smile slowly faded as her entire body seemed to wind down. She stepped over to the couch and plopped into it.

"Easy, hon."

It was a sturdy couch.

"Maria, get her a bottle of water." Her husband's authoritative voice.

"I'm fine, Scott."

"Your face just went pale."

She leaned her head back and closed her eyes to avoid staring at the ugly black paint streaking down the window.

Her thoughts paled. Her entire world paled. *Lord ... precious Lord ...*

She gratefully accepted the water bottle from Maria and drank from it deeply. Her eyes once again fell closed.

Oh, Lord, thank You. This could have turned out so much worse.
Another deep drink. And yet, her stomach burned.

Lord, where are they? Chris, Tema, Cappy ... are they all right? Please help them. Please ... ugh. The thought of what her friends might be facing overwhelmed her. *Lord, they're Yours. Please take this mess ... and make it right.*

★★★

THE BOYS SPLIT UP AS Chris and Bettema followed them, but Chris was sure if she could stay with the tallest one, he would speak for the rest of them. He seemed to be the oldest. And the fastest, unfortunately.

Bettema called her name.

Chris ignored her. The tone in her voice sounded as if she wanted Chris to stop. Chris had no plans of stopping. Not unless she couldn't keep up.

Even in boots and his jeans hanging low, the boy was too fast. He ducked through some bushes and crossed the back alley, then leaped the back fence of the next house and disappeared.

Chris pushed through the bushes but stopped in the alley. She couldn't jump that fence. Just the thought of it sent deep pains shooting through her lower back. Cursing, she leaned over her knees and tried to slow her breathing, staring at that fence.

Breathing hard, Bettema walked up beside her. "You still got some wheels, girl."

"They move pretty fast when I'm flat ticked off."

"I hear you."

Chris pushed up and headed back.

"Hold up, now."

"I've got to see Erin."

Bettema quickly followed. "All right."

Both women jogged at a quick pace, until Cappy met them on Kimberley Street, just two blocks from home.

Chris grabbed her friend's shoulders and struggled to catch her breath. "Is Erin all right?"

Cappy's scowl softened. "She's fine, *hermaña*. It's okay. They didn't hurt anyone. Just left a big mess."

"Mia?"

"I don't know, but I'm sure she's fine. Listen, you guys, Erin said they were Bandoleros." Cappy's scowl returned.

Chris pulled away and wiped the streams of sweat from her forehead. "Yeah, we figured that. What did they throw?"

"Looked like balloons full of black paint. One nailed the clinic's window."

She glanced at Bettema, then back at Cappy. "I've got to see Rin."

Cappy grabbed Chris's arm. "Wait. I just happen to know where the little ingrates used to hide out. They may still hide out there."

Bettema pulled Chris's arm from Cappy's grip. "What are you saying, Cap?"

"I'm saying, they're probably going to meet up to discuss their little adventure. Let's go see if the little creeps are there."

Chris rubbed her arm, then slowly lifted her eyes to meet Bettema's gaze.

Bettema looked at Cappy. "I don't know if that's a good idea."

"Hey, it's a totally better idea than you two running off after them."

For some reason, the idea left Chris intrigued. "Okay, Cap. We'll go." She stared her friend down. "But please. Don't tell me what you don't know, tell me what you do know."

Cappy smiled. "Will you relax? I know there's a huge mess to clean up, mostly on the window and floor of the porch. But I also know Erin is fine. When I left her, she looked more worried about the two of you than she did about herself."

"You're sure she's all right."

"Well, she's a bit shaken, I'd say. But Scott was there. Mia was crying, but Erin didn't seem too concerned about it. It wasn't like she was losing it."

"Why did they do it?"

A shrug. "I don't know."

Chris drew in a long, deep sigh. It seemed to reach into the depths of her soul. "Okay." She wiped the sweat from her face with the sleeve of her T-shirt. Looked up at her friends. "Yeah. Let's go."

★★★

"I'm not sure about this, Cappy." Bettema almost whispered the words as the three of them stood on the edge of Kelly Creek Park.

"Come on, Tee. They're just a bunch of little boys."

Chris studied the stand of trees at the far end of the park. The sight tightened the knot in her stomach.

"The creek is down there. In the trees. That's where they used to hang out. Back in, under the Cameron Street bridge."

"How do you even know this?"

Cappy grinned at Bettema. "I just know. And I'll bet you ten bucks that's where they're at right now."

"Always quick to place a bet, eh, lady?"

"It's not like I ever collect."

Chris lifted her eyebrow and gave Cappy a playful smirk.

"Oh, well ... okay. I did collect once. Pretty big score, actually." Cappy winked at her.

"Tema, last chance to back out." Chris waited to hear her friend's reply.

It took a few seconds. And came with the release of a deep breath. "Let's go see if they're there."

"Cool."

Chris touched Cappy's arm. "Not so fast, Cap. Come on. Think about this. We should go home and tell the cops to check this place out."

"Hey. Chris? We're here. Why waste the trip? Let's just go see what's up."

"Do you think they're armed?"

"They might be. But they're just kids. Not more than ten or twelve, I'd say."

Chris almost groaned aloud. At that age, if the cops moved in and hauled them away, they would all end up in juvy. What would it hurt to try to talk to them first? She looked up again at Bettema. "You sure?"

"Yeah." The word didn't sound convincing, but the firm nod and grin Bettema added to it solidified it.

"All right. Let's go see what's up."

"We should come at them from above. From the bridge." Cappy led the way through the park. "Um ... how many of them were at the clinic?"

Oh, now she asks. A laugh spurted out of Chris. Almost sounded like a grunt. "Four."

"Okay. That's not bad odds."

"You're sick, Cap."

"Recovering, Tema. I'm recovering."

Almost to the bridge, the three of them walked softly to cover their steps. A few seconds later, hushed voices carried to them. Cappy stopped. "Listen." A whisper. "It's them." Her brown eyes glittered. "Told you."

It could have been them. The voices sounded young. And male. Spanish. A bit frantic. Chris couldn't understand a word of it.

Cappy's chin lifted as she listened. "They're a little worried about their latest adventure." She tiptoed a few steps closer. Chris and Bettema followed. "They're ripping on each other."

"They sound a bit scared," Bettema whispered.

"They're scared out of their little minds."

"How can we get down there without them hearing us?" Chris leaned over the edge of the street and tried to see under the bridge.

"We can't."

She frowned at Cappy.

"We have to make enough noise to freeze them," Bettema said. "Then try to surround them."

Cappy gave her friends a thumbs-up. "Good plan. Glad I thought of it."

At the moment, Chris wanted to wrap her fingers around Cappy's neck and strangle the ever-loving daylights out of her.

The woman soft-stepped across the bridge and slowly leaned over the left side. Then soft-stepped back. "It's them, all right. And they're on this side of the creek. I'll go right. Tee, go left. Chris, that puts you in the middle."

"Why me?"

"You're the one with something to say to these little ingrates. They just targeted your best friend."

Cappy stared Chris down. Her piercing gaze, then her words, lit a fire in Chris's belly.

"Wait a minute." Bettema paused until Chris and Cappy looked at her. "We can't go in there hot. It'll just feed their hostility."

Breath rushed out of Chris. She used the bottom edge of her T-shirt to wipe her sweaty face. Struggled with what she needed to say. Didn't want to sound holier-than-thou. Didn't want to leave the words unsaid. Another deep breath. "Guys, if we go down there, we go as Jesus would go." She didn't think she spoke the words loud enough for them to hear. And if they didn't hear, she didn't think she had the nerve to say it again.

"Yeah. That's what I'm talking about." Bettema squeezed Chris's shoulder.

"Well, yeah. Me too."

Chris gave Cappy Sanchez, her good friend, rent sharer, and Hispanic sister in Christ, the goofiest look she could muster.

"What?"

"Nothing." Chris listened again to the noises and voices coming from under the bridge. Sounded like water splashing.

"They're making plans to hide out for the rest of the weekend." Cappy grew serious. "One just told the other to go home and raid his fridge and bring the food back so they could have something to eat."

Chris's heart fell. "Come on, let's do this." She peered over the edge of the street. A worn path led down to the creek. "Is there a path over there, Cap?"

A few seconds later, Cappy returned. "Yeah."

"Go that way. Like you said." Chris waited for her to again cross the street. "Ready?"

"On your signal," Bettema whispered to Chris.

"Wait."

A bit annoyed, Chris slowly looked up as Cappy tiptoed toward her.

"Should we pray first? Just to make sure ... we really should do this?"

"You're a trip, Cap."

"But she's right." Chris's voice cracked as she tried to whisper. The three women looked at each other.

"Go ahead," Bettema said to Cappy.

"Why me?"

"'Cause you put me in the middle." Chris bowed her head. "Come on, girl. Make it good. And make it snappy before they take off."

A deep whining sigh. "All right."

Chris closed her eyes and listened to Cappy's prayer. It was a good one, and even as she said, "Amen," Chris knew they'd be all right. This wasn't about seeking revenge, or even about seeking to make a power play. This was about talking to a group of scared and hungry children about how it was going to be from now on in Kimberley Square.

The place belonged to all of them. They all called the place home.

✳✳✳

OFFICER PHILIP MONROE ARRIVED TO ask questions and take pictures of the mess. Sitting on her porch swing, Erin tried to describe the boys, yet knew her descriptions sounded absurd.

A young Latino. Brown bandanna. Dark sunglasses. Hairnet. Baggy jeans that hung way too low on the waist. Black combat boots. Times four.

The officer wrote in a black book. "Yeah, they sound like the Bandoleros of old." His eyes lifted to take in the paint-covered window. "This is a shame. Do you have any idea why they'd do this? Do you know what set them off?"

Erin swallowed down the sudden lump in her throat.

The moment of truth. The moment she hoped would never arrive, especially not with her husband standing so close, hanging on every word she said.

Lord ... work this out. Please?

She smiled at her handsome man as she reached for his hand. He eagerly grabbed it and squeezed it. His eyes locked on hers.

"I do know why they came."

Surprise played out on his face, but it quickly soured into raw fear.

"They told me why. They said they had something to tell me." Erin pulled her husband toward her to have him sit on the swing beside her, then spoke to both men without allowing a hint of the fear she still felt to leak through her facade. "They said this neighborhood was their turf. Their hood. They came here today because I treated a young man Thursday night. A young African-American man who very well could have been an Eastsider."

Breath burst out of her husband.

Erin tried to give him a reassuring smile. "His name was Jamaal. And he was sweet, polite, and even a bit charming. In his own way." Her smile came more easily. "He had a deep knife wound on his arm that was starting to become infected. I cleaned it, stitched it, and he went on his way."

Scott seemed to be struggling to breathe. "When was this?"

"Thursday night. After you closed the clinic."

"While we were golfing?"

"Yep." She hoped her silly grin would help calm him, or at least help him draw in a breath.

"You said his name was Jamaal." Officer Monroe again wrote in his book.

"Yes." Erin turned to give him her full attention. "But this is not about him. He didn't do anything wrong. He was a perfect gentleman."

"Do you know his last name?"

Another thread of fear laced itself around her heart. "Please, sir. This isn't about him."

"You said that was why the Bandoleros came here."

"Yes. But they couldn't have known this boy ..." The words faded as Erin realized the truth. Somehow, the Bandoleros did know Jamaal was an Eastsider. But who told them? How did they know?

And, more importantly, how did they know he was here?

She glanced at the officer. He seemed to be deep in thought. Glanced at her husband. He didn't appear as if he could think at all.

"You didn't know this boy was an Eastsider?"

Erin answered the officer's question as she gazed into her husband's worried face. She knew it was the same question burning inside him. "No. He wore a long-sleeved T-shirt. No jewelry, no colors, no obvious signs."

"You said this was after the clinic was closed."

"Yes. I heard him walking around on the porch."

"How bad was his injury?"

"Took thirty-two stitches to close it."

"Did he say how he got cut?"

Erin turned to the officer. "This isn't about him, remember?"

"Do you have a copy of his medical release form I can look at?"

Her heart seized. She pulled her hand from her husband's grip, drew in a deep breath, then ran her fingers through her tangled hair. The breath rushed out as her hands fell to her lap. "We didn't fill one out."

The officer scowled.

"If I would have demanded it, he would have left. He needed care. End of story."

"We don't document every single patient that comes through this clinic." Scott pushed up from the swing and watched his step as he walked to the front edge of the porch. He turned, leaned back against the railing, and crossed his arms over his chest. "It's our policy to treat anyone and everyone who comes to us for care. No matter who they are. Even if they cannot pay." His authoritative voice again. "And sometimes, though we do not make a practice of it, if the situation warrants, we may choose to forego documentation."

Erin wanted to kiss her man right then and there.

"I understand, Doctor Mathis." Monroe studied a page in his book. "But in this case, that may not have been a good idea."

She wanted to push the officer back into his car and send him on his way.

"Yes." Scott glanced at Erin. "But as my wife said, this isn't about the injured Eastsider. This is about the four uninjured little hoodlums who came here to make trouble."

The officer smiled. "All right. I hear you both. And you're right."

Relief tamped some of Erin's fear.

"This really is a shame. But I'll get all this information to our gangs unit right away."

"Thank you." Scott reached to shake the officer's hand.

"If anything comes of the investigation, I'll be in touch."

"Thank you, sir." Erin stood and gave the officer a smile, but knew it was a poor attempt considering the mixed emotions churning her empty stomach.

Should she tell him about her three crazy friends out there somewhere doing who knew what? She glanced at her watch. Over an hour had passed. Where were they?

Monroe walked down the porch steps.

"Um ... sir?" Erin moved closer.

"Yes?"

"Three of my best friends took off after these boys when they saw what happened."

The officer's eyebrows rose considerably.

"I'm sure they're all right. I just wanted to let you know."

"Which way did they go." The question, not even a question at all, did not carry an ounce of enthusiasm.

"West. Down Kimberley."

He peered at his watch for a full five seconds. "All right. I'll drive around a bit. I'll let you know if I see them."

"Thank you, sir."

"Anytime, ma'am." His smile seemed sincere. "That's why I'm here."

✷✷✷

SPLASHING WATER AND FRANTIC DISCUSSIONS in Spanish covered Chris's movement as she eased her way as far down the path as she dared, ever so careful not to slip or give away her presence. She looked over the top of the bridge across the street and waited for Cappy to maneuver into a similar position. A few seconds later Cappy's eyes turned her way. At that same moment, Bettema laid her hand on Chris's shoulder.

On my signal, huh, guys? Oh, Lord ... help us.

She waited for the splashing to stop. Wanted at least most of the boys away from the creek so their first option wouldn't be to bolt across it.

It took more than a few heartbeats for that moment to arrive. When it did, Chris lifted her hand and gave Cappy one last look.

A nod from Cappy. A pat on the shoulder from Bettema.

Chris waved her hand and ran down the path, waiting until she heard Cappy's holler before she let out one of her own. She ran to stand in front of the tallest boy, between him and the creek, forcing him to step back against the hill under the bridge.

The boy on the left took a step to escape, only to stop when he laid eyes on Cappy. The boy standing in the creek started to move but froze when Bettema said, "No you don't, little dude." She herded him toward his friends.

Chris raised her hands and held them out in front of her, palms out and facing the boys, fingers up and relaxed. "Be cool. It's all right." She studied each boy. All were Latino, and all were wet to some degree. Two were barefoot, their feet caked with mud. She looked into their faces and saw worry in their expressions, fear in their eyes. Water dripped into puddles at one boy's muddy feet. His hair and clothes were drenched. The boy beside him looked so young, maybe only nine or ten. The tallest boy wasn't all that tall. Chris stood eye to eye with him. His eyes burned at her. His upper lip curled into a sneer.

"It's all right, you guys. Stay cool." Cappy also held out her hands. "Do you understand our English? *O prefieres español?*"

All four boys glanced her way, but none of them moved or answered her question.

Just as Bettema had said, their surprise entry effectively froze the boys in place. Chris was impressed with the two who tried to run. They had more guts than the tallest one, their apparent leader, who only backed away from Chris, effectively pinning himself against the hill.

She glanced at the boy on the far left, in front of Cappy. Her heart skipped a beat as a smile swept her face. "Hey. I know you. Is your name Enrique?" Her hands stayed up, imploring the boys to stay cool even as she relaxed her stance and tone. "Remember me? From the gym? And from the other day?"

The boy turned a bit green.

"You should remember her too." Chris wagged her thumb at Cappy. "She gave you a bottle of water at the church."

"What do you want," the tallest one said through his sneering snarl.

Chris shrugged. "We just want to talk. We're not cops. And we're certainly not your mothers."

A hint of laughter danced in the smallest boy's eyes.

"You paid a visit to my home. You terrorized my best friend and made quite a mess. I don't really appreciate that. And neither do my friends." Chris tilted her head to the right. "That's Tema." Tilted her head to the left. "And that's Capriella." She said the name with syrupy sweetness. Glanced at her. Those brown eyes bulged.

"Cappy. My name is Cappy."

The boys didn't care what her name was. The tall one maintained his sneer. And his glare.

"I'm Chris. What's your name?"

After a second, he opened his mouth and said four of the most vulgar words Chris had ever heard.

"Okay." She looked at the youngest. Gave him a small smile. "That's not your name too, is it?"

Another hint of a smile.

"Will you tell me your name?"

He glanced at the tallest boy.

This little exercise was going nowhere. "All right. That's okay." She sighed deeply. Let her hands fall to her sides. "Guys, we've got a huge problem. For some insane reason, you made a serious mess back there, and none of us know why."

"Ask your friend."

The words short-circuited her brain. "What?"

Vulgarmouth straightened and crossed his arms over his thin chest. "She took care of an Eastsider on our turf. We *own* Kimberley Street."

Chris blinked. She almost preferred to hear the boy's profanity. These words cut more deeply.

"What are you talking about?" Bettema moved in a step closer.

"The other night, your friend took care of an Eastsider and—"

"Wait a minute." Chris raised her left hand. "First of all, get this straight. My friend is a nurse. And if someone came to her asking for help, she'd help them no matter who they were." She tilted her head. "And second of all, did I hear right? Did you just say you owned Kimberley Street?" She glanced at Cappy. "Is that what you heard him say, Cap?"

"Word up, Chris. That's what the boy said."

"Tema? How about you?"

"Yep. I do believe you heard him correctly."

"Unbelievable." She slowly shook her head. Then glanced at the other boys. "That's a pretty bold statement, you know. But it's also the most stupid thing I've ever heard. Are you guys telling me you think you own my neighborhood?"

The wet-headed boy swallowed deeply as his eyes shifted away from Chris's gaze. No one else moved a muscle.

"Well, gentlemen." Chris lowered her hand and shook her head once more. "You better get this straight too. Because I'm telling you ... you don't. Do they own your neighborhood, Cappy?"

"You know? Chris? I don't think they do."

"Tema?"

"I know they don't own my neighborhood."

"Yeah. I thought so."

Vulgarmouth slowly reached into the front pocket of his jeans.

"Don't do that." Chris again raised her hand, palm out. Softened her voice. "Come on, kid, don't."

"Get outta here." The words squeezed through the boy's clenched teeth.

"What. You think you own this spot too? I'm not allowed to stand here and have a little conversation with you?"

He pulled a shiny steel switchblade out of his pocket.

Chris made a show of rolling her eyes and turning her head briefly away. "Aww, man. Now you've done it. Are you sure you want to do that?"

With a loud click, the six-inch blade popped up. "Get lost." More vulgar words. "Before I cut you up."

Chris glanced at the other boys. None made a move for their pockets. Standing there, gaping, they made no move at all.

"Son, you don't want to do this." Bettema's soft voice caused Vulgarmouth to blink. "Trust me."

"Hey, man," came from the wet-headed boy. The rest of his words meant nothing to Chris. Just a flurry of Spanish.

"Smart kid," Cappy said. "He wants his friend to put the knife away."

Chris gave the smart kid a reassuring smile. Pity swallowed her as the boy's bottom lip quivered. "Good thing you guys used a water-based paint, huh. You'd be in a world of hurt right now if you had gone with enamel."

Vulgarmouth took a step toward Chris. He laced both his English and Spanish curses with pure venom.

"Uhh ... I'm not gonna translate that for you, girl."

"Yeah. Thanks, Cap."

Another step. "You wanna get cut up? Just you and me." Another vile name.

Chris hated being called that name.

"Come on." The knife swung side to side in front of the boy's glaring eyes.

A twinge of pure rage twisted Chris's stomach. Her voice boomed, echoing back down on them from the roof of the bridge. "I helped your boy over there, slick. He ran at me for protection and hid behind me as the Eastsiders were chasing him."

A hitch in those glaring eyes.

She dared a glance at the boy she knew best. Pity again flooded her, spilled into her anger and tempered it a bit. But she kept her voice firm. "He was pretty scared too. Out of his mind scared." Her eyes narrowed to mirror Vulgarmouth's glare. "Want to see how scared? This is what your boy did to me." She pulled up the sleeve of her T-shirt to reveal her bruises. "See how scared he was?

This is where he grabbed me. And here." She pulled up the other sleeve. "Ahh ... but I was scared too. You better believe it. Clueless. That was me. We both just stood there like a couple of dummies and watched to see what they were going to do." She allowed a smile to pull her lips, to soften her glare. Yet she held the tall boy's gaze. "I stood there, slick, between your boy and that mini-assault rifle the Eastsiders carried." A quiet breath of laughter. "And I don't regret it. Not one bit. I'd do it again. But, you know? My only regret is that he did something to pull the Eastsiders into our neighborhood. And now we can't seem to get rid of them. They're like an infestation of ants or something. Always crawling out of their holes and making pests of themselves."

Giggles burst out of the youngest boy.

Chris looked his way and laughed with him.

Just as Vulgarmouth's switchblade flashed a few inches from her face.

SEVEN

Erin adored her husband. But she still couldn't look at him. They worked together out on the porch sopping up the worst of the paint with paper towels. Isaiah would soon arrive with reinforcements and equipment to finish the job. When he did, Erin would immediately excuse herself and escape to the kitchen to make sandwiches for everyone. When, not if, her three crazy friends returned, she knew they'd be starving. She was starving. Which was a good sign, since an hour ago her stomach felt as if she had swallowed a gallon of gasoline.

So far so good. Her husband had not asked her about Jamaal. But was that a good thing? How long would he stew? Was he stewing? Maybe he wasn't even thinking about it. Maybe his mind was preoccupied with cleaning up the mess. Maybe he had forgotten about the thirty-two stitches his wife put into the arm of an Eastsider. While he was off golfing.

Yeah, right.

She rocked back on her haunches and looked up at her husband, who struggled to wipe off the window without smearing black paint on his shirt in the process. She waited for him to look back at her. And she waited.

"You all right, love?" He stayed focused on his work.

"Fine."

"Have enough towels?"

"All I need."

"Isaiah should be here any minute."

Thank goodness. Erin pulled off one of her rubber gloves and reached up to scratch her nose.

Her husband finally peered down at her.

She felt her eyebrows lift.

"Can I ask you something?"

"Certainly."

"When were you going to tell me?"

A sheepish grin tugged at her lips. "I was hoping I would never have to."

Scott tossed his handful of paint-covered paper towels into the garbage bag, then pulled off his gloves and tossed them in too. With a sigh, he plopped down on the swing and gave his wife a long stare. "Please don't do that."

"Do what?"

"Conveniently forget to tell me things."

She stared at her husband's fifteen-year-old sneakers. "Where did you find those?"

He leaned over and took a look. "In the back of the shed."

"You're kidding."

"I was saving them for a moment just like this."

"They go in the garbage just as soon as you're done."

"That was the plan."

Erin loved the way his face always softened when he gave her that smile.

"Promise me something?"

She would promise him the world. The moon and the stars.

"Please promise to tell me everything that happens to you every single second of every single day from now on for the rest of your life."

Giggles overtook her. She pushed up to sit on the swing as close to him as she could get.

"Promise?"

"You know what they say about a promise."

"Yes, ma'am, I do." He pulled her in for a long kiss. "And I promise to love you forever."

The sun and the moon and the stars.

✯✯✯

CHRIS SHOULD HAVE SEEN IT coming, but she didn't.

She was getting old. At twenty-nine, her reflexes and peripheral vision just were not what they used to be.

But he missed.

And, with that thought reactivating her stunned brain waves, she almost thanked the little Bandolero for giving her another chance to reach thirty.

Thank You, Lord.

She glared at him, trying to keep a lid on the rage once again shooting through her belly. "That make you feel better, slick? Feel like a big man now?"

"Step back, son." Bettema sounded closer, but Chris didn't turn to look. "You made your point. Don't push it."

"Shut up!" The vulgar-mouthed boy lived up to his name, spouting off several more long strings of profanity.

"Oh, yeah. He's a big man." Cappy let out a grunt.

"No, Cap. He only thinks he is. His attempt to cut me didn't even come close." Chris took a step toward the boy.

His dark brown eyes flashed a hint of wariness.

Just what Chris was hoping to see.

He took a small step backward.

"Where're you going? Stand tall, big man. Try it again. Prove how big of a man you are to your homeboys here."

"Chris ..." Bettema spoke the word low and slow.

Chris blinked. Was she pushing her luck? Crossing a line? Her stomach burned. And yet, her hands were steady. Her heart thumped at its usual pace.

More profanity. At least it sounded like profanity. With that tone of voice, even in Spanish, it must have been something vile.

"Cappy?"

"Nope. Not sharing that bit of juicy verbiage with you either."

Chris's laughter spurted up from deep in her belly. "Tough man with his tough talk." She took another step closer.

Though the blade in his hand shook, the boy stood his ground.

Three feet between them. Chris lowered her gaze from his eyes to his chest, stretching her focus to take in his entire body. Slowly lifting her hands to a defensive position, she quieted her voice. "If you pull a weapon on someone, make sure you're ready to use it."

Curses.

"That was a nice attempt earlier. But here we stand. Go for it again, or put it away. Right now. It's your call."

One of the boys pleaded in Spanish.

Vulgarmouth's upper lip curled.

Lord . . .

His right arm swung at her. The blade came again at Chris's face.

She grabbed his wrist in her left hand, turned it, lifted it, and waited for the knife to drop to the ground. When it did, after some determined hesitation, the boy glanced her way. He stood on his toes, trying to ease the pressure on his elbow. His eyes didn't exactly plead, but they didn't glare at her either.

As quickly as she could, Chris pushed the heel of her right hand into the boy's face, but stopped just short of his nose. A gentle touch. That was all.

She lowered his arm and released his wrist, then pushed him away. Knelt down to pick up the knife. Held it in her hands as she stepped back a few aimless steps.

No one moved. Nothing was said.

Vulgarmouth stood slightly hunched, rubbing his wrist.

Chris again softened her voice. "You tried to hurt me, and you gave it a good effort. You've got an effective weapon here. In the hands of a master, this little chunk of steel can bring on some serious hurt." Even as she said the words, she regretted saying them. The last knife she saw used as a weapon tore open the chest of the man she loved. As she turned the blade to capture the light, a part of her cringed at the sight. Prayers whispered through her. But she needed to press on. "Yep, some serious hurt. But you're definitely not a master." She snapped it shut and tossed it at his feet.

He quickly crouched to grab it. Continued to stare at her as if she had just grown three more heads.

"My dad taught me how to take care of myself. He taught me to anticipate anything. To act before my enemy acts, forcing him to react. Or, in your case, to wait my enemy out to see if he does something stupid. Then, when he does do something stupid, to attack that stupidity and exploit the weakness created by it. Do you know what that means, slick? Exploit?"

Nothing. He only blinked. And swallowed.

"To take advantage of it. To use it *against* my enemy." She drew in a deep breath and released it slowly through her pressed lips. "Dude, I could have really hurt you just now. When someone pops the heel of their hand into the base of someone else's nose, not only will they easily break that nose, but if they hit hard enough, they can send broken pieces of it up into the sinus cavity. Can you even imagine how much that would hurt?"

He glanced away, disgust pouring from him.

"I had that opportunity. I could've laid you out, slick. Right here in front of your boys." She let her gaze fall over each one of them. To her far left, Enrique just watched her, as if trying to figure out if he could trust her. Holding the knife in one hand, Vulgarmouth stared at the ground. Wet-head looked so cold and pathetic, Chris wanted to wrap her arms around him and take him straight home to dry off. The youngest just stared up at her, eyes bulging, mouth gaping. She smiled at him. "Did you think that was pretty cool? What I did?"

He nodded.

"Guess where else I learned how to take care of myself."

Now his head shook. Slowly. But his mouth still gaped.

"The United States Army. I used to be a soldier." She let the words sink in. "And so did Tema. And Cappy." She gave her friends a grin. "Huh, guys."

"Why do you think we care," came from that vulgar mouth.

Chris ignored him. Gazed again at the youngest boy and used her thumb to point at Bettema. "She used to fly helicopters. Not just ride in them, but fly them. And Capriella over there used to work on Humvees. You ever seen a Humvee?"

His head again shook.

"Never? Well. It's like a big Jeep. It goes anywhere. And is it ever a kick to drive."

She enjoyed the sight of the grin on his baby face.

Another deep sigh overtook her. "Ahh ... man, you guys, you have so many cool things to see and do in your lifetimes. Please, please, please ... don't throw your lives away thinking you're all tough and macho. You don't own this neighborhood. You don't own anything! You only own what happens to your life. You own your future. And right now. You own this present moment. Do you understand what I'm saying?"

All four of them stared at the dirt.

Cappy talked to them in Spanish for quite a while. They asked her questions and she answered them, smiling from time to time. Vulgarmouth spoke up once and seemed to let her have it, but Cappy flicked whatever he said right back at him and he clammed up.

Listening to their exchange, watching them, hurting for them, Chris prayed. She glanced at Bettema and enjoyed the smile and the pat on the shoulder her friend gave her.

This wasn't about revenge. Not at all. And even though she couldn't understand the Spanish being spoken, the way the conversation dragged on—the way the boys interacted with Cappy—Chris knew good seeds were being planted. And that was why they had followed them to this place. To plant a few tiny seeds of hope into the hopelessness of their worlds as they knew it.

As Cappy continued to talk, Mr. Vulgarmouth Bandolero pocketed his switchblade and relaxed the glare in his eyes.

Chris smiled at him, but he didn't look her way to see it.

The crunching sound of car tires over gravel caught her attention. The car crept along the road above them much more slowly than the few who passed earlier. All of them standing there looked up at the underside of the bridge as if they could see through it and find out who just parked their car above them.

Cappy whispered a few words in Spanish, then said, "Let's all just stay cool."

The car's door slammed. The boys' eyes widened as they started to tense.

Bettema, standing closest to the path she and Chris ran down, waved to someone as if she wanted him or her to come down and join them. "Guys?" She gazed at each of the boys. "Don't be afraid. Just stay still."

A man's voice thundered over them. "What am I missing down here where those notorious Bandoleros used to hang out?"

Chris watched the heavyset man work his way down the path. Blue uniform, shiny black shoes, shiny silver badge, 9mm pistol tucked safely in its holster. He adjusted his heavy utility belt as he reached the bottom and turned to face them. His name tag read *Monroe*.

"Well, now. Ain't this cozy." His gaze swept Bettema, Chris, and Cappy. "I suppose you're the three friends I heard about." His gaze then swept the boys. "And I suppose you four geniuses are the Bandoleros who trashed the front of that clinic on Kimberley Street."

Glancing at the boys, Chris didn't know what to say or do. If the officer continued to push with that attitude, all the seeds they just planted would wither away and die.

"Yep. Lookee there. Black paint. Too bad you just ruined an eighty-dollar pair of jeans."

Vulgarmouth looked up to meet Chris's gaze. Wariness, or was it pure fear? Something transformed his glare into a look that stirred compassion inside her. She turned to the officer. "Sir?" She waited for him to turn her way. "Hi. I'm Chris McIntyre." She stuck out her hand. And waited.

The officer's blue eyes raked her up and down. "McIntyre, huh? I've heard of you."

She made a fist, then reached up to push away a strand of sweaty hair from her forehead.

"Yeah. You run that gym down on Kimberley Street. You're the one who faced down those Eastsiders."

Chris glanced at Vulgarmouth. With the pathetic look on his face, she needed to find a new name to call him. She didn't think he'd be spouting off any more vulgarities anytime soon. She turned once again to fix her gaze on the cop. "Sir? Yes. These are the boys who made the mess at the clinic. But we've been talking to them, and I'm sure if you'd allow them to return to the clinic right now to apologize to the owners, afterward they'd be more than willing to clean up their mess and make things right." Whew. She needed to talk fast to keep Monroe from interrupting, but she hoped the heavyset man kept up with her.

His lips pressed into a sloppy, frowning scowl. "Well, that sounds like a reasonable request. What do you all say?" He walked by Chris to stand in front of Vulgarmouth. "If I take you back there, will you apologize to the people you hurt and clean up the mess you left on their porch?"

Cappy spoke to the boys in Spanish.

Monroe gave her a questioning look.

"Just to make sure they understand," she said.

The three younger boys nodded. The oldest and tallest gazed at the adults. Finally, with a sigh of surrender, he nodded.

Monroe clapped his hands. "Good. I love happy endings. But let me lay down a few ground rules." He looked at Cappy. "You may translate."

She glanced at Chris and made a face as Monroe again stared the boys down.

"First. You must sincerely apologize. Not just mumble a few half-baked, 'I'm sorry's.'" He waited for Cappy to interpret. "Second. You must clean up every trace of the paint. Every trace." Again he waited. "Third. Today, this moment, marks the death and demise of the Bandoleros. Once and for all." He stopped and peered at Vulgarmouth. "What's your name, son?"

The boy swallowed deeply and wouldn't lift his eyes.

"I asked you a question."

He licked his lips. "Vince."

Chris smiled. Vulgarmouth now had a real name.

"Ahh." The cop grunted. "Yes. Of course. Short for Vincenté."

The boy's head jerked up. His glaring snarl returned.

"You're Miguel's brother, aren't you."

"Miguel is my brother." Slowly spoken. Deliberate.

"So, because of that you think you need to carry on in his footsteps? Keep the old gang together?"

"We are all brothers. We are Bandoleros."

"Not anymore." Monroe growled the words. "It's your choice, Vincenté Diaz, brother of the convicted murderer and drug dealer, Miguel Diaz. If you want to join your brother in prison, or the lot of his friends in juvenile detention, just say the word and I'll take you in so fast it'll make your little head swim. But if you and these boys get smart and make right the wrongs you committed over on Kimberley Street, then I'll take you all home to your mamas instead. So. What'll it be?"

Vince had no choice and he knew it. Even still, he waited so long to answer the question, Chris thought the cop might rescind his generous offer. But then, "Okay."

Monroe leaned toward the boy. "What? What was that?"

"I said okay."

"Okay to what?"

"We'll go apologize. And clean up the mess."

The other three boys seemed to breathe more easily.

"Every last bit of it," Monroe said.

"Yeah." Vince raised his eyes to look at the officer. "Every last bit of it."

"Well." Monroe turned to Chris. "Does that work for you and your friends, Miss McIntyre?"

A smile overtook her. Even made her laugh. "Yes, sir, it does."

"You're sure the owners of the clinic will agree to this?"

She nodded. "Yes. I'm sure."

"Well, all right then. Start walking." His grin looked more like a smirk. "I'll bring the guys with me and meet you out front of the clinic in about fifteen minutes. We've got a few more issues to discuss, but we'll be there. You can count on it."

She wanted to kiss the man on the lips, but restrained herself. "All right. We'll see you all later." She gave him one more nod, then followed Bettema up the path to the street.

As Cappy joined them, Chris heard the officer say to the boys, "All right now. I need all your names and addresses. Starting with you."

A sudden zap of terror froze the breath in her lungs. Would they tell him? Would they bolt in four different directions? But she heard one of the boys say, "Carlos Mercado. Three eight eight three Cameron Street, Portland, Oregon." And her breath released with a rush of relief.

Cappy grinned.

Bettema slowly nodded.

The three friends walked home, side by side by side.

★★★

ISAIAH SADLER AND BEN CONNELLY found Erin and Scott Mathis sitting on their porch swing engaged in a rather intense and highly public display of affection. As Isaiah politely cleared his throat, Erin almost fell off the swing. After exchanging pleasantries with her two dear friends, she hurried to the kitchen to splash cold water on her burning cheeks.

Mia slept on, but would soon awaken and demand her mid-afternoon meal. Stomach growling, Erin needed to eat, so she ransacked her refrigerator and laid out fixings for ham and turkey sandwiches. As her knife smeared mayonnaise on the last piece of bread, her screen door opened and three of her best friends in the world tiptoed across her living room floor.

They looked a bit worn out. Chris's face was flushed and her hair needed to be freed from its braid. Cappy grinned and detoured to Mia's cradle. After giving Erin a wave, Bettema followed the same detour and peered over Cappy's shoulder. Chris walked into the kitchen and pulled down a glass from one of the cupboards. "Hey, girl," she said as water poured into the glass. "You all right?" A long drink. Chris's dark eyes gazed at Erin over the rim of the glass.

"You bet I am." And she was. Now.

A satisfied, "Ahh."

"How about you?" Erin put lettuce leaves on each of the sandwiches.

"Never better."

"How did I know you would say that?"

"It's true."

"But you're hungry."

A faint laugh. "Famished."

"Well, have a sandwich. Oh, wait." Erin reached for a towel, wiped her hands, then pulled the Swiss cheese out of the fridge. "Almost forgot."

Chris's dark eyes glimmered. "You're the best, Rin."

She slapped a piece of cheese on one of the ham sandwiches and closed it up. Chris grabbed it and chomped a huge bite from it before Erin could even say, "Here you go."

Carrying the sandwich toward Mia's cradle and talking with her mouth full, Chris whispered to Cappy and Bettema, "Make a hole, you two. Go get a sandwich."

Erin could only laugh.

Bettema grabbed up one of the sandwiches as Cappy pulled a glass from the cupboard. "Have we got a surprise for you," Cappy said after a long drink of water. "You won't believe it."

Erin finished the last sandwich and wiped her hands once more on the towel. She leaned back against the opposite counter and waited for Cappy's big surprise.

The woman only chewed her sandwich and grinned.

"Come on, don't leave me hanging here."

A deep swallow. Another long drink of water.

Erin looked at Bettema for help, but the woman's mouth was so full she could only shrug her shoulder.

"The Bandoleros are no more."

She quickly met Cappy's gaze. "What? What. You hunted them down and killed them all?"

Cappy's grin widened. "Nope. But don't think we didn't want to."

"They're on their way here," Bettema said. "Can I get a drink of water?"

Erin's mouth fell open. She couldn't move to get her friend a glass from the cupboard. She could only stand there. And stare.

✳✳✳

WHAT A DAY. ONE OF those impossible days when her heart seemed to implode and explode all at the same time. Over and over. Not just once or twice.

Chris lay on her back in her bed, hands clasped behind her head on the pillow, staring up at the swirls of plaster on her ceiling. Outside her open window, birds sang and airplanes took off from PDX. Cars headed up and down Kimberley Street. Saturday night festivities were, without a doubt, just starting to liven up across the entire city.

She wondered what that handsome paramedic boyfriend of hers was up to. Maybe she'd call him later, after her heart settled down from its tumultuous day.

But the sight of those former Bandolero boys inhaling the sandwiches Erin gave them, not to mention Sonya's chocolate chip cookies that Ben brought over for them to devour, did more to settle her heart than anything. The sandwiches and cookies, all washed down with huge gulps of milk. And when Officer Monroe hauled the boys away afterward, Chris was sure each one appeared to weigh at least five pounds heavier than when they arrived.

Prayers once again whispered through her, and she closed her eyes and let them flow. Prayers for each boy, for their parents, brothers, sisters, and friends. For peace in their lives, families, and neighborhood. For peace in Kimberley Square.

Prayers of gratitude overwhelmed her. She savored the hope, cherished those tiny seeds planted earlier that day.

Each boy worked so hard to clean up the mess, and they actually started to relax and enjoy themselves once they got over their extremely tentative arrival. Chris would never forget the way Vince looked at Erin, as if his eyes could see into her very soul, as if he searched out every part of her inmost being for signs of anger, distaste, or rebuke. But he found none. Those things simply did not exist in her. Not long after that, the boy started to smile. An intensely sheepish grin at first. An honest reflection of what churned in his heart. But by the time most of the mess had been cleaned, his smile carried a sweet simplicity, simple happiness at not being rejected. Relief at being forgiven. Pure wonder in the joy of simply being loved.

I know that feeling, Vince. It's pretty cool, isn't it?

A smile worked its way across her face.

I'm glad I don't have to call you Vulgarmouth anymore.

The boy's profanity echoed off the walls of Chris's mind. Her smile faded.

Let go of it, Vince. Let go of it all. Don't follow the ways of your brother. Today you are free. Please know what that means. Don't fall back on the ways that'll just waste you.

She would have to leave that in the hands of her Lord. But what better place to leave it?

Ahh . . . Father God, thank You. Keep this kid close to Your heart. Keep them all close. Please? Like You keep me. Sometimes . . . it's like I can feel Your arms around me. I hope You can feel mine around You. I love You, my Father. Thank You for loving me.

She pushed up on the bed to sit on its edge.

Thank You for Jesus . . .

The Name hummed through her, reached in deeply to soothe her soul.

Thank You, Lord Jesus. You're so amazing. So true. Thank You for making me Your own, and for putting me here with the most amazing friends.

Her battered heart swelled.

And Lord? Please? Keep Your hand on those amazing friends of mine, and on those four little ex-Bandoleros. Please make them Your own. Please cause those new and tiny seeds we planted inside them . . . to grow.

✷✷✷

STARING OUT HIS LIVING ROOM window, Jason struggled to swallow a long drink of Pepsi.

He needed to call her. He needed to go over there and pick her up and maybe even drive her to the coast. He needed to walk on the beach with her tucked in beside him. Just walking, wading in the surf, and waiting for the sun to paint the sky.

He needed to calm down. What good would it do if he showed up at her place all steamed about the latest escapade she and her friends found themselves on earlier that day?

Did they actively seek out these little exploits? Didn't they know the war was over? They didn't need to be heroic soldiers anymore. There were highly trained and qualified people in Portland who got paid to be heroic. It was *their* job to fight the battles raging inside Kimberley Square.

"Let the police do their job, Chris!" He fought back the urge to throw his can of Pepsi against the nearest wall.

The phone rang. His heart almost burst out of his chest. He let it ring three more times just to be sure he wasn't dreaming, then walked over and lifted it slowly to his ear. "Hello?"

"Hey, you. Whatcha doing?"

Chris. He flopped on his couch and melted into it. "Hey, babe. I'm just sitting here thinking about you." And that wasn't a lie.

"Were you now."

"I need to come get you so we can go to the beach."

"The beach? Tonight? Are you kidding?"

Why did she always say that when he asked her that?

"Ahh, Jase, I really appreciate it, but not tonight. I've had a pretty hectic day."

Yeah. Tell me about it.

"Did you work today? I can never keep up with your schedule."

He laughed. "Me neither. And yes, I did, but just a half shift to cover Lansky's doctor appointment. Let me come get you."

A long pause. "I could use some ice cream."

"Done." He jumped up from the couch. "I'll be there in five." He clicked off the phone before she had a chance to object, grabbed his keys, and headed for his truck.

Was he calm? Did he want to innocently mention to her the fact that he knew all about her "pretty hectic day"?

His truck fired up with one turn of the key. He gunned it toward Kimberley Street.

Sure, those Bandolero brats started the whole thing. And didn't that turn out all fine and dandy.

Stoplights and pedestrians impeded his way. The sidewalks teemed with life, too many people, all out enjoying their night off. Jason forced himself to relax, to focus, to avoid any potential problem. To especially avoid those idiots who chose to drive drunk.

A sickening, familiar terror seeped into his gut. He shut his thoughts down. Gripped the steering wheel. Turned onto Kimberley Street. And let her face once again fill his mind's eye.

Chris. Will it be mint chocolate chip again tonight? A pretty hectic day. I'd say so. Poor Erin and Scott. They must have been terrified. It'll be good to see them again. And Mia.

Sharp pain stabbed at his heart.

Beautiful Mia. All of three months old. Wispy dark hair, big brown eyes. So cute. And growing so fast.

At a stoplight, he hit the brakes and mumbled a curse at an innocent pedestrian to break himself out of the moment. The stab left him aching. And whiny.

Why did his beautiful bride have to die? And his precious little one ...

Yep, she'll pick mint chocolate chip again. She always does. Why won't she risk trying something different?

No. Chris McIntyre took way too many risks already. Let her have the mint chocolate chip.

He needed to forget about Richardson's call. If things continued at their present rate, he'd have to tell his good friend not to call him when Chris found herself in another mess. Seemed as though Richardson called a lot lately.

Ahh, his good friend Sugar Ray. *The man had better practice up and get his game on, 'cause when we square up this Thursday night, Fire's gonna roast some Po-lice be-hind.*

His truck rolled down Kimberley. That huge church sat just ahead on the right.

She would ask him to go with her to that church in the morning. Sunday services at the beautiful Kimberley Street Community Church. All the good saints gathered round for the "Lord's Day."

Not his idea of a good time.

It was, once, wasn't it? What's happened, Jase?

He pulled his eyes away from the church. *Maybe it was. Once. But not anymore.*

Besides. Atlanta played Chicago tomorrow. And the Mariners were at Boston. Coop said he'd grill steaks and have his wife fix up a bunch of her world-famous grilled shrimp and veggie skewers. How could Jason miss that?

Maybe he'd ask Chris to skip church just this one Sunday and join them. How could she say no to grilled shrimp and veggie skewers?

He slowed his truck to a stop in front of Ben Connelly's house and peered at the big duplex across the street, up into that second-floor bedroom window. Wondered if he should lay on the horn. Then figured it wouldn't hurt to be polite and go on up. He'd say hey to Cappy if she was there.

His truck rumbled as his eyes surveyed the front of the house. From this distance, he couldn't even tell that a bunch of kids hurled black paint balloons at it earlier that day. A nice, happy ending.

Let's hope the Bandoleros are gone for good.

Chris bounded down the side stairs and crossed the porch. Jason's heart skipped about eight beats as she looked his way and smiled.

Girl. Girl, girl, girl.

Could it be possible she had become even more beautiful since the first time he saw her?

Another sick twinge ripped through his gut as the sight of her battered face—his first glimpse into her dark brown eyes—flashed through his mind. That deep cut on her cheek, all those tears ... and yet, even then she was beautiful.

The cut on her cheek had healed. Left only a faint scar behind.

Her scars ...

Shaking his head, he forced the nightmarish image out of his mind as Chris pulled open the passenger-side door of his truck and climbed inside. "Hello, you," he said as he leaned toward her. A hint of sweet perfume drew him in.

"Hello to you too, Mr. Sloan."

Her kiss was quick, but only because a car moved in behind them. Jason stepped on the gas and drove toward their usual haunt. Baskin-Robbins.

Chris snuggled up beside him, put on her seat belt, and then let out an incredibly long sigh. She glanced up at him with a bit of a shamefaced look. "Thanks for this. I think I'm needing some ice cream."

"You're very welcome." *I know you've had a hectic day.*

"We'll hit the coast one of these days soon. After Labor Day, okay?"

"Yeah. Anytime you're ready."

"I'm always ready." A pause. "Well, I guess that's not true, huh. Sometimes I wish we could move Kimberley Square to the end of the Cape Lookout spit."

Jason laughed. That sounded like a terrific idea.

Just for fun, they talked on about it for a while, then shifted their conversation to an analysis of the weather, the heavy traffic, and the crowd at Baskin-Robbins. And sure enough, Chris ordered two scoops of mint chocolate chip firmly packed into a waffle cone.

His girl. Big risk taker. Except with her ice cream.

Back in the truck, they slouched low in the seat and licked their cones, quiet and relaxed. And yet, Jason struggled with the moment. So far Chris had said nothing about her "hectic day." Would she? Was she waiting for him to ask?

She had no clue that he knew all about it and was dying to hear her version of the story. He could only hope her version sounded less intense than Ray's. And Ray got his story from Monroe. What a jerk.

As his last bite of cherry cheesecake melted in his mouth, a strange truth came over him. From Monroe to Ray to him ...

maybe the story got stretched a bit in the telling. Maybe it wasn't as bad as he was told. He needed to hear it from Chris. And he needed to hear it right now.

He started in on his chocolate peanut butter and let her work a bit more on her mint chocolate chip. He didn't want to start a fight, and he certainly didn't want to destroy the quiet moment they shared. Maybe he needed to seriously chill out and let things slide. Bottom line? The kids cleaned up their mess, Erin was fine, Chris was sitting beside him enjoying her favorite treat, and at the moment? Life was fine.

Between bites, she asked him what his plans were for tomorrow. He struggled to swallow, then said, "Don't know for sure." Though he did know. Very well. And he knew they didn't line up with her plans.

"Don't suppose I could convince you to come to church in the morning." No heat in her words. Not even an accusatory glance his way. Only a big bite of mint chocolate chip afterward. As silence fell over them.

He licked the bottom edge of his ice cream so it wouldn't drip and considered her words. Kept his voice soft. "No, I don't suppose you could." He blew out a breath of laughter to soften his next words even more. "Actually, I do have plans. Why don't you skip church and join us over at Coop's? We're gonna watch a doubleheader on his big screen, and he said he'd grill up some steaks for lunch. His wife's gonna make up some of her famous shrimp and veggie skewers." He paused. "Come with me. You'd love Coop's wife. She's great."

More silence.

Chris slowly turned in the seat, so completely that she pulled up her left leg and tucked it under her right, though she didn't look up to meet Jason's gaze. "I really don't want to. I'm sorry, Jase, but I don't want to skip church, or having dinner at Sonya's afterward."

It's not like skipping one Sunday will hurt you.

Her eyes finally lifted to meet his own.

He had to glance away. His lungs constricted, yet he forced in a long breath and let it out slowly before biting off a huge chunk of ice cream and swishing it through his mouth.

"You know how important this is to me."

More important than it should be. He swallowed deeply and tried to smile. "I know."

"It's not just about going to church. It's about learning all I can about God. Staying as close to Him as I can." She stopped to take a bite of her cone.

The silence unnerved him.

"The last thing in the world I want to do is push you."

He couldn't think of anything else to say except, "I know." It sounded lame to his ears, but nothing else that came to mind fit the moment.

She wiped her lips with her napkin and stared at her cone.

Jason tore off another huge bite of his and chewed it as he gazed over the parking lot. *Let her work this out on her own.*

"Jase, I'm afraid for you. I hate how you seem to be pushing God away."

The words slammed into him. He turned to stare at her, but she didn't look up from her cone.

"I know you're still hurting. Deeply. And I don't blame you. I hurt for you, for what could have been. My whole past ... the hurt is too much for me. It's only been because of God that I've been able to survive. I need Jesus in my life. I *need* Him. He loves me. And He loves you too. I need you to know that, like you once did. I need you to never forget it."

His first swallow wasn't enough. He needed another. "I do know that."

Her eyes lifted. Sadness poured out of them. "You do?"

"Sure I do. It's just that ..." He blinked. His mind stopped working, couldn't process the myriad of thoughts invading it.

Chris waited patiently, slowly eating her ice cream.

Jason wanted to toss his cone out the window. So much for a quiet moment.

"I know you're still dealing with ... everything. I know you're angry. I want to help you. I want to be here for you, to help you heal and move on. But I'm not strong enough to carry you out of the pain of your past. You may think I am, but I'm not."

Just what was that supposed to mean?

"You told me you love me. I believe you do. But it's so much more important for you to love God. To trust Him. Without God's love and healing ... you won't ever really, truly be healed."

She did know a few things about being healed, considering everything she endured in her past. Still, what gave her the right to say what she just said? Didn't she know how much loving her healed him?

"I want you to be free. Completely free. And only Jesus can give you that kind of freedom. Only He speaks truth. Only He can make us right with God."

"Chris—"

"I'm sorry, Jase." She took a bite of her melting cone. Spoke with her mouth full. "I don't want to nag you about this."

His own cone was melting. He licked at the drips, then pulled in a huge chunk. Chewed awhile. Then turned to study the expression on her face.

She was embarrassed. And looked a bit afraid.

"You think you're pushing, don't you."

"I'm afraid you'll hate me for what I'm about to say."

Oh, no. With a quick flip, Jason tossed the remains of his cone into the empty bed of his truck. He'd clean up the mess later.

Chris laughed. "Why'd you do that?"

He smiled. Her face, so tender and soft, revealed a sense of childlikeness. At times she seemed so innocent. So vulnerable. At times it seemed as if he could see into her soul as he peered into those glittering dark brown eyes.

"You're doing it again."

"I love you so much, Chris." The words slipped out. He didn't mind one bit. His hands lifted to caress her cheeks. "Is it okay if I love you?"

She lowered her head and again wiped her lips. And blinked away tears.

"What is it that you think I don't want to hear?" Even as he asked, he dreaded hearing her response.

She handed him her cone.

With a laugh, Jason tossed it in the back and then turned once more to caress her face. "You want to go somewhere more ... private?"

She nodded.

He started the truck and drove them to a park not far away. The place was packed on the beautiful Saturday night, but he found a fairly lonely spot under some trees and parked, then pulled Chris into his arms.

She pushed herself tightly against his shoulder, snuggling in as close as she could.

His heart just about ripped apart as he held her.

A few minutes later, she pulled away and wiped her eyes.

"Is this about what happened today?" As soon as Jason said the words, he regretted it.

She looked up at him, her eyes wide. "Did you hear about today?"

He could lie. He could say, "Well, you told me you had a hectic day." But not to that face. Not in this moment when she seemed crushed by some unseen force. He nodded.

"Ray told you." Just a whisper.

Again Jason nodded.

She let out a deep, trembling sigh. "That's okay."

"I pitched a fit when he told me what you guys did. But you know what?" He gently lifted her chin. "I'm over it. I'm slowly understanding what makes you tick. I may not like it, but I'm starting to understand it."

"They're good kids, Jase. And they're going to be all right."

"Thanks to you. And your friends."

"No." She seemed to steel her resolve. "This is what you must understand. If you see anything good in me or my friends, it's there because of Jesus. He's changed us and made us His own. That's why we tried to help those boys today instead of having Monroe haul them to juvy. Do you think I wanted to help them at first?" Her eyes burned. "When I saw them throwing black balls of who-knew-what at Rinny? No way. I wanted to kill them. The only reason I didn't was because I couldn't catch 'em." A hint of a smile.

Jason sat back and looked out over the park. Several Hispanic children kicked at a soccer ball while their parents laid out plates and food for a picnic.

What made these children different from the brats who used to call themselves Bandoleros?

Someone cares about them. Someone loves them.

"I'm so glad it all turned out like it did. The oldest one turned out to be Miguel's brother, Vince. Did Ray tell you that?"

Jason nodded.

"He's going to be all right. I just know it. He changed from night to day in just a few hours."

Would it last? How could a hardened little brat change so quickly?

"It was Rinny who changed him. Not me. Oh, and something Cappy said to him, but she talked in Spanish, so I couldn't understand a word she said."

"I'm glad too … that it all worked out."

"Jase, those boys were changed by Jesus in us. Vince stared Rinny down trying to find the usual meanness in her. Most human beings would have curled up their lip at him after what he did. But because Rin loves Jesus, He loved that boy through her. And she let Him. Does that make sense?"

What was she trying to say? He slowly turned to look at her.

"Please hear me out before you freak. I know you're going to freak, and that kills me."

Annoyance crept into his gut. "Just say what you think you need to say."

"Jase … in a way, you're like Vince. You're looking at me expecting to see meanness or whatever in me, and you don't see it. You see only love and concern. Yes, Jason, I love you. I've loved you since the first moment we met."

The words … he thought he would never hear them. He wanted so desperately to kiss her. But knew, somehow, there would be a *but*.

"That's why you love me. But I'm telling you, the love and concern you see in me comes from my changed heart. Jesus changed me into someone who can love someone else. Before He changed me, I wasn't capable of love. There was too much baggage and hatred blocking it."

"You're selling yourself pretty short."

"I know who I was."

"So. You're saying the only reason you are now the good and kind and loving and stunningly beautiful woman you are … is because of Jesus."

"Well, I don't know about the stunningly beautiful part."

Jason laughed. It felt good to laugh.

"But yes. That's what I'm saying."

"So tell me again why you're telling me this? Why should I care about this? You're changed. Right now you're a beautiful young woman very much capable of love. So what's the big deal?"

"The big deal, Jason, is that Jesus must be first in my life. I love Him for the changes He's made in me. I love you too, yes, but He has to stay first."

Something flickered again in his gut.

"I've given my entire life to Him. To love Him the way I need to love Him, He must remain first."

Jealousy. Plain and simple. He felt it before. When anyone looked at Jessica the wrong way.

"I know this can't be easy for you to hear. I know you're struggling with your faith now ... because of what happened."

He grunted. "Well, no. I guess it isn't easy to hear. You're telling me I have to compete for your love with the Savior of the world. The God of the universe."

"Then you've heard of Him." A grin.

"Oh, yes. I've heard of Him." A bit too sarcastic. Jason needed fresh air. He started to get out of the truck.

"Wait. Jase?" Chris grabbed his arm. "Please don't walk out on this."

He sat back and pulled his door closed. "I don't even know what I'm walking out on."

A sigh. "And I don't know how to explain it any better. I wish I could. I mean, I know what I must say, but I don't have a clue how to say it."

"Just go ahead. That's usually the best way."

Sadness flooded her eyes. "Jase ... if you don't move past your anger about what happened and learn again to love Jesus ... and let His love change you, I can't love you—not the way you want me to."

His jaw dropped as his mind sputtered.

"I'll always love you. You're the sweetest, most caring, most amazing man I've ever known. I loved Travis once. And you loved Jessica. We both know what love is. And now we love each other. I hope that never changes."

Her words made no sense.

"But I cannot have a future with you ... if that future does not include Jesus Christ."

Hearing the Man's name was starting to wear on him. His brain slowly processed what his girl just said.

"Please hear me. I will always love you. But I cannot be your wife. Not if you stay ... cold against God and His Son."

Rage overwhelmed him. He hated himself for it but couldn't squelch it. "Cold. Yeah. That's a great way to describe it. Only a cold-hearted God would sit back and watch what happened to Jess and Lizzy ... and not stop it. Or prevent it. Cold? Yeah. You better believe it." He pushed out of his truck and slammed the door harder than he had ever slammed it before.

EIGHT

"Jason, wait!"

No. He wouldn't wait. Wait for what? For someone who couldn't love him? Someone who was fully devoted to an all-powerful, cold-hearted, apathetic God?

Chris pulled at his arm. "Please. Stop."

He stopped. Turned to face her. Didn't say a word.

"Please …" Her eyes pleaded.

"What, Chris? Please understand? Please do exactly what you say so we can have a future together?"

She grabbed his other arm and leaned in to rest her forehead against his chest.

Her hair smelled so good, softly carrying on the breeze. He drew in a deep breath and tried to relax. Glanced around at the happy children playing, the parents talking and enjoying the night. Lovers. Best friends. Simply living life as it should be lived.

Jesus always talked about losing your life. If you lose it, you will find it. Something like that. What sense did that make? What was life if you couldn't live it the way you wanted? Why live life tied down to the demands of an ancient God who did what He pleased? Just a pawn in His sick little game.

Chris slowly pulled away and lifted her eyes to study his entire face.

She probably didn't like what she saw there. The thoughts flooding Jason's brain probably soured the expression on his face the same way they soured his stomach.

"I'm sorry, Jase."

He gazed over her head at the kids playing soccer. "Hey. No big deal."

"Please ..." Her forehead thumped against his chest. "I know I'm hurting you. I don't want to hurt you." She turned her head and wrapped her arms around him.

He ever so gently rubbed her back. "I know, babe. But you've got to do what you've got to do." No heat in his words. Just the truth.

"I'd die without Him."

A pretty narrow way of looking at things.

"But I don't want to live without you."

"So that's it, huh?" He pushed her away to look into her eyes. "You know, it's not like if you stay with me, I'm going to make you stop loving Jesus. You can still love Him. Can't you love us both?"

Her eyes glimmered with tears. "I do love you both. With all my heart."

"Then what is the problem?"

She didn't seem able to answer the question.

"Do you know? What's the bottom line here, Chris?" He eased his grip on her upper arms even as his tone sharpened.

Her lips shook. "I'm ... I'm afraid you'll pull me away from Him. I'm not strong enough to love Him the way I should by myself. I need to stay surrounded by people who love Him too. With their whole lives. It's not just about going to church. It's about strengthening each other to stay close to Him. That's why I've stayed in Kimberley Square when I've wanted to run away at least a quabozillion times."

"So? It's not like I'm going to pull you away from the church or your friends. We have a bunch of the same friends, you know."

"Bit by bit, Jason. If we get married and start a life together, we'll be as one. We'll be joined by our love and by the commitments we'll make to each other. But unless you walk with me closer and closer to Christ, I'll walk with you farther and farther away from Him. I'm not strong enough to make you follow Christ. If I marry you, and you don't want to follow Him, you'll pull me away from Him. If that happens, bit by bit ... I'll die."

His heart and mind struggled to keep up, to understand the logic. But he could hardly get past the first thing she said. She was already thinking about marriage?

But ... isn't that what you want? Don't you want to share this woman's life? And to have her share yours ... forever?

He let his hands fall to his sides.

Chris closed her eyes and seemed to crumple before him.

"Baby ..." His voice cracked. He reached to touch her once more. "I hear what you're saying. I want to marry you. I want to spend my life with you. I want you to be mine. But ..."

She blinked open her eyes and lifted them slowly to meet his gaze.

"What you're asking ..." Did he really want to say what he was about to say? Didn't he once love Jesus Christ and believe He was God? Did all that change the day Jessica died? In that same heartbeat? Then just how much did he love Jesus? If he could abandon Him so quickly when his wife was taken, did he ever really love Him ... at all?

A tear slid down Chris's cheek, leaving a trace across the faint scar. The sight tore at him. He reached up to wipe it away. She tilted her head to rest in his hand.

He wanted her. Wanted every part of her to become his own for the rest of their lives. But what she was asking ... he couldn't just let it go. What happened ... For God to just sit back and let it all happen ...

She didn't have to die. Not like that.

Raging heat overpowered him. His teeth clenched and he pulled his hand away. "Don't do this, Chris."

She stared at the ground. "I don't want to, but I have to."

"You can't make me love God again. Maybe I don't believe any of it anymore. Maybe now I know the truth about your *loving, compassionate* God."

She quickly looked up as her mouth fell open.

"Where was your compassionate God when Jessica and my unborn daughter were crushed to death by the front end of John Shadwick's car?" Saying the name sent a wave of nausea through him.

"The same place He was when Travis had his chest ripped open by the hunting knife in Wayne LeTrance's hand."

Jason refused to imagine it. "Then you should understand! How can you just accept it as His will?"

"I do understand what you're feeling. I've felt it too! But I refuse to let my feelings destroy me anymore. I choose to trust Him."

"That is such a laugh! Trust Him?"

"Jase—"

"After all you've been through, since the day you've been born. Look at all you endured as a child. Where was He? Huh? Why did He allow it? Why didn't He stop it?"

"He did stop it. And I'm here now, alive."

"Because you've surrounded yourself with friends who love you. And that's okay. That's great! But, Chris, this God you say you love and trust is the same God who stood by and let everything happen to you. How can you now accept His indifference?"

Her head slowly shook as her eyes lowered. "I can't explain any of this so you'll understand it. Or accept it."

"Why? Why can't you explain it?"

She quickly met his gaze. "Because you're too weighed down by your misery to see past what's got you so stuck. You can't see the truth anymore. You've lost sight of how big God is. And how good."

"No. Because of my misery, I can finally see Him for who He really is. And He's not about compassion and love. He's about control and having everyone doing things just the way He wants them to do it."

Her shoulders sagged. "What is faith, Jase? It's about trusting Him when we can't understand Him."

"I understand Him quite well."

"I'm sorry, but your vision of Him is clouded by your anger and pain. And human logic."

"Oh, really?" Jason glanced at the few adults nearby who turned their heads toward him and lowered his voice. "Well, excuse me for being human."

"He created us to know Him and trust Him."

"Why would I want to?"

She hung her head and slowly turned away.

"Chris, stop trying to make me believe. I know that's what you're doing. Like Erin made you believe."

That got her attention. She spun and stared at him. "What?"

"From what you told me, and from what Scott told me, I know Erin wouldn't let you leave that night."

Confusion swept her expression.

"She basically made you become a Christian because she knew that was what you needed. I'm not blaming her. In a way, she was right. You've said it yourself. Becoming a Christian saved your life."

Her eyes blazed. "No, Jason. Not becoming a Christian. That didn't do it. Anyone can be a Christian these days. Being a Christian can mean anything anybody wants it to mean. Giving my heart and life to Jesus Christ . . . that's what saved my life. Literally. If Erin hadn't stopped me from leaving that night, I would be dead right now. I was leaving that night to end it, once and for all."

The words hurt. He knew they were true.

"She did not make me do anything I didn't want to do." Chris softened. "I waited fourteen years to talk to someone about my past. For fourteen years I kept it inside. I didn't talk to anyone about it at all. Erin knew that. And she knew that was too long."

Jason swallowed deeply, trying to temper the anger flooding him.

"She knew I needed to talk to Jesus, to ask Him to help me, to give up everything to Him—everything I had been holding on to for so long." She wiped her eyes and blinked deeply. "I chose to do it because I knew there was no other way. The day I actually prayed and asked Jesus to forgive me, the only thing Erin did was make me sit there and hear the truth. She wouldn't let me walk out of the conversation until I heard it — all of it. And she knew the decision to believe it had to be mine. She didn't push me or make me do anything. The decision was mine."

"All right. I hear you."

"I cannot make you think anything about Jesus. This is not about me trying to change you. I'm telling you, I can't. I'm not that strong. If you won't let Jesus take the bitterness and anger that's eating at you, I cannot take it. Loving me will only make you think you're feeling better, but you'll still be hurting. You'll still be bitter. Only Jesus can help you with everything you're dealing with. It's too big for anyone else. Only He is strong enough."

It was all true. He knew it. But that still didn't make it anything he wanted to hear.

"You know what I dealt with. You said it yourself, it was killing me. Erin literally saved my life when she cared enough to find me again after all those years. Jesus Christ literally saved my eternal life when He used her to make me hear the truth about Him. But, in the end, it was all up to me. Once I heard the truth, would I believe it? Would I stay mean and cold toward Him because of everything He *allowed* to happen in my life? Would I continue to hate Him and be afraid of Him because I didn't understand Him?"

Jason's anger flickered out, leaving a sick heaviness in his gut.

"It's not about what I know or understand about Him. It's about how completely I'm willing to trust what He says despite what I'm feeling, or what I think I know or don't know. What I understand or don't understand."

"Okay. Whatever." He needed to sit down. His heart thumped.

If Chris didn't sit down, she looked as if she might collapse to the ground at Jason's feet.

"Come on. Let me take you home." He headed for his truck.

It took a few seconds, but Chris slowly followed. She hefted herself into the passenger seat and sat against the window instead of sliding to her usual spot beside him. She didn't cry, though she wiped her face with the sleeve of her shirt. Afterward, she slowly looked up to meet his gaze.

Weariness seemed to pour out of her. Jason felt it flooding over him. Without another word, he reached down to start the truck and then drove his girl home.

WHEN CHRIS TRIED TO SAY good-bye, thoughts tangled in her brain, making it impossible to say anything. Jason touched her hand but wouldn't say a word to her, not even a good-bye. She hopped out of the truck and it pulled away. As she stood on the curb watching it go, tears dripped down her cheeks.

This wasn't good-bye. She wouldn't lose him over this. He would come to his senses and realize she was right. He needed to believe again. Needed to trust the Father God he once knew and loved.

If he doesn't, Lord ... then this is good-bye.

His truck turned the corner and disappeared.

THE APARTMENT WAS TOO QUIET. The night, too young. With Erin and Scott off to an elegant dinner, Cappy off with Bettema to watch Bettema's boyfriend's softball game, and Sonya at the gym, that left Chris's options limited. No one would have guessed her night would have been cut so short.

She wished she could hold Mia, could tickle those pudgy cheeks and make the little sweetheart smile. Just thinking about those pudgy cheeks made Chris smile.

One more reason not to go with Jason to Coop's house for steaks and shrimp and veggie skewers. Tomorrow at church and later at Sonya's for dinner, Chris would only give Mia up to Erin at feeding time. Otherwise, she vowed to her Lord, she would hold her little namesake the entire, livelong day.

Sometimes, a sense of loneliness settled over her when the squirming baby was not nestled in her arms. She couldn't remember ever feeling that sense before Mia came along. Maybe ... she was being tugged into that aura of motherhood.

Oh, Lord, one thing at a time, please.

Laughter bubbled up from her belly, shaking her entire body. Lying flat on her back, again staring up at the swirls of plaster on her ceiling, she prayed and cried out the rest of her tears.

Jason would make such a good father. He's so kind. So sweet. Lord, he needs You so much. Don't let him wander too far. Don't let him stay cold to You.

As she prayed the prayer, the desperation she felt earlier eased. Quietness settled over her. She drank it in.

Peace.

Your peace, Lord Jesus. I know this is You. Your peace isn't like anything this old world tries to give.

Jason needed this peace. He needed to taste it for himself. Then he'd know.

Soon ...

The word slipped into her thoughts as soft as a whisper. She wondered if it came from her own heart ... or her Lord's.

It was a good word. Persistent. Full of hope.

Please let it be true, Lord Jesus.

And yet, somehow, with His peace weaving through her, she knew it was true. Jason Matthew Sloan would be fine. He wouldn't stay a pigheaded, cold-hearted windbag much longer.

My boy ...

Laughter again rumbled through her. She sat up and ran her fingers through her hair.

My Father God. I love You.

She pushed up from the bed and walked through her quiet apartment. On such a beautiful late-summer's night, she wanted to laugh and be crazy and bask in her Lord.

She pulled on her sneakers and walked down to the gym.

★★★

JASON PICKED UP THE TWO waffle cones from the back of his truck, threw them into the garbage, then uncurled his water hose and sprayed the melted ice cream into the street.

All that was left of this night. Washing away into the street.

Fine. She wants to love and trust Jesus? She can go right ahead. How can I stop her? But if she gives me up, she'll miss me. I know she will.

His heart ached as the green slime from her mint chocolate chip streaked down his truck bed and disappeared.

She loves me. I know she does.

He watched as several chunks of chocolate were caught up in the small rivers coursing toward the thin waterfalls cascading off the back of his truck.

Such a waste.

He released the sprayer's grip to shut off the water, then glanced toward the front of his house. Maybe while he had the hose out he should water the few stubborn rose bushes of Jessie's that survived his neglect. After that, maybe he should wash his truck. It needed it.

She loves you . . .

He leaned against the side of his truck and stared at a crack in his driveway. Over by the edge, one lone dandelion poked up through the crack. He shot it with a stream of water. The crazy weed stood tall. Oblivious. He shot it again. The force of the blast broke the dandelion's stalk. The fat yellow flower hung by an invisible thread.

She loves you . . .

He shot at it one more time. The stalk broke, sending the flower flying into the yard.

Such a waste.

He killed it. Poor little weed. But then he laughed. Nothing could kill a dandelion. Even if he dug it out by the root, it would still grow back.

Love could be like that. Relentless. Persistent.

Or it could be like good riddance to a bad weed. The whole ordeal amounting to nothing more than a waste of good water.

He glanced at Jessie's rose bushes, then tossed down the hose and went into his garage for a bucket, some soap, and a sponge so he could wash his truck.

✳✳✳

JUST A LITTLE BEFORE EIGHT, and laughter spilled from the gym's open doors. Chris leaned around the corner and watched the fun, savoring the joy on each face, both young and old.

Ben Connelly could not play volleyball. But even still, the grin on his face seemed to beam out his ears. Sonya sent over a nice serve that Jimmy Thurman promptly shanked. Kay patted his shoulder and said, "That's all right, Jimmy. Get it next time."

An image flashed through Chris's mind. Something had spooked Jimmy as he ran down the sidewalk earlier that day, almost knocking Chris and Bettema out of the way. She wondered again what was up with that, but let her concern fade as the cute little boy did indeed "get the next one." Everyone cheered, even though Ben promptly shanked Jimmy's volley.

Alaina, Jazzy, and Jen stood along the back row on Ben's team. The Three Amigos. Or, the Three Burritos, as Chris sometimes called them. They always seemed to be together. And all three seemed a bit out of their elements playing any game other than basketball. But their smiles were the same no matter what game they played. Bright, happy, full of laughter and life.

Lissa and David and Jeffrey were on Jimmy's team. Good kids. All of them.

In her perhaps overly eager optimism, Chris hoped to see maybe Enrique or Vince or one of the other ex-Bandolero boys out on the court. But she stifled a laugh as she realized they were all probably pretty much grounded for life after their ride home in the police car. *Maybe someday, Lord.*

A fresh wave of peace fell over her. Swept up in the tide, that word again whispered through her. *Soon.*

So sweet. Thank You, Father. She prayed one more time for it to be true — the "death and demise" of the Bandoleros, as Monroe put it.

One gang down, one more to go.

A shiver zipped through her.

She stepped into the gym, returned everyone's hello, and sat on the floor next to Isaiah Sadler. "Waiting for Jazzy, eh, Grandpa?"

A gentle laugh. "Yeah. It sure is fun to watch her play."

One of the best natural athletes Chris had ever seen. And since she had already said that to Isaiah at least a hundred million times, she didn't repeat it.

"Should be fun this fall."

Coaching the girls' AAU basketball team. "Yeah. I'm really looking forward to it."

Kay set up the ball for Ben to spike, but he boinked it into the net.

"And can you believe," Isaiah said, "he is the one who suggested setting up the net."

Chris laughed. "I never knew he was so bad at volleyball."

"The chink in his armor, I'd say."

She enjoyed the moment. It was just what she needed. Laughter, fun, friends, and finding out something new about her former commanding officer.

It didn't seem possible the man out there shanking and boinking the volleyball instead of passing and setting it used to be the commanding officer of the Fourth Brigade of the 101st Airborne Air Assault Division of the United States Army.

Hilarious.

And here she sat, five years later, in the gym she helped Isaiah build, working with her best friends at the inner-city community center she once called "Ben Connelly's little amusement park."

She didn't call it that anymore. Now she just called it home.

✯✯✯

EIGHT O'CLOCK ON THE BUTTON, the gym officially closed. Ben threatened to call Jimmy's mother if he didn't run straight home that minute. Laurie Walker sent her oldest daughter, Meghan, inside to hurry along two of the Three Amigos. The teenager gave Chris a sort of curious look, but it faded into a small smile. Chris quickly returned it before the girl glanced away. Maybe one of these days Meghan would stay longer. Maybe tomorrow at church she would say more to Chris than just her usual timid, "Hey."

If not, there would be another Sunday. That would give Chris time to think of something more substantial to say in reply than just her usual, "Hey, back atcha."

Almost at the door, ready to leave, Alaina turned to glance around the gym.

Chris watched her. Waiting . . .

Yes. The girl's blue eyes locked squarely on her. A huge smile swept that innocent face. "See ya, Chris!" she said as she waved. A quick wave, since Meghan yelled at her to hurry up.

Chris waved and smiled and struggled to breathe as her heart swelled to its breaking point.

Isaiah said his good-byes and walked his granddaughter Jazzy—and don't ever try calling her Jasmine—home. Ben and Sonya helped Chris and Kay take down the net and put it away.

Afterward, both gave Chris long bear hugs before heading home, hand in hand. As silence fell over the gym, Kay said, "Well, I guess that's it. And look at you. Back here on your night off."

Chris grinned. "This place feels like another room in my apartment."

"Too bad it's two blocks away."

"Yeah. That is one of its drawbacks."

Kay pulled her bag off the shelf in Chris's office. "Are you heading out?"

"No, not just yet." Chris sat in the chair at her desk and leaned back.

"Should I lock up?"

"Nah. I won't be long. Just pull the doors closed."

"Okay. Well, I'll see you tomorrow."

"See you, lady. Thanks again."

Chris listened as her friend unhooked the glass doors and let them close. A few seconds later, a car started in the back lot and drove away.

Silence fell so completely, she lowered her jaw to pop her eardrums.

And yet, the laughter echoed.

Ahh . . . Just the way she liked it. She kicked up her feet on the desk.

What was she waiting for? She should probably head home. She almost wanted to shoot a few hoops, but the long day had chewed her up and spit her out. She needed to walk home, get back into her comfie sweats, and finish the third Nevada Barr book Scott gave her last May. *Ill Wind*. Creepy tale of environmental sabotage in Mesa Verde National Park, not far from the place Chris used to call home. Perfect book to read before falling off to sleep.

Not.

Or maybe she'd study the Gayle Erwin book Scott and Erin both gave her for her birthday last April. *The Jesus Style*. More conducive to a good night's sleep.

Lord, what haven't Scott and Erin given to me?

She laughed at herself and pushed up from her chair.

Not much, that's for sure.

Time to call it a night. After a quick bathroom break.

Three minutes later, she crossed the office, grabbed her keys, switched off the light, flipped the lock on the door knob, and pulled it closed to make sure it locked. She turned, and fell back against it as her heart dropped out of her chest.

Scattered around the end of the gym closest to the doors, eight young African-American men walked around gazing at the floor, the basketball hoop, the lights hanging between the rafters. Most wore long chains of glittering silver. Some of the chains carried huge crosses at the ends. Most of the men wore jeans that looked as if they'd fall down any second. Most wore thin black skullcaps. The rest wore baseball hats situated at all different angles.

One by one as they gazed around, each man seemed to approve of what he saw. Heads nodded. Wide smiles appeared. One by one, they turned to meet Chris's gaze. She knew two of them — her friends from the other day. But she couldn't look at any of them for more than a heartbeat.

Her hand clenched, crushing her keys into her palm. If she could unlock her office door fast enough and get back inside before ...

She couldn't move. Her feet would not lift up from the floor.

Easy ...

Where she stood ... good. Her back to the door ... better than being surrounded.

One man carried a baseball bat. Another, what looked like a can of spray paint. She focused on the tall man's face. His eyes lifted to meet hers. And he smiled. His two front teeth sparkled under the lights.

Hello, Mr. Gold Cap. Chris glanced away. Locked her knees so they wouldn't give out.

Her shovel.

She blinked, then stared at ... her shovel?

One young man, wearing silver chains and a matching silver watch that looked at least five inches wide, carried her shovel in his right hand. He slowly walked up to her, shifting it into both hands, and held it out to her as if it were a peace offering. "Yo. Look familiar?" His teeth were perfectly white. His wide smile seemed genuine.

Chris swallowed deeply. Tried to drop her jaw so she could say something. If only the words would come. Any words. The young man seemed to be waiting for her to say something. Anything. If only she could.

"Yo. She's trippin' at your generosity, dawg."

Every single one of them laughed.

One man tilted his head at her. "Aw naw, boy, that ain't it."

And he was so right.

"She's buggin', dawg. Word up."

Again they laughed. Their hoots and whoops twisted her stomach into a knot.

"Yo. See, my boys here took this last time they was here. I told 'em we needed to get it back to you, so's you didn't get to thinkin' we was stealin' it or nothin'." Again, the shovel came at her as a gesture of peace.

Chris unclenched her fist and turned her keys, trying to poke them between her fingers. She pressed her lips open. Forced her words out. "You can leave it there." Her voice failed her. Yet she knew the man heard.

"Yo. Right here?" He pointed to his feet. "But don't you want it? Yo. You may need it later. To save your life."

Loud laughter. Profane taunts and shouts echoed off every corner of the room.

Chris glanced at each man, searching for the automatic pistol. No one carried one. No one seemed to be hiding one, not even the man who carried it before. Bones. Though, as small as the pistol was, it was probably tucked in the back of his waistband. He wore his jeans a bit closer to his hips than the others.

Several flicked gang signs at her and each other.

"Nah. Yo. I'd feel, like, totally better if you'd take it." The man held out the shovel and took a step closer. His dangling cross tapped its wooden handle.

Chris stared at that cross. Then reached out and let the man put the shovel in her left hand.

He did. Then backed up a few steps.

Grateful for his quick retreat, Chris glanced into his eyes. They seemed to smile at her.

"See? That wasn't so bad."

"She's buggin', dawg. She's buggin'."

More laughter. Though not from them all.

Was she buggin'? Could she keep it together? A whimper lifted up deep inside her. One word. *Lord?*

"Nah. She ain't buggin'. Yo. She's straight up. Fo sho."

This man ... was this man their leader? He talked the most. Seemed to hold each man's attention. But he seemed a bit short for the job.

Funny. How all of them, just a few days ago, seemed more like boys.

These men were not boys. This was not a bunch of Bandoleros standing here.

These guys were for real.

Jason tried to warn you ...

She switched the shovel to her right hand, her keys to her left.

"Aww ... watch out, dawg! She's posin'!"

"Nah." The leader's eyes still smiled. "Yo. She's grippin'. Not trippin'."

Loud laughter echoed across the room, unlike any laughter she ever heard echo inside the gym before.

"She's cool. Yo. Ain't cha."

Chris softened her expression and looked straight at the leader. "Thanks for bringing this back." She lifted the shovel just an inch.

"Hey." His hands spread wide. "We ain't no thieves."

No, just drug-dealing, terrorizing, vandalizing thugs.

You're grippin', Chris, remember? Get a grip.

The leader turned to gawk at the gym. "You got a nice pad here. We could use one of these in our hood. Yo."

Stifled laughter came from across the room. Chris watched several of the men walk the full length of the gym.

Surrounded on three sides now. Okay. But she still held an advantage. Glancing down quickly, she opened her palm and spotted her office key between the main door key and her apartment key. Again watching the men, she grabbed that key between her thumb and forefinger, let the rest drop, and regripped them in her palm.

Just in case.

Though she regretted the rattle the keys made as they fell.

One of the young men stared at her hand.

She pulled it behind her back. Very slowly. Gripped the shovel tightly. Then watched the leader as he continued to gawk.

He turned to face her. "So ... where's the Rock? Let's play!"

A quick swallow eased the bile creeping up her throat. "Um ... look, I'm sorry, but we've just closed up. Put everything away."

The leader scowled. "Straight up? But we wanna play some hoops! My boy Maal over there's gots good hops. He's a beast on da court."

Chris studied the beast for a second, then wondered why his face wore a faint scowl. Everyone else seemed to be enjoying themselves. She glanced back at the leader. "Yeah. I'm sure he does. And you all are welcome to come play anytime. As long as you wear the right shoes and come when we're open." Did that sound as stupid to them as it did to her?

"But yo. You're closed now."

She smiled. Or tried to. A fake one would have to do. "Yes. I'm sorry. But it's been a long day." And how.

He nodded. "I see. We're here, but you're closed."

A slow whooping sound came from the guy in the far corner of the gym. A second later, all his friends joined in. The terrifying sound continued for at least half a minute.

A sick thought flipped through her brain. She was suddenly very glad she had already used the bathroom.

When the whoops finally faded, one man hollered, "I think she's dissin' us, Cee Train."

The leader laughed. "Yeah-boy. I think she is."

Chris shook her head. "No way, guys. Really. It's all right that you're here. It's just that ..." She did not want to roll out any basketballs.

"Yo. Let's get outta here."

Her eyes quickly found the young man who just spoke the sweetest words she had ever heard. The basketball beast. Scowling boy.

He glanced up to meet her gaze, then turned his head away.

"Whassup, Maal? Had enough, boy?" And now Mr. Gold Cap scowled. "We done jus' gettin' started."

What did Richardson say this guy's name was?

One of them lit a cigarette. Another pretended to shoot baskets. Three others joined him. Soon a game broke out. Minus the ball.

They all wore sneakers of some sort. Would it be disastrous to give them a ball?

She glanced at the leader. Was his name really Cee Train?

His light brown eyes sized her up. "Are you buggin', girl?"

The question surprised her. "I'm ... trying not to."

He nodded. One time. "Yer doin' a'ight." He watched his homeboys play their pretend game.

Chris shifted her gaze to the man Richardson said was named Bones. She would never forget how the man's eyes burned into her.

The sight of the barrel of that automatic pistol pointed at her face. At the moment, the man stood watching the game, but he looked her way and caught her gaze. A smirk pressed his lips. He turned just enough to show Chris his back. Sure enough, the grip of the pistol stuck out from the top of the waistband of his jeans.

Chris's eyes closed as her heart struggled to pump her frozen blood. *Father God . . . Lord . . .*

Cee Train's voice startled her. "Yo! Two points, baby!"

"Aw naw, Cee, he missed!"

"Get back, boy. I saw it from here. Maybe even a trey!"

Sweat trickled down Chris's chest. Breaths filtered in and out. She desperately tried to keep the simple process from getting out of hand.

"Threeeeee points! Yo! Cee called it!"

She watched Cee Train as he watched his boys. His delight seemed real. It softened his eyes and carried out on his happy laughter. She glanced at Maal. He stood off by himself. The man had other places he needed to be.

Chris squinted slightly to focus. He wore a black wrap of some kind, looked like a bandanna, around his right forearm just below his elbow.

A loud curse. "Yo, Cee! Tell 'er to give us a ball."

She met the leader's gaze. Tried to think—what to say, what to do—but trembling overtook her, scrambling her brain, freezing her muscles into solid blocks of ice.

His delight slowly faded into questioning impatience. Then into pure disgust. "Yo. I don't think she's gonna give us one."

"We're closed," came at her in a mocking falsetto.

"Come on, y'all." Maal shifted his weight to his other leg. "Let's jet. Yo."

The game fizzled out. Each man walked ever so slowly toward Chris. The one stopped to pick up his bat. They moved closer. She couldn't look at any of them. Except Maal. But he wouldn't look her way. She gazed at Cee Train. Swallowed down the burning acid that had reached the back of her throat.

"Yo, now ..." Cee Train lifted his hand. "Be cool, y'all."

His words did nothing to stop his boys' approach.

Mr. Gold Cap suddenly shook the can of paint in his hand. The ball bearing inside rattling around mixing the paint sent shivers of panic through Chris's entire body. She turned to the leader. "Please." She didn't know what else to say. Didn't know if she could say another word without starting to cry.

"Yo." Maal took a few steps toward Gold Cap. "Don't, man. Come on."

Gold Cap sneered at him. "Come on, yo'self, boy. I'm jus' gonna leave a little token of my 'preciation for the girl's hos-pi-tal-li-ty." He rocked side to side like Stevie Wonder as he said the last word.

The ball bearing inside the can rattled.

Chris stared at Cee Train. Her heartbeat thumped in her eardrums.

The man watched his boys. Didn't say a word.

One moved in a bit too close to Chris on her left. She turned her head to face him, gripped the shovel, but kept her feet still, her knees slightly bent. Her thumb started to shake from squeezing the office door's key.

The entire gym swirled a bit. Chris struggled to focus. All eight men stood in her peripheral vision. The ball bearing rattled as the can shook. With her eyes open, jaw set, she slowly closed down and poured all of herself into that place where she could stand in her Father's presence. Head bowed before Him, she waited to hear His softest whisper.

She heard nothing but the rattle of the ball bearing.

But then she felt it. The soft whisper of peace.

Yes.

Breathe, Chris.

She breathed. Lowered her jaw and let it out through her lips.

Just breathe.

"She be buggin' again, Cee."

Ugly profanities, loud vile names. And she despised being called that worst name of all.

"A'ight, y'all. Looks like we ain't gettin' no ball. Looks like we gotta clear on out, so's she can close on up and go home."

"Yo, maybe we should follow 'er back to her crib. See where she's at."

Several of the men thought that would be a good idea.

A shiver of fear broke through the fragile peace in her heart.

"Yo. We's wastin' our time. Come on, Train."

"Ahh, that's right." Cee Train walked over to put his arm around Maal. He had to stand on tiptoes. "My boy, here, wants to finish off his little callout from the otha day. Wants to drop ol' Duncey good, yo. Maybe bust a cap on 'im, yo!"

The expression on Maal's face was one of pure fury. "Yo, don't be all up in my bi'ness, boy."

Cee Train pulled away and stared Maal down.

Maal's gaze dropped to the floor. "Yo, man." Silence fell over the room. "It's cool."

Cee Train cussed. Acted as if he wanted to punch his boy in the mouth. Then did. Hard. Maal's head whipped back as his arms flew out. But he caught his balance. Didn't fall. He stood and again stared at the floor. Not reacting in any way.

Chris's stomach heaved. Her eyes pinched shut as she tried to relax.

"Yo. Sho nuff, boy. Now it's cool."

She blinked her eyes open and tried to focus on the two men.

Cee Train appeared calm. He nodded sharply. Touched fists with Maal. And cussed again.

Whoops and hollers rang out from all corners of the room. Maal wiped the blood from his lip. Cee Train moseyed back in Chris's direction.

Silence fell. All eyes locked on her, until Gold Cap popped the top off his can of spray paint.

Chris's heart slammed to a stop.

The man crouched down and began spraying the paint on the floor.

"Hey, come on!" Chris forced her feet to slow to a stop and glanced around. She now stood at least ten good steps from her office door. A curse zipped through her. She quickly pocketed her keys and grabbed the shovel with both hands.

One of the men slid sideways to stand behind her, between her and the door.

Too close. She walked slowly, watching as many of them as she could as she took a few more steps out to the middle of the gym.

All the while, Mr. Gold Cap sprayed black paint on the floor.

The hissing noise as he sprayed followed by the ball bearing rattling inside the can as he shook it followed by more hissing as he once again sprayed—mixed with the silent screams ripping through her—almost plunged her over the edge. The shovel in her hands shook.

"Yo. Twoine. How's it comin', boy?" Cee Train crossed his arms over his chest.

Antwoine. Of course.

"You 'bout done?"

"Yo. Almost."

Chris bore her gaze into the leader of the group. *Please make him stop . . .*

"Yo, hurry it up, dawg. Maal's gots ta be somewheres."

Surrounded. Surrounded.

Trembling threatened to drop her. Yet she stood. Somehow. Staring at Cee Train.

It took forever, but the hissing finally stopped. A loud, "Boo-yah!" sent a river of bile into her stomach. She prayed it wouldn't burst its way up her throat.

"Yo, Twoine. Saawweeeet!"

Chris didn't turn around. Cee Train narrowed his eyes and continued to stare.

More hollers of delight assaulted her, mixed with loud, joyous shouts of profane language.

"Your boy just took you all down, Cee Train." The words growled out of Chris's burning throat. "You know there's no way now that I can keep this from the man who owns this gym. He's going to see your boy's brilliant display of artistry and immediately call the cops." She blinked. Where the words came from, she didn't want to know. Why she just included Ben in this mess, she ... hated herself for it.

"Yo." Cee Train walked toward her, exploiting his gangster's strut.

Chris quickly glanced at the few men she could see. All of them laughed at her. All of them watched their boy to see what he would do.

She wanted to turn and locate the men behind her. She could almost feel their eyes upon her. She had no idea where each man stood. How far. How close.

Surrounded.

Her back was totally exposed and at risk.

Deep in her heart, she started to weep. *Will You ... Lord? Will You please get my six?*

Lose the weapon.

She swallowed deeply.

Cee Train moved in to stand about three feet in front of her.

Keeping her eyes on him, Chris slowly knelt down and placed the shovel on the floor as far from her as she could reach. The blade clanged against the floor as her hand shook. She struggled to open her fist to release it. When it dropped from her hand, she pushed back up to stand face-to-face with the leader of the Eastsiders.

She breathed deeply. Let it out slowly. And waited to see what would happen next.

NINE

THE MAN'S EYES FOLLOWED HER every move. Then stared at her, hardened through narrow slits.

Wait him out. Just stand. Try to be strong. And breathe.

Chris breathed. Though, without the shovel, she felt as naked as the day she was born.

"Yo. Whacha do that for?"

She struggled to swallow. Her mouth was so dry it took effort to pull her tongue down from the roof of it.

Around her, no one moved. Silence bore down on her.

Wait...

And stand. Yes. She said what she needed to say. Ben would see the ruined floor and call the cops in a heartbeat. This entire mess was about to explode in all of their faces.

"Your boy ... who owns this gym?" Cee Train's eyebrows lifted just a tad. "Does he own dat phat church on the corner too?"

She needed another swallow, but at this rate, with nothing going down to stand in the way of what churned in her belly, with nothing to stop it, she was sure she would throw up any second.

Gold Cap's empty paint can clattered against the side wall, startling Chris so much she let out a shriek. "Answer the man's question!" he shouted, calling her two of the vilest names she had ever heard. Each word cut her to the bone.

She'd pass out if she didn't get a grip. Right now.

"Twoine, yo. Be cool, baby."

"Yo, Cee, take 'er out, man. Let 'er have it—"

The look in Cee Train's eye shut his homeboy right up.

Another desperate swallow as Chris's stomach churned. *God, help me . . .*

Those eyes narrowed on her once more. "Answer the question." Just for fun, Cee Train repeated the two names Gold Cap called her.

She forced the word out. "No."

That eyebrow lifted again.

"No one owns the church. Except God."

A slow nod. "A'ight. Dat's cool. But your boy does own this gym. Too bad."

Chris didn't know how to take that.

"You see, if five-oh finds out about our little . . . visit here tonight, we'll jus' have to come back and burn this place to the ground. And I'd really hate to do that, seeins how it's such a cool place. All the nice little neighborhood kiddies hang out here, I bet."

God . . . oh, God . . . no . . .

"And dat big fancy church too. Wit a few well-placed fire-bombs, we could easily light the whole place up." Those eyes widened. "Boom."

"Why."

The man leaned closer and tilted his head. "What? Yo. Didn't hear ya."

"Why? Why would you do that?"

He straightened and grinned. "Well, now, we cain't very well have five-oh all up in our grills about dis, now . . . can we?"

"You didn't do anything wrong until your boy ruined the floor." If she could only divide them somehow. She glanced at Maal. "It's a shame you're all going to pay for that."

"No. We're not."

Chris again looked back at the leader. She felt her gaze wither as his drilled into her.

"Yo. Nothin's gonna happen, sweetums, 'cause no one's gonna find out."

"You think I can hide what your boy did to the floor?" She still didn't dare turn around to look at it. She'd faint away dead if she saw it.

"Then you better get to cleanin' it up."

"Are you kidding? This floor can't be painted over like the back wall can. I have no idea how to clean off your boy's paint without ruining the floor."

"You's better get to figurin' it out then. My guess is you've got till Monday mornin' openin' time. Yo. So get biz-zy." And that name. Always that horrid name.

As laughter rumbled around her, Chris desperately wanted to slap a few names of her own right back into Cee Train's smug face.

"And yo. We'd love to stay and help you out, you know … but my boy Maal over there is trippin' to bust a cap in Duncey's fat trunk. Always somethin' goin' on." The man actually had the gall to wink at her.

Laughter once again surrounded her, but several of the men started for the door.

Relief gushed through her.

Cee Train stood still, but he waved his boys toward the door.

Chris glanced one last time at Maal. The man would not lift his head to look her way.

Fine. At least they were leaving.

Gold Cap hung around. He stepped closer and blew a breath of cigarette smoke into Chris's face. "Yo, see you." Again with the name. "Wouldn't wanna be you."

Clever. Think of that yourself? Her hands clenched into fists. *Keep cool, girl … at least until they leave.*

"Yo. Out."

"I'm goin'." Another cloud of smoke puffed her way.

Her stomach heaved at the stench. Her eyes teared up. She tried to blink to clear them. When she looked back at Cee Train, he stood closer than he had before. She took a step back.

He stepped with her. Stayed close. Spoke quietly. "Are we straight, girl? Do you fully com-pre-hend the seriousness of this sitch at hand? Let me break it down for you, just to be sure. Would dat be a'ight?"

She nodded. Slightly. One time.

"Yo. Here's how this thing breaks down. You may wanna call the cops and tell 'em we was here ... but do ya think they're gonna care?" A laugh. "They won't care. Yo, they'll just add it to their little list. Which ain't so little anymore. Yo." The cruelty in his grin narrowed his eyes. "But I'll care. Word up, girl. If I find out you's been talkin' to five-oh, I'll come back here. And I'll bring my boys. Alla dem. Yo. We'll burn dis place. And everything in it. We'll come at night." A whisper. "No one'll know it was us. In the mornin' it'll be a big ol' mystery. Everyone'll cry, 'Oh, boo-hoo, our little gym burnt down.'" His voice climbed another octave. "'Oh! Well, I wonda how dat happened?'" His hands covered his cheeks as his eyes widened.

She wanted to pick up her shovel and beat him over the head with it.

"But you know what else, girl?" Head tilted, he waited for her reply.

She barely shook her head.

"Dat same night ... we'll burn dat phat church too. And a few of the cribs next to it. Who knows. If I can posse up enough of my peoples, we may jus' light up yo entire hood." His eyes drilled into hers.

"I ... I hear you."

"Dat's good, girl." He leaned in even closer. "But do you believe me."

Fresh terror flooded her. It took all her strength to stand. Her eyes fell closed. "Yes."

"Good. I knew you was a smart girl."

She could not force up her eyelids. She did not get to see the man leave.

✯✯✯

TEN HEARTBEATS OF SILENCE. FIFTEEN. Twenty.

Her eyelids lifted. But she couldn't focus.

Two cars suddenly started, engines whining, thumping hip-hop booming. Squealing tires. Slowly faded. Silence. And they were gone.

Ten heartbeats of silence. Fifteen. Twenty.

God, my Father ... are they really ... gone?

Ten more silent heartbeats. Thumps against her eardrums. Hard pumps against the front of her chest.

They're gone.

She doubled over and fell to her knees, holding her stomach, waiting for the nausea to pass. Easing herself down to the floor, she curled into a ball, yet resisted the urge to have a good cry. She knew she'd get her chance soon enough—the instant she took in the sight of Antwoine's artwork sprayed all over her floor.

From where she lay she could see the paint can he had thrown against the wall. Dented on one end, it didn't roll far.

She closed her eyes and tried to draw air deep into her lungs. A faint hint of cigarette smoke lingered, along with the sharp biting smell of the paint. Her deep breath caught in her dry throat and made her cough. She needed to splash cold water on her face. Drink some down to quench her thirst and cool her burning stomach. If she could only get up. She quickly drew in another deep breath. Didn't move as it slowly leaked out.

What a night. What a seriously horrible night.

The whole day. Her whole entire week!

"Oh, Father ..." Just a whisper. "When? When will this end?"

Her shoulder ached against the hard floor. She pushed up to sit, facing away from the far end of the gym and the grotesque artwork she knew she could not take seeing. Not yet.

Breathe ...

She lowered her head and rubbed her temples.

She needed to get up and lock the gym's front doors. A little too late, but oh well. She didn't need anyone else helping themselves through the doors at this stage.

She pushed herself up the rest of the way, struggled to stay upright, and then forced her feet toward the doors. Tentatively peeked outside. The sun was just now starting to set. Fresh air swept over her. She stood outside and gulped the sweet-smelling air into her. Much better than the stench the Eastsiders left behind.

But after a few more beats of her heart, she trudged back inside and locked the doors. Tested them to be sure they were locked. Waited by the doors, listening, peering outside, watching for movement.

A white moth fluttered near one of the floodlights shining over the entrance. She watched its pathetic dance, mesmerized by its fascination with the light. She wished she could be so fully focused on the same goal. To be totally in the light.

Her eyes closed tightly. Tracks of the moth's path remained faintly illuminated against the black swirls of darkness. Then slowly, they disappeared. Only darkness remained. No trace of the light.

She turned and leaned back against the door. Kept her eyes closed. Tears leaked through her eyelids.

Lord, this isn't fair. What am I gonna do?

As if on their own, her legs carried her closer. Blinking away the tears, she took in the sight before her.

Down under the far basket, from nearly one end of the floor to the other, Antwoine Gold Cap, the stupidest human being she had ever known, had painted the word *EASTSIDERS* in huge black letters angled into sharp, violent points.

Chris dropped to her knees and gave in to her tears. Sobs overtook her, followed by deep, wailing cries as she fell the rest of the way down to the floor.

IF SHE DIDN'T GET UP, Cappy would show up looking for her. If Cappy found her in her present state, lying on the floor in the middle of the gym half conscious from crying and paralyzed by unbearable weariness, it wouldn't be good.

The whole block'll burn.

The very heart of her world.

If she could force herself up and make her way home, maybe tomorrow she could skip dinner at Sonya's and sneak back here to somehow try to clean up the mess. But where would she even start? What would remove glossy black spray paint from the glossy clear coat preserving the beautiful wood underneath? If she stripped away the paint, it would pull up the clear coat too. How would she replace the clear coat? And how could she do any of it without anyone else knowing about it?

Maybe I can tell Isaiah. He'd know what to do.

Fresh waves of anguish poured through her.

I can't! I can't pull Isaiah into this. No one can know. Oh, God ... my Father ...

Her sobs slowed as hiccups took over. Somehow, she needed to make her muscles move.

She pushed up to her hands and knees. Kept her eyes closed. Gritted her teeth. And started to crawl.

Not fair, Lord. I'm sorry, but this is just not fair. We worked so hard on this floor! I can't fix this. I've gotta tell Ben. And Isaiah. They'll call the police. Oh, Father, protect us.

She dared to blink open her eyes, slowly lifted her head. Sank back over her knees. And stared at the horrible mess.

Why did they do this? How could they be so cruel?

Her nose itched. She reached up to swipe at it, but stopped just in time. Something black, oily, had smeared on her fingertips. On both hands. A black, sticky mess.

Her head fell back. *Ahh, man! It's still wet! And these were my favorite khakis!*

Sure enough, the knees of her pants were as black as burnt toast.

Fine. She pushed up to stand. *Enough. What else, Lord?* She glanced around. *But ... why is it still wet?*

Her nose itched.

Fine. She pulled up the tail of her blouse and wiped her nose. Didn't matter anyway. With her pants ruined, who cared about her shirt? And with the way her nose dripped, she couldn't just sniff the stuff back up into her head.

She let her hands flop to her sides and raised her eyes to gaze into the rafters. Not long ago, she hung upside down from the very rafter above her, changing the light bulb that had turned out to be defective. *Remember that, Lord? I'll never forget the look on Sonya's face when she saw me. Even upside down ...* Quiet laughter bubbled up from her aching stomach. *She was not her usual joyful self that day. I thought she was gonna blow a fuse.*

Sweet Sonya. And Ben.

I've let them down. Big time.

Her head lowered. The sick artwork under her feet terrified her as much as it broke her heart.

It'll need to be resurfaced. Maybe even replaced. But how can we afford that?

Her nose again itched. Instead of walking to her office for tissues, which would have been the best thing to do, she started once again to lift her shirt. Pink patches of fairly clean skin on her fingers showing through the black smears caught her eye. She blinked. *Is it still wet? How is that possible?*

Rubbing her fingers down the front of her shirt left long inky trails on the pale green fabric. *It comes off. Does this mean ...?* Heart racing, she crouched down and wiped her finger across a line of paint. In some places where it appeared to be still tacky, it lifted off onto her finger with just a trace of a black smear left behind. In the other places where it had dried, it took a quick scrape with her fingernail to lift it from the floor. "Okay, Lord. What is going on here?"

With any normal kind of spray paint, it shouldn't have taken but a minute for it to dry completely. Sprayed on this type of surface, it should have been impossible to remove without the help of turpentine or mineral spirits, which would have also removed or at least damaged the clear coat underneath.

She pushed up, walked across the gym to grab Mr. Gold Cap's can of paint, and read the label. From what she could tell, it was normal glossy black spray paint. One of the more expensive brands, even.

So why, then, did it end up all over the knees of her good khaki pants?

Pulling her keys from her pocket, she hurried to her office for the roll of paper towels in the bathroom, then ran back out to the edge of the mess, fell to her knees, and started wiping. With firm pressure, after several passes, most of the paint lifted cleanly from the floor, collecting in piles of tiny rubbery flecks.

Mouth gaping, Chris sat back on her haunches and tried to comprehend the moment. *How is this possible? Can it really be this easy to clean up?*

She rubbed the paper towel over another line of paint. Though some of it smeared, most of it again came off cleanly, leaving two lines of flecks at the edges of each pass. Using the paper towel as a whisk, she swept up most of the flecks into one single pile that could easily be swept into a dustpan.

"No way." She sat on the floor and stared at the pile. "Is this for real?" A smile tugged at one corner of her lips. "Or ... Lord? Is this ... *You?*"

What could be more real?

Her entire being froze, until laughter spurted out of her. "Oh, Father ..." Lying flat on her back, she let her gaze wander through the rafters. "This is You. You're doing this." As her eyes closed, tears rolled down the sides of her face into her ears and hair. In her mind's eye, she crawled onto her Father's lap and snuggled in close against Him. "Thank You. This is too much."

The fingers of her right hand brushed the empty paint can. The ball bearing inside rolled back and forth for a second. A gentle sound. Much sweeter than when it smacked the inside of the can, mixing the paint.

Gentle and sweet. "You are too wonderful, my Father God. Too amazing." The words shook from her trembling lips. "I'll never get used to it. Ever." Tears in her ears made them itch. She laughed, pushed back up to sit, and used her shirt to dry them. Then let out a deep sigh. "Thank You. Thank You so ... so much."

But still a lot of work yet to be done.

It'll be okay. I've got time.

She worked her way back to her knees and started again wiping up the paint, but soon stopped. The magnitude of the job ahead would require a few more rolls of paper towels, a broom, a dustpan, and something to soften the floor under her knees. And one more very important thing. Tunes.

✳✳✳

WHEN MARGARET BECKER'S CD *Immigrant's Daughter* gave way to her *Simple House*, knees aching, arms shaking, Chris stopped for a moment to stretch out her back muscles and examine her progress. When *Simple House* gave way to *Soul*, she wondered if she had it in her to finish the job that night. When *Soul* faded out and silence once again swallowed up the gym, dizzy, sweated wet, and hurting, Chris struggled to push herself up to stand. Breathing hard, arms hanging like dead weights from her shoulders, she slowly turned in a circle, studying every bit of the floor surrounding her.

Still needing to be carefully swept, still needing work in places where the smeared paint left behind a dull residue, her beautiful floor was, nevertheless, still beautiful. The entire tag Antwoine Gold Cap worked so hard to lay down had been obliterated.

She couldn't believe it even as she stared at it.

"Father, this ... is awesome. How ...?" No words. No way to express it. "How can I ever thank You enough?"

Never. Not in a quabozillion years would she be able to love her Father God enough. Nothing would ever separate her from His love. Nothing could ever come between them.

I need You so much, Lord Jesus. May I always remain in You.

A huge, deep sigh left her arms tingling.

I can't wait to tell Cappy about this. You are so good! And Erin and Scott. And Ben! They'll be so —

A sudden truth struck her hard, stealing what little of her strength remained.

She couldn't tell anyone. Not even about this, one of the most amazing things she had ever seen. Wonderful and exciting and ... and she couldn't tell a soul.

A groan slipped out as her eyes closed.

This mess wasn't over. Nothing had changed. The threat still remained. No one could know about the Eastsiders' return visit. No one could know how Chris almost lost her lunch and dinner right there on the middle of the gym's floor.

It's okay. For now ... it's all right.

She peered once more at all that surrounded her.

Finish up. Go home. Go to bed.

Sounded like a perfect plan. She'd sleep like a rock tonight.

✳✳✳

DAMON LAMONT WAS SO DUMB, his daddy started calling him his Little Dunce way back in the day. Little Dunce gave way to Duncey not long after that. The boy wasn't the sharpest dawg alive, but he was, at the moment, the luckiest.

Seemed as if someone was watching out for the fool. Someone tipped him off. And the dawg knew enough to spread wings and fly.

Jamaal sucked in a deep drag from his cigarette and cursed as the smoke left his mouth. "Yo, man. Where is he? You said he'd be here."

"Yo. Chill, Maal." Twoine flipped Jamaal off. Then cussed. "Whachoo think? He was just gonna lay 'round waiting for ya?"

"If we woulda come straight here 'stead of takin' the scenic route ..." He tossed his cigarette into the gutter and stood tall as Twoine moved closer.

"Yo, man." Rummy pulled his keys from his pocket. "This reeks. Let's roll on outta here."

Jamaal ignored his bro. Curled his lip and narrowed his eyes.

"Don't be mad dawgin' me, boy." Twoine stepped up into Jamaal's face.

"You best *back off*, Twoine."

"Now, yo." Cee Train moved in. "Word up, yo. Duncey done tripped and skipped. But he ain't gone for good. Yo, Maal. He be back."

Shades of orange from the setting sun flickered in Twoine's eyes. Jamaal didn't blink.

"Now why you gotta be all hatin' on each other? Be easy, my brothas. Yo."

Not a twitch. Eye to eye, Jamaal stood Twoine down.

Cee Train put his hand on Twoine's shoulder, then pushed him away from Jamaal. "Won't do to have my brothas dawgin' each otha."

Twoine glanced away. "Yo, Cee?" His whiny voice. "Why we even here, man? Dis callout's been done called out. His-to-ry."

Jamaal lowered his head, but eyeballed Cee Train as he hit Rummy up for another cigarette.

A loud exhale preceded the cig, but Rummy coughed it up. Even handed Jamaal his light.

Cee Train only reversed Jamaal's eyeballin'. Though not with heat.

Twoine turned and skulked to Shree's ride. "Yo, Shree, let's bounce dis place." He stuffed his girl into the car and they all cut out.

Jamaal lit his cig and glanced back at Cee.

"Yo, man. You wanna lock up wit Twoine one of these days? 'Cause that, my boy, is the path you're traipsin' down. Yo."

Word up. It was true. He'd love to stuff those golden twins right down Twoine's throat. He sucked in a deep drag of the cig.

"Call 'im out, boy. I'll sanction it."

His head shook. "Nah, Cee. I don't wanna call 'im out." Not yet. But soon. After his arm healed. After he dealt a full measure on his dumb brotha Duncey.

"Be easy then, brah." Cee leveled his fist.

Jamaal pounded it. "Yo. Be easy."

"Word." Cee grinned. Then turned. Found his girl. And split with Dre and Rafer. All swallowed up in a cloud of dust.

Beside him, Rummy cursed. "Maal, I don't get you, boy. You're axin' for a world of hurt."

"Be easy, my man. Have a smoke."

"Ain't got none left. Thanks to you."

"Then let's go get some more." Jamaal stuck out his hand. "Yo. Lemme drive." He grinned when Rummy tossed him the keys.

"I'm just sayin', Maal ..."

They stood talking over the roof of the car. "Whassup, boy? Spit it out."

"Why was you all buggin' back at that gym?"

His cigarette made him gag.

"Boy, you don't mad dawg Cee Train twice in your lifetime and live on to tell the tale."

"I didn't mad dawg 'im."

"The only thing dat saved your skinny trunk was your 'mediate eye-fall."

His lip hurt where Cee clocked him. "Jus' get in, dawg." He pulled open the door and slid into the driver's seat.

Rummy dropped in beside him. "Jus' don't wanna see you go down, Maal. That's all I'm sayin'. Yo."

"Then consider it said." Jamaal turned the key and fired up the engine. "Now zip it. Let's go find Duncey."

"Thought we was goin' for more smokes?"

Jamaal just glared at the road passing them by.

✱✱✱

CHRIS COULDN'T SLEEP. HER KNEES ached, and her arms still felt like dead weights. Rolling from one side to the other only aggravated her. She resisted the urge to glance again at her clock. Five minutes had passed since her last glance. If even that. At this rate, it would be a long night.

Trying to pray only caused her mind to wander. When she realized where her mind had taken her, she tried to hurry back into her Father's arms, only to be enticed away and led down another wandering path.

Lord ... hold me ...

She needed to tell Ben about the Eastsiders' visit. He would find out soon enough anyway when he took a good look at the gym floor. Besides, the man had a right to know, and more sooner than later.

But he would immediately insist on calling the police, no matter how hard Chris tried to dissuade him. The whole neighborhood would burn. They'd find a way. She was sure of it. Cee Train would burn everything in sight, leaving no evidence, no clue as to who started the fire. Or how.

All a big mystery.

Gutting the heart of Kimberley Square.

Idle threats from a bunch of thugging wannabe gangsters.

"Chris, these guys are for real."

She growled and turned once more on her bed. If she heard Jason's voice one more time breaking into her thoughts, she'd scream.

I want to hear Your voice, Lord Jesus! Not my own, not Jason's . . . not even Ben's. What do You say I should do?

Silence.

She struggled to hear.

Silence. Her thumping heart. And the long growl threatening to let loose from her belly.

Fine. Okay. I hear You. I need to sleep. You're a God of peace, not chaos. A God of rest, not frustration. Fine. Okay. I'm going to sleep now.

Sleep.

Why did they bring my shovel back?

Sleep.

Ahh, Lord. Ol' Antwoine Gold Cap's little bloodshot eyes would bug completely out of his fat head if he saw how easy it was to clean up his latest tag.

Soft giggles helped cool some of the heat in her belly.

So what. You cleaned it up. Big deal. Doesn't change a thing. You still need to tell Ben.

With the empty paint can, the dirty paper towels, and the faint hints left behind, Richardson would certainly believe her if she ever told him about the tag. He may not agree that her amazing Father God kept the black paint from completely sticking, totally making her night. Her entire week. But the man would take notes of the Eastsiders' visit for his records, including the evidence of the tag that once defaced the end of the gym. One more Eastsider crime perpetrated against the peace-loving neighborhood of Kimberley Square.

Just another crime on their long, long list.

Lord, Cee Train is wrong. I know Ray would care. But what can he do about it? What can any of them do about any of it? Is the death penalty an option in Oregon for spraying a tag?

They would care. But they wouldn't be able to do anything about it, except make a note of it to put in a file somewhere. Then they'd just sit back and wait to see what the gang of hideous thugs would do next.

Not good enough.

Risking the welfare of her friends and family, not to mention the gym and the church, just so Richardson could add another entry into his little black book just wasn't good enough. Cee Train Eastsider was a man of his word. "Word up," he would say.

"Do you believe me, girl?"

I believe you.

She covered her head with her blanket.

Please don't look at me that way. Please don't stand so close . . .

"Do you believe me."

Please don't . . . "Yes. I believe you."

"Dat's good, girl. I knew you was a smart girl."

No. She couldn't tell anyone what happened earlier that night. Little by little, she would keep working on the floor, trying to scrape up what paint remained, careful not to scratch the clear coat. She could do it. It would take time. And no one would ever have to know about any of it. Not Cappy, not Ben, not Erin, not Richardson. Not Sonya. Not Pastor Andy. And certainly not Jason.

The thought brought another groan up from her belly.

Oh, Lord, Jason can never find out. He'd bust a gut. Go totally ballistic. No doubt.

She could not tell Jason. She could tell a soul.

Lord? This is between You and me. You got my six back there in the gym. I need You to get my six now.

Sleep.

She glanced at the clock. Yes. She needed to sleep.

She turned once more on the bed, fluffed her pillow for the twentieth time, then let out the deepest sigh of her life.

Just You and me, Lord. But, You know? I sorta like them odds.

Sleep.

They did bring my shovel back.

Sleep.

Thanks for makin' my week. That was so cool.
Sleep, My love.
Mmm. Yeah. Good night, my Father God.

BEN CONNELLY COULD NOT SLEEP. An energy surged through him.
A fire of some sort. Not heartburn, indigestion, or gas. He felt fine.
Invigorated. Even though it was half past three in the morning.

Sundays were busy days around this stretch of Kimberley
Street. Lots to do in the morning. Pastoral prayer, Sunday school,
morning worship service, afterglow ... He always hated that word.
Afterglow. Sounded like something a florescent green worm left
behind.

Then dinner and fellowship with his family and extended
family.

That thought made him smile. As his coffee dripped into the
pot, he stood patiently, holding his mug, waiting for the last drip
to fall so he could pour himself some. Scolded one too many times
for being impatient, for pulling away the pot and letting the stream
fall directly into his mug—which effectively ruined the hot plate
on the last coffeemaker he bought for his wife for Christmas—he
waited, mug in hand, watching for that last drip.

And he smiled.

Sonya had placed her savory mushroom meatloaf on the menu
for Sunday dinner. All baked to a golden brown with big chunks
of potatoes, long strips of carrots, and lots of extra mushrooms.
Shrooms, as Chris called them.

A laugh widened his smile. As coffee streamed into his mug.

Chris McIntyre. It didn't seem possible, but every time he
thought of the former medevac medic, that quick laugh spurted up
from his gut. A happy laugh. A laugh to savor. A laugh of gratitude.
Like the first sip of freshly brewed Colombian.

Excellent.

He padded in his slippers to the recliner in his living room and sat with his coffee, reading glasses, and favorite book. Then quieted his soul and listened. Opened the ears of his heart ... and waited. Listening. Resting.

That fire coursed through him.

"What is it, Lord?" His voice, just a whisper. "Is it Andy? Or Sarah?" Didn't seem like it. "Sonya?" He prayed for his wife. How he loved his beautiful, feisty, Southern belle.

The heat of the coffee fueled the fire. Yet didn't overpower it. "Hmm. Erin? The baby?" He prayed for Erin and precious little Mia. For Scott and the ministry carried out at the clinic. "Thank You, Lord, for handling that Bandolero mess." His head shook. "Wow, that could have been a disaster. Thank You for working through all of it. For bringing us through it safely ... and for making such an impact on those boys' lives. There's hope for them now. We'll see to keeping that hope alive. You've got my word on that."

The memory of Erin's laughter as the young Latino bandits scrubbed and erased their horrible deed carried sweetly into Ben's heart. No malice toward them. No contempt. Only the love of her Lord Jesus Christ, leaving behind the imprint of His mercy and unconditional forgiveness.

And the way they devoured those sandwiches. And Sonya's cookies.

"Lord, those poor lads. Ahh, please bring them back to us. Let us love on them with a fresh batch of Your love. And a fresh batch of Sonya's cookies."

Jamaal. The Eastsider boy Erin treated at the clinic.

"Lord, where is he right now? What is he doing? Please help him reflect on Erin's kindness. Please help him return here if he would ever like to receive a little bit more. We'll be waiting for him."

Chris McIntyre.

His heart settled. The fire coursing through him sharpened. Refined. He sat up straighter in the recliner.

Yes. This is about her, Lord. What is happening? She seemed so happy tonight when we left her at the gym.

Something happened.

"Lord? What? What happened?"

A car passed by on the street, the street still scarred by the ugly black tire tracks of the Eastsiders' last visit.

His heart seized. *Oh, Lord. Did they come back? Did something happen at the gym after we left?*

He glanced at the clock on the mantel of his fireplace. Squinted over his reading glasses to focus on the small hands. *They're getting smaller. Must be.*

Almost four. Should he go down there? See if everything was all right?

Not at four in the morning. If something happened, he would have heard about it. Chris had been duly warned to call immediately the next time something happened. She had her cell phone. And certainly, she was home, tucked safely in her bed, sleeping the night away.

Please let it be so, Lord. He wanted to call her cell. Then squelched that idea.

Cappy would have called if Chris hadn't come home. The two shared the same apartment. The two were good friends. Sisters in their Lord. *Hermañas*, as Cappy would say. *Surely, she would have called someone if Chris hadn't come home. Wouldn't she have called someone, Lord? And then called me?*

Relax. Yes. Of course, she would have called.

The fire in his spirit burned.

"Yes, Lord. Yes."

He sipped a long drink from his coffee, lifted off his glasses and set them on the table, then dropped his hands to his Bible and released a deep breath. *Yes, Lord. She's safe. She's sleeping. Thank You.*

Even so, Ben bowed his head, closed his eyes, and prayed for Chris McIntyre.

✹✹✹

"YO. JAMAAL. YOU 'WAKE, BRAH?"

Did his homeboy just call him *Jamaal*? It was hard to tell with the way his boy was laughing. All quiet-like. Like a fool. It slowly faded. "Yo. Whassup, *Earl*?"

More laughter. Like a little girl all wiggin'.

Too much weed. But never enough.

"Yo, Maal. Twoine's gonna ..."

His boy was bent. "Yo, Rummy. Ease up, brah."

"... bust you up, boy. Yo."

Jamaal would do some bustin' if his homey didn't shaddup. "Yo."

"What, dawg?"

"You trippin'? I'm trippin'."

Word up. Jamaal was trippin'.

"I'm tore up, dawg. Word."

Torn up. Worn out. Word.

Silence fell over the room, broken only by his brotha's soft snores.

Dat's it, Rum. Sleep, brah.

A quiet voice tumbled through his head. That lady at the gym. Standing there. Steady. Terrified. The same lady from the pictures on the clinic's wall. The lady soldier. Like that nurse. Like ... Erin.

Twoine's spray can hissing. The ball bearing rattling around inside it.

The sound sent him trippin'. He sucked in another long drag of his joint and held his breath.

His heart thumped. The room swirled. His eyelids fell closed as his breath escaped.

Trippin'. Seriously. Worn out.

Word.

TEN

HOME OF HER HEART. THAT was this place. The smell of it, the sound of it, the feel of it. The hope in it. The One honored through it.

Jesus. The One sent from heaven to give life to the world. And not just any old life. Life abundant and sweet. Life soaked in truth. Life that would never end.

Works for me, Lord.

Chris glanced Erin's way and enjoyed the quick grin her best friend gave her. It seemed weird to see her without a three-month-old baby-faced angel in her immediate vicinity. Erin and Scott both. Sitting there, they looked almost incomplete. And it had been only three months.

Chris felt almost ... lonely, once again, without the little one in sight. The ladies in the nursery had all the fun. Though Chris knew she wouldn't last more than five minutes in there. She wasn't too concerned about all the babies at the Kimberley Street Community Church that Sunday morning. Just one.

Her little namesake. Erin had, after all, named her brand-new baby girl Mia Renae. She even spelled it the way Chris's mother spelled it the day her brand-new baby girl, Christina Renae, was born.

Mia Renae. Chris's little niece. Scott and Erin were, after all, her favorite brother and sister.

Scott glanced at her, forcing her to meet his gaze. He barely smiled, though his eyes softened with it.

A bit embarrassed, Chris grinned, then again pulled her attention back to the book in her hands and the sermon Pastor Andy was preaching from it.

Jesus. The One sent from heaven to give hope to the world.

Yes, sir. Say it again.

Hope. What a wonderful word.

As in ... I hope the Eastsiders don't burn this place down. She coughed faintly to force the thought away. *Oh, Lord ... I hope that's not You telling me I have to tell Ben.*

Her stomach soured. She needed a couple more Rolaids. What a drag.

Faith. Confidently hoping for what we can't see. Standing strong in what we believe. Even if we can't feel it or fully comprehend it.

Especially ... if it gives you a sour stomach and you don't have the foggiest clue about what's going on. Or what Your plan is, Lord. But ... I know You've got a plan. Things are happening for a reason.

Soon.

That word again.

Fine, Lord. I hear You. A smile tugged her lips. *And I believe You. Even more than I believe that man named Cee Train. Wonder what his real name is. Probably something like Carlton. Or Clayton. Cecil, maybe. Or Cletus. Nah, probably not Cletus.* She focused again on the sermon. And soaked in every word.

Jesus. The One sent from heaven to bring truth to a world spoiled by the father of lies.

Truth. What else mattered in the universe? Believing truth beat believing a bunch of lies any day. And truth was a Man. Jesus Christ the Lord.

Do you believe Me, My child?

The whisper settled deep in her soul, sending chills racing through her.

Do you believe ...

She stared at the words printed in the book on her lap, yet couldn't read them through her tears. *I believe You, Lord Jesus. Father God. Yes. I believe. I love You. I trust You. I ... need You so much. Always.*

I will never leave you nor forsake you . . .

I'm counting on it.

Jesus. The One sent from heaven to bring love into the world.

As the Father loves Me, so I love you. Remain in My love.

Always. A giggle swept through her. She passed it off as a cough, then basked in the peace overwhelming her.

Peace. Even as a part of her cowered, terrified of what she knew she needed to do.

Later. She'd tell Ben everything. After the service. Maybe after dinner. Or tonight after church.

There simply was not a good time.

Soon.

Her eyelids fell closed as she let out a deep sigh.

Yes. Soon. But for now she would bask in the peace overwhelming her, and pray that peace would remain across Kimberley Square.

★★★

John Smoltz could throw a baseball through a brick wall. Alex Rodriguez could hit one so hard the thing would scream for mercy on its way out of the park. Roland Cooper could watch two baseball games at one time. The man never met a remote control he couldn't tame.

Roland LeRoy Cooper. No wonder everyone called the man Coop. His mother must have had some kind of vendetta against someone. Jason couldn't very well call his paramedic partner and best friend Rol, now could he?

"Hey, man. You ready for steaks?" Coop stared at the scantily clad women on the Bud Light commercial.

Steaks? Why not. Jason skipped breakfast. He shrugged. "I guess."

"Man, what is up with you?" Coop turned to give Jason a confused look. "You sick?"

"No."

"Well, show some life then. Here. Have another Mountain Dew." Coop reached into his ice-filled cooler beside the couch and tossed a bright green can in Jason's direction.

Jason caught it. Then glared at his friend. "Haven't finished my first one yet. But thanks." What he really needed was about ten of those Bud Lights. Or something stronger.

"Yeah. You bet." Coop changed channels to watch the Atlanta game. "You know, if they'd put vitamin C in Mountain Dew, it would be the perfect thing to drink for breakfast. It'd have all the important food groups: sugar, vitamin C, caffeine, and yellow dye number five."

"Man, you're the one who's sick." Jason perked up as his team turned a sweet double play.

Third out. Another beer commercial. Cooper flipped the channel to the Seattle game.

Enough to make Jason dizzy. He needed some fresh air. "Hey, I'll go light the fire." He pushed up from the recliner and headed for Coop's backyard, hoping his friend wouldn't follow.

"All right, man. Thanks. I'll have Lisa make up her skewers as soon as she gets back."

Yeah. You do that. Life just won't be complete without your wife's shrimp and veggie skewers.

A holler from the living room. "I'll have her bring you out some brew too, when she gets back."

Now you're talkin'. "All right." Jason tried to shout loud enough for his friend to hear. Tried to work a bit of enthusiasm into his voice, but knew he failed.

Out on the porch, the day was warm and sunny. Another nice one. He wondered if the nice weather would hold out for Labor Day, then grumbled again that he had to work. All weekend. Such was the nature of his job. A three-day holiday weekend brought out all the morons. And when the morons found themselves in trouble, as they often did, they called on Jason and his friends to save their day.

But he loved his job. It was just about the only thing that kept him going. Except for that brown-haired woman who ran the Kimberley Street gym. She kept him going. She gave him something to live for.

Except for today. Today he'd have to settle for Lisa Cooper's shrimp and veggie skewers.

With one hand holding his Mountain Dew, he lifted off the lid of Coop's barbeque and scraped off the burnt crust from the grill's rack with a long-handled brush. Back and forth. Black powder fell onto what remained of the previous fire's briquettes. Black upon black and gray. While the grill's rack, now scraped almost clean, gleamed under the sun's rays.

Easy. What once was a caked-on mess now glimmered. Just from a few aimless brush strokes.

If it only was that easy. To make something so dead, so burntout and caked with soot and ash, clean once again.

Is it that easy?

A dog's sudden barks pulled Jason from his musings. The neighbor's dog. A Rottweiler. And definitely not a happy dog now that someone on the other side of the fence would be standing there again preparing to grill steaks without the slightest intention to toss one over the fence. No wonder the poor thing sounded ticked.

Grateful for the fence, Jason gulped a drink from his can, then set it on the table and lifted off the grill's rack. He poured some new briquettes on top of the old ones, then squirted lighter fluid on the pile. He let it soak while he fished a match from the box Cooper kept beside his wife's gardening supplies in the cabinet on the porch. Jason studied the collection of colorful gloves, potting soil, pots, seeds, and fertilizer. Sadness tugged him down into a familiar miry pit. He sucked in a deep breath, hoping the biting smell of lighterfluid vapors would draw him again from his thoughts.

It didn't work.

He turned his head to stare out into the yard. He could almost see Jessica standing there. How many times had he grilled steaks in their own backyard while she worked in her garden or picked up apples from under their tree? He used to love to watch her when she fussed with the roses in their front yard. Every summer she'd clip the biggest and fattest ones and bring huge bouquets inside the house to brighten the living room or bedroom or dining room table.

She used to close her eyes as she leaned into the bouquets and breathed in their fragrance. She used to smile ... Jason's heart used to swell when she'd smile that way, stealing his breath and leaving him faint.

Yeah. Used to. He shook his head. Closed the cabinet. Lit one of the matches on the side of the box. Watched it burn. All the way down to his fingers. Watched it flicker out against his skin.

Sharp, sudden pain shot through him. First-degree burn. Dark powdery mess, all that remained of the small piece of wood.

Another deep breath. Lighter fluid vapors mixed in with the smoke trailing off the extinguished match.

To breathe is to live, Jase. His precious bride's voice. *To live is to love.*

To live is to feel pain, Jess. His own growling voice. *To feel pain ... is to know this pathetic life goes on. Without you. Without our sweet child.*

His teeth ground. *I'll never trust You again, God. Why should I? Will You take Chris away from me too?* He flicked what remained of the burnt match onto the briquettes. *Without You, I can't have her anyway. You've already taken her from me.*

Sounds of laughter carried to him from inside the house. Jason leaned closer to the window and peered into Cooper's kitchen. His friend's wife, Lisa, carried several bags of groceries to the counter. She squealed again as her husband grabbed her from behind and kissed the side of her neck. Danny, their ten-year-old son, ignored their antics, reached for one of the bags of chips, and headed back toward his bedroom. Lisa called out, "Not too many of those until we eat." But her words carried no weight, as they were swallowed up with giggles and loud kisses.

Jason leaned away. Wanted to smile. But he couldn't. The weight crushing him seemed to drain him. He turned, lit another match against the side of the box, and tossed it onto the pile of charcoal. Then squirted more lighter fluid on the tiny flame.

The eruption sent a fireball a few feet into the air. Dancing waves of orange and yellow. Mesmerized, Jason watched. The fire dropped to a more sensible level. The briquettes caught and slowly started to burn. Shimmers of heat lifted high into the air.

The neighbor's Rottweiler barked.

Later, Jason would throw a chunk of his steak over the fence. Just because. No reason for the poor dog to go hungry. No reason for both of them to be miserable on this beautiful day.

SHE HAD TO DO IT. Right now. She wouldn't find a better time. There wouldn't be a better time. She didn't want to ruin the man's afternoon, but she couldn't pretend any longer. Something happened last night, something that Ben needed to know about. It would be wrong not to tell him. But yet, did she dare tell him? If she told him and he called the police, what would be the consequences? And then, when those consequences played out, how could she stop them? Or live with herself afterward?

People moved around her, grabbing their purses and Bibles, talking and smiling, slowly filtering toward the front doors of the church. The service was over. And yet Chris stood. Still. Staring up at that cross.

Lord, it can't wait. Not another minute. Ben has to know. I have to tell him.

She definitely needed more Rolaids.

How can I tell him? I know what he'll say.

Maybe she could convince him not to call the police.

Yes. That's it. If I can just tell him what happened and convince him it wasn't that big of a deal ...

That wouldn't happen. As soon as he heard only the first half of her story, he would be racing for his cell phone to dial up Richardson.

By now, I'm sure we all have the man's number on our speed dials.

Not funny. She sat on the pew, put her elbows on her knees, and leaned over to stare at the floor.

Erin sat beside her. Close. "Can you tell me?"

Her voice, asking the question she always asked when she sensed something wrong, washed away some of Chris's queasiness. A long sigh helped to wash away a bit more. Chris lifted her head and gave Erin a smile. Leaned back in the pew. "Wish I could, Rin."

A sad look. "Me too." A smile.

"It's nothing major." As if saying that would help.

Erin leaned back. The two of them sat quiet and still as the remaining crowd shuffled out of the church.

"It's nothing a little Mia time wouldn't fix." And an all-out raid by the entire city's SWAT teams.

"She should be arriving soon. I'm sure she'll be glad to see you."

"No, don't stick around. I've got to talk to Ben first, then I'll head over to Sonya's. Well, after I change."

Erin turned to meet Chris's gaze. Her eyebrows lifted. "Nothing major? You sure?"

"Yeah." A nod.

"Okay. I'll take your word for it."

Chris dropped her gaze. Should she tell Erin too? At the same time she told Ben? The question sat in her heart. Sat there. And sat there.

Erin didn't move. She seemed to be waiting for something she knew would eventually arrive.

Chris swallowed. Glanced up. "Um, no. I mean ... yes. Nothing major." A laugh. "You go on. I'll see you at Sonya's."

"Okay." Erin patted Chris's hand, then pushed up to leave. Walking away, she said, "But if I find out it is something major ..."

Chris could only laugh and shake her head. Later, when Erin did find out about everything, Chris would have to suffer those consequences too.

Much to suffer later. Or not. *Lord ... it's all up to You. I'm just along for this ride.*

She stood, gave the cross one more long look, then went to find Ben. And found him standing in his usual place, saying good-bye to his friends. At that moment, saying good-bye to Erin and Scott and their little sleeping one snuggled deep in her carrier.

Erin glanced Chris's way before turning to leave with her family.

Yeah, yeah. I hear you, Rinny. There'll be consequences.

Chris walked up to Ben. The man stuck out his hand. She shook it firmly.

"Mushroom meatloaf today. Come hungry."

She laughed. Couldn't help it. "Yes, sir. That will not be a problem." She held his hand a second longer, then released it as her fragile good mood slipped away. She couldn't look up at him. "Um, sir? Can I talk to you for a minute?" Her eyes lifted to meet his gaze.

"Certainly." He glanced around. "How about in here?" He pointed, then led her to the soundproof room beside them for mothers with crying infants. He turned on the light and held the door open for her.

Erin's favorite room. Chris sat on one of the glider rockers and tried to get comfortable as Ben pulled the door closed and sat beside her.

Silence fell over them. Deep silence.

She needed to say something. Mushroom meatloaf would soon be pulled from Sonya's oven. Sonya may need her husband to mash the potatoes or something. To make gravy. Or set the table. Well, that was usually Sarah's job. And Cappy's.

"Whatever it is ... you know you can tell me."

Chris glanced up but couldn't hold Ben's intense gaze. "Yes, sir. I know. It's just that ..." The words ended.

Ben shifted in his glider rocker. He seemed a bit out of place sitting in it. "This is about what happened last night, huh."

Chris's heart seized. She looked at Ben.

"Something kept me up last night. Is it the same thing that kept you up?"

"Sir?"

"You didn't sleep well last night. Did you."

She blinked. "Um ... no, sir." Nothing could hide the bags under her eyes.

He smiled. "Chris, we're done with the army. You don't have to call me 'sir' anymore."

She almost laughed. "Hard habit to break."

"Well, break it. And that's an order." Two seconds later, soft laughter filtered out of him.

Chris let hers escape. And it felt good. But it faded. Too quickly.

"So, tell me what happened last night. Why didn't we sleep well?"

How to proceed? Abort the entire spectacle? Cut to the chase and get on with it?

Ben's head tilted slightly.

"The Eastsiders paid me a visit last night at the gym."

A long, deep breath. Slow nodding.

"They brought back my shovel." She milked that fact for all it was worth. Optimistic to a fault.

"But what else did they do?"

"Painted a tag on the gym floor."

Ben's face scrunched into a hard frown.

"Which"—Chris waited for his eyes to open—"cleaned up easier than I would've thought. There are still some traces of it, but it cleaned up fairly well."

His right eyebrow lifted.

"Yes, sir. It was pretty amazing actually. Almost as if the paint didn't dry completely. With a little work, most of it came up." A little work. She almost laughed. She could still barely lift her arms.

"Most of it?"

"There are still some places that I haven't yet really ... worked on."

More nodding. Ben appeared deep in thought.

"I saved the paint can. And the paper towels I used to clean it up." She said the words, then wondered why she said them. Ben's silence caused her to want to ramble on and on. But she stopped and waited for him to say something.

"What else did they do."

Chris swallowed. Looked away.

"Did they threaten you?"

Her heart thumped.

"Chris."

She slowly met his gaze.

Ben waited. A stern expression played out on his face.

"Yes, sir." A whisper. Chris struggled with the moment.

"Did they hurt you in any way." Spoken more like a statement, in a tone starting to sound just as stern as the expression on his face.

"No, sir. They didn't hurt me."

"How did they threaten you?"

"They said they would burn down the gym and the church if I told you or anyone. If we called the police."

A growl. "You know we have to call them."

How could she argue with this man? "Do we, sir? Can't you just let this slide? Since it cleaned up so easily ... it's all done and over with."

He slowly shook his head. "I don't think so. It won't be over until someone stops them."

"Or something. Like sheer boredom."

"No. They're not going to stop. If we do nothing, this will only get worse."

"Please, Ben." Chris slid forward to sit on the edge of her seat. "Exactly what did they say to you?"

Painfully, she told him. She told him everything.

"We have to call Richardson."

"We'll be taking a huge risk if we do."

"If we do nothing, the risk remains."

Silence. Deep, eardrum-popping silence in the soundproof room. Chris stared out the window at that cross on the wall above the pulpit. "What else can we do?"

"This is bigger than us, Chris. We can't stop this gang by ourselves." A pause. "And I will not allow them to threaten you again. The next time ..."

A shiver zipped through her. She lowered her gaze to stare at the floor.

"I will not ..."

She looked up at him.

His shoulders sagged a tiny bit. "... do nothing. I cannot do nothing, Chris. You cannot remain at risk. The gym, this church ... We must fight back. We must get help in that fight."

She nodded her agreement. Didn't know what else to say.

"Tomorrow morning, Cappy will open the gym. You and I are going to see Richardson and talk to their Youth Gangs Unit." His eyes bore into hers.

"Yes, sir."

He visibly relaxed. "Are you sure?"

Chris smiled. "Yes, sir. I'll go with you." No matter what happened. No matter how the mess would end. She would stand beside this man and fight.

He was, after all, the man in charge.

"But let's pray about it. Right now."

She wanted to hug him.

The man in charge. Answerable to his God.

★★★

MAD MAX REWOUND IN THE VCR. Cooper turned on the couch to face Jason and said, "Hey, man. You need to call her."

Jason glared at his friend. "And you need to mind your own business."

"Go over there. Spend some time with her."

"You kicking me out?"

"You've been here all day."

He pushed up in his recliner. "And she's been at church all day. Or with her friends."

"Since when are you not her friend?"

Since she put all of them before me. Jason didn't give voice to the thought. He only sneered.

"Come on, man. You don't wanna lose this girl."

"And how do you know what I want?"

"I don't know what you want. But I do know what you don't want. You obviously didn't want your steak today, since you tossed it over the fence for Rocky."

He thought he got away with that.

"And you don't want to let Chris get away. She's the best thing to happen to you in a long time."

He stood up and grabbed his keys. "And I don't want to sit here and listen to you anymore."

"You know I'm right."

Jason told the man what he knew for sure. Rambled off a few choice words. Not a very nice way to end the evening.

"Yeah, go ahead. But when you lose her for good, don't come crying to me."

He slammed the door on his way out. Stormed to his truck. Climbed in. And sat there. Staring at Lisa's rose bushes in the front yard of the house.

A deep sigh drained what little remained inside him. Completely empty, he wondered for a split second if he could even make it home.

Coop was right. And yet, he was wrong. Jason had no plans of losing Chris. He wouldn't let that happen. And yet, he couldn't figure out how to keep her. How could he hold something tightly enough to keep from losing it, without crushing it in his hands ... and killing it?

He pushed his key into the truck's ignition and glanced back at the house. Coop was right. Even if Jason didn't plan on losing Chris, wouldn't let it happen, it would happen all by itself if he didn't do something. And soon.

Did Chris love him enough to wait for him to figure things out? How much time would she give him? How much longer could he put off dealing with the issues he knew he needed to deal with?

The questions made his brain spin.

Not tonight. He couldn't deal with anything more tonight.

Small steps. And maybe he just took his first one. He would figure this thing out. Deal with his issues.

Later.

He got out of his truck and walked back inside the house. The opening credits of *The Terminator* flashed on the big screen.

"Back, huh?"

Jason tossed his keys on the table by the door. "Got any more beer?"

Coop rummaged through his cooler by the couch and held one up.

Jason grabbed it, then plopped back into the recliner. As Arnold the Terminator strutted buck naked across the big screen, Jason downed half the beer. As beautiful Linda Hamilton appeared, smiling, her curly blonde hair falling softly down to her shoulders, Jason downed the other half. As he hit Cooper up for another beer, he vowed, deep in his heart, to prove his best friend wrong. Jason would not lose Chris. He'd do whatever it took to keep his own beautiful lady right where she belonged. Next to his side. Forever.

Even if it meant giving her God a second chance. The God who used to be his own. The God he knew he couldn't run from forever.

His second baby step.

Exhausted from the effort, he settled back on the recliner, drank his beer, and watched beautiful Linda take down her android nemesis.

CHRIS SAID IT WAS NOTHING major. Of course, Erin didn't believe her. Not for one second. Not when Chris first said it. Not at dinner that afternoon. Not through the rest of that night. At church. Late last night. And now this morning.

Standing on her porch, Erin now knew for sure she was right not to believe Chris. Whatever had been bothering her best friend yesterday, it definitely was not something trivial or minor. She watched Ben's Explorer take off down Kimberley Street carrying him and Chris toward the main part of town. She didn't know where they were going, or why, but she knew whatever it was that pulled both Ben and Chris from their work, it had to be, indeed, something major.

As they drove away, they didn't see Erin standing on her porch. She didn't want them to see her, didn't want to pry. Yesterday, at dinner and all night afterward, Chris and Ben seemed content keeping their secret from everyone. But by now certainly Sonya would know what was happening, wouldn't she? Should Erin cross the street to find out? Make a quick phone call?

She let out a deep breath and then walked back inside her house and closed the door. If Ben or Chris planned to share their secret, they couldn't do so until they came home. Erin could wait until then. Everyone would find out sooner or later.

She had a nagging feeling she already knew what it was.

Dressed in a white onesie adorned with pink puppy dogs and lying on a folded blanket on the floor by the couch, Mia batted at the shiny plastic Winnie the Pooh, Eeyore, Piglet, and Tigger hanging above her from the crossbar of her play gym. Erin lay down on the blanket, propping her head in her hand, cherishing that happy smile, those adorable giggles of pure delight.

Her heart ached, so full of love and wonder, yet wrenched with concern. A thread of terror as sharp as barbed wire seemed to wrap itself around her, even as she opened her entire being to the peace and strength of her Lord.

Mia turned her head to share with her mommy the full force of her radiant joy. Erin could hardly breathe at the sight. Those little feet kicked the air as if they couldn't wait to plant themselves firmly on the floor and start running. Or dancing. A pudgy hand reached toward her, and Erin lifted her own to meet it. Tiny fingers latched onto her thumb, pulling her entire hand toward that ever inquisitive mouth. Erin turned her hand and curled her pinky finger so her babe could draw in the small knuckle. Hesitant slurps gave way to full chomps as toothless gums clamped down on it.

"That's the idea, my love."

Chewing and sucking, Mia seemed to stare at Erin's bright smile.

Erin widened it. Clicked her teeth together. "These are teeth, little boo, and soon you'll have them too." Her smile faded a bit. *But not too soon, I hope.* She dreaded the misery her little one would endure as that mouth slowly filled with teeth. No way to avoid it. Nothing she could do to prevent it. "You're growing so big and strong." She almost wished the process would slow just a tad, that her little one would remain this little for at least another year. Maybe two.

Something twinkled in Mia's eye.

"Oh, no. I saw that. Are you planning on being a little terror in your 'Terrible Twos'?"

Mia spit out her mommy's finger and turned her head away to laugh.

"Oh ... wait until I tell your daddy." Erin wiped her finger on her shirt and then patted her daughter's diaper-covered bottom. "I think you're just teasing me. You'll always be my sweet little boo."

More kicking and batting at Winnie. More adorable baby giggles.

Erin wiped her eyes on the sleeve of her shirt and drank in the moment.

Even as that jagged thread tugged at her, nothing could separate her from this precious little one. Nothing could work its way between her and her husband, or any of her friends. Nothing could ever separate her from the love of her Lord. His love sustained them all. Nurtured and protected them. Nothing could ever pluck any of them from His hand. The thought brought a settling peace over her. *We are Yours, Lord Jesus. I am Yours. Mia and Scott ... Chris, Ben, Sonya, and Cappy. Tema and Isaiah and every other dear friend You've given me. We are all Yours. No matter what happens.*

The biting thread tightened.

No matter what has already happened that Chris didn't want to tell me about.

Mia gave Tigger a hearty slap. He took it well. Came back for more. Judging from her bright smile, Mia loved him for it.

No matter what, Lord. We are Yours. We're in Your hands. Always.

Coo-cooing noises.

Thank You, Father. Thank You so much.

Whirls and woos.

Erin moved in as close as she could to her daughter and listened to the lively one-sided discussion playing out between her and Tigger, complete with bubbles and giggles. "Is that right?" Those big brown eyes turned to meet her own. "Really?"

Pure baby talk. Giggling grunts and soft woo-woos.

"You do? Yeah. I miss Daddy too."

Sudden silence. Mia stared and blinked.

"Daddy? Did I say the magic word?" Erin tried not to laugh. "Daaah-dee. Daaah-dee."

Definitely her daddy's girl.

And no wonder. You've been his from the moment you slid into the world. Into his hands. All slippery and screaming.

Back to batting at Pooh.

Memories of that day flooded over her. She patted the soft behind and enjoyed the replay in her mind's eye, seeing again the awe on her husband's face as he held his newborn daughter in his hands for the first time. Although Erin didn't know it was their daughter at first — it took her doctor husband a full ten seconds to look his wife's way and give her the news.

"Mia Renae." He repeated the name over and over as he cut the cord and carried her to the table to wipe her clean. "Oh, Lord. Thank You, Lord." Over and over. Then finally he turned. Beamed. And laid their screaming, wiggly, pink, and wrinkled little daughter on her mother's chest. Close to her mother's heart.

A moment to last forever.

Her beautiful daughter. Not so wrinkled anymore, yet just as wiggly. Perfect in every way.

"Oh ... Rin ..."

Her eyes closed as another sweet memory played out.

Late that first night in her hospital room with Mia in her arms and her husband asleep on the recliner beside her, Erin waited for Chris to make it home from a quick trip to Colorado. Waited, praying, hoping it would be soon, while Mia was awake and quiet and happy.

Chris did walk in then, only to walk out a few seconds later, obviously overwhelmed by it all, much to Erin's delight. But when she walked back in a few minutes later, her eyes were swollen, her face red and splotchy.

Erin's heart, so full from that day, nearly shattered.

And yet, those dark eyes stared with wonder and joy. Ever so gently, Chris sat on the bed and moved in close. So slowly, she reached up to touch the blanket swaddling the infant. "Rinny ... she is ... so ... *beautiful*."

Erin tilted her head as if to listen to her babe. "What's that? Oh, okay." She smiled at Chris. "She wants you to hold her."

Terror flooded those swollen eyes.

Quiet laughter spurted up from Erin's belly. "Come on. She's been waiting for you."

Chris hesitated, fidgeted, swallowed deeply, and gave Erin several worried looks.

"It's all right. Just open your arms." Erin tried to lean forward, but soreness hindered her effort. She sank back, relaxed, and laughed again. "And come get her."

"Rinny ... I'm not sure ..."

"You're gonna say no? You want her to be sad?"

A long look.

"You want me to be sad?"

"No." And finally, Chris seemed to relax. "Wouldn't want that."

"Come on, then."

Chris leaned in closer, then met Erin's gaze once more. Whispered, "You really did good. But I knew you would."

Erin could only smile. So much to say at that moment, so many questions to ask about Chris's trip, how she was, why she had been crying ... all of it could wait.

Chris gathered Mia into her arms and settled back on the bed. Touching the tiny hand, barely lifting each finger with her own pinky finger, then glancing up at Erin and laughing as Mia closed her fist around it. Whispering to her, telling her how beautiful she was, how perfect, how much she would be loved ... Tears slipped down Chris's cheeks. She tried to blink them away, but couldn't seem to keep up with their flow.

Erin handed her a tissue, which Chris gratefully accepted.

As they sat in the darkened room, Scott softly snored from his position on the recliner. Mia fell asleep in Chris's arms. Erin struggled to keep her own tears at bay as she savored the sight before her, hoping the picture would engrave itself permanently into the deepest reaches of her mind.

As she blinked her eyes open and saw the happy smile on her little babe's face, she knew she would need another tissue. Fast. She couldn't keep using her shirt.

She didn't move to get up. She needed to stay close to her wiggly child and to hold onto the memory of Mia that night, so tiny and sweet, swaddled in the blanket, sleeping so peacefully in Chris's arms. The memory had, indeed, engraved itself in Erin's mind.

She really needed a tissue.

Her heart slowed, seemed to struggle as dread swept through her. And concern. She caressed her daughter's silky hair and let her prayer carry out on a whisper. "Lord ... thank You for this moment. For my sweet, beautiful little girl." Such soft, dark hair. Would it eventually turn blonde? Would it stay brown like her daddy's hair? "Lord, thank You for this moment. For all the moments. So many to treasure for the rest of all time. And so many more to come."

Mia pulled her fist to her mouth and started to suckle.

"You're getting hungry, aren't you, little boo. Well, it's about that time."

And still those feet kicked.

"Lord, thank You so much. There is no way I can say it enough. Feel it enough. Show you enough." She patted that round behind. "No way."

Mia gave her a concerned look.

Another pat. "What are you thinking about, boo? Are you worried you won't get to eat soon?" Erin leaned in to playfully nuzzle a onesie-covered arm. "Little worry wart. Of course Mommy's gonna feed you." More nuzzles, that switched to outright kisses on those pudgy cheeks.

Which was Mia's cue to let Mommy have it for all the pats on her bottom. Both of the tiny hands came up to pat Erin's face.

Laughing, Erin pulled away. "My goofy girl. You're pretty funny, you know that?"

A huge smile.

"Rinny, she's too beautiful. I can't stand it!"

Erin pushed up to sit cross-legged, then moved the gym away and pulled her daughter up to blow loud raspberries against the plump belly. When her arms shook with the effort, she pulled Mia in and held her close, leaning back against the couch, listening to her daughter's playful grunts and coos and soft breaths.

And still her heart ached. In this quiet and playful moment, Chris and Ben were off doing something ... though deep down Erin knew where they were and what they were doing.

A deep breath washed through her as she gently rubbed her daughter's back. "Lord, this has something to do with the Eastsiders. Something happened. And Ben took Chris to see Richardson. Please set me straight if I'm wrong. But I don't think I am."

Mia once again sucked loudly on her fist.

"What are we going to do, Lord? If the Eastsiders come back here looking to make trouble, how can we stop them?" Even as she spoke the words, she retraced her thought. "No, Lord, that's up to You ... and Richardson and his friends. I'll let You and them stop the Eastsiders. So I guess my real question is ... how can I stop Chris from getting herself neck deep into the thick of it ... again?"

She waited for an answer, desperate to hear anything. But heard only the silly grunts and suckling noises coming from her hungry baby.

"All right, little boo. I hear you." She let out a soft laugh. "And I hear You too, Father. Your silence speaks pretty loud." Another laugh. "So may I just say this? When Chris gets herself once again neck deep in the thick of the trouble, like I know she will, I'm going to trust You to see her through it. Like You always have before. Okay? I trust her to You. No matter what happens. No matter how thick it gets."

Mia squirmed just enough to gently pat Erin's cheek.

Erin pulled the hand to her lips and kissed the palm. *Thank You, Lord. Forever I will trust You, love You, and thank You.* She patted that soft bottom once more, then leaned back to give her daughter a look. "Ahh, my dear. You may be hungry, but first things first, all right?"

Laughing, she carried her wiggling armload to the changing table.

ELEVEN

Another vow broken.

As Ben drove his Explorer away from the police station, Chris turned in her seat and watched the big building disappear behind them. Jason once said how it sometimes helped him to forget about a particularly difficult run if he could watch the scene disappear through the back windows of the ambulance as Cooper drove away from it. He didn't always have the luxury, but when he did, he took advantage of it.

The last time Chris sat in Officer Ray Richardson's interrogation room she vowed she would never be back. Never again would she step foot inside the building, not even if they asked her to come to their Christmas party and put the star on the top of their Christmas tree. And how long did that vow last? Not even three months?

She needed to quit making vows.

She turned back around in her seat and tried to relax.

Ben gave her a small smile. "Are you hungry? Should we stop and have lunch?"

Over the course of the morning, her stomach had tied itself into a huge knot. "I'm not exactly hungry, sir. But thanks anyway."

He nodded. "Let's just head home then."

She let out a deep breath and watched the street roll along under the truck.

It had been a productive morning. Richardson drove Ben and Chris out to the Youth Gangs Unit headquarters and showed them the file the unit had collected on the Eastsiders over the past two years of their most active existence. The file had to have been at least six inches thick, full of reports, statements, photos, mug shots, and the like. Chris wasn't sure if seeing the file offered her reassurance or discouragement. With all the information that had been collected about the gang, why were they still roaming the streets selling their drugs, vandalizing private property, and basically terrorizing entire communities?

Her friend from the gym, Cee Train, wasn't the leader of the gang, though he was high up on their chain of command. Some guy named Rafer ran the organization. And from one glance at the mug shot on the man's rap sheet, Chris knew he was one man she never wanted to lay eyes on ever again.

Antwoine was a lackey, though loud-mouthed and violent. And a terrific artist. Loved to spray his Eastsider tags all over the place.

Chris could attest to that.

Bones was one to keep an eye on. The officers in the gangs unit made a special note in the file when Richardson passed along the bit of information Chris had given him about the young man kissing the barrel of his brand-new fully automatic pistol.

According to their records, several of the gang members carried weapons, mainly 9mm Berettas and .44 Magnums. All carried knives or shanks of some sort. Most used, sold, and otherwise distributed marijuana, though some were actively engaged in use and distribution of the harder drugs: heroin, crack cocaine, or methamphetamine. None were older than twenty-five, with the youngest official member weighing in at eleven. At least from the information the gangs unit had collected. There was still so much they simply did not know.

It was that particular item of discussion that disturbed Chris the most—what the gangs unit did not know. When she told them about Cee Train's threats to burn down Kimberley Square, two of the officers laughed quietly, and another smiled. Only Richardson seemed to believe her. Richardson didn't laugh or even crack a hint of a smile.

Though the gangster's threats were probably just empty threats. Still, to see the anger and concern on Richardson's face both enflamed the ache in Chris's stomach and eased it at the same time.

Richardson cared about Kimberley Square. He said he would step up his patrols of the area and press the gangs unit to keep applying pressure to bring down the worst of the Eastsiders' criminals. Chris wasn't sure how much pressure one man could apply, but since that one man packed his own collection of heat and could summon the entire cavalry if needed, she was grateful beyond words to have him on her side.

She watched Ben as he steered the Explorer onto the street behind the church. Her heart swelled with gratitude and relief. "Thanks for making me do that."

Ben glanced her way and smiled. "Thank you for telling me what happened. I know it was hard for you. Especially when God's little miracle made it even that much more enticing for you to not tell anyone." A faint laugh. "And now you know you need to tell everyone else."

Chris groaned aloud. "Can't you just tell Sonya and let her tell everyone?"

"Nope. Once you come clean with everyone, so to speak, you'll feel better."

"Yeah. I guess."

"Remember that. Until this is all over, don't keep anything to yourself. No matter how trivial. And keep your cell phone with you at all times."

Where had she heard that before? "I will. I promise."

"Good." He pulled the Explorer into the private parking area behind his house and parked next to Chris's own Explorer.

She laughed to herself when she saw it. Thick dust covered it from end to end.

Ben must have heard her laugh. "Looks like the youth group will have at least one customer at their next car wash." He pushed himself out of the truck.

"As spoiled as I am around here, I should just sell it." Though Chris knew she never would. She followed Ben onto his back porch and through the screen door into his house. The sight of Sonya's happy smile coupled with the sudden overwhelming aroma of freshly baked bread completely unraveled the knot in her stomach and almost blew her away.

STANDING AT THE GYM'S GLASS doors, ready to turn off the lights and head home, Chris stopped to take one more long look around the cavernous room. The day had been busy with a large crowd of neighborhood children enjoying the last of their summer vacation. The week had been quiet. But canceling tonight's rec league basketball games had been a good idea. On the eve of Labor Day weekend, all the teams would have been short players. Chris could have suggested the remaining players organize themselves for a couple of pickup games, but giving everyone the night off proved to be the better option. Even without the league games, she could stay and leave the gym open the rest of the night for walk-ins.

She could do that. She probably should do that. But she needed this night. It was only five o'clock. The night was still young. Even though the week had been quiet and uneventful, she needed to go home, take a long shower, curl up on the couch in her living room, and just chill. Finish reading her book. Or maybe take a nap. Or maybe just sit there and soak in the silence. Praying. Basking in the moment with her Lord.

Maybe later she'd get in a little Mia time, after Erin and Scott made it home from their pre-holiday trip to the coast.

A faint smile tugged her lips. She needed all the Mia time she could get. But with Scott working most of the busy weekend, she'd let them spend the rest of this night together before things got out of hand. She could survive a few more hours without holding that wiggly little one in her arms.

Chris flicked off the lights in the gym, pushed herself out one of the doors, and turned to lock them, pulling on them to make sure they were locked. Slowly, she walked toward the back lot. All was quiet. The breeze lightly fluffed her hair. She let her small backpack drop to the ground, reached up to release her hair from its braid, then gently shook it free to fall over her shoulders.

Though tainted by recent bad memories and ugly bare patches of dirt, this place still held her in its grip. The place of light, of soft breezes and ladybugs and evergreen trees. She wished the rhodies would bloom all year long. So beautiful.

She looked over her shoulder to take in the long strip of bare dirt by the gym's back wall. She'd be back to replant flowers. Or maybe grass this time. She'd figure something out. Soon. Later.

Smiling, she turned, grabbed her pack, and headed for the front of the gym, for the sidewalk that would lead her home.

Her smile pressed into a playful smirk when she saw the familiar truck parked across the street, the familiar man leaning back against it, dark sunglasses on his face, arms crossed over his chest. The man just stood there. Could he possibly be waiting for her?

Still smirking, Chris walked across the street and leaned against the man's truck as well, facing him, though he faced the gym. She ran her fingers through her hair, then propped her elbow on the upper ledge of the truck's bed and rested her head in her hand.

Jason finally turned his head toward her, a tight grin reflecting amusement.

Even through his dark sunglasses, Chris could tell his eyes studied every inch of her. Top to bottom. "Find what you're looking for?"

"Maybe."

Chris glanced down to see what had so interested him. Scruffy white sneakers. Dark blue Nike sweatpants. White T-shirt that said *Kimberley Street Gym* on the left shoulder. Curly brown hair just freed from its braid. Black pack. She lifted her eyes and shrugged. "Not much to look at."

"Beautiful."

A grunt of laughter spurted out of her. "You need new glasses."

"These work just fine."

Yeah, as long as they don't offer x-ray vision.

"Heading home?"

She tilted her head. "How'd you guess?"

Another tight grin. "Want a ride?"

"With you?"

Laughter. Finally. Jason looked away and rubbed his whiskery chin.

"Where are you headed?"

"Anywhere you want."

Was she willing to give up her quiet night?

"Have you eaten yet?"

No, and her stomach had been growling for the past hour.

Jason's head turned toward her. "You want to go get something? My treat."

Hesitation swept over her. She regretted it. Then wanted to deal with it. "Can I ask you one question first?"

"Sure."

"Did Richardson tell you that Ben and I talked to him?"

Jason nodded. "Yep."

"Did he tell you about what happened last Saturday night?"

A deep sigh. "Yes, Chris. He told me."

"Are you upset that I haven't called you to tell you about it?"

"You said one question."

"These are follow-ups."

Laughter.

Chris savored it.

"No. I'm not upset. I haven't exactly called you either."

"Are you upset about what we talked about last time we talked?"

"Can we just go get something to eat?"

She lowered her head and struggled with her own selfishness. "I really wanted this night to ..." Her words faded. She stared at the ground. "I guess I just wanted to relax tonight."

"I can understand that."

Slowly, she looked up to meet his gaze, wishing she could see his eyes through the dark glasses. "Are you working this weekend?"

"Yup. All weekend."

She cringed. And gave in. "Yeah. Okay. Let's go get some dinner."

Jason turned to face her, still leaning against his truck, arms still crossed. "Do you think I'm upset with you?"

Her thoughts tangled. She really wished she could see into his eyes.

His head lowered, as if he stared at the ground. "I'm not. Really."

"I said a lot of things the other day that were hard to say. Hard things for you to hear."

"Yeah. And I've been thinking about everything you said."

Chris turned to lean into the truck, folding her arms over the ledge of the bed, resting her chin over her arms.

Jason moved in closely beside her. "That doesn't mean I'm upset."

"I know."

"I'm trying to understand it." His fingers brushed her hair away from her face. "I need you to help me understand it."

How could she help him when she could barely understand it herself?

"I don't want to lose you."

She turned and leaned into his embrace.

"I feel like I just found you." He held her close against him. Lightly rubbed her back. Slowly, up and down.

Panic ripped through her, turning her stomach and stealing her breath. She pushed away, struggling to fight off the multitude of old ghosts.

Jason held out his hands. "I'm sorry."

She couldn't look up at him. "No, it's okay." Her heart thumped. She dared a quick glance into his eyes, then waited as he slowly lifted off his sunglasses. The sight of his deep blue eyes, the level of concern pouring out of them, left her floundering. "No." Just a whisper. She touched his lips to keep him from speaking. "It's all right." Caressed his cheek.

"It's still too soon for you. I'm sorry."

She didn't want his words to be true, but she knew they were true. When would she ever be free from her past?

"How about if I just take you home."

Her hand fell to his chest. She spread her palm over his heart and felt the strong pumps of each beat. She stared at the back of her hand.

"If it's too soon, it's too soon. I'm not going to push you." Impatience. Frustration.

And how could she blame him? She couldn't ask him to wait forever.

"Chris, look at me." He raised her chin with gentle fingertips. "It's all right."

Was it? His eyes softly gazed at her, yet traces of disappointment flickered in them. She lowered her head, closed her eyes, and turned away to lean once more over the edge of the truck bed.

Would she ever be able to fully return this man's love? To fully satisfy his needs? How could she, if simply accepting his love was such a struggle? Everything she told him before about belonging to Jesus first and needing Jason to be His as well ... was it all just a cover for her pathetic inability to allow this man standing beside her to fully express his love for her in the ways he wanted to express it? Did she tell him all that about Jesus hoping he would stop loving her because of it? That he would stop wanting her, would just go away and forget about her?

But how could this man love her that way? Didn't he know how tainted she was? Hadn't she explained it all to him enough? Hadn't he seen it for himself?

With a loud sigh, Jason leaned back against the truck. He put on his sunglasses and once again crossed his arms over his chest. "Tell me what you want from me, Chris."

She squeezed her eyelids so tightly stars appeared.

"Do you want me to leave you alone?"

"No." The word croaked out of her.

"And yet you don't want me to touch you." Definite frustration. "You want me to be a Christian just like you. I can't love you until I love Jesus. And then, when I love Him, I can't love you more than I love Him. We'll both love Him with everything we've got, and then settle for what's left over for ourselves."

She lifted her head to look at him, but he didn't turn to meet her gaze. "No. That's not what I want."

"But that's how it works."

"Not all the time."

His head turned. "Most of the time." A bitter laugh. "Yeah, Erin and Scott are the happy exception. But most of the time in Christian marriages something's gotta give. There isn't enough love to go around, and someone gets the short end of the deal."

Chris didn't hide her confusion. "Jason, in Christ, there is always enough love."

He grunted and looked away.

"Please don't judge me right now. Not at this moment. I ... I freaked out about ... and I'm sorry." She had to force in a breath. "Maybe this is all still too much for me. Too soon. But I'm learning. I'm getting over things I've never dealt with before. You have been helping me so much. I don't want to lose you either."

His sour expression didn't change.

"Jason, as I learn more about loving Jesus and accepting His love for me, He'll teach me more about how to accept love from others. He'll help me learn not only how to receive it, but how to give it. The way real love should be given."

"You give it just fine." His voice was a growl. "There's just not enough of it."

Chris drew in another long breath and let it out slowly. "What do you ... want from me?"

"Right now, all I want is for you to let me take you to dinner. Then maybe to a show. I just want us to have a nice night. Together. Is that too much to ask?"

It sounded nice. Very nice. And yet the tone of his voice angered her. She struggled to restrain several sudden and bitter replies, to corral the heat coursing through her. Words jumbled in her mind, leaving her thoughts tangled. She couldn't look at him. The silence dragged on.

"You know what? Fine." Jason turned and pulled open the door of his truck. "And you know what else, Chris? *I* can teach you a few things about accepting my love, if you'd give me half a chance. But if you keep trying to stuff God down my throat, I may just have to move on." He froze for a second, as if the words startled him.

"Jase ... come on. Don't leave." Chris didn't have the energy to sort through her thoughts. "I'll go with you. Just let me change my clothes."

"Forget it."

Her jaw dropped.

"See ya later." He climbed in the truck and slammed the door.

Chris stepped back as the truck's tires spun. Standing in the street, she watched the man she thought she loved leave her behind in a cloud of fumes and dust.

✷✷✷

DEFINITELY A NIGHT FOR PRAYER. Curled up on the couch, her hair wet from her shower, Chris focused on feeling, on hearing each beat of her heart. Cars passed by on the street. Echoes of her own voice trying to explain things to Jason invaded her mind, followed by echoes of his voice trying to tell her how crazy her words sounded, how little sense it all made in his larger scheme of things.

But it does make sense, Lord. It makes perfect sense to me. And if it means Jason needs to move on and find someone else to love ... The thought twisted her stomach. Just what did it mean? Did it need to come to that?

Did she really love him? Could she live without him?

Oh, Lord ... I guess I could, if it came to that. But I can't live without You. I know that. Oh, Father ... Her throat tightened. *I'd wither and die without You. I need You so much. More than anything.*

So what really mattered?

In Your scheme of things, Lord Jesus. What do You want from me?

A flurry of words tumbled into her mind. Bits of verses from the Word. Bits of songs. *Abide in Me. Remain in Me. Remain in My love. Follow Me. Be Mine.*

Like a Valentine.

Trust Me. Don't let your heart be troubled. Don't be afraid. My love, come away with Me.

Come away with Me ...

Yes, Lord. Always. Rest flooded over her, and she let it overtake her. *Thank You, my Savior.* And yet, her heart ached. *But, Lord ... what about Jason?* Tears burned her eyes. *I've made such a mess of this, trying to explain things to him. How can I make him understand?*

You can't. He said it himself. It's something he must figure out for himself.

The thought weighed her down. *But what if he can't? Or won't? If I can't help him, and he won't even try ...*

Then she needed to let him go. It was his decision to make.

Please, Jase. Please. Don't keep your back turned to Him. I can't ... I can't let you go.

✳✳✳

JAMAAL CLIMBED INTO HIS RIDE and laid some serious rubber in his wake. He had better places to be on his Friday night than listening to his homeboys spouting off. Twoine and Bones, all loudin' off about that church on the other side of town. Of course that lady told the cops about Twoine taggin' her floor. Why wouldn't she? The fool didn't need to do it. So now, let him pay for it. Five-oh would nail his skinny trunk to the wall. Suited Jamaal just fine.

So why couldn't he let it go? Why didn't he hang at the crib long enough to tell Twoine where to stick his loudin' off? Shree and Cee Train and Bones. Even Rummy getting all down with it. And that little hottie hanging on Twoine's arm. Little Sharnisha. It was her hood she was dissing. Her own peeps. Didn't she care? Or had Twoine bent her all up with his talk? Just who was feeding who?

But Rafer. That was too much. Pushing Twoine past kilt. Point of no return.

Something was going down. And for the first time since his beatin'-in, Jamaal bailed on his homeboys. Let them have their fun. He'd make his own fun with his own hottie. Vanessa. She was off da hook fine. Wicked sweet. And looking to hook up.

Word. Ditching his crew tonight was his best idea in a long time.

He cranked up his hip-hop and cruised the strips in his hood looking for fun. Turning the corner just down the street from Vanessa's house, he knew he would soon find it.

✳✳✳

ON SUNDAY AFTERNOON, WITH THE rest of the world insanely squeezing every last drop of excitement out of the final weekend of their summer, Chris lay on the floor of Ben and Sonya's living room engaged in the one activity she wouldn't trade for anything. Her entire day had been quiet and peaceful. Outstanding in every way. From the morning services at the church to Sonya's delightful dinner of grilled seafood salad sprinkled with tons of fresh crab and crunchy croutons. And tomorrow Ben promised to actually pull out his barbeque and grill steaks for everyone to, as he put it, "officially celebrate all the hard work everyone has contributed over the past year to strengthen the outreach ministry of the church and to serve the residents of our community, Kimberley Square."

Chris wasn't too sure about how hard she had worked since arriving on the scene last January, but she was most certainly sure about grilling the steaks.

And even more sure about the little one lying on the floor beside her playing happily with Ben and Sonya's baby gym, grabbing at the little stars and moons hanging down, laughing and smiling just as cute as cute could be.

Way too cute.

Just the way Chris loved her little niece. Fed, changed, and happy. Kicking and squirming as if she simply couldn't take being still when there was so much to see and do and touch and hold.

Chris could take a lesson. She leaned closer to whisper in Mia's ear, "Don't ever get old. Stay just like this forever."

Mia looked at her and let out the goofiest little giggle, as if to say, *"Yeah, right, Auntie Chris. You think I wanna be like this forever? Don't stand in my way, 'cause I wanna grow up to be big! And drive Daddy's car!"*

Chris laughed. "I hear you, little babe." She grabbed a flailing hand and loudly kissed the back of it. "I hear you."

Sitting in his recliner, Ben lowered his paper and grinned down on them.

Chris enjoyed how his grin gently crinkled his eyes. "Have you ever seen a happier baby, sir?"

"No, I don't think I have. Nor have I seen a happier adult. Not in a long time."

He lifted his paper before Chris could reply. She didn't mind when she felt the rush of heat to her cheeks. "He's a funny guy, isn't he, Mia my love." But she knew he was right.

Sonya walked by, carrying another pitcher of water toward the collection of plants basking in the sunlight pouring through the front picture window. "Well now, Amanda was a pretty happy baby. And no wonder. We spoiled her from the moment she was born."

Following Sonya and carrying a small step stool, Erin faked a loud gasp of outrage. "Surely, my dear friend Sonya, you are not insinuating that my precious daughter is happy because she's being spoiled." She flashed a wink and a grin at Chris.

"Oh, Erin, I would never say that." Sonya stood under one of the hanging plants by the window and waited for Erin to stretch out the stool. "If Mia is spoiled, it's certainly not because of your excellent parental skills."

"Chris is spoiling her," came from behind the newspaper.

"Hey!" Chris pushed up to sit, then leaned back on her hands, waiting for the three of them to stop laughing. "It's my job to spoil her. Then send her home to her mom and dad."

"Can't wait to return the favor, lady." Erin held the pitcher while Sonya climbed the stool to stand on the top step.

"Yeah, like you'll ever get the chance." At the rate Chris was going, it would be a slim chance at best.

Erin lifted the pitcher to Sonya, then steadied her by putting a hand on Sonya's hip.

Something slapped against Chris's arm. She glanced down to find Mia lying on her right side reaching both hands out, trying to grab Chris's arm. Chris fell to the floor and played patty-cake with her. That smile, those happy little giggles ... Chris couldn't imagine heaven being any better than this. *You are just way too cute. And you love me, don't you, you little cutie. You know I'm your Auntie Chris. And you know how much I love you. I'll always love you, sweet Mia Renae.*

Big brown eyes. Long dark lashes. Pudgy dimpled cheeks and that little round nose. Big happy smile showing pink gums and a tiny pink tongue. Giggles. Then, with a kick and a squirm, the babe rolled once more onto her back and reached to grab the toy sun, moon, and stars dangling above her.

Reach for those stars, little babe. Let her pull a few down, Lord.

If the moment continued to swell, Chris would need to get up and grab another tissue. Maybe one of these days she would learn to carry a box with her when she spent time with her niece.

Erin and Sonya talked softly about the state of the philodendron they watered. Watching Mia, listening to them talk, hearing Ben turn a page of his paper—Chris felt her heart slam to a stop.

Thumps of rap music carried toward her, from where, she couldn't tell. She looked up at Ben as he slowly lowered his paper. Their eyes met. Erin and Sonya talked on.

The thumps grew deeper, louder, then suddenly stopped. Staring at Ben, Chris's mouth fell open as she strained to hear any sound.

Mia reached for the stars. Her goofy baby noises didn't ease the stranglehold on Chris's heart.

Several cars. Racing closer.

She turned to meet Erin's gaze. Then Sonya's.

Screeching tires.

Ben folded his paper and dropped it to the floor. Chris couldn't look away from the concern flooding Erin's eyes.

Pattering sounds. Sharp. Unmistakable.

Chris tossed the play gym away and fell over Mia with her entire body.

Gunfire. Several weapons, fully automatic, sprayed bullets into the front of Ben Connelly's house. Loud smacks and thumps. A hideous shatter as the front window imploded.

Breath squeezed out of Chris in a crying wail. "Please … God!"

Tires screeched once more. Loud taunts and hollers followed. Laughter.

Silence.

God, help us … help us …

Nothing moved.

Mia wiggled her hand, freeing it from Chris's weight, then patted Chris's arm. A quiet wooing sound filtered out of her.

Chris forced her eyes to open. Blinked. Slowly lifted her head.

White stuff fell like snow around her. She couldn't comprehend the sight.

"Chris?" Ben's voice. Breathless. "Mia?"

More pats on her arm. Chris lowered her head and studied the most beautiful eyes she had ever seen. They peered back at her as if to say, *What are you doing, Auntie Chris? Is this a new game?*

"Chris?" Ben worked his way up to his hands and knees.

"Good. Mia's fine." She struggled to breathe. Slowly pushing away from the baby, she took stock of each wiggling appendage. "She's fine." Her voice shook so hard she didn't think anyone could understand her. "Mia's okay."

"Sonya?"

Oh, God . . . A bolt of lightning lit up her belly. *Where they were standing . . .* "Rinny?" She turned—the window was gone. The falling white stuff? Disintegrated foam padding from the love seat. The entire front of it. Obliterated. *Exit wounds . . . Oh, God . . .*

"Sonya?" Erin's voice. Soft.

Ben crawled to the edge of the love seat.

Chris swallowed deeply, forcing her throat to clear so air could flow into her lungs. She turned to give Mia a long hard look. Eyes wide, the baby's lips were curled into a perfect O. "You okay, boo?" She felt every inch of the little body, praying nothing was wrong. "Boo? Please, God . . ."

A burst of happy giggles. Waving hands and kicking feet.

Breath gushed out of her. "Thank You, Father. Thank You."

"Sonya!" Erin shouted the word. "Dear God!"

Ben's cry. "Sonya!"

Chris jumped as the back screen door burst open. Cappy ran through with Bettema right behind her. "You guys?" Cappy stopped and gaped. "What the . . . ?" Bettema headed straight for the phone.

"Cap!" Chris grabbed the play gym and lowered it back over the baby. "Watch Mia."

When Cappy fell to her knees beside them, Chris crawled past the love seat to the front of the room. Erin and Ben knelt over Sonya. "She hit?"

"No sign of it." Erin quickly palpated Sonya's entire body.

Chris pushed Ben away, then moved in and lowered her head, her ear, against Sonya's chest, listening over the thump of her own heart. "Breathing sounds clear. Strong heartbeat." She ever so gently lifted one of Sonya's eyelids.

Sonya turned her head and grimaced. "All right, y'all ..."

"Sonya?" Ben pushed against Chris.

She moved to Sonya's head. Palpated it gently.

A weak groan. "I'm fine, y'all. I'm fine."

Ben lifted his wife's hand to his lips.

"Sonya? Where do you hurt?" Chris spoke softly to Erin. "No indication of head trauma."

"Her collarbone's broken." Erin's voice barely carried the words. "Sonya, stay still." A pause. "Don't move."

Chris glanced at Erin. A line of sweat trickled down the side of her face. "Rin?"

No reply.

Ben's breath rushed out of him. "Sonya? Sweetheart?"

"I'm fine." Smiling weakly, Sonya gave her husband's hand a squeeze. "Really now. I'm fine, Benjamin."

"Keep ... still. Don't ... move your arm." Erin's face paled. She lifted her eyes, but looked past Chris. "We need a ... a brace of ... some tape, maybe." Her eyes shifted to meet Chris's gaze. Lost their focus. Then fell away.

Chris slid around Sonya and grabbed Erin by the shoulders.

Erin looked down at her left arm. Slowly pulled it away from her side.

Chris gasped. "God ... no ..."

Bright red blood covered the inside of Erin's forearm.

TWELVE

"Oh, God ... Rinny ..."

Erin leaned into her.

Chris held her for a second, then eased her down to the hardwood floor, brushing away several shards of glass from where her arm and shoulder would lie.

"Erin? Chris? Is she shot?" Cappy peered over the top of the love seat.

"Throw me a pillow, Cap. And stay with Mia." Chris started to lift Erin's blouse, but Erin's hands stopped her. Cappy set the pillow on the floor beside them and hurried back to the baby.

"Mia's okay?"

Chris squeezed Erin's hands. "Yes. She's perfect. It's you I'm worried about. Let me look."

"Scott's ... at the church."

"He'll be here any minute. Please, Rinny, let me look."

Ben gently lifted Erin's head, placed the pillow under it, then smoothed back her hair from her face. Erin turned to gaze at Sonya. Fear filled her eyes.

"Rin, it's all right." Chris pulled her hands from Erin's grip. The way they trembled, she struggled to unhook the bottom three buttons of Erin's blouse. Her teeth clenched. She tried to force herself into work mode, to forget it was her best friend's blood smearing on her hands.

She needed a towel. And help. Lots of help. *Scott, where are you?* Her stomach twisted as she lifted the blouse. Blood oozed from a jagged hole in Erin's side, close to her bottom rib. *God ... why?* The bullet almost missed her completely. "Gotta turn you, girl. Need a quick look." Breath grinding, Erin rolled just enough for Chris to see an ugly exit wound. "All right. Relax, now. Breathe."

Did she speak the words to Erin or herself? Her hands trembled so hard, she clenched them into fists. *Lord, help me do this . . .*

Erin grabbed Chris's hand. Blood on blood. Slippery grip. "Hey." The word cracked, yet a weak smile softened her blue eyes. "It's all right."

Chris nodded. "Yeah." A deep breath. "They got you. But it's clean. In and out."

"Okay." Erin licked her lips as her eyes fell closed.

Bettema knelt beside them. "Cops are on the way. They said they'd send everyone they could."

"Good. That's good." Chris needed to put pressure on the wound. She tried to pull her hand away from Erin's grip.

Erin held on. Her eyes blinked open and found Bettema. "Tee, could you go find my husband? Please? He should be at the church."

"Yeah. I think I know where he is." She pushed up and ran out the front door.

Chris stared at the hands gripping hers.

"Okay. We're okay."

She slowly lifted her eyes. "Yeah." Tried to smile. "Cappy, I need a towel. Something to . . ." The words faded. But Cappy would understand. Chris tried again to pull her hands from Erin's grip.

Erin once again held on. "It's okay, lady. Breathe."

She nodded. Then smiled easily. "Who's the patient here?" Erin eased her grip and their hands slipped apart. Chris caught the towel Cappy tossed to her, folded it, then eased it under and over the wound. "Little pressure now. Just a wee . . . bit." She winced when Erin tensed.

Quick stomps up the front stairs. The screen door opened. Scott appeared. Then froze. His mouth fell open. He walked a few steps closer, falling to his knees at Erin's side. "Baby?"

"In and out, clean." Chris moved back so Scott could take over.

He lifted a corner of the towel. "Okay. Okay." Gave his wife a brave smile. "You've got yourself a bullet wound here, love. But it's nothing. Just a little inconvenience."

Chris wiped the blood on her trembling hands on the bottom of her shirt. She watched Erin's eyes as they stayed on Scott.

He studied the wound. "Everyone else all right?"

Chris glanced at Sonya but couldn't settle her thoughts long enough to reply.

"She said Sonya broke her collarbone." Ben grimaced as he said the words.

Scott gave Sonya a sad look. "Is that right? What a pain, huh?"

"I'm all right, y'all." Grunting, Sonya started to get up.

Erin yelled at her as Chris moved in to help Ben push her back down. "Cappy, throw me another pillow. A flat one." Chris smiled at Sonya. "Don't do that again, okay?" Cappy threw the pillow. "Don't lift your head. Let us do it." Chris tucked the pillow under as Ben lifted his wife's head. "Better?"

"Yes. You're so sweet, Christina."

"Now stay still and do what she says. Don't be stubborn." Ben held his wife down with a long kiss on her forehead.

"Sonya being stubborn. Imagine that." Scott let out a quick laugh as he caressed Erin's shoulder. "Sweetheart, let's pull your legs up." He kept pressure on her wound and helped her lift her legs, bending them at the knees.

Chris helped as much as she could, then pushed up to stand by what was left of the window. Her shoes crunched on the glass. With the hardwood floors, Sonya repeatedly harassed her guests about running around in stocking feet. At the moment, Chris was grateful for the harassment.

A warm breeze carried through the open wall, fluttering the curtains. The city's haze and long streaks of con-trails tainted the blue sky. When she glanced again at Erin, her friend was looking up at her.

"And my little boo? Where is she?" The tone of Scott's voice remained conversational, professional. Chris wanted to scream and shout and kick something.

"Over here, Scott." Cappy's voice came from behind the love seat. "And she's just fine. Aren't you, you little cutie-babe."

Scott let out a deep breath.

"They, um ... they hit the church too, Ben."

Startled by the words, Chris pulled her gaze away from Erin and glanced at Bettema, who stood by the front door.

Ben's eyes fell closed. "Aww, no."

"No one's hurt, though. They didn't seem to hit anything ... vital."

He nodded. Kissed his wife once more.

Faint whimpering and crying, then loud knocks on the screen door startled them all. Bettema pushed the door open and knelt to gather Jimmy Thurman into her arms. "What is it, little man? Are you all right?"

The boy worked hard to sniff back his tears. Hiccups tore at his words. "My sis—she's hurt real—they hurt her ... real bad!"

Erin reached out to him. "What, Jimmy? Tell us again."

He wiped his eyes and turned to Erin. "Shar's wiff 'em." His eyes bulged. Blinking deeply, he glanced around the room. His gaze fixed on Erin. "You okay, Miss Erin?"

Teeth clenched, she waved him closer. "Come here, you."

The boy took a few steps toward her and stopped. Then chewed on his thumbnail.

"What about Shar? Tell us, sweetheart."

"She's hurt real bad, Miss Erin." Jimmy's eyes widened even more at the blood on Scott's hands.

"Where is she." Erin put strength behind her words.

"Up in dare crib. They been hangin' near our house."

Stomach quaking, Chris crouched to look the boy in the eye. "Who, Jimmy? Who's been hanging near your house?"

He acted as if he had just been caught pilfering his mother's cookie jar.

Erin reached for his hand and he gave it to her. She pulled him closer. "Jimmy, please. Tell us who it is."

Sobs burst out of him. "Eastsiders, Miss Erin. And Shar's been runnin' wiff 'em."

Hanging near his house. Three, maybe four blocks away. Chris lowered her head and rubbed her eyes with the back of her hand.

"You have to go, Chris."

She blinked deeply, then stared at Erin.

"You're the only one who can. If she needs help ..."

Chris glanced around the room. And knew it was true.

"Go help her."

"Rin ..."

"Go." Erin nodded one time, then ever so faintly smiled. "I'll be all right."

Don't make me leave you ...

"Go."

Chris glanced at Scott. At Jimmy. Tears streaked his ebony face.

"Take my cell phone." Erin lifted her eyes to look at the back of the love seat. "Cappy? Dig out my cell. It's in my purse." She leveled her gaze on Chris once more. "Take it and go. And be careful. Call in whatever you find. Put that handsome boyfriend of yours to work."

The room swirled. Chris shook her head to clear it. Cappy handed her Erin's cell phone. Chris looked up at her. "Stay with Mia."

"Yeah." Cappy grinned. "I used to think you were the one who got all the cushy jobs. Not anymore."

"Don't enjoy it too much. I'll be back to take over ASAP."

"You better." Cappy gave Erin a tender smile, then hurried back to Mia.

Erin grabbed Chris's hand. "Nothing heroic, lady."

"Yeah, yeah. I hear you."

"Get to her, get help to her. Then get out."

"Erin ..."

A long, hard look.

"All right. But ..." The words stuck in Chris's throat as it tightened.

Erin squeezed Chris's hand. "I'll be waiting for you. Somewhere." Her faint breath of laughter was cut short by a wince.

Overwhelmed by the moment, Chris rubbed her forehead, then leaned down as far as she could and touched Erin's cheek with her own. Her eyes pinched shut as she whispered in Erin's ear, "Be all right, girl. Please."

Erin pressed her cheek against Chris's. "Good as gold, girl. You know that."

Trembling, keeping her eyes closed, Chris pushed up to her knees and drew in a sharp breath, then turned to Jimmy. Blinked to see him clearly through her tears. And gave him a smile. "Let's go get your sister. Okay?"

The boy nodded.

Chris started to stand but Erin stopped her. She gazed once more into those blue eyes.

"*Vaya con Dios, hermaña.*"

The words sifted through her as sweetly as a spring rain. *Go with God, sister.* She squeezed Erin's hand and smiled. "Yeah." A laugh. "Right back atcha, lady. Right back atcha."

✷✷✷

JAMAAL PARKED HIS RIDE AGAINST the curb and got out, slamming the door behind him with all his might.

"Yo, be easy, brah," came from inside the car.

"Zip it, Rummy."

"Whatever, dawg. Yo."

He walked a few steps into the quiet street, his fists clenched at his sides.

Why did he ever agree to it? Rummy said he was all bored and wanted to make a trip downtown. Dre and Emmin wanted to ride too. Nothing else going on. Just a quick trip to town to see what was up.

Yeah, right. To see what was happening with Twoine and Bones and the rest of the crew. They was all hanging out at some pad off Cameron. Twoine's little hottie's hood. Said she picked the place out all by herself. Wanted a crib for all of her boys to hang with her and chill. Maybe get a quick buzz on. Sho nuff.

Leaf was plentiful at the crib. Jamaal didn't puff a toke but still had a buzz from the contact high.

Then they all cleared out. Heading for a hit. He wanted to head back to the hood, back to his crib. Do some chillaxin with Vanessa. Watch something on her mama's big screen. But he agreed to ride along.

Why? Why did he do it?

"Maal? Yo." Rummy leaned toward the open driver's side window. "Any day now, foo."

Jamaal ignored him. Shook his head slowly as his teeth ground.

"Train said to meet 'em—"

He spun around and whipped out his blade. "Rum, I'll slice you up if you say one more word."

"Yo." Rummy cursed and leaned back into his seat, mumbling something Jamaal couldn't hear.

He clicked the knife shut and dropped it back in the pocket of his lowriders.

Why. All of this mess. He knew something was up—Twoine had been jawin' for days, ever since 5–O posted across the street from his crib. They was tailing Bones too. Looking for a reason. Any reason.

The fools were determined to give them one.

The last thing Jamaal wanted was to be tailed, nailed, and jailed with them.

So why did he go? Why didn't he head home when the thought hit him?

And then they led him toward that place. In the last car, he could have turned away and drove off. Not followed them. But they would have dawged him and let him have it for not playing his part, for not backing up his crew.

A little dawgin' would have been worth it.

The last thing in the whole wide world Jamaal wanted was to be joyin' with his homies down Kimberley Street. Especially past that gym. And that clinic. But when Twoine and Bones and Q-Tee all whipped out their heat and sprayed lead all over that big church and the crib next to it, that was it. Bent up and jacked. Totally messed up.

He couldn't stop it. He had no clue this was the big hit Twoine had been all calculatin'.

The entire scene left him tore up. Shaking. Wanting to go back to his crib and get his fo-fo to shoot someone dead himself.

Twoine.

Yeah, Twoine would be first. Right upside that big ol' head of his. Boom. Then Bones. The fool. Then maybe he'd take out Cee Train and Rafer. Take 'em all out. Do the world a favor.

Then maybe … why not. Maybe he'd turn his fo-fo straight up on himself. Word up, he'd end it all. It would straight up kill his mama dead. But then … if anyone got kilt back there on Kimberley Street, every homeboy in the crew would be as good as dead.

Jamaal wasn't down with spending the rest of his life with his homeboys rotting away in some jail. They already lived in a world holding them as captive as any jail.

Breathing deep, his heart pounding in his chest, Jamaal cursed it all.

Somehow, someday, he would find a way to break free.

★★★

CHRIS POCKETED ERIN'S CELL PHONE and gave Scott's shoulder a squeeze as she walked around behind him.

"Be careful," he said to her. "And remember. Leave all that brave stuff for the boys in blue."

"Don't worry." She steered Jimmy toward the door. "Learned my lesson the last time. Remember?"

She could almost hear the man's thoughts running through his mind. *And the time before that ... and the time before that ...* She loved him for not giving them voice.

But, yes. So. Did she really learn any lesson at all?

Bettema touched Chris's arm. "I'll go with you."

Chris shook her head. "Stay here. I'll be back soon."

Jimmy pushed the door open and headed down the steps, but Chris stopped in the doorway to give Erin one last look.

That soft smile remained.

Chris savored it. Then followed Jimmy down to the sidewalk. Once she got there, he started to run, but it took Chris a few seconds to force her trembling feet to work. "Hold up, Jimmy. Just a second." She walked as quickly as she could. The boy turned to look at her as he walked backward. "Exactly where are we heading?"

"Past my house. Come on." He turned and tried to hurry her along.

Chris hoped she could keep up with him.

He ran down the side street to the corner of Cameron Street, then turned right and ran past Velda's house to his own house, near the middle of the next block.

Breathing hard, sweat dripping off her face, Chris slowed to a fast walk.

Jimmy turned and ran back to her. "Come on, Chris. We're not there yet."

"Sorry, buddy. All the excitement has got me a bit flustered."

"Please? We gotta help Shar."

"I'm right behind you. Lead on." He took off again, and she followed him another block to a large rundown house in desperate need of a new paint job. Among other things. "In here?" The place looked inhabited, though not by anyone who had the means to live in a nicer house.

Jimmy ran through the side yard to the back porch where he climbed a rickety lattice that may have once supported roses or vines of ivy. Whatever it was hung withered and dead, woven through the wooden crosspieces. At the top, Jimmy crawled onto the porch roof, then stood on tiptoes to pull himself through a small window into the house.

Chris stood in the yard, sweating, gasping for breath, staring at the vacant spot on the roof where Jimmy just stood, at the small window he just pulled himself through. No way did she want to climb that lattice. And the window didn't look big enough for her to crawl through even if she wanted to.

Jimmy's head popped out the window. "You comin'?"

Chris glanced around, then lowered her voice. "Are you crazy? I'm not climbing that thing."

He sucked in his bottom lip to chew on it. "Okay. Wait a sec." He disappeared once more.

Chris sank to her knees in the soft grass, shaking her head and trying not to give in to the urge to run straight back to Kimberley Street. Her hands itched from the dried blood on them. Erin's blood. Her eyes pinched shut. "Oh, God ... Lord God, please ... let her be all right." A deep breath helped settle her. She blinked open her eyes and drew in another.

"Hey, come in here!"

She leaned a bit to her right and squinted through the collection of junk on the back porch. Jimmy held a door open for her, waving for her to come closer. She forced her feet once more to carry her. Tried not to think about anything else. She walked toward him, picking her way through the junk in the yard and on the porch to the door. As soon as she reached it, Jimmy took off down the hall to the front end of the house, then ran up a flight of narrow stairs.

Chris followed him. Slowly. Listening. Gazing around. Trying not to breathe the musty air too deeply into her lungs.

It looked as if the house had been divided into four fairly large apartments. Was anyone else home? She stepped around a bicycle leaning against the wall, staring at the huge collection of junk piled under the stairwell.

Just what was this place? It reminded her of a funky college frat house. Or a drug house. Everyone cohabitating peacefully, all pitching in a percentage of their profits from dealing crack or cooking meth to keep the electricity flowing.

Lord, I don't want to be here . . .

"Chriiiisss, come on. Hurry up!"

She usually enjoyed being around Jimmy Thurman. How many times had she joined him and Benny Connelly on the floor of the church's basement, pushing Tonka trucks around the imaginary city they created? But when he said her name that way, it always made her want to reply, "Hey, Jimmy. Want a little cheese to go with that whine?"

The boy was six years old. Would he even get the joke?

"Hurry! She's still here!"

"Okay, Jimmy. I hear you." At the end of the hall, Chris peered up the stairs. The boy stood out front of a door leading into one of the top-floor apartments, but quickly ducked inside as Chris climbed the stairs. At the top, she peeked through the door.

The sickly sweet stench of marijuana almost knocked her over.

Just what she needed. On top of everything else.

Maybe that was it. Maybe Jimmy had gotten himself high somehow and was imagining all of it. Maybe Sharnisha sat at home on a big couch in front of her TV watching the Disney Channel with all her friends.

Carefully, Chris stepped into the room. The floor creaked and groaned under her, beneath threadbare and filthy carpet. The room was open and large with the living area to her right. Dirty windows let in some light. A scruffy couch sat against the far wall. To her left was the dingy kitchen. No other furniture at all. Crumpled sacks from Taco Bell and Subway littered the floor.

Jimmy's voice pleaded with someone, probably his sister. The sound drew Chris to the back bedroom. Slowly, she walked toward the hall, then stopped long enough at the open door of the first bedroom to realize the boy wasn't imagining anything. Two teenage girls lay on the floor in the bare bedroom looking worked over. And sky high.

She pulled Erin's cell phone from her pocket and punched in 911. But waited to push the button to send the call through. The heated discussion brewing in the back bedroom couldn't wait. She moved toward it, then stood at the door struggling to see through the smoky darkness.

"Get outta here, Jimmy! Leave me alone!"

Two girls sat on the floor in the large, completely bare room. One leaned against the wall by the bathroom. The other, Jimmy's sister, sat curled in a ball in the corner beside her. Chris ignored the first girl to glare at Sharnisha Thurman, then crossed the floor to open the dusty curtains and push open the window. Fresh air fell over her, but the light pouring in blinded her for a second.

"Yo. Don't do that."

Squinting, Chris turned. Sharnisha covered her eyes with her hand, her thick makeup smeared all over her face. With her other hand, she pushed her little brother away.

Jimmy sniffed back tears. "She can help you, Nisha."

"Chris?"

The first girl knew her name? She was young. Blonde. And now, in the light, very familiar. Chris walked toward her. Her heart seized. "Meghan?"

Alaina Walker's sixteen-year-old sister, Meghan, slowly worked her way up to stand.

Chris steadied her by the shoulders. "Are you all right? Are you hurt?"

The girl had been crying but otherwise appeared unharmed. "They said they'd be back. We gotta get her outta here."

"Straight up, they'll be back." Sharnisha let out a raspy laugh. "They my boys. They be comin' back to take me home wit 'em."

"They ain't your boys, Nisha." Jimmy tried to move closer to his sister, but she pushed him away hard enough to send him sprawling.

"Hey." Chris wanted to slap the girl, but Jimmy bounced right up, unfazed. Chris turned and rubbed Meghan's shoulder. "Are you hurt? Did they hurt you?"

Her head shook, but she couldn't look Chris in the eye. "They didn't even touch me. They said they don't do white girls."

Chris's stomach heaved. Thoughts tumbled through her mind, meshing into pure chaos. Two heartbeats later, the sound of several cars pulling up to the curb froze her. Froze her entire being.

Jimmy ran to the window. "It's dem! Dare back!"

"Told ya they'd come back for me." Sharnisha waved a hand at Chris, as if telling her to go away. "They ain't finished wit me yet. I gots lots more for 'em. Come on up, boys!"

Jimmy grabbed Chris's arm. "We gotta git! Dare here!"

Tears dripped down Meghan's cheeks. "I can't leave her like this ..."

Chris swallowed down the bile in her throat. "No. Get out. Right now." She put the cell phone in Meghan's hand.

"No! She's my friend! I'm not leaving her!"

"You have to get out!"

Meghan shoved Chris away and tried to pull Sharnisha up from the floor.

The front screen door of the house opened with a loud squeal. The main door burst open. Laughing voices flooded the stairwell.

Teeth clenched, Chris grabbed Jimmy by the shirt. "You know how to use one of these?" She handed him the cell phone.

He checked it out. "Yeah. My mama's got one."

"Get out of here. Now. Get away from the house and call the police. 911. Do it."

"'Kay." He took off into the bathroom to crawl out his window.

Chris pulled Meghan's arm. "Girl, please go. Follow him out the back."

"Nisha, come on!"

Sharnisha pushed her friend away. "Git, Meggy. I'm done wit you."

Stomps up the stairs, in the apartment. Lots of them. Creaks and squeaks as the floor struggled to carry the weight.

How many of them?

Chris stopped breathing.

So many laughing voices. All of them moving her way.

✷✷✷

"I KNEW IT WOULD COME to this. I knew it!" Jason didn't wait to hear Cooper's reply. He let out a string of hard curses, letting each word spit from his mouth.

"All right. Calm down, bro." Cooper parked the ambulance in the middle of Kimberley Street, directly in front of Ben Connelly's house.

Jason jumped out, grabbed his kit, and ran to the front door. Ray Richardson's partner, Gloria Mallory, waved him inside.

Richardson stood by the door. "We just got here. Watch the glass."

Jason thanked his friends but wasn't sure if it sounded convincing. With the way his mind and stomach churned, he knew a scowl played out on his face. He walked through the door, turned—a gasp stuck in his throat.

Erin.

He couldn't move.

Scott worked at her side. Blood covered her shirt. His hands.

She turned her head toward Jason and smiled weakly. "Hey, you. Welcome to the show."

His feet carried him closer but only after Cooper gave him a shove from behind. He knelt by Erin's side, next to Scott. Let another curse slip.

Scott took the kit from Jason's hand. "Just a tiny inconvenience here. Got a Band-Aid in this thing? That's all she needs." His smile was aimed at his wife, but Jason drank it in.

Erin grabbed Jason's arm, yet looked at his partner. "Hi there. Could you ... please take good care of my friend? This is Sonya. She broke her collarbone."

Cooper stepped around them all to kneel at the woman's side. "Well, then. Hello there, Sonya."

Jason shook his head to clear it. With all the goodwill floating around, he wondered if someone would soon make up a batch of popcorn. Maybe ask him if he would like a nice cup of tea.

Erin's grip on his arm tightened and she turned to zero in on him. She froze for a second, wincing sharply, as Scott started to clean the wound. Blinked, then drilled her gaze into Jason once more. "Chris ... went with Jimmy Thurman. Somewhere. We don't know where. He said his sister ... was hurt bad by the Eastsiders. That they were hanging out ... somewhere around here."

Jason's mouth fell open.

"Do you have any idea where?"

"No. None." He turned to Richardson. "Hey, you know of anywhere around here where the Eastsiders may be hanging out?"

The man shook his head. "Not around here. Their hood is miles from here."

Jason couldn't take the disappointment in Erin's eyes. He turned once more to Richardson. "You hear of anything else called in around here lately? As in the last hour or so?"

He conferred with Mallory. "Well, yeah. Monroe just took a call for out on Cameron Street. Dispatch said it was an unknown situation."

Erin pulled Jason's arm. "That has to be it. Go to her. She may need you."

"Demanding when she's bleeding, isn't she?" Scott grabbed the blood pressure cuff from Jason's kit. "Hold still, love."

"Jason ..." Erin swallowed deeply, then licked her lips, her strength fading with exertion. "Jimmy said his sister was hurt bad, but who knows what Chris will find. Jimmy lives on Cameron Street. He said the Eastsiders were hanging ... close to his house."

Jason turned once more to look over his shoulder at Richardson. The man nodded, then grabbed the radio microphone hanging from his shoulder. "Dispatch, charley five-five-two. Did charley five-five-seven just take a call for Cameron Street?"

The dispatcher's voice crackled through the mike. "Ten-four. Unknown situation, possible medical to four-eight-oh-seven Northeast Cameron."

"Roger that."

Jason turned and waited for Cooper to look at him. It didn't take long. "Can you handle things here?"

Cooper shrugged. "I'd say so. I think we're ready to transport. What say you, Doc?"

Scott unwrapped the BP cuff and tugged the stethoscope from his ears. "Immediately."

Erin squeezed Jason's arm. "Please go."

Jason held her hand in both of his. "I may owe you for this."

"I'll be sure to collect."

He smiled at her. Then gave Scott a long look.

"You better get going." Scott grinned. "If I know Chris, she's probably gotten herself into something over her head."

Jason wanted to laugh but knew the words were true. He squeezed Erin's hands once more, then pushed up and turned to Richardson. "Take me to Cameron Street." He headed for his friend. "Please, man? Take me there now."

Richardson hesitated only long enough to glance at Mallory. "You stay here?"

She nodded.

He pulled Jason by the arm toward the door. "All right, then. Let's go."

✯✯✯

Too late to run. Chris grabbed Meghan and pushed her into the bathroom. "Stay in there. Do not come out." She pulled the door closed and turned to lean against it. And immediately stood face-to-face with her good friend Cee Train. Her insides dropped to the floor.

"Well, now." His grin carried pure amusement. "Yo, brothas. Lookee lookee at who we got here."

Seven of the man's smirking homeboys slowly filled the room around him. Most of them looked familiar. Same ones from the gym.

"Too sweet, dude." Antwoine's smile flashed his golden teeth. "Ahh ... we gonna have us some fun now."

Laughter rumbled out of each man.

"Gentlemen?" Chris's heart thumped so hard, her voice shook. "Be easy, now. Please?" No pleading. Just a simple request.

Cee Train held up his hand to quiet the laughter and taunts. "We be easy, girl. Yo. Don't worry 'bout it."

Nothing in his words convinced her.

Eight of them. With a few others hanging back in the hall. In and out of the other bedroom. One of the girls in there laughed. Chris didn't want to think about what might be going on.

Bones stared her down, caressing his automatic pistol. He lifted it to his lips to kiss the barrel, then rubbed it against his cheek.

Chris's stomach twisted at the sight. Her teeth clenched so tight her jaw ached. *Easy . . .*

The way he was toying with her, she would just bet he was the one who fired the shot that ripped through Erin's side.

On the floor to her left, Sharnisha rolled onto her hands and knees and tried to stand. Her legs wobbled, and she crashed back to the floor. Loud laughter shook the walls of the room.

Every man laughed. Except one. Standing back by the door.

Chris blinked hard, then studied him closely. Yes. The one from the gym. Mr. Serious. The one Cee Train punched in the mouth. The one he called Maal. Short for Jamaal? Maybe. He stood, arms crossed over his chest, glaring heavily at his friends. His right forearm was still wrapped with a black bandanna.

Yes. He was the one Erin treated at the clinic. Had to be.

Sharnisha tried again to stand. No one made a move to help her. She dropped back to the floor with a soft cry.

Ahh, girl. These are your boys, huh? Chris looked at Cee Train, tried to keep her voice light. And steady. "I'm surprised you guys came back here. You should be long gone by now, considering the mess you made not far from here."

The man's upper lip curled into a vicious sneer, twisting his thin moustache and goatee. "Yo. Why you care?" He called her a few hideous names.

She swallowed. Forced breath into her lungs. "Cops will be covering this entire area, if they aren't already. If I were you, I'd be clearing out of here fast. Not making myself comfortable, but making myself seriously scarce."

"Well, you ain't us," came from Bones.

"Unless . . ." Chris pushed down some of her fear. Turned her eyes to meet Cee Train's gaze.

The man stared at her. His head tilted. "Unless?"

"You want to get caught."

More laughter. Curses. All in pure fun.

None of them cared one bit about getting caught. Except maybe Jamaal. He didn't laugh. But maybe the man didn't know how to laugh. Maybe he wasn't the same man Erin treated after all.

And maybe none of them cared about getting caught because they had all been caught so many times before and then almost immediately released.

Anger fueled her words. "You shot two women today." Not exactly the truth, but not far from it. She held out the bottom of her shirt. Wavered a bit at the sight of Erin's blood. "See?" Her voice, that one word, shook.

Something flickered in Cee Train's eyes.

"Yeah. That's right. At the house next to the church. You shot my best friend ..." The words wrenched her heart. Her teeth clenched. She struggled to find the strength to finish. "And you hurt one of the sweetest ladies in the world. They never did anything to you. In fact, one of them, my best friend, even helped one of you. When you were hurt." She glanced at Jamaal.

His sudden surprise followed by a cruel glare confirmed it. This was the man Erin treated in the clinic. But all she could talk about was how nice he had been. How polite and—

"What she sayin'?" came from one side of the room.

"Yo. Who she help?" came from another.

"Yo! Dat's *it*, Train. Step off." Antwoine moved toward her, pulling out a switchblade from the pocket of his baggy jeans and flashing it in her face. "Yo. I'm gon' slice you up." Vulgar names. "Inside and out."

Cee Train swung out his arm and caught Antwoine in the gut, doubling the man over. "Be easy, T. Yo. She jus' talkin' trash. Don't let it trip you out." A grin. "Ain't no need for a slice-n-dice. Not yet."

The rage in Antwoine's eyes as he struggled to straighten and breathe left Chris lightheaded. She pinched her eyes shut and tried to stay upright on her feet, pushing back against the door to steady herself.

"Yo, Twoine." Sharnisha's voice stumbled over the word. She sounded as if she was about to be sick. "Commere, baby. Don't be buggin' over her—"

A rush of movement and a loud grunt cut off her words. Chris's eyes flew open as Sharnisha screamed. Twoine kicked her again. "Yo! I ain't buggin'!" He swore at her. Called her a string of ugly names.

Chris wanted to push the man away from the girl. She needed to move, needed to push him away, begged her entire system to move into the man's way to push him back. She couldn't move. Her jaw hung open. Yet breath barely found its way into her lungs.

As Sharnisha cried, Twoine wiped his mouth with the back of his hand. Spit on her. Then slowly turned to glare at Chris.

Sharnisha wailed, her arms covering her face.

Chris stared into Twoine's intense glare, then tried to soften her eyes until nothing remained in them except pity. And great sadness. It wasn't difficult. Tears blurred the man's face. She licked her lips and swallowed against the tightness in her throat. "You told me these are your boys, Sharnisha." The words barely escaped, yet carried across the heavy silence that fell over the room. "Aren't you glad they came back for you?"

THIRTEEN

JASON LEANED FORWARD IN THE front seat of the police cruiser as Richardson slowly drove onto Cameron Street. Monroe's cruiser blocked most of the street. The rotund officer hiked up his utility belt and approached the car. Richardson reached to quiet the squawking radio.

Monroe nodded one time. "Ray." He bent over to peer into the car at Jason. "What are you doing here, Sloan?"

Richardson ignored the question. "What do we got?"

Jason tried not to snarl at Monroe. The man wasn't exactly one of his favorite people.

"Three cars out front of the residence. Ran a trace. Guess who all three belong to. And your first guess doesn't count."

His heart slammed against the front of his chest. He squinted down the street toward the house and saw the cars parked in a row at the curb, but the house was hidden behind some trees.

"Mohler's cordoning off the block from the east. Talley and Cordelay should be blocking off the cross street from the north and south."

"How many do you think are in there?" Richardson's face bore a heavy frown.

Monroe lifted off his cap and scratched his head. "Well, say three or four at least per car ... I'd guess twelve at most. All armed and considered extremely dangerous. Of course." He slicked his thin hair back and replaced his cap.

Jason closed his eyes and sat back in the seat. *Twelve Eastsiders, all armed and dangerous ... with Chris right there in the middle of them.* "We gotta help her." He couldn't do more than just mumble the words.

"Huh?" Monroe leaned down to peer again into the car.

"Chris is in there."

Richardson nodded, then turned to Monroe. "There's probably a civilian in there. Chris McIntyre. She works at the gym on Kimberley."

Monroe straightened and looked out over the top of the car. Then smirked. "Yeah. I met her once."

Jason leaned against Richardson. "And maybe more than just her. She went into the house to help a girl who might be hurt."

"Fine. Great." Monroe cussed. "So what are we talkin' here? Two civilians? Maybe more? And at least twelve bad guys." He nodded. "Yeah, we better get SWAT in on this."

Richardson glanced at Jason, then turned back to Monroe. "You call and request it?"

"No. Thought I'd leave that up to the captain when he gets here."

"How long will that take?" Jason grunted as Richardson's elbow pushed him back. He leaned away, then whispered a curse.

"As long as it takes, son," Monroe said.

Don't call me son. Jason stared out his window. His eyes were drawn to the front yard of a nice bungalow-type house. Yellow and red roses swayed in the breeze.

As long as it takes. How long will that be?

Breath squeezed through his throat.

Oh, God ... please ...

He blinked.

Are you praying, Sloan? Crying out to God now that things are getting desperate?

A deep sigh rushed out of him. *Father God ... have You given up on me?*

The roses swayed and danced on the breeze.

⋆⋆⋆

ANTWOINE SCARED HER THE MOST. The way he glared at her. His eyes seemed to pierce her skin wherever they fell. Cutting her deep. Leaving her weak and numb.

Two of them walked out of the room. Jamaal moved just long enough to let them pass, then returned to his spot by the door. Watching.

Chris watched him, hoping he would meet her gaze, hoping to stir up at least a little bit of sympathy in him. But the man glared at Antwoine. Followed his every move.

Cee Train backed up a few steps to lean against the wall and pulled out what looked like a joint. Lit it. Then sucked in a deep drag. Two of his smiling homeboys walked up to him with their hands out, wanting a turn.

Chris glanced at Antwoine. He continued to glare at her.

They wanted to get caught. They were all just standing here practically daring the police to show up and take them in. No one cared. Unless ...

The thought struck like a sharp jab to the stomach. Breath gushed out of her.

Unless Jimmy didn't make the call.

Her eyes closed. *But he's a smart kid! He can use a computer. I can't even use a computer!*

A presence startled her. She blinked open her eyes to find Antwoine standing so close his breath fluffed her hair.

"Yo. Wassup?" The hideous name he insisted on calling her slashed through her. "'Fraid, girl? You lookit. Yo. Well, guess what. If I were you, y'know what? I'd be scared too." A laugh. More like a wheeze. "Yo." That name again. "I'd be buggin' outta my head if I was you right now."

The stench of Cee Train's joint filtered toward her. Slow, burning rage inched up from her gut.

"Word. I'd be buggin' so bad ..." More laughter. His vulgar, horrible words created images of filth she could only hope would soon fade from her mind.

"Yo, girl. Wanna hit?" Cee Train reached out to her, offering her the joint.

She shook her head. With Antwoine so close, the back of her head ground into the door. "No thanks. But you go ahead."

Laughter.

Burning, building rage.

Easy ...

If she couldn't control it, it would control her.

Father ... please—

Antwoine leaned in to lick her cheek. Her eyes pinched shut as her mind short-circuited. She didn't breathe or force open her eyes until the man pulled away.

Her cheek itched. She couldn't move to wipe off his spit. White hot fury swept through her.

Enough of this was enough.

✳✳✳

"RAY, DON'T EVEN TELL ME to calm down." Jason used a pair of binoculars to peer through the windshield of the police cruiser at the huge gray house about a half block away. They had moved a bit closer than before to get a better view of the house, but that was it. In the last ten minutes, no one made any attempt to enter the house. And no one made any attempt to leave it. "How much longer are we gonna sit out here and wait?"

"Sloan, I told you. Until enough backup arrives to take them all down. Come on, man. You want to walk into the middle of a hornet's nest?"

"Right now Chris is in the middle of that hornet's nest. She needs our help!"

"Jason, if you don't take it easy, I'm gonna cuff you to the cage and leave you here all by yourself. I'll go wait with Monroe."

"You don't need to cuff me to anything." Jason lowered the binoculars and pinched the bridge of his nose. "I'll calm down when you guys finally make a move and go in there."

Richardson checked his watch. "Chastwick's on his way. And Jeffries. We won't need SWAT. When those two get here, we'll have enough to take down the entire house."

"Right. So, until then, we're just gonna sit out here and wait."

"Keep your eyes on that window." Richardson pointed to the house. "Let me know what you see. And say a prayer they don't leave until we're in place. If they leave now, we'll miss a golden opportunity to take them all down."

Say a prayer. Right. *You're forgetting how out of practice I am.* He growled. "You sure we're not going to need SWAT?"

"We can take them. Once they see us, they'll bug out like a bunch of cockroaches caught in the light."

"Yeah, but will they bug out shooting? Or taking hostages?"

Richardson shook his head. "That's not how these guys react. They're all more into self-preservation than sticking together for the good of the crew."

"Well, that contradicts what you just said. If they're into self-preservation, won't they come out shooting to save their own skins?"

A deep sigh. "Who knows. All I know is if they come out shooting, we get to shoot back. We're wearing armor. They're not." A pause. "I'm hoping it won't come to that. But if it does, we'll be ready for them."

"Yeah, but will Chris be ready?"

Richardson met Jason's gaze. They shared a long look of resignation. "We'll just have to wait and see."

"Yeah. Great." Jason pulled the binoculars back up to his eyes. "Just great."

✯✯✯

CHRIS SLOWLY RAISED HER LEFT hand and spread her fingers wide. She kept it close to her chest, her elbow against the door.

Twoine watched her.

She tried one last time to catch Jamaal's eye. She needed an ally, or at least the assurance he was not a hostile, but the man wouldn't look her way.

Forget him. He's dead weight. He's not gonna help you.

Cee Train laughed and smoked his joint. The two others didn't seem to care what was happening. Bones tucked his pistol into the back of his jeans, then lit his own joint. Or maybe it was a cigarette. At this point, Chris didn't care.

Sunshine poured through the window facing the street. A light breeze ruffled the dirty curtains. All around her, life merrily traipsed along on Labor Day weekend. Birds sang. People grilled steaks on their barbeques, played volleyball or lawn darts out in their backyards.

But if six-year-old Jimmy Thurman, for whatever reason, did not make the call, life as Chris once knew it would end. Because what she was about to do would probably get her killed. But if she could pull it off ...

As the plan wormed through her mind once more, doubts crept in to squash her slim hopes. Could she shove Antwoine away hard enough to give herself time to grab Sharnisha and pull her into the bathroom? Doubtful. Would Meghan, if she was even still in the bathroom, know enough to help, then to lock the door behind them all in time?

The flicker of hope died away on her next breath.

No. No way.

With the way her arms shook, she'd be lucky to push the man back more than a few feet. Not enough time to grab Sharnisha. But maybe time enough to dive through the door alone?

Maybe.

Then again, maybe not.

And if that door opened at all, or if she even moved away from it, Meghan would be vulnerable.

Not acceptable.

Other options?

She racked her brain for anything. All hope tumbled and died on her myriad of fractured thoughts.

No other options. None.

Trembling overtook her as her eyes fell closed. She relaxed her arm, lowered her hand, and used it to help steady herself against the door.

There had to be other options.

Antwoine laughed at her. She didn't open her eyes to see it.

Pray. The only thing she could do. In that one moment, she was as helpless as she had ever been.

"Always so helpless. My little Chrissy . . ."

Rage rekindled in her belly.

Use it. Do something with it.

"Hey, Chrissy . . . you want another beer? Nah, you lost the taste for it, huh. Wonder why?"

God . . . help me . . .

If this continued, she'd pass out. The stench of Cee Train's joint, Bones's cigarette, Antwoine's sweat—

"Yo, dawgs. Wassup in here, y'all?"

A new voice. Loud. Deep. Did she dare look?

"Yo, man. It's about time you got here. We's jus' hangin'. Dat's all." Cee Train hissed out a giggle as he said the words.

"It be time to clear out. Yo. Five-oh cain't be far."

This new voice spoke with authority. Chris dared a glance.

Her knees gave out. She slid down the door to land on the floor.

Rafer. And his mug shot did not do him justice.

Tall. Older than the rest. Chiseled face. Long scar above his left eye. Black nylon skullcap. Silver chains riding over his solid chest. Dark brown eyes bearing down on her. Amusement flickering in them.

Father ... God ...

"Yo." A horrible slur. "Who are you?"

She shook so hard, her head bumped against the door.

"Yo. She's a present, Rafe." Antwoine kicked the bottom of her shoe. "She was here when we got here."

Rafer's eyebrows lifted. "Fo' real, T?"

"Sho nuff. Yo."

His eyes raked over her. "You want her?"

Antwoine's smile curled into a sneer. "Yeah. Yo, man. I'll take 'er."

Rafer didn't seem impressed. "Well, whatever. But if you're gonna get some, you better get it quick. Yo. We about to roll." The man threw Chris a dismissing wave, then turned and backhanded Cee Train for the last hit of his joint.

Antwoine crouched so low his silver chains rattled against the floor. He looked Chris in the eye. "Yeah. I want you." His voice grated low out of his throat. "And I'm gonna get me some right now. Yo. Fo sho." He flicked a gang sign at her.

Or what looked like a gang sign. Chris couldn't tell. She couldn't look away from the man's shiny gold teeth, mesmerized by how they glittered as he smiled.

✳✳✳

FINALLY. JASON FELT AS PENT up as a greyhound before a race.

"Now listen to me. Wait for my 'all clear.' I mean it, Jase."

"I hear you." It was only the twentieth time Richardson said it.

"Stay close, but stay out of sight. If you get in the way, man ... if they don't kill you, I will."

"All right, Ray. Come on."

"I should give you a gun."

Jason snarled at his friend. "Don't want one or need one." He gripped the portable first-aid pack. With the tools rolled up inside the pack, it felt like a thick club in his hand. "I'll be all right."

"Stay forgotten."

"You got it."

Richardson slapped him on the back. "See you when the dust clears."

"Yeah." Whatever. Just get the dust flying in the first place.

Biting the inside of his cheek, Jason waited for the officers to set up their front line around the house. When Richardson gave him the signal, he ran across the yard to his assigned waiting place by the back porch. Once the thugs made a break for it, most would head straight for their cars. Jason would give them two minutes to clear out ... and then go in and find Chris.

He hid behind an old washing machine and watched as the cops around him prepared to go in.

Chris.

Her face appeared in his mind's eye. He wiped a fat drop of sweat from his eyebrow.

If anything happens to you ...

His hands shook. On his knees, he leaned around the washing machine. The cops still had yet to move.

Come on! What are you waiting for?

On his knees ...

His eyes closed as his head lowered. If he didn't control his breathing, he would hyperventilate.

He loved her.

Terror clamped down on him.

God ... I love her! I can't lose her!

Crashing steel upon steel. The paleness of death. Blood so dark and so cruel.

I can't lose her too. Oh, God ... please ... please hear me. Please keep her safe.

Her voice echoed through his thoughts. *"You've lost sight of how big God is. And how good."*

His eyes pinched tightly as his teeth clenched. *I know You are good, Father. I've always known it.*

"Only Jesus can help you with everything you're dealing with. Only He is strong enough."

Jesus . . .

A squeak startled him. He wiped his forehead with the back of his hand and leaned again around the washing machine.

Yes.

The cops were just now, finally, starting to move in.

✷✷✷

RAFER'S LAUGHTER BROKE THROUGH CHRIS'S daze. Startled, she blinked deeply, then lifted her gaze from the glittering gold teeth to Antwoine's eyes. Filled with delight, they seemed to glitter as brightly as his teeth.

She couldn't wait. If the man made a move, she'd miss her chance.

Rafer turned to walk out the door.

Chris popped the heel of her right hand straight into the base of Antwoine's nose. The crunch of bone, his screams, left her instantly sick. She struggled to push up from the floor, to turn and reach for the doorknob of the bathroom.

Hands grabbed her feet and pulled her down. Her cheek thumped off the floor, slamming her teeth together.

Shouts, curses . . . someone roared with laughter.

Screams. Deep inside her. Pure rage lit her on fire. She tried to kick away, but the hands on her feet held firm and pulled her across the floor, away from the door. She lifted her head just enough to keep the carpet from burning her cheek. One of the men sat above her, at her head, then grabbed her left hand and twisted it up behind her.

280

Pain in her wrist and shoulder froze her solid. Breath stuck in her throat as prayers screamed up from her soul.

"Yeah, boy. Like dat. Yo. Hold her down."

Curses, then terrifying sounds scattered her prayers.

"Straight up. Yo." That vulgar, hideous name. "You're mine."

Loud hollers and cheers reached her from every corner of the room. Whoops of encouragement. Then one shout broke through the rest. "Yo! Step off, T! NOW!"

That voice. *Jamaal?*

Antwoine's hands grabbed at her, proving he had no intention of stepping off.

Shouts of pure rage ripped across the room.

Jamaal ... Father ... help me ...

Antwoine let out a long line of curses and pushed off, bruising Chris's hips and kicking her knee. Soon after, sounds of a furious fight filled the room.

She tried to move, to see behind her, but the grip on her hand tightened, pulling her arm higher against her back. Pressure on her shoulder built, grinding her breath in her throat. She watched Sharnisha as she lay huddled, ignored, in the corner. Chris wished she could join her. Ignored. Alone.

The fight wore on. Her stomach wrenched as fists pounded flesh. Someone kicked her feet. She tried to pull them up, but the grip on her hand and wrist tightened. Her arm was pulled higher. A cry zipped through her.

"Yo, man. I'll take her!" Laughter again mixed with the sounds of the fight.

Higher yet. Her shoulder reached its breaking point. She fought back a scream, not daring to move, not even to breathe.

"Right now. Yo." One of the men, his voice sounding like Cee Train's, sat on the back of her legs. Her arm moved, pulling at her shoulder. Another shift of his weight on her legs. Her arm moved again. *God, no!* Another ... her shoulder popped. Chris's free hand clawed the carpet as agony shut her down.

Laughter and shouts gelled into nothingness. Only blackness, swirling, total chaos. Hands grabbed at her. Pushed up the back of her shirt.

Then nothing. No movement, no voices.

Complete silence.

The weight on the back of her legs shifted once more, then moved away. The grip on her hand eased, moving her arm, stirring another groan of agony deep in her belly. Tears fell into the musty carpet as she ground her forehead into it.

"Yo, BACK OFF!"

The shout tore through her. Cee Train's shout. The tone of command in it quieted her sobs.

"Right now, Shree! Do it!"

The man gripping her hand released it. Laughing, he pushed up to stand.

"Back off. Yo. Get away from her."

Another shout from across the room. "Clear out! Five-oh's here!"

Shuffling and shouting broke out from all over. From outside. Downstairs.

None of it mattered. Holding her breath, fighting back the cry racing through her, Chris pushed up enough to work her arm back to her side, then grabbed it and rolled onto her right side, hoping to ease it back into its socket. Whimpering, she gasped when the bone slipped into place. Relief flooded her, followed by a hard rush of nausea. Holding her arm, she curled into a ball, breathing deeply, swallowing down the threat of bile until it passed.

Someone stood near her. A presence.

She forced her eyelids open, blinked away tears, tried to focus.

Cee Train.

The man just stood there. Gaping at her. Chris couldn't believe the expression on his face. Concern? Fear?

He breathed heavily. Didn't move.

He's stoned. Watching him, Chris worked her way up to sit against the wall. Teeth clenched, she wiped her face, then held her aching shoulder, forcing back a whimper.

"Yo." Softly spoken. And the man still stared.

Chris breathed, letting the rhythm of incoming-outgoing air settle her nerves. She barely shook her head against the wall. "You better split, man." Her voice shook. "Five-oh is here."

His eyes narrowed. His mouth gaped. "You ...?"

What was there, in his eyes?

"Who did that? Who would ...?"

She looked away and laughed. Just a faint grunt. *Yeah. You saw it, didn't you. Serves you right.*

"Man ..." His head slowly shook. "Dat's messed up. I mean ..."

You're messed up. Just leave me alone. She glanced toward Sharnisha. Laughed again. Just another grunt.

The girl was gone.

Moved pretty quick when you had to.

A groan caught her attention. She peered across the room, forcing her eyes to focus.

One of the Eastsiders lay on the floor, his back to her.

Was he stoned?

Cee Train took one look, then bolted for the door, only to run into a fully uniformed policeman. He shouted, the officer shouted ... Chris focused on the man across the floor. Lying still. Not moving at all.

Jamaal?

She tried to work her legs under her, but the pain in her shoulder and the sludge in her blood dragged her down.

"FREEZE! Don't you move!"

A different officer stood in the middle of the room pointing a gun at the man on the floor, as if he thought the guy would jump up and tackle him.

Chris rubbed her eyes, trying to comprehend the moment.

Was it Jamaal?

Who was fighting? It had to be Antwoine. Someone pulled him off her.

She stared at the young man's back.

Jamaal. You pulled him off. That's why you two fought.

That was why he lay on the floor. Groaning.

Lord God ... Chris pushed up and crawled closer.

"Stay back, ma'am." The officer still pointed his gun.

"He's hurt. Get a medic."

"Ma'am, stay back!"

Chris leaned over Jamaal's side even as the cop grabbed her right arm. Her left arm fell, grating her shoulder. Dragged to the floor at the cop's feet, she kicked up to her knees and screamed at everyone, at everything ... at the cop, at Jamaal, at the pain ... everything crashed down on her.

Blood soaked the carpet under Jamaal.

And still the cop held Chris by the arm. "Let me go!" She wrenched free and slid across the floor, moving around Jamaal to assess his injuries.

No ...

His eyelids flickered. He breathed, though each breath sounded horribly ragged and shallow.

She scowled at the officer. "Get a medic up here now! Is Sloan here?"

The officer scowled back at her. "Yes, by chance, he is." He holstered his pistol and relaxed his stance.

"Jason!" Chris screamed the word loud enough to explode her eardrums. Dizzy, she turned back to Jamaal. She couldn't move him, and with her useless arm, couldn't figure out how to staunch the blood flowing in rivers out of him from the deep stab wounds in his chest.

He struggled to wet his lips. His breaths were just gasps. His eyes lifted only enough to meet Chris's gaze. "You ... you're ... the one."

Holding her arm, Chris leaned in closer. "What?"

"You ... in the ... pictures." A cough brought bubbly pink blood to his lips.

Oh, Lord ... Father God, I can't help him. Please. I can't—

"At the ... on the ... wall. Pictures."

Fresh tears flooded her eyes. "Yes. At the clinic. In the pictures." She lowered herself to the floor close beside him. Took his hands in her own. And squeezed them.

"Army ..."

She tried to smile. Her tears fell into her hair. "Yes. I was in the army."

"Erin ..."

"Yes. We flew helicopters. A medevac Huey. Erin and I."

"Erin ..." His eyelids faded shut. Breath hushed out of him as a smile faintly pressed his lips. "Wooorrrd ..."

Chris held his hands against her cheek as sobs overtook her. "Breathe, Jamaal. Please?"

He didn't breathe. Antwoine's knife punctured both his lungs. He couldn't draw in a breath even if he wanted to.

"Please? Maal?"

He died at that moment, his hands resting in hers.

Chris lay on the floor beside him. Weeping. Wishing for just one more breath. Just one more heartbeat.

But it never came.

✯✯✯

SHOVING MONROE OUT OF THE way, Jason ran into the room. Johnson stood there, thumbs hooked into his utility belt. His face bore a smug half smile, yet he spoke softly. "He's gone."

Jason moved closer. The sound of Chris's sobs tore his heart out his chest. He knelt behind her. Quickly studied the young Eastsider lying in front of her. Touched her shoulder. Then lay down on the floor behind her. He wrapped his arm around her and held her tightly as she cried.

FOURTEEN

Ever so gently, he swept back the tangled hair from her face, pushed it back off her forehead, then leaned in to kiss the soft spot just under her ear.

They wanted to clear the room. The entire house. The coroner had been called and would arrive soon. The young man beside them would be placed in a body bag and taken downtown to the morgue.

Another horrible, senseless waste.

Cops like Johnson, Monroe, and a few of the others didn't mind one bit that the gangsters were killing each other off. Good riddance. Jason couldn't blame them entirely for their attitude. In a way—a shallow-minded, ignorant, and incredibly sad sort of way—it made sense. If anyone had to die this day, if it ended up being one of the criminals ... so be it.

Even still, the woman he loved lay holding the hand of one such criminal, crying as if her world would never again be made right. The young man was a gangster. A thug. He and his friends terrorized her and her friends, vandalized a place she cared about, randomly shot holes through her church and her good friend's house. Almost flat-out killed her best friend.

Sweet Erin. How close the bullet came from missing her entirely. How close it came to killing her instantly. Or painfully slow.

To be gut shot. Jason couldn't even imagine how horrible that would be.

And here lay this thug, slain by his own friends. His brothers, he had probably called them. What a joke. For taking his life, one of his *brothers* would spend the rest of his life in jail. If justice prevailed. Maybe even life for life.

And still she cried on. Such desperate weeping. Jason wanted to pick her up and hold her against him, closer than he had ever held anyone or anything in his life. His heart ached, a deep slicing ache making it hard to breathe.

He loved her. In every way.

Especially now. Here, in this disgusting place. Here she lay weeping for this lost soul while everyone else around her wrote it off as good luck. Good riddance. And good-bye to another criminal.

"Hey, man. Come on."

He lifted his head to look at Johnson.

"Get her up. Let's go."

He spoke as quietly as he could, hoping the man would hear him. "Give us another minute."

"One minute, Sloan. That's it." The cop left the room.

Jason leaned in to kiss his love once more under her ear. "Take your time." The faintest of whispers.

Chris drew the young man's hands to her face. The dark skin touched her flushed cheek, then her swollen lips.

Jason's hand shook as he caressed her hair.

"Jamaal." Spoken softly through her sobs.

He leaned in again. "I'm sorry. What?"

"His name ... was Jamaal."

Familiar name. Jason's mouth fell open. "Erin's friend?"

Chris reached to pull down the black bandanna wrapped around the young man's arm. A long line of stitches had been neatly sewn into the smooth skin, closing a clean, straight wound. A knife wound. "Thirty-two. Some of Erin's best work."

"Ahh ... Chris ... I'm sorry."

"He died ... saving me."

His eyes widened.

Chris let go of the man's hands and pushed them away, then grabbed her upper arm. "He saved me." Just a whisper.

Jason gave the man another long look.

"Oh, God ..." Chris rolled onto her back.

Jason moved so she could lie comfortably, though she still held her arm. "Are you okay?"

Her entire face was wet. Sweat drenched her hair.

Jason unrolled his kit and grabbed out a small ice pack and a triangular bandage. He mixed the ice and wrapped it in the bandage, then placed it against her forehead. "Shh ... It's all right."

She let go of her arm only long enough to wipe the tail of the bandage across her face and nose.

"Are you hurt, Chris?" He slid the ice closer to her eyes. Just a little.

Her hand lifted to massage her shoulder. "I could use another ice pack if you've got one."

"Just this one. I don't have my full kit." He pulled it away, but she stopped him and pressed it back against her forehead.

"I just need another minute."

"Take all the time you need." He watched as she grabbed her arm again. "Chris, what happened to your shoulder?" He sat up and gently palpated it.

Her hand covered his. "It's all right."

Swelling. "Did it dislocate?"

She released a huge breath. Swallowed deeply. "Yeah."

Jason pulled the ice down to cover the top of her shoulder with it. His teeth ground as a million angry thoughts, most of them questions, flooded his mind.

She wiped her eyes with the back of her hand and looked up at him. Swollen and horribly bloodshot, her eyes gazed at him with such tenderness, sadness, weariness. "We should get out of here."

"Not yet. Lie still."

Her eyelids closed. "I need to see Rinny."

"I know you do. She's fine. You know that."

"Yeah. I know."

"Tell you what. Let me brace your shoulder, then we'll go find Ray and get the ..." He let his voice trail off, then grinned at her instead of finishing his statement. His choice of remaining words wouldn't have been appropriate.

She smiled at him. "Yeah. That sounds like a plan."

LYING ON AN EXAMINING TABLE in the Emergency Room at Good Samaritan Hospital, Erin wondered what exactly it was she lay on. It felt more like a concrete slab than foam padding. She turned her head and watched her normally rock-solid doctor of a husband study the list of her initial lab results, his shaking hands rippling the paper as his eyebrows remained scrunched in a deep frown. Just for fun she said, "You were right."

Her simple words seemed to fluster him even more. He turned to look at her. "What, sweetheart?" A quick smile. His eyes once again studied the sheet of paper in his hand.

Erin waited.

"I was? About what?"

Silly boy. His concern tickled her. The best medicine she could ask for.

He finally lowered the paper to the table and gave her his full attention. "What was I right about?"

"This being a little too inconvenient. I need to get out of here."

"Me too." A mischievous grin. "It is my day off, you know."

"Yeah. I know. You've already mentioned that maybe ... fifteen times?" Erin laughed, then instantly regretted it.

"Oops."

"Yeah, oops." She tried to lower her jaw. At this rate, if she didn't quit grinding her teeth, she'd very quickly need a whole new set.

Scott fussed again with the thick bandage covering Erin's side. "Everything looks good, sweetheart. There's no reason for them to want to keep you overnight."

"Great. So get me out of here."

"Not quite yet." A tender smile softened his firm expression.

"I need Mia."

"Me too. But she's fine with Cappy."

Erin raised her eyebrow. "Did you hear what you just said?"

Her husband bit into his lower lip. "Um ... yeah. I'd better go see if I can get you out of here."

"Yeah. Go. And hurry."

He kissed her deeply. She let him. When he pulled away, his hand caressed her cheek. His eyes took in every bit of her face.

Erin's heart melted. "I know, love. I hear you."

His hand shook against her cheek.

"I know."

He drew in a deep, quivering breath. "I'll be back. Just relax. Rest."

She nodded. Prayers whispered up from her soul as her eyes closed. *So much to thank You for, sweet Savior. Ahh, Lord ...* A deep breath refreshed her. And didn't really hurt. *So much. For everything. For absolutely everything. Thank You, Lord.*

She needed to hold her daughter. Her arms ached with it. Urgency. Pure longing. *She's all right. She's okay.* She would be getting hungry soon. Erin needed to get home. To hold and nurse her daughter. No matter how much it hurt.

Hurts worse to be here. Lord, please. I need to go home.

And Chris.

Lord, I need to see her. Where is she? What happened?

The last thing Officer Mallory said before she left the hospital to head back to Kimberley Street was that her fellow officers found the house where the Eastsiders were located and were in the process of staging a raid. But that was over a half hour ago. By now it had to be over. By now ...

She tried to relax, but her prayers of thanksgiving turned to desperate cries for help. *Please, Lord ... let her be all right.*

How many times had she prayed the same prayer? Since that first day in the parking garage at King Fahd International Airport in Dhahran, Saudi Arabia. Always the same prayer for the woman with such dark brown eyes, the friend she grew to love in the opening days of Operation Desert Storm, the friend who had since grown closer than a sister.

My hermana. Oh, Lord Jesus, hold her close. Keep her safe. Please? Bring her home to me. If I ever get out of here ... may she be waiting for me. Please, let her be okay.

✳ ✳ ✳

HARD AND COLD AS A concrete slab. Did they steal this examining table from the morgue?

Where was her husband? Anybody? This place had lousy customer service. Where could she lodge a formal complaint?

Her daughter would be starving by now. Her daughter needed her mommy! Why didn't Cappy bring Mia in so Erin could hold her? Where was Cappy anyway? And where was Chris?

Erin slowly lifted her right hand and ran it through her tangled hair. *Lord, please. Where's Chris? If someone doesn't arrive soon, I'm getting out of here. I'll take a taxi home. Hitchhike if I have to.*

She rubbed her eyes. Her side throbbed.

Stupid dumb creeps. What did I ever do to them? What's their problem anyway? Who put the humongous chips on their skinny little shoulders?

Jamaal.

Sweet kid. He didn't have anything to do with all this ... did he, Lord? Please say no. Please ... let him be sitting at home watching a baseball game. Anything. Don't let him be wrapped up in all this.

Gritting her teeth, she lowered her arm, then gently poked at the bandage covering the two new holes in her body.

Like I needed two new holes. Just great. I've just had my love handle pierced. Who knows? I may have just started a new fashion trend. Everyone from coast to coast will be running to their local malls to have their love handles pierced!

She wanted to scream. Her hand again rubbed her eyes.

Someone stepped into the room. Quietly. Soft footsteps. Erin pulled her hand away and blinked deeply.

Chris.

Her heart flooded with joy, then broke into a million pieces. Chris's face, the sadness there, the brace pinning her arm ... Before Erin knew it, her feet came around and she sat up on the table. Waylaid by the pain, she tried not to wince, waited for it to ease, then pulled her best friend into her arms.

"Hey, lady." The softest of whispers.

Lord Jesus ... thank You. Erin couldn't let her go. Her arms refused to release their tight hold.

Chris's head rested against Erin's shoulder. Several deep breaths shook her.

"Are you okay?" Erin's tears fell against the back of Chris's shirt. "Girl ... what happened?"

"Rin, I've got some ... bad news." Chris pulled away.

Erin blinked to see clearly. Wiped her eyes with her fingertips. Barely nodded.

Chris lowered her gaze to the floor. Her bottom lip trembled as she seemed to struggle for control.

"First tell me ... are you hurt?" Erin touched the bright white Velcro strap around Chris's wrist. Let her eyes follow the bend of Chris's elbow, up to her shoulder. "What happened?"

A faint smile. But Chris didn't look up. "Things got a little ... hairy."

Erin forced in a painful deep breath and held it long enough to settle her racing heart before letting it out slowly.

"They got them all. At least they think so. The main guys, anyway."

"Sharnisha?"

A weak grunt. "She ran off. The only one they didn't catch."

"Did they hurt her? Like Jimmy said?"

"Not more than she asked for."

Oh, Lord ... Erin closed her eyes only long enough to whisper the prayer. "Chris ... did they hurt you?"

"They ... tried."

She touched Chris's good arm. "Please look at me."

Those dark eyes, swollen and sad, pinched shut. "Rinny ... Jamaal's dead."

Erin's mouth fell open as her heart dropped like a lead weight inside her.

"He saved me. He totally saved me. He pulled Antwoine off me. They got into a fight." Sobs stole Chris's breath. "Antwoine killed him. Stabbed him several times in the chest."

Erin couldn't breathe. The young man's face, his smile, filled every part of her mind. Her eyes slowly closed.

"I'm so sorry, Rinny."

Chris leaned against her. Erin blindly pulled her in once more.

The memory of that day ... his brown eyes taking in the pictures on the wall, his smile of approval at Erin's handiwork, the gentle way about him. Polite. Sweet. For a gangster.

He had put off his gangster ways to seek help from a stranger. Treated that stranger with dignity and respect. Allowed that stranger to see a glimpse of the beautiful young man he was at heart.

And now ... he was dead.

Miserable. Senseless. It wasn't fair. Wasn't right.

"He saved me. He totally saved me. He pulled Antwoine off me ..."

Holding onto her best friend with every ounce of her strength, Erin cried as hard as she had ever cried.

Jamaal ... thank you. Thank you. Thank you.

✯✯✯

RAIN PELTED JASON'S UMBRELLA AS he leaned against the front of his truck. It had started raining the day after Labor Day. The kids in his neighborhood didn't seem to mind. It always stunk anyway when beautiful weather teased everyone stuck inside on the first day back to school.

Many times that summer Chris had said how the city needed a good, hard rain. "To clear the air," as she put it. "To cut the dust and wash out the haze."

The rain falling today would probably do just that. But it could never clear away the haze left by the events of the past few days. That haze would remain. Thick, dark, ugly. Hovering over Kimberley Square for a long time to come.

Jason wondered again who came up with the name *Kimberley Square*. It had a nice ring to it. Especially when he allowed his heart to consider the place as his home.

The house where he lived sat officially outside the limits of the Square. If there even were official limits. Considering the generous nature of the people at the heart of it, by their definition, the Square probably incorporated the entire city. If not the entire world.

Generous. Caring. Loving. Tenacious.

All of them. The Connellys. Erin and Scott. Cappy and Bettema and even Isaiah, the kindly old groundskeeper.

And especially ... Chris.

Especially now.

Standing in the rain, she held an umbrella with one hand while the other lay pinned firmly against her stomach by the thick brace wrapped around her waist. She tried to ditch the brace several times over the past four days, said she didn't need it anymore. But Jason would nag her and Erin would nag her until she finally relented and kept the thing wrapped around her. Her shoulder would eventually heal but would always be weakened by the trauma. Her spirit would heal. But always be shaken. Wounded. Haunted by all that happened.

He would do all he could to bring her through this. Even ... pray.

A few short years ago, prayer used to be an easy thing for him. Talking to God. Telling Him what he needed and waiting for His reply. Throwing in a well-meaning thank You from time to time. Sweetening the pot by praying "in Jesus' name."

What a sham his faith had been. How quick he had been to discard it.

He cursed more now in Jesus' name than prayed in it.

How much longer did he think he could continue to curse the all-powerful One who held all things in His hands? And get away with it?

Jessica. His sweet bride. They had been married only two years. She was the love of his life.

Taken, God. You took her from me. Why shouldn't I hate You for that?

The word churned the acid in his stomach. He shifted his umbrella to his left hand, his weight to his right leg.

God ... I'm tired of hating You.

The rain smacking the umbrella left a soothing melody in its wake. Thumping off the hood of his truck. Splashing into the puddles at his feet.

How can I keep hating You? You've taken from me, yes. But now ... You've given me so much.

Up the hill not far away, she stood, holding an umbrella, capturing his complete attention. Concern for her burned his already aching stomach. Deep, hard concern. He had never cared for anyone more. Except Jessica. His high school sweetheart. The love of his life.

But I'm breathing. I'm living. This is my life now. And Jessie's gone. Oh, God ... The words still sliced through him. *She's gone.*

Dressed in black, standing beside her friends from Kimberley Square, Chris McIntyre stood in the rain to pay her respects to a young man who didn't deserve her respect. The gangster they placed in that body bag deserved to die, along with every one of his *brothers*. For all the terror and pain they caused, they each deserved to die. For the way Chris still carried her pain. For Erin, hurting the way she hurt. For all Scott had to endure. Ben Connelly. Sonya. All of them. Agonizing over all that happened. Forever scarred by the events.

Jason wanted to kill every last one of the worthless thugs who called themselves Eastsiders. If there were any left.

Stupid thought. Of course there were Eastsiders left. The raid gutted most of the organization, but not all. The gang would regroup. And be back.

But not to Kimberley Square. They learned their lesson about dealing with these people. These people knew what they believed, and they fought for it. With everything they had. These people knew how to fight. They were soldiers. Warriors all.

God ... I wish I knew what I believed. Do I still believe You are true? Do I believe You are who Chris says You are?

The casket was slowly lowered into the ground. Jason's heart ached as Chris awkwardly held her umbrella with her strapped-down left hand and tossed a flower down onto the casket with her right. From the distance, the flower looked like a white rose.

Erin tossed hers. Then Scott. Then Ben. Then Sonya. A few others tossed theirs. People Jason didn't know. And then the woman he thought was the thug's mother. Her shoulders shook as she cried. As she tossed the final rose.

God ... she loved her son.

But who else did? No one else tossed a flower into the hole. None of the thug's homeboys turned out for his burial.

Lord Jesus, You loved him.

"He saved me. He pulled Antwoine off me."

The words seared a swath through Jason's brain. Chris's voice. Choked by sobs.

Yeah. He drew in a deep breath and let it out slowly. *I'll give the guy that.* His teeth clenched. *If you really did save her, man . . . yeah. I'm grateful. If I had a rose, I'd toss it.*

Why was he even here? Just because of Chris? Why did he refuse to join her beside the casket? Why did he insist on staying down here, all alone by his truck?

Why.

Too many whys. All these years. The unanswerable question. Ever plaguing, ever taunting, the word stood like a huge, thick wall between him and everything he once knew to be true.

Let it go, Jase. Hold on to what's real. Right now.

He still believed.

You're real, God. You're real . . . and You're big.

Just being around Chris, hearing her talk, watching love and life play out in her dark eyes . . . God was real. Alive. And true. If Jason didn't see that, didn't know that from looking at anyone else in the world, he saw it and knew it from looking at Chris. Everything about her exuded love and truth and faith. Peace. Hope.

Even now, weighed down by all that happened, such hopelessness for an entire group of troubled kids, still, there she stood. Tossing a white rose. Showing respect to the one young gangster who died trying to do the right thing.

God . . . I love her.

His left hand tingled. The blood had drained from it. He switched the umbrella to his right hand and stuffed his left into the front pocket of his jeans.

It's true, Lord. All the things I love most about her are there because of her love for You. Do I want to change that? Who would she be, without Your love coursing through her?

It was all so true.

She'd be just like I've been for the last three years. Bitter. Angry. Living a life that's already dead.

Slowly, one by one, the group turned away from the gaping hole swallowing up the body of the young Eastsider.

"His name was Jamaal."

"Yeah." Just a whisper. "Jamaal."

After hugging the young man's mother, carrying her umbrella, Chris stepped carefully down the hill. Jason pushed away from the front of his truck and waited for her.

The words echoed in his thoughts. *"His name was . . . Jamaal."*

Yeah. God . . . thank You. I know the guy did what I couldn't do. He saved her. I believe it.

He blinked deeply as the cold wind made his eyes water. He needed to see her clearly. Wanted each step she took to be sure and safe.

You saved her, Lord Jesus.

He let out a deep sigh.

Savior. My Savior. You saved me. You're not dead. You're alive. You're not coldhearted and indifferent. You are the one true God.

Maybe you're finally starting to get it, Sloan.

Finally starting to get it. *God . . . forgive me . . .*

Chris stopped at the bottom of the hill to wait for Erin and Scott. Jason wanted to join them but held back. He gave Erin a smile and a wave when she turned his way.

Her smile did his heart good. And Scott's quick wave. Jason returned it. And yet he didn't move.

Erin eased into their Mustang as Scott held his umbrella above the open door. When she was in, he pushed the door shut, hurried to the other side, and climbed in.

Jason shifted his eyes to the lady walking toward him. Beautiful. Though sad and weary and a bit pale. He didn't like seeing her in black.

She walked with her eyes down, avoiding the puddles. Avoiding his gaze. Until she couldn't any longer. Her head slowly raised. Her gorgeous dark brown eyes lifted to meet his own. That smile. That voice. "Hey, you."

"Hey back atcha." She taught him to say it like that.

The smile widened. "Thanks for being here. It means a lot."

He shrugged. "I'm sorry I didn't join you up there."

"Nah. It's enough that you're here."

He struggled to find a way to force out what he wanted to say. "Um ... you know, I really am sorry he died. He seemed like a good guy. From what Erin said."

"Yeah."

"I'm grateful to him. I'll always be."

She only smiled.

Rain battered their umbrellas. Her free hand must have been numb by now. He quickly lowered his umbrella, then reached out to take hers. Moved in close to her side. "Want to go somewhere?"

"Scott and Rinny said for you to come back to their place. They were going to hit Boston Market on the way home. Scott said there would be plenty."

"Sounds tempting."

"Wish I was up for something more exciting, but ... I'm not."

"It's okay." He guided her to the passenger side of his truck and started to open the door but stopped to gaze into her eyes. "Are you okay?"

She nodded. "Good as gold."

Not convincing at all. But Jason smiled anyway.

Chris lifted her head and drew in a deep breath as if smelling the air, pulling it in to sit full in her lungs before letting it escape. Her eyes closed as she seemed to enjoy the moment.

Jason leaned down and lightly kissed her lips.

She peeked open one eye. "Did you mean that?"

He wanted to shout his reply for all the world to hear. Finally, in every way, he meant it. But he only whispered so she could hear. "Oh, yeah."

"Prove it." Something twinkled in her peeking eye.

Jason touched her cheek with his fingertips, then leaned in and kissed her again, full and deep.

She reached up to take the umbrella from his hand.

Startled by it, Jason broke off the kiss, but she pushed her lips into his, not letting it end. Overwhelmed, he touched her cheeks with both hands as rain fell over their heads and trickled down their faces.

She slowly pulled away, then snuggled in against him. His arms surrounded her, holding her close.

So many things he wanted to say. So much to tell her. He wanted to grab the umbrella to keep them both from getting soaked, but she had tossed it behind her. Out of reach. Laughter rumbled up from his gut.

"Jase?" Her voice was muffled against his chest.

"Yeah?"

"You mind getting a little wet?"

He pulled in a long, deep breath. The air, heavy with the rain, smelled clean. As it flowed out of him, he let another laugh escape. "No. Not at all."

"Really?"

"No. I kind of ... like it." He laid his head back to let it fall on his face.

Chris leaned away and looked up at him.

He blinked the rain from his eyes. Gave her a smile.

"Are we ... going to be all right, you and I?"

Water coursed down her face. Dripped off her nose. Jason lifted his hand and brushed his thumb across the faint scar below her eye. "I was wondering that same thing, but I didn't really know how to ask."

"You want to know what I think?"

"You bet I do."

"I think we're going to be all right."

"Really?"

"Yeah." A gentle smile softened her eyes. "You want to know why I think that?"

"Yeah. I sure do."

"I know that God loves me. And I know He loves you too. That's enough for me." She squinted to keep the rain out of her eyes. "You want to know how I know that?"

Almost laughing, he wasn't so sure if he wanted to know. But then he said, "Yeah. I do."

"I know He loves you because He ... gave you to me. To love."

His mouth dropped open. The words fell over him as sweetly as the rain.

"Does that make sense?"

He barely nodded. "Yeah. I think it does."

"Okay." She leaned against him once more.

He wrapped his arms around her and held her tenderly.

As the rain continued to fall.

THANKSGIVING DAY
2007

EPILOGUE

SITTING ALONE ON THE COUCH in their living room, wearing soft cotton sweats, sipping freshly brewed coffee, Chris savored the moment. Her family still slept. Her husband's snores softened the silence. Sweetened it. The moment swelled.

With the turkey in the oven, she could crawl back into bed and cuddle up beside him. Two more hours of blissful sleep would be heavenly. But this moment was special, one she had cherished since her daughter's first Thanksgiving nine years ago. Silent and still, the next two hours were hers alone.

Madison Jane had arrived in late August of 1998, and in the chaos following, it took Chris three months to start working on her baby book. The morning she finally found time to start it, Thanksgiving morning, she had just put the turkey in the oven and sat, exhausted, on the couch in their living room, wearing soft cotton sweats and sipping freshly brewed coffee. From that moment, chronicling each event, pasting in picture after picture, Chris worked on that book for five years. The very last picture placed on the last page of the book had been taken on Maddy's first day of school. The new era in her daughter's young life demanded an entirely new book to chronicle it.

When Jase Junior arrived two years and three months after his big sister, Chris worked on both books for the first time in the quiet stillness of his first Thanksgiving morning. Five years later, when he ran headlong into his kindergarten class completely overjoyed at finally being able to go to "real school," Chris barely had time to snap a picture. The last page of his book contained a blurry figure of a child someone else may not even have recognized as Jason Sloan Jr.

But his mommy knew.

Though he looked quite different now. At seven years old, he was growing into a handsome replica of his dad. Thin and strong. Minus his dad's meticulously cropped facial hair, of course.

She laughed quietly, then sipped her coffee, careful not to spill even a drop on her son's precious book sprawled open on her lap. She flipped the pages back to her favorite photo, the one of her sleeping newborn baby boy tucked safely in his sleeping father's arms.

So safe there, my big boy, in your daddy's arms.

So safe. Held so tenderly in her Father God's arms.

Her eyes closed as she basked in the moment.

All the years, He had never let her go. Nothing hummed more sweetly through her than her Father God's love. Combined with the love of her husband, family, and dearest and best friends, nothing could compare to the moment she savored. As the turkey baked in the oven. As her family slept on.

Maddy's book was starting to show wear from all its use. Precious and fragile. Chris lifted it with both hands to her lap and then slowly flipped through the pages.

My beautiful little girl. A snapshot of the night they brought her home from the hospital. One of her grinning dad, holding her close to his chest. *You look so happy being so close to his heart.*

The last page, that last picture. Maddy crying and holding tightly to her mommy's legs.

My not-so-brave little girl.

But Alisabeth cried too. Erin's daughter wasn't any more brave than Chris's, not when it came to starting school. That same day, both girls eventually quit crying when they realized that, together, they could face the unknown. As they turned away from their mommies and started that new chapter of their young lives, their mommies started to cry.

The memory brought a laugh bubbling up from Chris's belly.

Both she and Erin hurried out of the school that day as they wiped tears from their eyes and tried not to look at each other.

Mia Renae, Alisabeth Rose, Zander James. Scott and Erin's three little ones — not so little anymore.

Chris closed her daughter's book and set it on the coffee table next to her son's. In the bedroom, her husband snored.

One more hour to savor before the day's rush began. Getting everyone up, fixing breakfast, then heading off to church for the Thanksgiving service. Then back home to put the finishing touches on the turkey before hauling it to the table for her family to devour. Turkey and stuffing and gravy and mashed potatoes. Peas and corn and hot buttered rolls. Milk and iced tea and fresh hot coffee. Apple, peach, and pumpkin pie. An almost mirror image of the meal they shared that past Saturday in the parking lot of the church with all their friends and family and fellow residents of Kimberley Square.

Then, after dinner, after the dishes had been put away, as the men settled in for their three-day "Football Frenzy," Chris, Erin, and the girls would head off to Eugene for the two-day women's basketball tournament at the University of Oregon. The first few games of Alaina Walker's sure-to-be-fabulous senior year. Already she had been chosen as the team's Player of the Year for her sophomore and junior seasons, and found herself fully deserving the Pac 10 All-League honors she received last year. The way things were going, Chris didn't doubt for one second the girl had a chance at making a WNBA team. Even though Alaina talked about letting it rest and becoming a high school teacher and a coach.

Chris slouched low and kicked her feet up on the coffee table.

With all that lay ahead, she had much to savor in the next hour. Much to be thankful for.

Difficult times left her more determined than ever to remain her Father's own. Though her dad passed away not long after Maddy was born, he was at least able to hold her one time in his arms. His first and only grandchild. A tiny baby girl not ever to know how much her granddaddy had changed in his last year. How much she changed him. She would never know how much her mommy welcomed that change, treasuring it as death stole him away, even as she screamed in agony at his stubborn refusal to accept forgiveness and believe.

Jason's loving words that day still echoed faintly in her mind. *"You did all you could. It was his decision to make."*

Maybe if there had been more time, if the cancer hadn't moved so quickly through him.

But you had your whole life to decide, Dad. Now you have to live by the choices you made.

It all still tugged at her. All she could do was give it to her Father God.

Things quieted after that for a while. Until Ben had his heart attack. The news left everyone devastated, though he fought back like the true warrior he was. Slowed a bit by his medications, he still commanded with a gentle hand, freely showing true love and respect in the simplest ways to all who crossed his path. Maddy and Jase Junior could not have had a more loveable grandfather. And Sonya still kept everyone in line.

Closing both the clinic and the gym almost tore the heart out of Kimberley Square. But with financial concerns, Ben's health concerns, and Scott advancing through the ranks at Good Samaritan, both closures turned out to be wise decisions. Chris still missed that old converted warehouse that once echoed with bouncing basketballs and joyous laughter. The huge building was now, once again, a warehouse. And the back lot had once again disintegrated into a deserted, overgrown, trash-covered lot.

Erin and Scott were able to remodel the clinic's half of the duplex to accommodate their growing household. Not long afterward, Jason and Chris jumped at the chance to buy Mrs. Taylor's house when she moved to Arizona. As if it had been destined, best friends became, once again, next-door neighbors. Chris still couldn't think of any other place in the entire world where she would rather live and raise her family.

The fortieth birthday party they all threw for her a few months ago proved that.

What a night that had been.

How in the world can I already be forty?

Thirty more minutes before Jason's alarm sent the morning into a chaotic whirl. Plenty of time to cherish again the moment that had stunned her just a few days ago.

After the drenching rains at the tail end of last week, Saturday morning dawned crystal clear. The clean, fresh air carried on a light breeze, just enough to ruffle the few dead leaves that remained here and there on the ground. It wasn't difficult to convince Ben and Andy to move the community dinner outside under the trees and warm sun. Hauling tables and chairs, then enough food to feed two army divisions, people from every corner of Kimberley Square sat down together to eat a glorious meal.

Afterward, with several members of the worship team playing softly on guitars, most of the children playing impromptu games of Catch Me If You Can, most of the men congregating around three tables under the trees, and most of the women gathering up dirty plates and leftover food, Chris and Erin stood next to Sonya and Sarah, carefully sealing the leftovers with plastic wrap. Ben moved closer and beckoned Chris and Erin to join him.

"What's up?" Chris asked as she wiped her hands on a paper towel.

"Someone I want you to meet." Ben's eyes twinkled. "Again."

Chris glanced at Erin, but Erin only gave her a look of confusion. They followed Ben to one of the tables set up on the outer edge of the festivities, farthest from the music and children's ruckus.

A man and a woman, both fairly young, African American, and obviously in love, stood by the table. Ben walked over to them and put his hand on the man's shoulder. "Chris, you may want to sit down. When I tell you who this is, you won't believe it." He turned to grin at the couple. "Though there might be a slim chance you may recognize him." A laugh. "But I doubt it."

The young man's shyness made Chris smile, but she saw nothing in his features she recognized. She had never seen him before.

Ben turned to meet her gaze. "God has done this. Only He could bring this man back into your life in such an amazing way."

Was there something there ... in the man's eyes ... she had seen before? Did she know this man?

Still looking down, he rubbed his nose. "I don't blame you if you don't remember me. I'm ... not the same guy I once was."

That voice ...

Chris glanced at the woman. She had definitely never seen her before. Pretty, smiling, and holding her man's hand in a fierce grip, the woman seemed to be enjoying the moment almost as much as Ben.

"And I'm not hangin' around wit my usual crowd."

The woman giggled.

Chris didn't know what to say. She glanced at Erin, but Erin offered no help.

The man slowly lifted his eyes and looked at Chris. His head tilted just a bit to the right. "My name is Calvin Tracy. But you may remember me as ..."

His pause triggered a memory that shot lightning bolts through Chris. Her jaw almost dropped to her chest. "No."

Calvin grinned. "I go by Cal now. That was my grandpapa's name. I never really liked it much. Not until I got older. And a lot smarter."

A bit dizzy, Chris's voice rose about three octaves higher than normal. "Cee Train?"

The man's head fell back as he laughed. "See, I knew you'd remember me."

She could only stare.

Cee Train, now eleven years older, carried not the slightest trace of the man he was a lifetime ago. His head slowly shook.

"God help me ... Chris, you gotta know how sorry I am about ... everything. I ain't wit dat crowd anymore." More shaking. "No way. I went clean after gettin' out of jail. I've been clean now for 'bout five years. This is Mekelle. We gonna be married soon."

Ben said to Mekelle, "Tell her what your name means."

Grinning, the woman leaned against her man. "It means, 'Who is like God?'"

The words stunned Chris, until a breath of laughter spurted out of her. "This is too much."

"I heard that you was still around here." Cal slowly lifted his hand. "I've been wantin' to come by to apologize to you, Chris. I knew since that day ... I needed to make things right wit you."

She studied his outstretched hand for another second. Then reached up to shake it. "You just have ... Cal." Laughter overtook her. "Though I may still call you Cee Train from time to time. That name is ingrained in my mind."

"Ever since dat day. Yeah. I understand." He released Chris's hand as his head again shook. "But dat ain't me no more."

The words brought tears to Chris's eyes. "Yeah. I can see that." She stuck her hand out. "Nice to meet you, Cal."

Laughing, Cal once again shook her hand. "Nice to meet you too, Chris."

★★★

JASON'S ALARM BREAKS THROUGH THE silence, pulling her out of the moment, bringing her back to the world of here and now. Soon two hungry children would be bounding down the stairs. Soon that big hungry child of hers would need coffee and his good-morning kiss.

Even so, for a few more seconds, sitting low in the couch with her feet kicked up, she savors the moment.

Her heart thumps, pumping blood all through her. Her stomach lets out a huge growl, making her laugh.

Life. Full and abundant and free. Surrounded on all sides by love and peace and hope, she breathes in the depths of the moment, as the very essence of her Savior fills her. Nothing to fear. No reason for worry or doubt. Tucked safe in the crook of her Father's arm, fear no longer finds her. She hears His heart thump, and gentle laughter seems to find that sweetest part of her soul.

She hears a squeak but keeps her eyes closed. Tries not to grin. Another squeak. Her lips quiver. She holds her breath to force back the smile. Waits for the impending …

A huge weight slides onto the couch beside her, too big and too quiet to be one of her kids. A warm, gentle hand cups her cheek and slowly turns her face. She blinks open her eyes.

He is close. Very close. He smiles. "I was gonna really scare you."

"Squeaks gave you away."

"We should get them fixed."

"When we get new carpet?"

He breathes a faint laugh. "There's nothing wrong with our carpet."

"It's worn out. And ugly."

His head shakes. His eyes stare at her lips.

"We could use new tile in the kitchen too."

He leans closer.

"And new windows."

Their kiss is long and slow. He barely pulls away. "Good morning, my love."

"Right back atcha."

"We don't need new tile in the kitchen."

She laughs.

He kisses her again.

Thumps and stomps bring her two little ones down the stairs and into the kitchen. A second later she hears, "Mom, are we outta Corn Pops?"

Her husband slowly opens his eyes and stares deeply into hers. "Remember when they used to be called Sugar Pops?"

"Pantry," she says, again restraining her grin.

Her son races to the pantry.

"My love, why do we allow our children to eat Sugar Pops?"

"It's better than your All Bran," comes from their sassy little nine-year-old.

"Ouch." Chris laughs. "She got you there."

Jason's right eyebrow lifts. He lightly touches his wife's nose, then jumps up and gorilla-walks into the kitchen to scrub his daughter's tender cheek with his whiskery chin.

Maddy squeals with delight. Jase Junior pokes the tip of his tongue through his lips as he struggles to open the new box of Corn Pops.

Chris's stomach growls. She pushes out of the couch to begin her day but stops near the kitchen and looks over her shoulder.

Her special time, those two quiet hours, flew by way too fast. They always did. But the memories, the moments she cherished, would stay with her for all time. On this, another Thanksgiving Day, the gratitude overwhelming her becomes an offering she lays down at the feet of her Lord.

Yahshua. Thank You so much. Her eyes fall closed. *My Savior. My Lord.*

She turns and walks into the kitchen, watching her son hold up a Corn Pop to study it closely in the light. "Daddy," he says, "are these really made of corn?"

Maddy snorts. "They wouldn't be called Corn Pops if they were made out of something else."

Chris gives both her daughter and son a kiss on the cheek and a quiet, "Good morning, you." She waits for her husband to finish filling the coffeemaker before tickling his ribs. "I'm gonna go take a shower."

He turns to get one more kiss.

She plants a solid one on him, then heads for their bedroom. "Well," she hears him say to the kids, "they really did used to be called Sugar Pops. That should tell you something." Laughing, Chris pulls the bedroom door closed and walks over to sit on the edge of her side of the bed. A deep breath washes through her.

Lord ... thank You. This life You've given me ...

What more can she say? She slowly shakes her head.

I love You so much, my Father, my God.

Her eyes wander to her nightstand, to that framed picture sitting back behind the lamp and her Bible, the picture taken in 1996 at her twenty-ninth birthday party. She reaches for it, dusts it off, and pulls it in close to study it.

Her eyes once again take in every grinning face. A wall of women. Side by side. Arms entwined like a daisy chain.

Bettema and Cappy and Erin and Chris. The Four Warriors, as Corissa Foley used to call them.

Bettema so tall. Married with children now, and living in San Diego. Cappy so crazy. Crazy enough to sign up for a stint with a defense contractor to find herself back in the desert wrenching Humvees and troop carriers. Erin so pregnant. Eight and a half months pregnant at the time, carrying that squirming little babe who is now eleven years old. And Chris. Looking so ... *alive*. She still thinks so. Just starting to really live back then, after living for so long ... dead.

What a party that had been. A complete surprise. "You only turn twenty-nine once," Erin had said. "But you can stay twenty-nine for at least eight years."

And now I'm forty. How is that even possible?

She takes another long look at that grinning, ridiculously pregnant woman in the picture.

Father God ... oh, Lord. This woman ... if it wasn't for her ...

Almost twelve years ago. That knock on her door. The soft words spoken through it. *"Chris?"* That pause. *"Chris ..."* That longer, unbearable pause. And then, the two words that literally saved her life. *"It's me."*

Tears cloud the picture in her hand. *Rinny ... Oh, Lord, thank You. Thank You for Ben putting her in our crew. Thank You for the way she stood by me. Thank You for sending her to Colorado, to my doorstep, at the time I needed her most. I was so hateful to her, but she never left, never gave up on me. She brought me to You, and You made me Your own.*

After one last look, she places the picture back on her nightstand.

You made us all Your own. And we'll be Yours, together, forever. It's totally too much. Too wonderful. Just like You, Father. Thank You.

Laughter erupts in the kitchen, widening her smile. Her stomach growls, long and loud. Pushing up from the bed, she decides to postpone her shower. She heads back to the kitchen and says to her son, "Did you save me any of those Corn Pops?"

Three ways to keep up on your favorite Zondervan books and authors

Sign up for our *Fiction E-Newsletter*. Every month you'll receive sample excerpts from our books, sneak peeks at upcoming books, and chances to win free books autographed by the author.

You can also sign up for our *Breakfast Club*. Every morning in your email, you'll receive a five-minute snippet from a fiction or nonfiction book. A new book will be featured each week, and by the end of the week you will have sampled two to three chapters of the book.

Zondervan *Author Tracker* is the best way to be notified whenever your favorite Zondervan authors write new books, go on tour, or want to tell you about what's happening in their lives.

Visit *www.zondervan.com* and sign up today!

ZONDERVAN.com/
AUTHORTRACKER
follow your favorite authors